Maria Louisa Charlesworth

Oliver of the Mill; a tale

Maria Louisa Charlesworth

Oliver of the Mill; a tale

ISBN/EAN: 9783337024369

Printed in Europe, USA, Canada, Australia, Japan

Cover: Foto ©Andreas Hilbeck / pixelio.de

More available books at **www.hansebooks.com**

OLIVER OF THE MILL

BY

MARIA LOUISA CHARLESWORTH

BY

MARIA LOUISA CHARLESWORTH,

AUTHOR OF "MINISTERING CHILDREN," ETC.

MONTREAL:

DAWSON BROTHERS—PUBLISHERS

—

1876.

Dedicated

TO THE OLDER LIFE OF

RONALD, EDWYN AND OSCAR BARCLAY,

THE INFANT CHEERERS OF

MY SOLITUDE.

> " Grace begun shall end in glory ;
> Jesus, He the victory won ;
> In His own triumphant story
> Is the record of our own."

" Wherever Jesus came when upon earth He brought peace and happiness. Wherever He trod He seemed to dissipate grief. It could not, therefore, be possible that sorrow could ever intrude into His presence in heaven. Sorrow and sighing are often as the Christian's convoy on earth, but they quit him for a better convoy the moment the disembodied spirit escapes from its earthly tabernacle.

" Oh think !—to step on shore, and that shore Heaven —to take hold of a Hand, and find it God's Hand—to breathe a new air, and find it celestial air—to feel invigorated, and find it immortality. Oh think !—to pass from a storm and a tempest for one unbroken smile ;—

" To wake up and find it glory !"

> " My heart is resting, O my God !
> I will give thanks and sing ;
> My heart is at the secret source
> Of every precious thing."

PREFACE.

AFTER a period of ten years, the writer meets the wishes of many friends, and offers another Tale, in the trust that it may prove an interest and aid to some youthful minds.

It has not been easy for the writer to select a subject which seemed in harmony with her own feelings. The buoyancy and beauty of earth's morning existence are left far behind her; the deeper emotions and Diviner loveliness of its receding life are in view—the eye following those who, having done the will of their Father in Heaven, are departed or departing to be with Him for ever. The glories of the sunset sky are attractive to every mind, but the sunsets of human life may be oppressive to those who have no assurance of the radiant morning to follow. Yet, to be written truly, a tale must thrill with the deep impressions of life on the writer's own spirit. The light of the morning of Childhood is bright and diffusive in its influence; but the gleams that break through the clouds to older life's sobered eye, revealing the Heaven beyond them, have more power to arrest and penetrate the soul.

May it be allowed to the writer to say to any wishing to use a tale such as this for mothers' meetings or schools, that there is no need to pass over portions as above the range of the class in view? Higher thoughts than once lay before the minds of our people are welcome to them now. The wonderful dissemination of the Bible opens the mind of the class who most value and read it, to the grandest conceptions of thought and feeling; and though it may be that intellectually they do not rise to them, yet the soul receiving them expands to a capability of interest in the reflections which may unfold the moral or spiritual life of a tale.

The shadow of evil lowers over the scene; but such is earthly life! No parish in which it is not known; few families who are unacquainted in some form with its saddening gloom. There is but little unconsciousness of the existence of outward forms of evil now; the novel and the newspaper circulate in every class. The need is, not to attempt to hide its existence, but to let its darkness and misery prove a beacon to warn that "the way of transgressors is hard." Truth also requires that the contrast be given —the parish struggling alone as to earthly guidance in Divine life, of which so many are found! with the change when the light of a Christian life and a Christian ministry form the centre and bond.

"O Lord, are not thine eyes upon the Truth?"

The Cottage, Nutfield.

OLIVER OF THE MILL.

CHAPTER I.

"By what name shall we call him?" asked Oliver Crisp, as he leaned over the bed where his young wife, Naomi, lay, with his infant son in his arms. The face on which the husband and father intently gazed was chiselled into that perfect form that the Angel of Life often leaves impressed on the features when the silver cord is loosened, and the golden bowl is broken. Naomi waited a few moments in silence; this silence was natural to Oliver Crisp, who was himself slow to speak; if a quick reply were given him, he took the longer to consider its bearing. He gazed stedfastly on his wife, without a glance on the infant she had placed in his arms. Then Naomi looked up into the face of her husband, tears trembled in her dark eyes—his were calm and clear as they met hers overflowing with deep emotion; but his bowed form, the trembling hands, and quivering lip told that the strong man was no stranger to strong feelings.

Naomi's cheek flushed a moment as she said, " I should wish that thou shouldest call him by the name that may seem best to thee."

Again all was stillness in that chamber; its casement open to the west; the September sun was setting, and its golden light rested on Oliver's bent head, gilding the baby's robe of white, and filling the glistening eyes of Naomi. She did not close her eyes against the radiance of the setting sun, nor seem to heed it; she had seen beyond the portals of that land where " the sun shall be no more thy light by day," and earthly light or shadow were little now to her.

Oliver made no reply; Naomi said slowly in a tone that seemed reflecting on the past—

" I had thought that I would like to call him Malachi, for he was last of all the prophets before Messiah came; and if Messiah's return be near, our son may be the last of all your house before His second coming ! "

Still Oliver made no reply, and Naomi held out her arms for her child.

" Thou wilt kiss thy babe ? " she said.

Oliver bent lower and laid a kiss on the infant head, and breathed a quiet blessing; then gave him back to his mother's arms, and rising, stood at the open window. As he looked on the earth and sky, he thought on the same aspect of all things seven years before, when village bells at evening told the gladness of his marriage-day. He looked on the earth—the harvest glowed as then in the rays of the setting sun; he looked on the sky—its glory had not dimmed—heaven knows no fading hues. With a heavy sigh he turned again to her, "his lamp on earth;" the brightness of that light was flickering, and would soon expire for him; then earth, how dark, how drear! The strong man struggled with his grief, but his cheek was white with anguish, as he took his silent place again beside the bed. Naomi laid her hand upon his knee, and softly said, " When I sit in darkness, the Lord shall be a light unto me." He in sad undertones replied in words he had heard her murmur on her bridal day, " Thy sun shall no more go down."

This silent man, with all his strong reserve, seemed understood by Naomi as readily in silence as in speech. With the quick instinct that devoted love can give, Naomi often answered to her husband's thoughts, until he would forget he had not spoken; his thought and feeling so clearly read and fully understood by her responsive spirit. Words from her lips that had ever lighted the present, now shed a gleam on the future, as she murmured low once more, " When I sit in darkness, the Lord shall be a light unto me." Her husband yielded his spirit to them, as he always did to words from her, and believing, he beheld by faith the form of Him who is " the Resurrection and the Life," of Him who hath abolished death; from whom, and in whom, there is no separation.

The old woman came who nursed Naomi, and gave her wine and bread. Naomi smiled, they knew not why. Then looking up adoringly, she took it as though to her it were the supper of the Lord.

The aged woman took the infant and stood beside the bed. Naomi had closed her eyes, her hand laid in her husband's; they watched awhile. " She sleeps," he said. At his dear voice she looked back again, as if half unconscious what she saw; yet in her eyes the spirit depths of light and love. Her eyelids closed again, and with one sigh her spirit passed away. The old woman's tears fell on the infant on her arm. " She sleeps ! " again her husband said, more audibly, as though to assure himself that she would wake. "'Tis the last sleep!" the old nurse answered. Unable to bear the thought, Oliver Crisp broke through his reserve, and uttered the precious words, " He giveth His beloved sleep ! " Then said, " Good mother, take the babe away." And Oliver was left alone.

Yet not alone ! Another Eye is watching; another Heart is throbbing, when the loved depart. " Precious in the sight of the Lord is the death " (now the " sleep ") " of His saints." When we take the cup of bitterness from the hand of Him who drank its very dregs for us, we find that He who was Himself " the Man of sorrows and acquainted with grief," has mingled for us the balm of life in that cup of bitterness. The heavens were opened above the Son of Man on earth; they have never closed again. Where Jesus stands, beside the child of sorrow, the heavens are open still; and though at times the mists of earth may dim the eye, yet it is freely given to look with open face into the heaven of heavens, to follow whither Christ hath led, to see the light, and feel faint earnests of the life of immortality.

Oliver Crisp took his farewell look on the face that had been the sun and centre of earth's gladness to him; so still in its beauty, the hush of expectancy on it, as though awaiting with listening joy and awe the voice that would awake it from sleep! Oliver Crisp stood long with fixed and earnest gaze; then said—

"My jewel! there is One who sold all to buy thee. I give thee to Him!"

Then turning away, he wept tears that eased and softened the heart whence they flowed.

CHAPTER II.

"Hast thou thought on a name for thy child, my son?" Oliver Crisp was slow to answer. Who could wonder! The question drew back on a sudden the veil that closed in the earthly sanctuary of his heart—that scene of overwhelming feeling, the last on memory's page; that scene, every touch of which was graven in his heart for ever, whose record lay apart from every other, which nothing could efface, nor, he thought, relieve with the softening mist of distance; standing out clear in the reality of its earthly agony, its heavenly tenderness and glory. In the secret of his soul it was ever present, and there, he thought, through earthly life's long years it will ever lie, in the forefront of all things, until, through the same separation of soul and body he should pass to eternal reunion. In the freshness of bereavement he did not know how, as the distance lengthens behind us, and our solitary steps advance on the "Better Country," the ties broken here brighten before us there; and we learn to say with ever-deepening thankfulness, not only, "I shall go to him," but also, "he shall not return to me!"

Oliver Crisp could not reveal that sacred scene to

other eyes; he did not know how to enter on the question, so he was silent.

"The poor mother might well have named him Benoni, 'the son of my sorrow;' and thou mightest call him 'Benjamin, the son of the right hand;' for if the boy be like his poor mother, he will full surely be that unto thee."

Oliver Crisp rested his elbow on the arm of his chair, covering his face with his hand. Mistress Crisp, seeing that the subject troubled him, said no more.

Was the term "poor" then to be the one used for the future to describe his Naomi, his wife, the mother of his child? She who ever seemed to him the richest creature that walked the earth, in all her human skill and tenderness, and heavenly grace and love, and was she now to be called "poor," because she had passed from the sin and suffering and sorrow of earth to her eternal rest? A stranger and a pilgrim here, now she was with the Father in heaven, the absent gathered home; the child of Light and of the Day had passed from earthly shadows to the life on which darkness cannot lour. Thus thinking of her, the sad word "poor" fell with a strange bewildering sound upon his ear; but as the struggle passed he reverted to the question, saying—

"Not the son of her sorrow, mother; rather say the son of her joy; for she is gone to all that was more her own than anything here."

Oliver Crisp was the fifth generation bearing the

same na   The last three had owned the Mill where they now lived and worked. His father attended the parish church, though the highest lessons he learned were not taught by man, but direct from the Holy Word. He had married early into a Quaker family, in the neighbouring town. In the first years of married life they often drove to the Quakers' meeting in the town, but this custom gradually dropped, and they went together to the parish church, or Mistress Crisp sent all beside, while she kept house. She was a woman of most upright mind; erect in figure, rather hard in countenance, but of a kindness of heart that sometimes showed itself in outward expression to the surprise of those who did not know her well. Her opinions and feelings were many of them narrowed and stiffened by early pressure from without, instead of being freely expanded from within. This want of early expansion of heart and mind caused her the loss of many touches of feeling and thought that would have moulded her strong nature with more beauty and delicacy. Yet, true in Christian principle and feeling, she lived to win the respect and regard of those who knew her; though her influence over others was not what under freer and fuller training it might have been. Her home was the undivided centre of her earthly love, though her kindness extended to many. During her son's married life Mistress Crisp had occupied a small but pretty cottage at the foot of the green hill on which the Mill and the Mill-house stood, but now in his bereavement she had returned to make her home with him and his motherless infant.

Oliver Crisp was the first of the name who had not been baptized in infancy. It would have been a strain of feeling to his mother, to which his father would not subject her; but Mistress Crisp knew that Naomi's feeling was strong, and concluded it would probably have its influence. Wishing not to add any difficulty to his mind in his circumstances of sorrow, she herself began the subject when some weeks had passed away, saying—

"Dost thee mean to sprinkle the child?"

"Baptize, mother, they call it."

"I know it," she replied; "but Baptism is of the Holy Spirit, which many have had who never were sprinkled. I am well assured thou hast been baptized of the Holy Spirit, my son; but thou never wast sprinkled."

On this subject Oliver was ready with an answer. He had often listened silently to the fervent words of Naomi; he had pondered and read on the question, seeking counsel from the one only source of true Wisdom; and now, to the surprise of his mother, he replied at once—

"We may be sure God doth not tie up His grace to the outward forms, so that they cannot be parted if it so pleaseth Him; but if He, who was man for our sakes, did use water when the Baptism of the Spirit came on Him, we cannot be wrong if we follow in His steps, who hath laid Baptism on us as a command, and a means of salvation. He stood for us all the way through, and who can say but we should be wrong, if we slighted the sign, when we sought for the grace?"

"Dost thee mean for thyself, son?"

"Well, mother, the child and I are left alone, and we must stand as one. God grant His grace may keep us one for ever!"

Mistress Crisp was silent, and Oliver was considering what he had said. The October twilight was growing duskier as they sat beside the fire; it was perhaps an easier time to Oliver Crisp for converse than the light of busy day. A feeling came over him as if he might have seemed to shut out his mother; she had made no comment on his declaration; and presently he said in a low tone, "Mother, might not you be the third?"

"Ah, son! I never would at the word of thy father; he asked it of me when thou wert an infant. I have sometimes wished I had not denied him; but when we have looked only on one side, 'tis not easy to turn for the other. We seem to have a born knowledge that our way must be right; but I have come to believe we should look into the Scriptures to learn from the Word and the Spirit; and then, may be, we should not always stick fast where we were!"

"Then, mother, receive the outward sign with the child and with me; and who knows but an added grace may come to us with it!"

"How could I turn for thy word, son, when I stood out against thy father's?"

"Not my word, O mother! but His word, who said, 'All power is given unto Me in heaven and in earth: go ye therefore, and teach all nations, baptizing them in the Name of the Father, and of the Son, and of the Holy Ghost.'"

"Ah, son! if it be His word, I have stood against Him so long, I dare not turn as persuaded by thee."

"Yet why not?" asked Oliver Crisp. "He who stood as son to His mother on earth, would never be against a son prevailing for good."

The days passed on quietly until Oliver Crisp said, "I would not see October out without the child being christened."

"Well," answered Mistress Crisp, "I can tell thee I have scarce thought on anything else. I think I can see light in it for thee and for me; but for the poor babe who cannot tell one thing from another, it seems to me superstition and nothing less nor more."

Then Oliver Crisp answered slowly but readily, as one might who spoke from a book, or from long consideration and settled conviction, "The grace that receiveth the poor babe that departs this life, is free to the infant at all times. It is His grace who knoweth no change nor shadow of turning. Thou must deny the dead babe His mercy, or grant it free to the living. The question of responsibility and free-will belongeth not to babes. It is a simple case of mercy for infants, through Him who took their nature that they might be received in God's mercy through Him. The case of neglecting salvation or rejecting the blessing doth not touch them. Mercy floweth free to the babe; thanks be to Him who was the sinless infant of Bethlehem for them!"

As he spoke he turned his eyes on the sleeping infant, and the fervour of Naomi's voice came over his soul as she said, "Did He not command that the children should be brought unto Him? Did He not blame those who would have kept them from Him? Did He not take them up in His arms and lay His hand upon them and bless them, and exhort all to follow their childlike spirit, if they would inherit the kingdom? O, Oliver," she added, "if when we were yet without strength Christ died for the ungodly, there surely is a welcome for the strengthless babe to His arms and His covenant! What would Naomi have felt if Obed, born to Boaz, might not have received the outward sign of God's covenant with Israel his people! And what would every Naomi, from the birth of Messiah down to your own Naomi to-day, feel, if their infants were denied the tender seal of the covenant of peace that now embraces their parents!"

Naomi had spoken to this effect, and the feeling of her words came back over the soul of her husband. Her Jewish fervour had been roused by the question, yet she asked no promise, and never named the subject again. Left free, Oliver Crisp felt the personal responsibility which led him the more earnestly to consider, and more fervently to act, when conviction had come to his mind.

His mother listened, but made no reply. After a while Oliver Crisp took up the subject again, increasingly anxious that his mother should see and act as appeared right to him.

"You would hold, mother, that while we are constantly seeking for the Holy Spirit to enlighten our minds in the Scriptures, and the knowledge of Christ, who is Himself the Word, you would hold we are bound to act up to the light that we have, without regard to the past of our life, or to man, wouldst thou not?"

"Yes, thy words have a right sound," she replied; "but I fear I have thought a deal of the past, and the way I was brought up in, and had much respect to man. I like thy discourse, and would have thee say more. I often wish now that I had let our poor Naomi speak more freely with me; somehow something rose up against it when she tried to begin."

"Ah, mother, that leads us back to the babe, and to Him who said, 'Whosoever shall humble himself as this little child, the same is greatest in the Kingdom of Heaven; and whoso shall receive one such little child IN MY NAME receiveth Me!' How then should not the little child be baptized in His NAME?"

"But they say baptism signifieth believing."

"So it must," replied her son, "for those of older years, such as were those whom the Apostles were to teach. Nor can baptism avail aught to the child in after years if it be not followed by faith. But baptism acknowledgeth the death of nature and the raising up to a new life in Christ, who both died and rose again that we might die in His death, and be raised in Him. This baptism signifieth; and this the believing parent may desire to show forth in his child. I do ofttimes see that a word is taken and made a block in the way, hindering and shutting out, when the blessed Truth is opening its arms on one side and the other."

The name he should give his infant cost Oliver Crisp many a thought. He said over and over, "Malachi," "Malachi," as breathed from the lips of Naomi; but though a name revered in the Bible, it had a strange unnatural sound to his ear in the familiar life of every day. Many times, when alone, he repeated it aloud to try whether he could get accustomed to the thought that one named Malachi could be the child of Oliver Crisp; but he always found his mind led by the name to some inspired words of the prophet, and never to the infant son of his home. He remembered the reason which Naomi had given for her choice of the name, but that reason was one Oliver Crisp failed to take in.

Naomi's mother was a Jewess by birth, the daughter of Jewish parents of foreign nationality. Receiving the Christian faith she had lost all that family ties could provide; she had married a Jewish missionary and had come with him, in his failing health, to England; led by his native ties to this village of the West, which was the dwelling-place of the Crisps. Left a widow, and losing all that had led her husband there, she earned a maintenance for herself and her child by her skill in embroidery— embroidery of the needle being in great request in those days.

Naomi's mother, passing from the intense expectation that pious Israelites held of a coming Messiah, had found a still higher hope in the blessed expectation that Jesus Christ, whom she now knew as Israel's true though rejected Redeemer, was coming again — that He was coming again, not first to receive to His glory His people Israel, His typical Bride ; but to receive first His Church to Himself, "the Lamb's wife"—that the day and the hour of His coming no man knew ; that all were to watch lest coming suddenly He should find them sleeping. Naomi's mother had but changed her expectation from a first coming to a second coming in glory ; when the children of the Light and of the Day would be "caught up on clouds to meet Him in the air, and so would be for ever with the Lord."

The Jewish week of six thousand years having nearly expired, Naomi's mother dwelt in thought on the seventh thousand — the Sabbath of rest and blessing—and she stored the heart of her daughter with the prophetic visions of millennial peace.

This intense personal love and expectation of Him who had once been despised and rejected of men, this hope full of immortality, steeped the fading years of earthly privation to Naomi's mother in the glow of life everlasting ; and gave to her child, Naomi, an elevation of thought and feeling,

which raised her above the depression of early circumstances, enabling her to tread in "blessed hope"
the pathway of life, daily waiting and watching for
the Messiah's return.

Oliver Crisp had never caught the inspiration of
this hope. He rested in the work wrought for man's
salvation, and believed it was a finished work. He
trusted his daily life to His Providence whose grace
had saved his soul. His spirit was restful, his life was
consistent; but it lacked the onward, upward tendency
that strong expectation gives. His life lacked the
spiritual brightness given by constantly turning to
One whose return is ever drawing nearer, One in
whom every hope is to meet its infinite and eternal
fulfilment.

On the day of the infant's baptism Oliver Crisp
said finally to himself, "Malachi! She must have
been dreaming some old Jewish dream, or had some
vision of things to come which I cannot understand!
She said, 'I should wish thee to call him by the
name that may seem best to thee.' She was always
the wisest of women; she knew she was leaving this
world for a better, and was more likely herself to
judge by that world than this! I know of no name
for honest trading like Oliver. It is a name that has
stood well for generations gone by, and may for
generations to come. It was my father's name, and
he gave it honour—for a worthier man never traded
in flour. It must be settled to-day. I shall be glad
when it is done with. I am sure I had best name
him OLIVER!"

CHAPTER III.

IT was the last day of calm October. Oliver Crisp
did not go to his Mill. The day of his motherless
infant's baptism was sacred to him as a Sabbath.
The old nurse who had tended the mother looked in,
asking leave to dress the baby, to which Mistress
Crisp gladly consented, for her mind was on the
strain with the events of the day, and she hardly
trusted her servant girl on a day so special! But
when she found the old nurse fixing tiny rosettes of
crape on each little sleeve, and on the band of the
white robe which Naomi had made and embroidered
in anticipation of that day, she was displeased, and
bade her keep such conceits for those who made
mourning a question of dress. The old nurse was
hurt, and said it was unchristian to let the poor babe
go out into the world with no signs of its sorrow
and loss. Mistress Crisp might have spoken
severely, for her feelings were much on the strain,
but her son came downstairs dressed in heavy black
cloth, which made a striking difference in him, as he
wore, except in deep mourning, corduroys and top-
boots; and his hat was covered with crape. This
satisfied the old nurse, and his presence calmed his
mother. People have a way of saying, " What a sin

to put yourself out when going to a holy service! " not considering that in the weakness of nature it is often deep feeling keeping the spirit on the strain which makes self-control so readily lost. Self-control is a cold victory; but the quivering spirit, if stayed on the Lord himself, can be kept by Him in perfect peace.

Oliver Crisp took his infant on his arm, and wrapped it up in Naomi's shawl with as much tenderness as a mother. He said to the old nurse, " Pass on, and we will follow." Then, in a voice that struggled with emotion, " Mother, we are going to show forth that we receive the kingdom of heaven as little children to-day; let us kneel at His feet whose blessing we seek." Mistress Crisp kneeled by her son; it had not been her custom to kneel, she sat on her chair at morning and evening prayer, but now she felt it a comfort to take the outward posture of supplication. Her son kneeled on one knee, on the other lay his infant asleep on his arm; quiet tears fell from the mother's eyes, calming and softening her spirit in prayer.

" Lord Jesus, we come in Thy name. We are slow of speech, and slow of understanding Thy love; but here we offer and present ourselves, our souls and bodies, to be unto Thee a reasonable sacrifice, praying Thee that we may be filled with the Spirit. We bring this infant to the arms of Thy mercy, beseeching Thee that as one whom his mother comforteth, Thou wouldest receive, keep, and comfort him, both now and evermore, to the glory of Thy grace, O God, our heavenly Father, in our ever-blessed Lord and Saviour. Amen."

Then Oliver Crisp put on his hat, and stepped slowly and cautiously down the threshold-step; he walked as one carrying a burden; it was not the weight but the treasure he bore that made him tread so heedfully. They said he had never taken the infant in his arms before that day; they did not know the secrets of Naomi's departing hour.

As Mistress Crisp passed her own cottage gate, she said, "I will be up with you in no time;" and hurrying to the casement of the now deserted dwelling, she plucked a red rose, that hung its head as if it mourned the summer. She laid it in the white folds of her neckerchief, and hastened on. As they trod the winding lane to the church, they saw one and another gathering there. Farmer Caxton, in his Sunday coat of black; Keziah, the servant girl, followed him, with a child dressed in mourning in her arms, Baby Meg by name; Mistress Caxton hurrying after, with her prayer-book in her white pocket-handkerchief. Mother Dumbleton, the village help. Old Joe Richards, with his thin bent legs, leaning on his oaken staff; he looked hard at Mistress Crisp, for his small eyes were keen, he could read fine type without glasses, and he was pretty sure he caught a sight of the red rose that was not meant to be seen. It was afternoon-school time, but children were watching down the lane to see the baby come, and, walking slowly on before was Dame Truman, the village schoolmistress; she held up her hand and looked to heaven as the baby passed, as though to ask a blessing on him.

Near the church porch stood a figure never seen there but once before—a Jew, with long black beard : he was not an old man, but he stooped as though he were, with downcast looks. Oliver Crisp had not spoken all the way, oppressed, it might be, by the sight of a gathering company, but now he said, " There's Benoni ! " Mistress Crisp replied, " Sure he will never come in to such a service ; thee will not ask him ; he is one who resisteth the Spirit ! " They passed in silence under the old church-porch, but as they passed Benoni clasped his hands ; he did not speak nor look up. They left him there, and when they returned Benoni was gone.

They entered the church, close by where the old font stood, typical of admission by baptism to the outward and visible church. The sponsors were already standing there, the children of the old Castle, whose tower and turrets rose above the forest-trees that clustered high upon the eminence on which the Castle stood ;—Isabelle and Conrad, eldest son and daughter of the Colonel and Madame Gray, sponsors for Naomi's child, and witnesses of the elder baptisms.

The three generations—mother, son, and infant, with the youthful sponsors, gathered round the font. It was beautifully wreathed with creepers and white chrysanthemums, but the flowers were lost on Oliver Crisp ; nor did he see the friendly people, nor the outer wreath of clustering children, awed from pressing nearer by Dame Truman's lifted finger, and the tears she wiped away—he only saw the little chamber in the sunset's golden light, the young beloved wife, the extended arms holding his infant to him, the dark eyes swimming in their tears, and heard her low tones—earth's only music to him! Yet was the service real; and as its holy words drew back his absent heart, they led his downcast eye to mark another presence there;—even His who gathers the lambs in His arms, folds them in His bosom, and gently leads the burdened ones.

When the minister gave back the infant, Isabelle took him in her arms, and her gentle kiss on the sleeping brow left her lips wet with the sprinkled dew. "Oliver," Naomi's child, her first god-child; it was hard to give him up when all was over, but friendly greetings were gathering round the font; she gave him to Mistress Crisp, who folded him closer than ever before, with the secret feeling of "one Lord, one faith, one baptism." Isabelle and Conrad turned for the Castle, and a group of many friends trod the lane to the village with Oliver Crisp.

Oliver Crisp walked, thoughtful and almost silent, in the midst of his friends. It might be singular that a man of such silent reserve should be so much thought of as was this man. A stranger would not have called him a pleasant man; but all who knew him felt his worth. You might not be sure of his words, but you might be sure of his heart; and when his words were given they were pretty certain to be right words.

Mistress Crisp hastened on, glad to find herself alone with the infant, now drawn to her heart by a spiritual tie. She could not be alone in company as her son could, and her heart was overflowing with feeling; her mind was relieved; a blessing had come in her desire "to fulfil all righteousness." Her son had read the fourth of Matthew in their early service that morning, and above her the heavens seemed opened as never before, and the words passed and repassed through her mind, how, when John forbade the Saviour to seek baptism of him, the divine Redeemer answered, "Suffer it to be so now, for thus it becometh us to fulfil all righteousness. Then he suffered Him." And truly she felt more one with Him, her gracious Saviour, on whom the out-poured water was the sign of the fulness of the indwelling Spirit.

In her deeper tenderness of feeling she was sorry she had wished to shut out Benoni. Still she thought that a wandering ped'ar, an unbelieving Jew, could not be in the right place in such a service, and, was it not said in the Acts, of such unbelieving Jews, "Ye do always resist the Holy Ghost!" Yet, for all that, she felt kindly now even to him. It was strange that an outward rite that seemed meant to shut her in to the faith by a visible sign, instead of making her feel more divided from those outside, should draw her closer in feeling to such outcasts: she could not understand this; but she felt she had none to inquire of save her silent son; so as usual she let the question alone.

She did not know, and she had none to tell her, that every act of simple obedience, faith, and love draws us closer to the Lord himself. God is Love! and he that dwelleth in Love dwelleth in God, and God in him. Whether the act have an outward form or be only a spiritual exercise, none can set their heart to keep the words of Christ, without finding the promise of Christ fulfilled, "My Father will love him, and we will come unto him, and make our abode with him." This was the secret of the deeper tenderness, whether flowing through an appointed sacrament or any other means of grace;—the deeper consciousness of the indwelling Christ in the soul.

And then, as small things mingle with great, when undressing the baby, she thought of her displeasure at the little crape-rosettes and at mourning in general. She recollected the heavy mourning of Isabelle Gray—her son's deep mourning did not appear unnatural to her —Isabelle had been left fatherless only a few months before; and it seemed to Mistress Crisp, in her softened feeling, that the deep mourning made a silent appeal to those around her to remember her sorrow, not to expect from her what at other times would have been given—special greetings to all assembled there; it made a softened barrier, a shield from the outer world, for which the sorrowing heart was unready; and she thought she would not again condemn the raiment of sorrow.

When Isabelle gave back the infant, Mistress Crisp said, " Wilt thee come and see him sometimes ?   1 know thou hadst a kindness for his poor mother."

The word "poor" took young Isabelle by surprise; she had loved Naomi as the friend of her soul —a brief friendship, from her tenth to her fifteenth year. She stood there enriched with the treasures of Naomi's heart, and the wisdom Naomi had learned from the Only Wise; the pitying word " poor " could never be linked with Naomi's name ! She did not know then that those whose thoughts cleave to the dust of the mortal body, who see not the glory and feel not the power of the "present with the Lord," in Whose presence is fulness of joy and pleasures for evermore, can only speak in pitying, though tender, terms of the departed.

Isabelle gladly accepted the invitation; and, taking her brother's arm, they turned up the long avenue of old chestnuts that led from the church to the Castle.

It was one of those autumns that linger in the mind as a perfect ideal of the season. The sky was intensely blue, the trees in full foliage of gold, untouched by the wind, the stillness of the autumnal air only more felt for the caw of the rooks floating high overhead, and the nearer song of the robin— that old song of hope and trust, though wintry days may be near, heard often but slowly learned. The children of the Castle sat under the trees on one of the many seats placed at fine points of view. The uplands of the park opened before them, and they wondered at the glory of the golden foliage, and watched the stately deer as they browsed under the trees, and the touch of autumnal decay blended with their sorrow.

The sense of being suddenly left fatherless is a strange surprise to a young heart. Conrad was yet only in his seventeenth year. The shield that had always been raised between him and the world had suddenly dropped; the hand that had held it lay buried cold and deep and could not raise it again. The heart that ever responded warmly was silent; he must enter life's battle fatherless! As he thought on this, how poor seemed all the wealth at his command, and all the outward means of advancement and pleasure, weighed against that one buried heart, to whose wisdom and tenderness he could not now return or appeal! But Conrad knew a Father in heaven of whom he could say, "Thou hast given me the shield of Thy salvation; and Thy gentleness hath made me great." Of all that his father had left him, the richest and most sacred inheritance was, he knew and felt, the life that father had lived, and the prayers that had been offered for him.

They sat in the stillness and beauty until Isabelle rose with thoughts of her mother, and they hastened home. They had spent the early morning wreathing the font with bright flowers for Naomi's sake ;— Naomi—who had entered on an inheritance incorruptible, undefiled, and that fadeth not away.

As Oliver Crisp walked home through the lane to the village, Mistress Caxton remarked on the beautiful flowers adorning the font; he had not noticed them, a flower had no natural attractions for him; but an ear of corn was a marvel to his mind—its structure, growth, and perfection. You might often see him lingering in a corn-field, examining, admiring, and, we may say, adoring the bounteous Creator. "This also cometh forth from the Lord of Hosts, who is wonderful in counsel and excellent in working."

Oliver Crisp asked his mother, in the evening, if she had noticed the flowers, of which the people in the church made such admiring mention.

His mother had noticed them; but she thought them out of place! Mistress Crisp had a saying, "Things out of place are more hurtful than helpful." She always had a wise reason to give why they *were* hurtful; yet it made the lines drawn round her appear very strict, as many things in her view were thought out of place, and too often it might be that they were so in reality. Brought up in the strictest discipline of Quakerism, strongly bound in feeling by its outward regulations; then placed in the midst of those who entirely disregarded them, cut off from strict membership from the body of Friends by her marriage, she held the more strictly to all that outwardly belonged to that religious section. She had none to lead her above and beyond forms and systems, to show her that the letter alone killeth; but the spirit giveth life. Believing the principles of the society in which she had been brought up to be more spiritual than those of any other, she had clung to outward regulations and observances as though the shell of necessity held the kernel. She was one whom all felt must follow her own views; whom no one endeavoured to move or influence; until Naomi called her " mother ! " and unconsciously drew the stiffened spirit into the softer blendings of truth, natural and divine.

It was not long after the happy union of her son with Naomi that others began to find they could awake a new response in Mistress Crisp, even on subjects on which they had known her mind to have been made up before. You could penetrate the surface now, and the pure water of the heart's true feeling instantly sprang up to view.

Old Joseph Richards was one of the first who discovered in Mistress Crisp a greater readiness to listen with interest, and fall in with the feelings of others. It was natural that old Joseph should be one of the first to discover a softening response ; as he was a great lover of conversation, when the subject matter could be of his own choosing and conducting.

A conversation arose between them when Mistress Crisp had passed her first winter in the cottage at the foot of the hill on which stood the Mill. The cottage garden had been gay in past years—much admired by the passers-by. Its hedge of close-clipped yew, and yew pyramids, closely cut, on each side of the gate, only threw into brighter relief its gay borders, where every standard cottage-flower might be viewed in its season. Mistress Crisp's first work on entering was to clear out the borders; a heap of leaves and roots slowly consuming, was the last relic of that gay little garden. It was then well dug up and closely planted with vegetables and fruit, with a bed of herbs large enough to have supplied the kitchen of the Castle.

The passer-by felt the change a dull one; it added to the retirement of the cottage, as no stranger now stopped to gaze; the only added company it brought was the birds; they at once increased in number, the larger supply of fruit being attractive to them; they crowded the trees that skirted the garden, and paid their tribute of song. It was impossible for Mistress Crisp to have a cultivated taste for music, and having no natural love for it, she often found their harmony oppressive, beginning at early dawn, and the nightingales in full chorus by night; but to shoot them would be a wanton outrage, and to deny them their share of her fruit, even though she found it a large share, would have been contrary to her benevolent feelings; so the birds sang on, and Mistress Crisp only expressed a regret when her black currant and red currant jelly ran short in supply for the sick.

It was a warm evening in spring; the first season of the change in the garden, when old Joseph Richards passing by, stopped to greet Mistress Crisp, who was carefully watering her herbs. Mistress Crisp knew how welcome a talk was to old Joseph, and asked him in to take a seat in the porch. Joseph entered the gate, and stopped at every step, remarking the change.

"Where be the grand old pi'ny that used to roll out his red balls from yon corner? He was king of the garden! Did the frost nip him up?"

"There was no need to wait for the frost," replied Mistress Crisp; "there is a fine bed of leeks in that corner, and many a poor body, I hope, will know the difference this winter between a piony and a leek."

"Well, mistress, for all you could neither boil him nor bake, I liked the old tree."

"Flaunting colours have no favour with me," replied Mistress Crisp, with decision.

"Well, now," said Joseph, who had taken his seat in the porch of the cottage, "when I was in the seafaring service, I saw a deal of foreign parts, and I'll be bound you'll scarce think it creditable" (meaning credible), "but the birds there are as gay as any blossom; decked out, I can promise you, as gaudy as can be. Why I have seen red and yellow and green, all laid on together, and a touch of black, as if to show up the colours. They were the cheerfulest fowls you could think to see for colour; but never a piper amongst them! I'll be bound, mistress, He that made them so gay is wiser than we!"

"But, friend, hast thou no notion of the difference between birds of the air, and mortals, who put on their finery for pride and conceit?"

"Well, now, mistress, don't take me amiss; you see I have travelled amain, and that stirs a man up to take notice. How it hurts me to see our poor fellows by dozens just lay by their plough or their sickle, as may be, for their platter, and their pipe, and their pillow!   I do twit them with never looking off the brown earth; but they keep their eyes afore them, and never look up nor around!"

"But what has that to do," asked Mistress Crisp, "with the parading of colour?"

"Deary me!" answered old Joseph, "I don't know.   I suppose I was wandering.   I am given to that sort of thing; it's a bad feeling when your recollection has broke away from the bridle, and you get pulled up, and don't know where you be!   But as I was thinking, for I do remember that, I never liked my old woman so well as when she was dressed out in her blue gown; it was home-spun by her mother, and dyed a real blue; and her red ribbon pinned round her head!   Her hair was as white as the snow, turned right back off, as good, aye! and as handsome a face as ever I wish to see!   Sometimes she would grow thrifty, and pin on a ribbon of black.   Wouldn't I soon have it off!   I always was a man for colour, and, mistress, you'll not think the worse of me," said old Joseph, in a pleading tone; "but I do think if our old dears and our young all travelled the waysides in black, we should look as if we followed a funeral!"

"Thee may have brown, friend, and grey, without seeking for show!"

"I know it, mistress, I know it; but only to see how the red cloaks warm you up by the look of them, all the same as a sunbeam!   And I have sat by the firelight, and taken notice of the red poppies on my old woman's print-gown until I have felt like taking a walk on a gay summer-day! Deary me! if it had been nothing but black, I should have thought she was sitting there mourning for me! But beside this, I find a blessing in it too. I have got a rose as red as any pi'ny; it covers my chamber-window. I am not much for sleep now; I always wake with the sun, when the first bird gives its twitter under the eave. There I lie, for it rests my old bones, and what should I do up? So I watch for the first red rose that blooms, and the next, and the next; and you may believe me, as I lie there, with the rising sun shining full, they mind me of the great drops of blood that were shed in the garden from Him who kneeled in anguish for us! You may not see how they can show up like that; but they are as like to great drops of blood as two things can be; and when you have once taken the notion, there is no doing away with it. I used to weary and weary of the sun up so early; but now he might shine all the night, and I should not complain, for when I open my eyes and see the red roses there, I am away in that garden! I think of Him there, then the cross, and the grave, and the angels, and the village where He turned in to sup, and the room with the doors shut, and the shore, and the hill where He went up, and the clouds hid Him, until they open again and we rise up to meet Him. I finish one part before I begin another, and now, by my thinking it over so often, it runs as clear through my mind as yon brook, and I am scarce ready when I ought to be stirring and down ! "

" Couldst thou come at a small tree for me that would run over my window ? "

" I could graff one," replied old Joseph.

" If thou couldst I would thank thee."

" Yes, yes, I can do that as well as the trained men. I have always had nature in hand all my day. The top gardener at the Castle, he would say to me, ' Joe,' says he, ' I can trust ye, and a little trust goes further than a deal of skill.' I have known him set me to open or shut the vine-houses, when an inch too much or too little might ruin the fruitage. ' Be very particular, Joe,' he would say; he knew very well it was just what I was, or he never would have set me to do that. I had been used in my time more to favour plantations. How glad my lady was to get me with my bill-hook in hand! I used to feel vexed to hack away as I did, for I thought, Who had made them ! but she would look wonderful pleasant, and say, ' They will only grow better, Joseph!' I did think that was a lesson for me, to see how one bough after another has been lopped off from me; but I believe it was true; for my thoughts were all upon them when they grew about me, and now my old heart is just resting wholly in Him.

" But as I was saying, I can see to the tree. We must just get a wild stock from the wood, put in a graft off my good tree, and the wild stock will change its nature. Is not that written out as clear in the truth as if writ in a book, to teach us that the old nature must be changed to the new, not of itself but of a gift from above! Yes, yes, a graft from the one tree of life, that is He who died and rose again, in whom our life is hid; we live if He live in us! Ain't it so, Mistress Crisp?"

"Yes, friend, thy memory must be a great comfort to thee."

"It did not come out of my memory," replied Joseph; "it came from Him who gave me the gift. O, mistress, 'tis an unspeakable gift! Haven't you found it so?"

"May be it will come fuller to me when I have thy rose-tree! But few can have memories like thine."

"Ah, mistress, so they say; but I tell them we are fashioned alike, but folks let their memories go napping when they should be at work. I know well 'tis easiest to get slothful and stiff, and doze away in my chair; but I say, 'Wake up, old Joe, and stir about, or thy limbs won't long serve ye!' But folks won't do that with their memory, as I tell them; they say 'tis gone, when 'tis no more dead than I am, but only just sleeping for sloth. I say to them that make that excuse ready, 'Wake it and work it, and you'll find there's life in it yet!'"

"I don't know, friend Joseph; thy advice is good, no doubt, but there is a weakness comes over, that when you would remember good things you cannot."

"Well, mistress, I am always hobbling about, having a word with one and then with another. It is all I can do, for I am seventy-three if I am a day. And if I would sit and listen, folks young and hearty, aye, children to me, would talk by the hour and tell me all things that had happened, aye, and things that had never happened too; and then when I try to turn them upon good, they say their memories are weak. Well, I take them at their word, and I say, No doubt that they be! Then they are just satisfied and comfortable like; for there are plenty have a notion that if old Joe will agree with them they must be right. It ain't the thing to set up a poor sinner like that, but that is their notion. So when we be all agreed that their memories be weak, I put it to them, 'How do you serve a weak body? Do you starve it because it's weak?' 'No,' they say, 'we feed it.' Then I say, 'Don't you crave to nourish it up with meat and with wine?' 'Yes,' say they. 'Well then,' I say, 'for why do you starve your weak memory? Don't He say who is the Truth, "My flesh is meat indeed, and my blood is drink indeed!" Ah, dear souls,' I say, 'if you did feed upon Christ you would find your weak memory grow stronger to think upon Him! Read of Him, speak to Him, speak of Him, and hear of Him when you can and where you can, and you will soon find that whatever else you forget your memory will be strong to think upon Him.' I put it many ways as it seems to come at the time, and sometimes I seem to think it helps them a bit!

But, mistress, I be ashamed talking here for this while. You see I be an old man, and my heart's been filling so long that now it runs over; but I thank you kindly for the discourse we have had, and I won't be slow to see after the tree. I wish you a good night." And old Joseph raised his hat and bowed low as he rose to depart, for no persuasions of Mistress Crisp had ever succeeded in constraining the old man to forego the respect he felt due, by uncovering his head.

"Fare thee well, friend Joseph; I hope thee will call in again."

The rose-tree was planted and flourished, and it lacked not care. Mistress Crisp tended it with affection, and old Joseph often looked in. He was still a pilgrim six years after, and able to reach the church on the day when Naomi's infant was baptized, with father and grandmother, the day when Mistress Crisp hid the red rose in her neckerchief. Across the little pathway from where the red rose grew over the lattice, Mistress Crisp had a border of tall white lilies: when in bloom they formed a beautiful contrast to the crimson blossoms of the rose, and she preserved the lily petals in brandy for cuts and bruises; so in one way or another the little garden became both useful and ornamental.

CHAPTER IV.

In real life there is no such thing as monotony. An occupation may be monotonous, or affliction may exclude the endless variety naturally open to all, but life itself has no monotony. The secret of the stage holding such power to interest and enchain the mind, is because it supplies in an exaggerated form what every human being ought to be able to find, in due proportion, through the emotions and perceptions of life.

Susceptibilities that have not their healthy exercise always demand compensation in an unhealthy and exciting form. There is more true tragedy and comedy in real life than can ever be found woven into the drama ; year by year they open their varied scenes and blend their influences. Comedy is but the ripple of the surface, catching the fitful play of light ; tragedy the depths below. Wit or humour, if true to the human heart, has its grace and tenderness ; if devoid of purest feeling it may amuse the fancy, which is itself a misshaping tool, but cannot charm the imagination, the soul's creative faculty. Tragedy has its emotions of joy as deep as those of sorrow. Tragedy and comedy often blend even as we see the tear and the smile. It is difficult to give

either in strict truth with human nature; but comedy
more difficult than tragedy. Its ripple on the surface is often so slight, the light that plays in it so
changeful or so fleeting, that words fail to embody
it ; in its richest, purest form its essence is so subtle,
it cannot be caught and confined in the written
page; it is soon robbed of its delicate grace, and
becomes exaggerated and coarse. But it may surely
be affirmed that both are found existing in all fully-
developed life; whether rich or poor, learned or unlearned.

It was the deeper emotions of life that were
aroused in Naomi's mother. She had been the
daughter of wealthy Hebrews, brought up in a home
of learning and elegance, enabling her to impart
much to her child that raised her, both in mind and
heart, above the ordinary level even of those whose
means enabled them to command the education of
the day. Yet as the child of poverty, Naomi was
trained in all the simplicity and homely duties of
cottage life. No village " help " was seen in her
mother's home ; it was Naomi who kept the floor of
cold cement, common in those parts, so clean ; who
polished the old furniture, left by her father's parents,
until you saw the bright reflection of fire or candle in
it. All was done so neatly that the little working
woman never looked untidy, nor had anything untidy
round her. It was a happy life she lived, too young
to remember any other. She was her mother's
earthly all; a child clothed with humility, and her free
and loving nature made her a general favourite. At

home in almost every cottage, she had many friends; while her constant companionship with her mother, who most carefully taught and trained her, kept her from the danger that her free childhood might have found, in association with many who lacked the grace of mind and heart that adorned her mother.

Naomi was an English child, and dearly loved her native home; while the dreamland of her heart was the fair inheritance of Israel's scattered race; and its horizon the blissful scene of bright millennial years. Naomi's mother had never lost the feeling of a stranger in a strange land; she could not blend with her own life the ties that clustered round her child; living so intensely in feeling, shortened her years; few and evil life's days seemed to her; yet the little moment wore a halo of glory in the love that redeemed from all evil. Naomi was the one flower in life's wilderness for her, the one only object for which she still toiled. At times she almost lost sight of the past, and lived only in the present and future, while she cherished her child.

The village miller, Oliver Crisp's father, felt from the first the high claim that the widow had to respect and attention. His kindness had cheered the last days of her husband, and then became the solace of the widow. He was a plain man, living in the same house that his father occupied before him; not caring, with better means, to enlarge his expenses; but with a heart to feel and a hand to aid in distress. Mr. Crisp (he too was an Oliver) some-

times found he had a bushel of flour " on hand,"
or half a sack of potatoes " not wanted ; " or flour
had risen in the market, and Naomi's mother must
share the benefit. A grave and somewhat gruff
man to strangers, he had a blunt, kind way of giving
gifts that made them seem so natural that the re-
ceiver was never surprised, and had to think over
the event before the favour was exactly understood.

The last visit he paid her she could never forget.
It was winter, a cold snowy night ; but he looked in
on his way from market ; he could not stay, only
inquiring kindly, as he had not seen them at his
house for a while ; then as he turned from her little
fireside, he said—

" I met the agent on his way yesterday for the
rent. I said you were but sadly, and would not
want to be bothered, so I paid it up ; don't think of
it more, it makes no odds to me ! "

He never crossed that threshold again. An
illness of a few weeks removed him from the midst
of the busy life he led, and the deeds of kindness in
which he delighted. The miller's son, Oliver, was
fully able to take his father's place ; he was a son
worthy of his parents, thoughtful, true, and good to
all. Ten years older than Naomi, he had been to
her a brother, a friend, and almost a young father.
Naomi had never known life without her friend Oliver
as her playfellow.

The Mill-house was a palace in those days to
Naomi, for the farm-houses were not open to her
and her mother. It was a singularly bare abode, for

Mistress Crisp removed even the few quaint conceits of its former days; but the much larger room, the white bricks neatly sanded, the old oak furniture from past generations, the great eight-day clock, the upstairs rooms with their far-reaching view, and the wonders of the Mill, the terror of the sails that came round so inevitably, with that strange low swoop, her hand safe in her friend Oliver's whenever she went near; the live stock—two horses, a dog, two cats, and a poultry-yard, a large rabbit-house, and occasional additions of little silky pigs—all this was great advancement to Naomi; and always enjoyed under Oliver's fostering care, his father's grave yet tender kindness, and Mistress Crisp's cordial welcome, what could it lack to charm the child.

Yet this was not all, for Oliver was bent on pleasing Naomi in her cottage home. Her canary, looking like a drop of amber, sung in her low thatched cottage, in a cage that Oliver had made. Her own little rabbit-hutch was his work, and every woodland walk she took with him, he carried her across the streams dryshod; and while he climbed higher, he let down a hand to help the little active girl to the lower branches of the trees. Neither had a friend beside, a sister nor a brother; who could help rejoicing that they found all this in each other!

As Naomi grew into her tall girlhood, the intercourse changed; they did not meet less often, but it was not now for free joys of childhood. But Naomi could still tell all their daily life to Oliver, and he still cared for every want and wish.

He was seven-and-twenty when his father left him, his widowed mother's stay. It was his first bereavement, his first sorrow. All he wanted he had found in the two homes, and the few hearts that made the circle of his inner life. He had no idea of sorrow until his father went; the loss fell on him like a blow. Strong man as he was, he could not rally; he turned from the Mill, turned from the market, he seemed to turn from all; while Naomi and her mother wept together the loss of such a friend as Oliver's father had been.

It was many days before Oliver crossed their threshold; and when he came, though he sat there as of old, he scarcely spoke; yet he came again and again, as if their starting tears and few brief words of sorrow had power to soothe. "He is a true man," said the widow, "who mourns so for a father!"

Naomi looked up, and her full heart drank in her mother's praise of Oliver.

It was at this time that Mistress Crisp felt called upon to counsel her son, saying, "Is it thy mind to know whether thy visits are acceptable to Naomi? If it be, thou hadst better go forward at once; if not, keep thy distance; thou hast been free long enough!"

The cloud of bereavement that had hung so heavily over Oliver Crisp now seemed to deepen, and the lights that had lighted his pathway went out one by one. Too sad at heart to seek earthly happiness while the sods were scarce welded on the grave of his father, he withdrew from his friends of the cottage; and a heavy reserve, that seemed a chilling coldness, took the place of his once friendly manner.

Then it was that Naomi started into womanhood, and knew what her past life had been, what her present was not, and what her future was never likely to be! A desolation stole over her young heart, that her mother's tenderness, though it soothed, could not cheer. The widow's soul was pierced with a deeper grief than she had known before; her wan cheek grew paler, and her strength declined. They were not left to want in temporal things; in some way—they hardly knew how—every want was supplied.

Mistress Crisp, quite surprised at the turn things had taken, often called in. She never imagined that the chilling separation could in any way have arisen from her desire to bring things to an issue, to make both happy, or save both from misery. It was, and always had been in life her one desire to do the right thing; she had no second purpose ever to serve; no inferior reason; only this one object;—to do, and help others to do, the right thing. Therefore, perhaps, it was, that she never felt conscious of a mistake. If a thing took a wrong turn, she always felt she had done the utmost to keep it right; if it could have been put right, what she had done would have accomplished that end. This was not any conscious self-assertion, but the result of her one single aim and desire, always to do right. Any one of less integrity would have readily supposed the possibility of a mistake, where Mistress Crisp felt assured she had done all for the best. She was disappointed and sorry, for no one to her equalled Naomi. She could not follow a stream that flowed rock-bound out of sight.

Oliver sometimes looked in on the widow and her daughter, but the visits were brief. and the heart-ache deepened under his civility. He must be concerned in many kindnesses done, yet they could not tell how. Oliver now became a far more reserved man than his father. Many kindnesses were still shown around; but you could seldom trace his foot-steps, and you seldom heard his words. He would make suggestions to his mother, who was ready to follow them out; she would sometimes say, " I don't know how it is, but the things my son can see do not seem to strike me ! "

No one could take a liberty with Mistress Crisp; her high-minded character and decision kept people at a distance. All the village felt disappointed in the failure of their expectations, and many rumours were afloat. Now and then a word on the subject reached her; and if it were from any to whom she felt called to reply, she said at first, " It's just my son's honour; he is breaking off to leave Naomi free ; and then, if she is constant, he will ask her outright." But when two years ran their slow round, her heart became troubled, and she said, " If ever man sinned by honour, 'tis my son ! I believe he will carry it on until it meets where it begun, right round in a circle, and love clean shut out! And if he does, I for one will maintain a man's honour may harden his heart; for it keeps apart two sent on earth to be one—if ever there were such a thing as two made for each other! And for all that I have asked her, she has not been in this house for a twelvemonth!"

"May be," said Mistress Caxton, who was the one engaged in a friendly talk at this time in a call at the Mill-house; "may be, your son thinks of you, and fears to break up your home."

"I wish he did think of me," replied Mistress Crisp, with some sharpness; "he has heard my mind often enough to have made up his own, and been married, aye, twenty times over! I have given it up now; for, as they say, love can't be driven. I never felt so sure of anything as of him and Naomi. I have vexed and fretted, too, until I have now let it alone."

Naomi was seldom seen out; her mother required her constant care; and except for their little purchases, and the pint of new milk she now daily fetched at evening milking from Farmer Caxton's cow-byre, she was seldom seen abroad. The childhood she had kept so long in happy freedom of thought and feeling, was gone; her very youth seemed passing away, and womanhood, with all its depth, was hers. Her mother was fading day by day, bearing now a broken heart, that bowed resigned, but seemed to have no power to rejoice, feeling that her child must soon be left quite unprovided for—to a cold, evil world, without a friend. Her longing eyes were bent so sadly on the dark future of her daughter, that they failed to see or seek the blessedness awaiting her own departing spirit.

This was one of those strange pauses that sometimes come in human life, when the very wheels of existence seem locked, dragging heavily, and all stagnates within and around. The solemn pressure of a heavy hand is laid on the spring that governs life; it weighs heavier and heavier; there seems little hope that it can ever be lifted, and the heavy-laden spirit toils on in the dead calm of existence. So it was with Naomi and her widowed mother; and so it was with Oliver. He was naturally a man of close reserve, and when once he had shut himself up in his sorrow, and lost the living play of Naomi's life on his own, his natural reserve grew and strengthened; he nurtured the gloom that a father's lost presence in everything cast over him; and had not, it seemed, the spirit or the energy of will to launch out into any new interest and blessing.

Old Joseph's keen eyes had long been observing all that troubled his friends; but true religion imparted true feeling to him. He often said, when others were impatient to judge, or to hurry anything, "Remember there is a time to speak, and a time to be silent! Let be, let be; don't be meddling too soon; meddle and mar are words to hang always together. Sometimes when I am in a heat to be doing or speaking, I strike down my old staff and spell out the word, 'wait.' 'Tis a wonderful word! Tens of tens of times it has held me back from mischief. I have lived a long day, and most of the troubles I have seen folks come out the wrong side of, was just for the want of laying down at their feet that one little word 'wait.' If they had but known the meaning of that word, they would have ended right instead of wrong. I always hold with teaching the young; there's nothing like it, I say. Well, you know I am old Joseph, and there is never an urchin but can give me the slip; so I say I must not set up for a teacher! But when I have a few odd halfpence, I just buy up a few goodies, and when I happen of a child handy, I fish one out, and I say, 'Now, youngling, I'll give you this goody when you can spell me a word;' and then I spell, w-a-i-t. How quick they catch it up, to be sure, with their eye on the goody! And it's got such a hold on their memories, that there is scarce a child when they meet me but cries out, 'I can spell wait.' Then I say to them betimes, 'Now, you will find that word, WAIT, is one of the main secrets of life. Old Joseph will soon lie under the green turf; but when you are big lads and girls, and men and women, you come and stand by where he sleeps, and spell his word, WAIT; and what's more, you look in the Book where he found it, and you will find a blessing laid on it there.' I have known the time that I have given them a goody for every separate WAIT they would find in the Book. The poor rogues! I had nothing better to give them, and they took it kindly from me."

He was at this time a busy labourer in the Castle

plantations, but often found time to look in at Naomi's house, to inquire for her mother. In the early spring of the year, more than two years since the loss of the kind miller, he called in one evening, and finding the widow alone, and in weakness and pain, he sat with her awhile. Her spirit was desponding, and old Joseph encouraged her to tell out her trouble.

"Master Richards," she said, "I have never spoken to a creature of the heavy weight on my mind; but we two are alone, and I believe I may speak safely to you. I am dying, my days are few now; and I have not a friend to whose care I can commit my Naomi! An orphan and friendless is a terrible thing for one only nineteen, in an evil world like this!"

"Have ye thought on the words, 'Leave thy fatherless children with Me! I will preserve them alive, and let thy widows trust in Me?'"

"Yes, I have read, and thought, and prayed over every promise I could find; but the rest and the peace do not come."

Then old Joseph sat considering awhile, as though he took counsel with a wiser than himself. At length he said kindly, "I know the trouble must be great! To our thinking, an earthly protector was provided, and now that blessing seems gone!"

"Indeed it does," said the widow.

"Have they said one another nay?" asked old Joseph.

"No, never a word but of kindness between them."

"Be there any obstacle laid in the way?"

"No, I am sure of that; there is nothing."

"Then," said Joseph, "it is but a darkness raised up by the Evil One! Many a time I have known him raise up a chill mist, that has crept over poor souls, they did not seem to know how; and it's nipped them up like a frost-bitten rose, the beauty just gone, and they can't tell how it came. Sometimes it takes them with a chill to Him that's above them, and they can't get the better of it, because they think it's in them; whereas it's no such thing, but it's just round about them; and if they would believe it and strike through it, they would get above it in no time. Sometimes it just comes between them and folks here, and makes a coldness and a gloom that keeps on troubling their minds; and they say, it is this, or 'tis that, when it's just no such thing, but only a cold mist that's risen up round their spirit; and if they would only strike through it, there's peace and love just beyond it. It's a net for the feet, and it holds many a warm heart fast bound against this or that; and there is only one Deliverer; but thanks be to God, there is a Hand, if they would but take it, would lead them out in a step, and that chill left behind them for ever."

"I think it must be so, Master Richards; but I see no help for it?"

"Well, now, I am not of your mind in that;

there is always help for them who know where to look for it; but may be, you have been asking and asking to have it done from above, when it's just left to you to do it below?"

"O, Master Richards, I could not do anything!"

"Why not? are they not both as your children, the one almost as much as the other? Have they not both taken your word, and minded your way in days that are past? You are bound to speak up as much for the good of the one as the other. I will not say any more, for that's my word of advice, and I can't add to it nor take from it; but you see, if I am right and if I am sent with this message to you, the opportunity will full surely be given, and you do your part and use it. But let come what may, hold your trust to Him who has promised all shall work together for good."

The widow waited and watched. It was not long before Oliver called in to inquire how she was; she was alone, and he sat down and seemed to speak more freely than before. Any one who had anything to say to Oliver Crisp was sure of many an opportunity in the silences between his few sentences. Gathering up the courage of faith, the widow said, with strong effort, "My days are numbered now—the life you have nourished so long has well-nigh run its earthly course. I have only one care——" she paused. Oliver neither spoke nor looked up—"one treasure!" Oliver looked at her. "To whom shall I leave my Naomi?"

The stillness that followed was terrible to the

widow; it was only of moments, but how long they can be!

Then with a voice of deep emotion Oliver answered, "To me!"

The widow clasped her hands in unspeakable thankfulness. But when they sat silent again, the answer seemed so natural—it was the answer given of old more often than any,—"Leave it to me;" the words might mean no more than His care for the orphan. The question arose in her mind, but was at once answered by Oliver rising and asking, " Where shall I find her ? "

" She is gone to the farm for the new milk for me, and will now be returning."

" Does she often go there ? " asked Oliver, with an eagerness not natural to him.

" Most days, we have no one to send, and I live on it now."

In absence of mind Oliver forgot to take leave of the mother, and left the cottage. He took the wood that skirted the fields, and saw Naomi returning, with Jonathan Caxton, the farmer's eldest son, at her side. Hastily retracing his steps, he re-entered the cottage, saying in hurried tones, all unlike himself, " Naomi cannot be mine! yet, believe me, I will guard her, though it be with my life!" and having said this he left the cottage as hastily as he had entered.

The mother watched for Naomi's return with feverish anxiety. She came with her pitcher, but no trace of any trouble on her face. The mother could not question, she knew not what to ask; she had no clue to guide her; and she feared to tell Naomi what had passed. Days came and went, and Oliver did not return. At length he came before the usual hour of the evening milking, bearing in his hand a new can. Taking off the lid, he held the can to Naomi, saying, "I have cows on the Mill-field now; can they save you your evening walk?" He looked into her face as he spoke, not with the old free glance, but with an earnest, searching gaze.

"That is good!" said Naomi, "isn't it, mother?"

The milk now came daily, sometimes brought by Oliver himself, sometimes sent; but all hope seemed likely to sink again into the same troubled waters as before. Yet not the same; one was nearing the shore where no tempests break nor rough billows swell. The last sands of earthly life ran out quickly. Old Joseph called again, and sat once more alone with the widow; he had often looked in when Naomi was there, now she was absent. "Have ye been able to settle the question between them?" he asked.

"No," she answered; "I took your good advice, and it seemed to prosper, but it has all fall'en out wrong, I cannot tell how; but I have no care left now. The Lord will provide! that word is enough for me now. He may grant me to see that desire fulfilled; if not, I can leave it with Him. Master Richards, my trust is wholly wound about Him who loved me and gave Himself for me: it cannot fail now!"

"That's right," said the old man. "Hold on, He you trust will not fail you!"

It was evening, late in June. The mother had not risen that day, and Naomi watched with faint heart the sundering of her one only earthly tie. Her ear caught a step she knew in the cottage room.

"Mother, Mr. Crisp is come in;" she had called him so of late.

"Ask him in here," said the mother.

Oliver entered the little inner room, and stood by the bed, looking down with silent sympathy.

"I know Who sent you!" said the widow.

"No one sent me," replied Oliver; "I have been absent these two days, and came to inquire."

"You know not who sent you, but I know! Kneel by me," she said, looking first at Oliver, then at Naomi.

They kneeled on either side; then reaching out her thin, transparent hands, she waited for a hand from them, they gave it; then laying Naomi's hand in Oliver's, she slowly and solemnly said, "My children, ye are one! God bless and make ye blessings!" Oliver trembled, Naomi was calm and cold, but he felt the slight pressure of her hand in his own, and said, "NAOMI!" She answered, "OLIVER!" he clasped her hand in both of his, and they rose up one from that hour.

Oliver saw that with the peace of every hope fulfilled, the long-tried spirit was passing to its rest; and saying, in a low voice to Naomi, "I will fetch my mother, and return directly," he hastened home.

On entering the Mill-house, he took his mother's hand, saying, "Naomi is mine!"

" Nay, son, but hast thou spoken ?"

" It is no time for words," he replied; " her mother is departing."

Mistress Crisp tied on her sheltering bonnet, and hastened to the cottage. She watched through the night with Naomi. The stars shone out in the azure sky, scarcely dimmed by the one taper's feeble ray. For many nights Naomi had had only snatches of feverish sleep, while she tended her mother's broken slumbers. Each dawn she had seen the morning star rise over the hill, it came like a messenger from heaven to her, bringiug home in their freshness the words, " I AM the root and offspring of David, and the bright and morning star ! " As she waked and watched in that lone chamber, while a world was sleeping unconscious of her grief, the star arose to greet her; it seemed to say, "O child of sorrow, thou art not forgotten ! The voice that rolls the stars along, spake all the promises ! " This night she did not watch for the rising of the star, she was alone no longer; but as the dawn broke over the sky and slowly brightened, her mother said, " He calleth me ! " Instinctively Naomi raised her eyes towards the hill; the morning star had risen, and its soft splendour full in view, was linked for ever with the last breathings of a mother's voice, and a husband's dear embrace. In strange confusion in her young heart the thrilling words blended themselves with every mingling feeling—" I will give him the morning star "—her mother's, her own, and Oliver's !

CHAPTER V.

Naomi would not leave her now desolate home until she left it as Oliver's bride. Mistress Crisp, with a mother's care, divided her time, always spending the night in the widow's lowly cottage. She had a noble nature. To her it was nothing that her son's wife was chosen from so humble a dwelling. Naomi was her own fortune;—her lowly mind, ever seeking heavenly grace and wisdom; and her pure and devoted heart, were the richest dower. Three months she kept her cottage home, and then consented to the marriage-day.

Oliver brought her the wedding-dress. Long and far had the wandering pedlar Benoni sought for one that would satisfy Oliver. It was soft in texture and hue as the wing of a dove, and woven of finest wool. Naomi had always shunned all finery and fashion, and became her simple garments well—true woman, daughter, wife.

"My daughter, wilt thou give these garments of thy grief away, now that God hath given thee rest in the house of thy husband?"

"Yes, I will not take them there," said Naomi; "my mother is beyond the shadows, and we will not cling to them here."

They wandered under the forest-trees in the evening hour before their marriage-day, and Naomi said, "Thou wilt not have the bells to-morrow?"

"So my mother says," replied Oliver; "she calls them tinkling cymbals! I will not have them rung against thy will, but why dost thou say so?"

"It is not that I do not like the bells," she said, but it was such a little while ago they tolled so heavily, it brought me back from my mother's joy to our own loss and the dark grave."

"All shall be ordered as thou wilt," he answered. "To-morrow is thine own day, and no one can unsay thy will. But if happy spirits could list our village bells, I know that there is one to whom they would be dear! She thinks on thee in Paradise, and to-morrow will fulfil her wish."

"The village would wonder," said Naomi, "that I could be glad so soon!"

Oliver smiled and said, "That's a long task, to look out against other folks' wonder! Keep thine own heart true, and let them wonder on!"

"Well, I don't know, I am sure," she said; "but would not you feel it,—ringing over that grave?"

"Ah!" said Oliver, "I have sinned enough over a grave not to wonder at thee; but the thoughts that never came to my help seem to rise up for thine! I was thinking but now that when we sow the corn in the earth we don't think of its lying in the darkness; we think of its springing up again in the blade and the ear, and the full corn in the ear; like the harvest-fields we are looking on now."

They wandered on in the beauty of evening and the fulness of converse, as long ago, each feeling a change in the other. In Naomi there was now the quiet depth of a woman; the free gush of her childhood and girlhood was gone, but a power was there that the heart of her husband could safely trust in. He felt that her love and truth would water his life, and leave their well-spring only deeper within. Oliver had less surface readiness than before; he seemed to have taken a step back from his fellows in distance and reserve, but it was not really so, for he who draws nearer to God can never really be more distant from man, but equally nearer, though the surface may not reveal it at sight. It was well that they had been parted thus, to meet in greater depth and power. Could we see the end of the Lord in every trial, we should inscribe "It is well" at its close.

Mistress Crisp dressed the bride, tied on her close straw bonnet, trimmed with white; pinned her shawl of white crape; and then finally added a plain gold brooch she had had prepared with her mother's hair. This Naomi welcomed with a tear; and then Mistress Crisp led her to the church, where her bridegroom awaited her. As they entered and saw the gathered people, Naomi trembled; but courage returned when she stood at Oliver's side, and they took the marriage vow, and prayed the marriage prayer, and received the marriage blessing, and she was Oliver's wife, and they returned to his home.

All was prepared, as could most comfortably be

done, for Mistress Crisp in the cottage, which it was
her settled purpose to enter at once; but she spent
the day at the Mill-house, where she had prepared a
dinner for their friends. Many came from far and
near who could not be received; invitations had
only been given to a few, but so many greetings,
congratulations, and good wishes met them on their
way that it took a long time to accomplish the walk
to the Mill. Old Joseph uncovered his white head
as they passed, and a tear glistened in his grey eye.

The entertainment was abundant, and warm
friends sat round the hospitable board, which lacked
nothing that good feeling could supply. After their
meal, Oliver took his guests to the Mill; the wives
and daughters remained with Naomi and Mistress
Crisp, but the latter took all the strain of the
day on herself. She talked with one, appealed to
another, and then drew all into some general subject; her motherly feeling for Naomi made her
eloquent. The head can make an orator, but eloquence is the voice of the heart; and the most
unlearned are found eloquent when the heart is
deeply stirred. It must not be thought from this
remark that Mistress Crisp was unlearned. Her
education had been a superior one, but she seldom
put forth her powers of conversation. It took her
guests by surprise; while Naomi felt the kindness of
the shield extended over her.

Mistress Crisp arranged an early tea, after which
with many warm benedictions, yes, many a heartfelt
God bless ye! the guests departed; and many re-

marks were made from one to another to the effect that they had never seen Mistress Crisp so pleasant before! "She must be mighty pleased to get her son married, and shift herself to the lone cot," said one, with a touch of sharpness in her tone.

"Ah," said another, "it is Naomi! there's none such as her; she has got her son a prize, and she knows it."

When the guests were all gone, Oliver, who seeemed to share his mother's animation, said, "Now, good mother, take a rest in your chair: if none but you could prepare, there are plenty to clear!" then taking Naomi's hand, he drew her arm within his own, and gathering up his mother's shawl, said, "Let's take a turn to the old Mill."

She trod the soft turf; there were no swooping sails coming terribly round as of old; the Mill had not worked on that day; yet her hand was in Oliver's, as safe as when long years before he had held her back from any fear of venturing too near. The mill-steps stood facing the valley on that glowing September evening.

The large white shawl wrapped Naomi's head and shoulders, her fine Jewish features were not less striking so enveloped; the breeze that blew over the hill had all the softness of summer, though it bore to their ears a band of reapers' first song of harvest-home. Few fields were yet cleared, and much corn was still standing; the white-shirted men were pressing steadily on in a field below them, the corn falling before that unwavering line, and the sickle gleaming on the shoulder, as each reaper raised his hand of wheat-ears for the bind.

She sat as of old on the steps of the Mill. It was a lovely scene to watch when every feeling of the soul was rest, peace, and home. The valley opened in its autumnal glory at the foot of the steep grassy hill on which the Mill stood, then widened and stretched away in the distance; while broken lines of hill caught the fast declining rays of the sun; —now in deep purple, then suddenly suffused with a golden mist, then a rose tint, and as the sun's rays sank lower, the deep solemn blue of the hills became contrasted with the pale evening sky; when suddenly the sinking sun threw up a radiance that covered the western heavens with crimson, and tinged the soft clouds of the eastern sky. It was like a grand exhibition before the eyes of the two who sat almost silently there, watching the closing splendours of the day—impressed by the magnificence above, and the beauty and bounty beneath.

In the valley at their feet every spot had its interest for them. Every cottage nestling under the trees was familiar to Naomi, and supplied by Oliver with flour—for each cottage in those days had its oven and baked its home-made bread. Naomi could see the roof from under which her mother had entered her rest; the old church-tower within the shadow of which they had made her grassy grave. The river winding under the trees, gleaming in the radiance of the sky. The water-mill where the stream flowed deepest, and the turrets of the old castle on the height to the left, amid the glory of its trees; while the forest, scarcely touched by autumn's golden fingers, stretched beyond it to the far distance. Naomi caught the sunlight on the castle, and wondered in her heart whether any one in its grandeur could be as happy as she was!

Often in childhood's first glee Naomi had sat on those Mill-steps with Oliver. They had sat there together when she numbered more years—when first a feeling woke up in her heart of a love more than a brother's, and a protector that would always shield her! Two years had passed since then, the wintry time of her life; now she sat there in the rest of a love that seemed to her nothing new, but the old trust given back without a fear. As the sun dipped behind the hills, she murmured softly the blessed word, "Thy sun shall no more go down!" Oliver answered them not, but long after, when the sun of earthly joy was setting for him, Naomi heard them again from his lips, his assurance to her!

The evening star rose in the sky, her eyes rested upon it; she remembered the messenger of peace that the star of the morning had been to her, and she silently thought on those words of tender remonstrance, "Why sayest thou, My way is hid from the Lord, and my judgment passed over from my God. Lift up your. eyes on high and behold, Who hath created these? That bringeth out their host by number? He calleth them all by names, for that He is strong in power, not one faileth!"

Suddenly, in the stillness, the sound of bells broke on her startled ear, smiting the soft evening air, awaking a thrilling emotion. "O, Oliver!" she exclaimed, overcome by the peal that rose over village hearts and homes to greet them on the hill; "O, Oliver!" But Oliver's face was all one pleasant smile as he said, "Well done, old boys! Naomi, you won't mind them now!" Out they rang a true heart-peal, clear and glad, from hands determined that Oliver should find that village men knew how to tell out the day. Bravely they rang, rising and falling on the ear, reverberating from hill to hill—the only voice of the twilight, and that voice filling the air with happy melodies for them.

"'Tis lovely!" said Naomi.

"'Tis grand!" replied Oliver; and he began to call up in the silence of memory what special cause the men had to ring wedding-bells for him? Then a few pleasant facts rose up in the gladness of Oliver's heart, as he listened to the pealing of those happy bells. Naomi loved them up there, where no one was near; and as the sound floated away to the distant sea, the light on whose waters she had caught before sunset, the words of Bunyan's Pilgrim came back on her spiritual mind—"And all the bells of the city rang again for joy."

Famous bells they were; a peal, the gift of the last maiden possessor of the Castle, and each bell bore its own inscription :—

1st bell—"Let Christ be known around."

2nd bell—"And loved where'er I sound."

3rd bell—"Then shall true joys abound."
4th bell—"Before Him lowly fall."
5th bell—"And praise Him Lord of all."
6th bell—"Whene'er I lift my call."

The men were trained; and this evening it seemed as if every influence combined to stir the hearts and nerve the arms of those stalwart ringers. Old John was not much over seventy years then—the oldest of the men, and not very strong on his legs; but his arms, long practised in ringing, had a wonderful power, and he would not give up his soft tenor bell. Oliver had no ear for music, but he knew the old man would be there; and to Naomi's gifted ear, his silver bell held the music of all.

Over the woods of the Castle they rang. Its happy circle was unbroken then. Conrad and Isabelle were playing bowls on the lawn. She stopped to listen, exclaiming, "How pretty the bells sound! I wonder why they are ringing?"

"Now come on!" said Conrad; and the bells rang over their young heads unheeding.

The same sound had touched two hearts—the child's, amid the glory of her ancestral woods; and Naomi's, on the high steps of the Mill. The voice of Naomi was soon to be sweeter than evening bells to young Isabelle, but as yet Isabelle had never spoken to one who was to become her first friend.

Another ear caught the peal, and knew well the occasion. Jonathan Caxton had turned out alone when the bells broke on his ear. Now he buried his face in his hands; those marriage bells rang a knell to his heart.

But on the bells rang, never heeding who heard; or rather, as determined that all should hear and know that village men can make their warm congratulations to be heard, when, not for gold, but for hearty goodwill, they ring out their peal.

Then Naomi said, "Let us go! I shall cry if we stop here—the bells seem so glad!"

Oliver turned; her eyes were swimming in tears. "Let us go," he said, cheerily, "and see what my mother thinks of the bells!" and with the stars brightening above in the blue sky, they hastened home.

Mistress Crisp, fatigued both in body and mind, had had a long sleep in the arm-chair. She woke up at their entering, and suddenly hearing the peal, exclaimed, "What a clatter of bells! I call it just folly to rouse up a village when children and old folks are sleeping!"

So it is that the same sound awakens feelings so varied! The heart-echoes are drawn from the life, not only by evening bells, but by every voice both of nature and grace. With Naomi at her side, Mistress Crisp soon regained her motherly composure and tenderness, while Oliver went to shake hands with the ringers. They each wished him well; but old John raised his hand as if to invoke a blessing as he let go of his quivering rope, and said, "May ye live long and be blessed, and be, as thy father was, like unto the Father of fathers!"

CHAPTER VI.

THE quiet flow of happy life—two lives blended
in one, a noiseless current in its depth, and less
observed, because more complete—this life of Oliver
and Naomi leaves us free for a time to turn more
fully to others.

Mistress Crisp had decided at once to make her
own home a separate one, though still on the Mill-
property. She said it was of no use to put young
folks in the good ways of the old; for you have no
sooner taught them, than something new was sure
to turn up, making them wish for a change! Her
decisive sentence was, "Let them meet the world
as it is, and find out for themselves; for that is not
half-learned that Experience has not had the teaching
of!" Yet she dwelt not far off, with a motherly
heart. She tended her herb-beds and vegetables;
such quality you could find nowhere else; and her
single border of white lilies, multiplied year by year,
you would have supposed it the flower of her heart,
and so it was; and its purity might well make it dear to
one pure in spirit as she was; but when you saw her
pull off petal by petal in the prime of the blossom,
and carry them in to steep in bottles of brandy, you
knew that the compassions of her soul exceeded her

admiration of the white blossoms courting the sun. When Joseph Richards planted the red rose, no one diminished its beauty; it blossomed abundantly, as if it knew that it held an unequalled place.

There was not a hurt in all the country round but Mistress Crisp shared in the credit of the cure; and many a sufferer would trust no one but her. She had never quite understood the ways of her husband and son. A lone widow's, or a sick man's bill written on " Paid," when no money had been received, was to her mind a confusion, and not quite the right thing. But she always said that business ways were beyond her, and she left them alone. We need not dwell on the exact differences of opinion in such cases; as Mistress Crisp settled the point by saying, " Men have their way, and women have theirs; and let that end the question; for we have not to look after each other in the things that belong to the right hand and the left ! "

Yet she had the highest esteem for her husband. She often said, " Thee know I was ' read out ' for marrying with Oliver Crisp; but what ' Friend ' in all England would not have done so if Oliver Crisp had been the reason ! And the whole Society, had they but known him, might have been glad to keep him on second hand ! "—She in, and he out ! She kept strictly to the dress of the " Friends," and the Bible use of personal pronouns; and she taught the same kindly form of speech to her son. Her son had been brought up with no strict association with any ceremonial of worship. " To do justly, love mercy, and walk humbly with God," was the motto and the life of the home he grew up in.

Fully to know Mistress Crisp, you must ask of the poor; they best know the eloquence of praise for those whose remembrance dwells in their hearts. It is a strange thought, the different registers of earth! There are the grand state records that tell and that test the history of nations. In the palace homes and the hotels of Old England when you pass in or out, you write your name in a book. In the homes of the rich you leave a card, when you call, which may be read, to tell who are the acquaintances and friends of the family; but ask of the poor who their friends are, and you read the name graven on the heart;—the fervent tone, the tearful eye, will tell you that their friends are friends indeed!

Dress was then, as it is now, a subject of frequent remark; and the villagers would say, " Did ye ever see Mistress Crisp in a bran new thing, or yet in one to say old ? " Her perfect neatness kept everything without spot; and her erect, quiet movements preserved her garments long in wear. Her great love for flannel and unbleached cloth for the poor made her very unwilling to think anything new a necessity for herself. Mistress Crisp had attended most of the sick-beds in the village for thirty years; and few had departed without her ministering aid to body and soul. Once she failed;—it will be remembered that she was not with Naomi in the last hours of earthly life. When Naomi was sinking slowly in her brightness and beauty, Oliver Crisp said, " Mother, thee wilt be with her?" But Mistress Crisp answered, weeping, "It is no slight on thee, my son, but I can't see her depart! She has been the light of my eyes, and the life of thy heart; and if I looked on, it would finish thy mother! Thou hast sore need of a better helper than I am, and He will not fail thee when that hour has come."

As far as Mistress Crisp understood others, she spoke with kindness and truth. Yet it was not the less a fact that many a word from her fell with the strength and weight of a stone into the under-current of deeper natures than her own. Such words would sink, raising circle after circle of thought and feeling, that would have been incomprehensible to her. Such stone-like words in life often descend into the deepest current of feeling, troubling the still waters, and sometimes lying in the bed of the current like a block, always making an eddy in the stream; but this does not prove the speaker to be hard or insensible, but only unconscious of that which lies hidden under the surface. Moreover, there is a great difference between dropping a stone unawares, and throwing a stone. Mistress Crisp did the former, but seldom the latter.

The one whom, perhaps, she never really troubled was Naomi. The latter's life was a crystal; you seemed able to see the very well-spring of her thought and feeling. Mistress Crisp had never had a daughter, and she looked on Naomi as a rare thing, to be handled with care. She always softened under the beam of Naomi's full eyes, and the angles of her sentences and sharpened tones of her voice melted and dissolved into tenderness for her. She kept to her principle of allowing young folks to learn by the mistakes that they made; and passed no comment on the slight changes that gave a grace and a finish to the once singularly plain home of Oliver Crisp.

Children had a pleasant awe of Mistress Crisp; however fretful in sickness, they were patient when she sat beside them, and they told their bad feelings to her in a way that could not be drawn out by their mothers. She never failed for want of a remedy; that it was not always successful is the lot of all who administer medicine. Her good broth of boiled bones and herbs was often her most restorative aid, and no sick nurse could equal her barley-water and gruel. She had also a closet filled with shelves, on which were strong sheets and linen for the poor in their sickness. It was one of her chief personal pleasures to add to this store, and everything she possessed was mended and repaired to the last with such neatness by herself, or her well-instructed servant, that it was a question whether the garment was not more to be admired at last than at first. The keys of this village linen-closet, of a chest of drawers, of a closet of preserves, and her small cellar, with its home-made wine and other stores,—indeed all her keys, she carried in a large buckram pocket; and another ample pocket contained ginger and peppermint-lozenges for the aged, and sweetmeats for the children—when the children were good! Mistress Crisp always took it for granted that children were good, and this well-known expectation, or persuasion, or almost certainty, together with the bulls'-eyes, sugar-candy, and other sweetmeats, which somehow found a place in her capacious pocket, went far to produce the good behaviour expected.

There was no personal effort that Mistress Crisp so carefully avoided as the finding fault with old or young. Many a fault she did not see; not from any indirectness of vision, but because she thought an escape might prove a warning. But when she undertook to train a young servant, for whom she felt responsible, nothing escaped her remarks, though she did not make every fault a subject of censure. Her domestic arrangements were always kept in such order that they never wanted putting to rights, and the best of household maids were those who began with Mistress Crisp. It must be remembered that it was far easier in those days to train a young servant than in these; for girls then made their place of service their home; they felt its interest and its welfare their own; their quiet and becoming dress went on much the same year after year, they did not hurry into fashion and folly; their attraction lay in themselves, and not in their dress; and many a servant became a trusted friend, loved and cared for to the end as one of the family.

Mistress Crisp put her servant-girl well and patiently into the way of doing everything, and then expected her to attend to all that she had taught her. She had but one penalty for inattention—it was a singular one, but it answered. If dust were left after the duster, or a litter on the floor, or a wrinkle on the bed-quilt, or spots and marks on furniture, or a smear on the china when washed—her old china was choice, and she used it, but it did not signify how common the ware if the smear were upon it—for any failure of this kind Mistress Crisp put on her tortoise-shell spectacles the next day, and sat in the centre of the room watching the whole proceeding ; and unless you had once seen her in this position, you could scarcely imagine how effective it was. There was a saying amongst the village mothers, " Get your girl to Mistress Crisp, and you have made her for life."

It would not now be easy to find such a one as Mistress Crisp. Some fifty years ago such characters were not so uncommon. The waves of restless thought and action that now everywhere agitate life flowed with comparative stillness then. Personal character had time to take form, and there was space and leisure for others to observe the form that it took. But now, when crowd meets crowd, when distance is reckoned by moments, when events lose their order of succession, and claims press in on all sides, how can marked character be readily formed? Or, if formed, who will pause to observe and record ? We may write of the past, and find it easy to trace the foot-prints of souls calmly treading life's path, and living out for others the experience they had won ; but will the future give these again, or far other pictures of life ? Eyes that looked around half a century ago return to the past for quiet portraits ;— portraits of those high enough in general excellence to be models, yet low enough to be left in the sweetness of seclusion.

We turn now to Jonathan Caxton. He it was to whom Naomi's marriage-bells were but a muffled peal, ringing backwards the hope of his heart. He was the eldest son of the largest farmer of the place—a man who, though rich, kept up all the habits of a plain farmer's life. His sons went out for their day's work, and all that was done on Farmer Caxton's farm was well done. Jonathan had felt an early attraction to Naomi. Her birth graced her lowly station, and carried into it a simple dignity and gentleness rare even in those quieter days of England's daughters. The village never doubted the love between Oliver Crisp and Naomi; but when Oliver appeared a changed man, reserved, and with a shadow hanging over him, it was supposed he must have been denied, and young Jonathan's hope grew strong. But Naomi's was no heart to change. Oliver was cold, but this might yet pass, and he, and he only, she felt, could be one with her life.

Jonathan asked not her hand, but showed her what kindness he could in friendly manner. Yet, meeting no encouragement, he determined to get the question settled by speaking to his mother, through whom all appeals were made to his father, and then asking Naomi, who could not refuse him when no other suitor urged his prayer. He knew not the strength that can repose beneath gentleness. But it never came to this point; for Farmer Caxton, a successful maker of money, had also acquired the love of money.

On any subject involving money he was very hard to approach; no one in his family could venture it except his wife, and she with great caution.

"Farmer Caxton," said Mistress Caxton—for on grave occasions she would so address him—"our Jonathan has set his mind on the girl Naomi. I am well assured he might look higher, and not do better, and shall be as glad for my part as the lad if you will not say him nay."

"Jonathan marry the widow's daughter! I should like to know when? When he has made both ends meet for himself, I can tell him! Shall I work my life out, that my sons may go and take up with paupers! You may tell him Naomi shall never darken my door, nor he either, if he stirs a step after her." And Farmer Caxton turned out.

Naomi darken a door! She who came as a sunbeam from heaven! There are souls on earth whose very presence attempers the atmosphere around them. Sent from God, they have more than an angel's mission here. They come to minister to others' need. They come to walk in love, and dwell in love; for they dwell in God, and God is love. And such as these was Naomi.

"Mother, I can't be denied! Here or otherwhere, I must have Naomi."

"Lad, it is of no use; your father never changes his mind. I was dead set against marrying him myself; I told him over and over that I never would; but he just held on till I found myself his. It is no manner of use speaking of it again; you might as soon move a rock as turn your father from one way to the other."

"Well, mother, I have told you the end; so you had best let him into the light of it too."

Mistress Caxton watched her opportunity for many a day, then said, in a pleading tone, "Father, have you any young woman in sight for our Jonathan?"

Now Farmer Caxton was a plain-spoken man, and he answered, "Not I! But I have this thing in sight—that a farmer wants capital to do any good, and a farmer's wife must bring money. Do you suppose I would have made you Mistress Caxton if you had brought me no money? Young folks take a liking, and they think that reason enough to go marrying. Our eldest son, too, and half-a-dozen younger ones after him, treading on each other's heels! What's a father for but to look out for his son; and to begin with agreeing to a thing like that, where, pray, would it end, but in ruin and want?"

"Well," said Mistress Caxton, with a touch of displeasure in her tone, "I think you have proved, if ever man did, that it is a head and a good pair of hands that are worth every bit as much in a farm as the money a woman brings. And it's my mind, and I'll speak it, that if ever woman had the gift to make much out of little, it is Naomi."

"I have said it," said Farmer Caxton, "and I'll not hear of it again."

"Then I had better warn you the lad may be off;

for he has got a will like his father's—not given to change."

" Let him go," said Farmer Caxton, in the coldness of anger; "his brother shall stand in his shoes."

Jonathan heard the decision from his mother. He waited awhile in doubt, dreading his father's hard nature; and Naomi was given where alone her heart could give its affection.

CHAPTER VII.

IF it be the strong influences that govern, it is the
gentle influences that mould into beauty. The
strength of the wind may be irresistible, and its
purifying fury a blessing; but it is the soft breeze and
balmy air that expand nature and bring it to perfection. The rushing torrent cleaves a pathway
through rocks, but it is the gently-flowing river and
gliding streamlet that fertilize. This is the Divine
teaching in creation: it is the same teaching by the
Word of God. Green pastures and still waters are
the experience of blessing in following the Good
Shepherd. Elijah stands out in Holy Scripture with
a grandeur unrelieved by the softer touches of nature;
yet even to him the Lord came not in the strong
wind that rent the mountains and broke the rocks,
nor in the earthquake, nor in the fire, but in the still
small voice; at that still small voice Elijah wrapped
his face in his mantle and went out. The great
lawgiver who had dwelt alone with Jehovah, amidst
the flame and thunder of Sinai, uses the gentlest
imagery to describe the Divine Word, with the
grandest introduction ever penned or breathed—
" Give ear, O ye heavens, and I will speak ; and hear,
O earth, the words of my mouth. My doctrine shall

drop as the rain, my speech shall distil as the dew; as the small rain upon the tender herb, and as the showers upon the grass." The same truth is summed up in the declaration of Jehovah—" As one whom his MOTHER comforteth, so will I comfort you;" a MOTHER'S name being the central point of earth's tenderness. And this is acknowledged in the declarative response of the human heart to Jehovah, "Thy gentleness hath made me great."

Over the Mill-house there now reigned a tenderness of quiet peace. For two years before the settled engagement with Naomi it had been a grey atmosphere, where nothing brightened in warm sunshine; now a deeply loving nature—that richest sunshine of earth—made the life of the home; and its atmosphere therefore expanded all that was tenderest and best in those who dwelt within its influence. Naomi's light step glided through work which another might have made a labour. She had not only the home-work on her hands, but two cows in her dairy—Jess, and Bobtail,—called so from a misfortune that robbed the good cow of the useful tuft at the end of its whisking tail. A poultry-yard soon increased under her care, and the Mill became the resort of hucksters for young fowls and eggs. She had a tall pigeon-house, and she sometimes stood quietly to watch the white pigeons sweep under the sky, and turn in their rapid circles, catching the sunbeam. She had geese fed on the green hill, and soon added bees to her garden; they flew the valley's length, bringing back on their toilsome ascent of the high hill the nectar from every

flower. Cats, of course, there were, but not indoors.
Mistress Crisp had trained them well; a pretty race
of cats they were, pure white, with cypress tails.
And a noble dog, a gift when quite young to Oliver
Crisp at his marriage, from " a well-wishing friend :"
Though not allowed indoors, the dog attached itself
greatly to Naomi; its name was Aleppo. Naomi
had wished for a golden canary, in memory of the
one dear in her childhood, but Mistress Crisp had
said that a bird in a cage was a thing out of place;
and Naomi would not willingly strain a single feeling
of her mother-in-law's; and truly never home less
needed a singing-bird, for Naomi's voice was a carol
of joy, and oftentimes when she sat at her embroidery
on the door-step of her cheerful room, leaning against
the side door-post, where she could see the Mill and
her husband's white figure at the door when the Mill
steps turned that way—oftentimes she sat there at
her embroidery and sang. It was at first always by
herself that she sang; for she feared that singing
might not be pleasing to Mistress Crisp, and Oliver
had no ear for music; but Naomi discovered that he
had a voice, and after a time she would persuade
him to sing hymns with her.

Naomi's skilful hand, and her eye for tasteful
arrangement, soon gave a simple charm to the Mill-
house it had not had before. Her indulgent mother-
in-law had left a supply of old china, which Naomi
removed from the closet-shelves, and displayed on
the high mantelpiece and dresser, and she nailed
slips of blue cloth with small brass nails on the edge

of the worm-eaten book-shelves; such novelties as these Mistress Crisp did not see—we mean she did not comment upon, except to herself. "A young thing's fancies! even she can't be perfect!" It might be questioned whether Mistress Crisp was ever conscious of an error or mistake in herself; her upright, blameless life, her kindness and consistency, were faultless. It might almost have been wished that she could commit a fault, and feel that she had; her strong nature would have been opened and softened by the sense of failure.

Only one thing Naomi pleaded for in her new home, and that one was flowers. There was not a flower in the Mill-house garden, save the grand old white lilies. Oliver could not deny her, but he said, "I thought such things were more bother than good!" still he freely consented. But when creeping rose-trees and other climbers were begged for, he replied, "They will only grow to make litter." Yet Naomi prevailed, and the house, walls, and garden began to feel a brightness when the summer sunshine fell on them.

And so she lived as wife and daughter there, a life of love and blessing; busy in daily work, yet with a hush upon her spirit, as of one listening in heart for what any moment might bring—the coming of the King of kings! in whose presence groans would cease to mar creation's peace, and love would blend its discords into harmony. Sometimes she would read with her mother-in-law from Holy Scripture; none save Naomi could have asked for this from the reserved Mistress Crisp; but when Naomi's radiant eyes looked up at prophet voices, that told of millennial blessedness, Mistress Crisp would firmly, though gently, answer to the appeal, "I do not tamper with such mysteries. It is best to suppose them spiritual." Her husband loved to hear her read the Bible. At evening, when the great ledger was put away, he would say, "My jewel!" for that was what he called her, "Where's the Book?" There were many books upon the shelves, yellow-leaved and old, but they puzzled Naomi's head, and Oliver could not understand them when she read them aloud; so they had the more of the one Book whose words are as silver purified seven times in a furnace of earth. There were some volumes of Owen, Baxter, and Bunyan, and these were her personal delight. Her Bible and her Pilgrim's Progress had both been gifts in her happy childhood from Oliver, and now he had her all his own, trained by their heavenly teaching.

As the winter passed away, Mistress Caxton of the farm felt uneasy at her son making more frequent excuses than she could account for, to ride to the distant town.

"Why so unsettled, lad? What's the town company, that you cannot rest in your home?"

"I am after pleasing father, if it must be told," he replied.

"What, a wife, Jonathan? be ruled by your mother, and bide your time yet. Lad, you neither know the world nor yourself, and you will set your foot in a net, and then there's never the hand that can loose it again!"

"I can't help it, mother; father never thought of me; he only cared for the purse. I can't find another heart, and no use if I did, if the purse were not equal. So I will have no more contention, but buy his free will!"

"O, lad! 'tis no good buying and selling like that! Work on steady awhile, and father will put you in a farm; and if there has been one true heart in the world, you may be sure there's a second, for there never was a thing in creation that hadn't its fellow. And what's more, you will happen of it, too; for they that will put up with anything, why let them take it; but they that wait for the best, and know where to look for it, 'tis certain to be given. Dost know, lad, where to look?"

Jonathan made no reply.

"I mind you, lad, 'tis never said a wife is from the Lord, but 'a PRUDENT wife is from the Lord.' When He gives, He gives what's worth the having; but that's a poor fate that just takes anything."

"Well, mother, if father talked like you, I would not stir without his word. But you know it is plain enough to be seen when it is not to be heard, that it's just what *money* a thing will fetch or lose. I have often thought I hated money; but I am changed now, mother—I am going in for it, too!"

"Why so hasty? Don't you know one step will take over the rock, and where are you then?

There's no taking it back to stand where you once stood before ! "

" What account would you give, mother, of the woman for me ? "

" Three things, lad, 'tis your need to consider. First, what's the worth of her spirit ? will she turn a fair face on you when, may be, life turns a dark one ? A holiday wife is a poor toy at the best ! Next, what's the worth of her head ? Can she tell which you need, the bridle or spur ? and how to use them, and not chafe you either ?—And can she make both ends meet when the measure runs short, as well as when it is full ? I can tell you, it takes a good head to do these ! And then, what's the worth of her hands ? Can she turn them to one thing when another won't do ?—Will she go quietly on it until work lies under her power ? When you have settled those three things, you are pretty safe for this world ; and you have not learned yet to look beyond it ! Take your mother's word for it—you may empty a full purse, but you will never drain a heart that is true ! "

" Ah, mother ! 'tis too late ! I want you to tell father that I have fixed my mind on Alice Cramp ; he knows there's money there ! "

The mother's counsel was in vain ; and the town bells rang merrily for Jonathan Caxton and his bride. They were married as summer came in ; and a farm engaged for them in the next parish.

Farmer Caxton had taken no notice of Oliver's marriage ; but this did not trouble Oliver Crisp. His jewel was brightening in his home day by day ; and he gave his kind word upon Jonathan's marriage, when he met Farmer Caxton, as pleasantly as if no slight had been put on himself. Naomi, too, expressed her best wishes for Jonathan's happiness, having been no stranger to his feeling for herself, though she could not respond to it. But Mistress Crisp, who had heard, as probably all the village had heard, of Farmer Caxton's word about Naomi—" As that he should say, she should never darken his door!" This was a word she could never pass over. It was not only Naomi,—though were it her alone it would be quite offence enough not to pass over; but it applied equally to her son and herself; and even to her departed husband; for had not Naomi been as free of their house as any child could be of her home ? "

Mistress Crisp, after that saying was reported, took no further notice of Farmer Caxton. She gave no recognition when they met, and if he attempted it she would not see it. She did not consider whether even a strong utterance of displeasure might not be better, than to cut off a neighbour from life's courtesies because of a wrong feeling and wrong utterance on his part ; or whether the better course might not be to pass it over as an error, that some day might be repented of. Life is too short, and mutual needs are too great, to wait for repentance in those who do us wrong, when the wrong is of a nature that only requires a personal overlooking. Naomi could well understand the hard feeling of the farmer, and was not surprised at it. Those who have right on their side can best afford to pass over an offence; and the higher the nature, the more readily will it take in view the standing-point of the offender, which will often account for the offence. A low range of vision cannot understand, and, therefore, fails to excuse, or forgive, or forget. But, any way, an outburst of indignation or displeasure is far better than a cold isolation.

Isabelle, the eldest daughter of the Castle, at that time in her tenth year, often rode with her father over the green hill crowned by the Mill. It commanded a most extensive and lovely view, and was a point to which the Colonel often took his friends. His frequent visits to the spot increased his acquaintance with and regard for the Crisps, who had held the Mill for several generations; and young Conrad, only son of the Castle, had early formed a friendship with Oliver, the Mill becoming a special interest to him as a child; and his frank, warm nature won Oliver's regard. Conrad was two years older than Isabelle, and full of youthful energy.

The courteous Colonel did not forget to offer his congratulations soon after the evening bells had rung the marriage-peal. Dismounting from his horse, he entered the wicket-gate to greet Naomi; and then invited her to the garden-paling to speak to Isabelle. Naomi curtseyed to the child. Those were days when English women and English girls knew how to curtsey. It appears now to be a courtesy peculiar to the Court; and in lowly life a crooked bend takes the place of the significance of a curtsey. Isabelle shook hands from her pony, and looking at Naomi, said, "I am so glad you are come!" Why should the stranger-child be glad? She could not have told why, yet this first meeting linked her with a secret sympathy to Naomi. They met at intervals on the hill, or in the village, or in Mrs. Gray's morning-room, when Naomi sometimes took an order for her lovely embroidery; which, though the wife of Oliver Crisp, she still liked to employ herself in; and thus the feeling strengthened between the child of the Castle and the wife of the miller.

The second summer of her home, Naomi gathered courage, and asked if the young ladies and the young gentleman would please to come and partake of her strawberries and cream. Isabelle's face flushed with pleasure, and Mrs. Gray gave consent. The forest that stretched away to the left of the Mill, when you stood facing the valley to the west, had no doubt once covered the hill. It still clothed the neighbouring Castle-height; and just below the white Mill-house an oak-tree had been spared. It had grown to a splendid size, quite unsurrounded, and its low branches spread out a close covering overhead. It was under this spreading canopy, on the soft turf, that Naomi prepared for her friends. The little girls were shy, and kept with their nurses; but Conrad was soon in the Mill with Oliver Crisp, and Isabelle slipped her hand into Naomi's, and went with her to look at the creatures.

Then Naomi, to please the little ones, called her cows to follow her, and they came and stood under the far side of the oak-tree, and Naomi milked little old-fashioned tumblers full of frothing milk, which delighted the children. Then the geese came flying at her call, with their outstretched wings skimming the ground, and the little ones clung to their nurses at the cackling approach of such a formidable body; but as soon as they were gone, they wanted them back again. Naomi wisely called her white pigeons instead, who flew to the ground, and one, more tame than the rest—a white, fan-tailed pigeon—lighted on Naomi's shoulder and took the bread from her lips, and then sat on her finger, to the delight of the children, who shouted to have it. Its mother had by some means been shot, and Naomi had brought it up from a nestling. It so pleased the children that Naomi, always ready to give pleasure, presented it to Isabelle, to the delight of the child—her first living possession. She carried it home in a basket, and it had a wicker-cage in the hall.

Conrad had no young friends near at hand, and Oliver Crisp most safely shared his confidence. The boy talked over the past, present, and future with the miller. Many a long, earnest talk they had at the top of the Mill-steps. A willing listener is a gift to a young heart, and Oliver's few words, when he gave a reply or a comment, were not forgotten by the ardent boy. These summer visits became a frequent treat, though Naomi was not allowed to be taxed; a basket came with provisions—not half so good, Isabelle and Conrad maintained, as the first feast provided by Naomi!

Of all the performances under the oak-tree, Aleppo's were the most amusing and most constantly asked for. At first, when Naomi said, " Aleppo, fetch your master ! " Aleppo ran up the Mill-steps and tugged at his master's coat, and Oliver and Conrad came gravely down, greeted by a burst of happy laughter from the children. But at length, when the dog was sent up, Oliver only looked and smiled when Aleppo pulled and tugged. Aleppo himself was soon up to the cheat, and when told to go, at the request of the children, he pretended not to hear ; and if compelled to take notice, he only wagged his tail, and pushed his nose into Naomi's hand, as if saying, " You know you don't want the master !" Then Oliver's stick was put in some place difficult of access, and Aleppo was desired to fetch it. All the different attempts of the sagacious dog, and the ingenuity with which he accomplished his task, delighted the eager children : especially when Aleppo climbed the Mill-steps of his own accord, and laid the stick at his master's feet, and Oliver Crisp stooped and took the stick, and gave Aleppo a pat of commendation, guessing at the expectant eyes below.

The visits to the Mill were varied by Naomi being invited to the nursery-tea at the Castle; and then the visit to Isabelle's room, and the sitting in Isabelle's chair to look at her treasures.

" Have you any treasures ? " asked Isabelle.

Naomi's full eyes met the eyes of the child as she answered, " In Heaven ! "

Isabelle was silent, and Naomi said, " Does it

not say, 'Where our treasure is, there our heart will be'?"

"Yes," said Isabelle; "but I meant pretty things here."

"I have some," answered Naomi, "but very few. I have a little old china; but that is all, I think."

"What have you in Heaven?" asked Isabelle.

"My mother is gone to be with Christ, and my father went before I can remember; and the Lord Himself is there, who loves us more than father or mother!"

"Does He really?" asked Isabelle.

"Yes," answered Naomi. "We may learn to say, 'He loved me, and gave Himself for me!'"

"How do you know He loves you?" asked Isabelle.

"Because I love Him, and the Bible says, 'We love Him because He first loved us!'" and seeing the child was forgetting her earthly treasures in the light of a treasure in the Heavens, Naomi went on, "Once I had no other love to look to. My mother was dying, and I had no one else; and then I found that the love of Jesus was near, and strong enough to keep me from being afraid of being left all alone in the world."

Isabelle sat silent in her little chair before Naomi; and Naomi, fearing that the subject was weighing too much on her young heart, said, "There are a great many treasures in Heaven—harps of gold, and crowns, and palms, and precious stones!"

"I don't care so much for them," answered

Isabelle, " as to hear of Him whose love could make you happy all alone."

" Yet they must be very beautiful," said Naomi; " but I never saw a precious stone."

" Did you never see a precious stone?" asked Isabelle. " I will ask mamma to show you hers when you come again. You will come soon again?" she asked, for Naomi had risen to go. " Do come soon, Mrs. Crisp!"

. " Will you not call me Naomi? I am, or, at least, I used to be, Naomi to all the village!"

The lady of the Castle engaged Naomi to instruct Isabelle in embroidery—a work much in favour with ladies in those days. These lessons took Naomi once a week to the Castle, and many a hallowed talk passed between the two, leaving the needle less busy sometimes than it might have been; but Mrs. Gray saw enough of Naomi willingly to trust her child to the happy hour of work and converse. Naomi saw the jewels, and her delight was great in really looking upon the ruby, the emerald, the sapphire, the diamond—all stones of the High Priest's breast-plate; and not less so, the pearl of the New Jerusalem. The reality of these things to Naomi brought them home with a new feeling to young Isabelle.

One day, to her surprise, Isabelle discovered that Naomi was looking for the second coming of the Lord.

" But will He come," asked Isabelle, " while we are living on the earth?"

" No man knoweth of that day nor of that hour," answered Naomi. " He may come while you and I are quietly working here! He said Himself, ' Watch, therefore, for ye know not what hour your Lord doth come!'"

"Does it make you glad?" asked Isabelle.

"Do you not think," replied Naomi, "that if One who was worthy of all love had died for you, and lived again, and was coming back to take you with Him,—would not your heart watch day and night for His return?"

"Yes, if I were not at all afraid!" said Isabelle.

Naomi replied with her tenderest smile, "If you are afraid of Him, it is only because you do not yet know Him! You have a little Bible there—if you read of Him when you are alone, and ask Him to show Himself to you through its blessed words, He most surely will; and when you know Him you will love Him more, and perfect love casteth out fear!"

"Shall I read with you?" asked Isabelle, who seemed in some degree a stranger to her Bible.

"Yes," answered Naomi; "we can always read when I come, if I may keep you so long; but you will learn it best alone. Don't you know that you get to know any one with whom you are often alone? And so we learn to know the Lord when we are alone with Him. And though you will always want the help,—which may God give you!—of being taught by those who best can teach, yet to learn to know the blessed Saviour, you will find to be easiest to you when in His own Word you see Him, alone with Him, and learn His love for you—learn to know and believe the love He has for you. He says, 'He that loveth Me shall be loved of My Father, and I will love him, and will manifest Myself unto him!'"

IT passeth *knowledge !* that dear love of **Thine,**
Lord Jesus ! Saviour ! yet this soul of mine
Would of that love, in all its depth and length,
Its height and breadth and everlasting strength,
     Know more and more.

It passeth *telling !* that dear love of Thine,
Lord Jesus ! Saviour ! yet these lips of mine
Would fain proclaim to sinners far and near
A love which can remove all guilty fear—
     And love beget.

It passeth *praises !* that dear love of Thine,
Lord Jesus ! Saviour ! yet this heart of mine
Would sing a love so rich—so full—so free—
Which brought an undone sinner, such as me,
     Right home to God.

But, ah ! I cannot tell, or sing, or know
The fulness of that love, whilst here below :
Yet my poor vessel I may freely bring !
Oh ! Thou who art of love the living spring,
     My vessel fill.

I *am* an empty vessel ! scarce one thought
Or look of love to Thee I've ever brought ;
Yet, I *may* come, and come again to Thee
With this—the contrite sinner's truthful plea—
     " Thou lovest me !"

Oh ! *fill* me, Jesus ! Saviour ! with Thy love !
May woes but drive me to the fount above :
Thither may I in childlike faith draw nigh,
And never to another fountain fly
     But unto Thee !

And when, Lord Jesus ! Thy dear face I see—
When at Thy lofty throne I bend the knee,
Then of Thy love—in all its breadth and length,
Its height and depth and everlasting strength—
My soul shall sing, and find her endless rest
     In loving Thee !

CHAPTER VIII.

Farmer Caxton had but one standard in life, provided always that outward propriety were observed; and that one standard was the abundance that a man possessed!—provided also that the man had made his money by his own industry, skill, or good fortune. Therefore, he now slighted Oliver Crisp, because Oliver might have done well for himself in the world, and matched money to money; instead of which he had let himself down in the world; which Farmer Caxton thought reason enough for casting him off. Mistress Caxton had a different view, and tried to show every civility in her power. Yet, with all his love of money, Farmer Caxton was by no means a miser, in the general sense of the word. He educated his children, paid his men well, had the best workmen, the best farm-buildings, horses, and cattle on the Castle estate. He was a thorough man of business; but he would rather hold back until he got his price, than sell at a lower. He knew how to drive a hard bargain; but he kept his cottages in good repair, and did not neglect his men when disabled. Yet money was his idol; what could be gained or lost in any transaction was his chief consideration.

Jonathan's marriage pleased him well. Mr. Cramp was the largest tradesman in the neighbouring town. His shop was one of those comprehensive places more common a century ago, which on one side served groceries of all descriptions, candles and cheese, and on the other side, drapery of all sorts. He also dealt in corn and hay; and, of late years, he had added a banking-business. He was quite the chief tradesman of the place. Mr. Cramp gave an allotted sum to each daughter on marrying; on the express understanding that under no circumstances would another penny be added. "I have sons and daughters enough," he said; "and when I marry a daughter, I consider her off my hands, and done with!" but the marriage portion was large enough to satisfy all parties concerned.

Farmer Caxton pursued much the same plan, for he stocked his son's farm—a very costly thing, then; this done, in addition to the money that Alice Cramp brought, he considered his son well off his hands. Mistress Caxton furnished the house.

When the short absence after the wedding was over, Mistress Caxton received her daughter-in-law at the new farm; all was in beautiful order, a servant-girl engaged, and everything ready to hand.

"Now you will not need to churn again until Friday," said Mistress Caxton. "I will send over that day to put you in the way."

Sally Dumbleton was the village help at Farmer Caxton's. She arrived, brushing away the dew with her hasty step by six o'clock on the summer morning; but the farm was asleep, the men were waiting outside, no master to direct. Alice Caxton and her husband had been at a late party the night before, in the town; and Sally Dumbleton did all the dairy-work alone. On the following Tuesday she made trial again; but Alice Caxton had given a return party at the farm, and it was seven o'clock before a master in slippers looked out to set his men on.

"None of the old go here, I can see!" said a man transferred from the parental farm to this; "they say the women can make or mar, and 'tis plain our new mistress don't come of farm-life!"

"I tell you what, Cely," said Sally Dumbleton to Cecilia, the farm maid, "your pans tell the lack of hot water; sour cream and sour milk will just ruin your dairy!"

The warning was true, but there were none to heed it. Mistress Caxton herself grew hot in remonstrance; but Alice, her daughter-in-law, said, "I think it a hard case if the purse that I brought is not long enough to find me help!"

Alas, for the farm! The butter came back from the market unsold; the village women gave up any regular coming for milk that was sour. Jonathan was angry. His wife cried, and said she was not born to labour! Sally Dumbleton gave up, and one help proved only worse than another. Jonathan called up the yard-boy for bringing no eggs. "Please, sir, I was just to and fro the town with mistress's band-box; and the day afore I walked in and out for sweet pies for the supper."

It was not dairy produce alone; the home was a scene of continual discomfort. Alice's mother, Mrs. Cramp, was a bustling, active woman, but she had not trained her daughters to household work; they gave their attention to dress and visiting; and when the daily duties of an active farmer's wife came on poor Alice, she could not tell at which end to begin; nor how to handle work. She made her farm-parlour gay, and in frequent visits to the town tried to amuse herself as well as she could.

"I cannot eat these lumps of lead!" said Jonathan, throwing down a cake of bread.

"Cely," said Alice Caxton, "you know I told you to make it light."

"Yes," answered Cely; "but you called and called for me just between the rising and the sinking of the dough; and that is how it came heavy. It was not my fault, I am sure!"

Mar the dairy, and the comfort of home, and you will not find the fields continue to flourish. Jonathan began to take to company, and often spent his evenings out, and Alice fretted at home. One infant after another only added to her cares and her helplessness. Farmer Caxton seldom went near the farm, and Mistress Caxton had given up her good counsel in despair.

Their truest friends were Oliver and Naomi. Oliver's heart smote him, for he remembered the past—he remembered his long-cherished grief for his father, and how his mother's words, falling on a heart at that time unready, had led him to slight Naomi, and to give reason for Jonathan's hope. He was not slow to think that disappointment might have led to an ill-matched union. He tried to win Jonathan's confidence, and to advise him for a better course. It was an effort on Oliver's part; not from lack of good-will; but because he never went out of his way in life to win any one nor anything; though he often went out of his way to aid in other need. Jonathan responded to the feeling of kindness, and several times Oliver saved him from rash resolves. Naomi, too, became a welcome visitor at the farm. Poor Alice Caxton felt herself ill-used in being expected to attend to duties for which she had never been trained. She was not true woman enough to know that it is a chief point in woman's life, to be ready for any and every variety of daily duty ; to apply both heart and head to each small task, and never to measure the present or the future by the past.

"You see," said Naomi, " you were not born and bred to these things. I am more in the way of them, and might help you a little."

" 'Tis past help, Mrs. Crisp ; I often tell Mr. Caxton there is nothing for it but giving up farming."

" No, sure, not that ! " said Naomi ; " you will get into the way of things before long, that seem strange to you now."

"I am not made for work, Mrs. Crisp ; I brought him a fortune, and 'tis hard to be expected to slave as if I had not had a penny."

"I think I could find you a good sort of body,

who would just take your dairy in hand, and make your butter your pride."

"I am sick of the dairy, it is always turning sour, and I cannot help it! I always knew milk did not keep more than the night. I say, sell the cows, it is but one thing less, and that one no end of bother; then Mr. Caxton breaks out, and says you may as well sell the farm, for the dairy's the gauge of the whole. Sell it all then, I say, and let us live on in peace."

"Shall we," said Naomi, "take a day through in our minds, and see how we could order so as to give you more quiet?"

"Take a day through? why, that's nothing new! It's what I know by heart to my sorrow and care. Here, the first of the morning, just the best hours for sleep, there is such a turn-out all over the place—the cocks are all crowing, and the squeaking of pigs, and the yard-boy will hollow out the names of the cows, until I hear them all in my dreams; as to sleep, it's no rest! it drives me to be late; and when I come down there is such an outcry in every direction— there rumbles the old churn, and the butter won't come! Then the women crowd to the door, wanting a penny off here and twopence off there, for milk that they say turned sour. Cely has got her arms in the cheese-curds; and there's the beat, beat, of the linen doll. Then in comes the yard-boy with a dead duck, and a hatful of young ducklings just out of the eggs, and their mouths all a-gape, and I never know what to put in them! I had heard say peppercorns were good things, so I fed them with those, but they died everyone. Then a horse or a cow is sure to be ill ; or a man comes on business and Mr. Caxton has been off and two hours away, and no one knows where, and little Joe comes crawling down-stairs in his night-shirt, and the baby screaming above. Such a drive !—it knocks me up before I have so much as turned round in it. And as to my being mistress. and not a creature to wait on me, nor to make the cold breakfast hot! I should like to know who would not give up in despair!"

Even Naomi was hopeless! Still she often went to the farm; it eased poor Alice Caxton to pour out her troubles, and the baby got a comfortable dressing and nursing in her ready arms.

A third infant added to their difficulties. Four years had now been passed in the farm, and the case was proved hopeless. It was at length settled that the only thing for Jonathan Caxton to do was to sell his farm-stock, pay his debts, and with the remainder of his wife's money try his fortune in America. The farm was re-let, and in September, four years and a half from their marriage, they were to wind up and sail from their native land. Mistress Caxton took the boy Jonathan. Alice was to go with her parents, and Naomi begged to keep baby Meg ;—at all events, until the parents were settled, and might be able to send for her out to them.

The question arose where the last days before they sailed should be spent. Jonathan dreaded his father, but his poor wife was afraid of both her father and mother. Those whose pride it is to make money, have seldom much sympathy for those who lose. It was settled by Mistress Caxton that they must come home—as she called it from her maternal heart, and spend the last days at the old Farm. Naomi went over to help on the day of winding-up; it was a sorrowful scene, and the confusion of all things made every one useless. Farmer Caxton's large gig came in time to fetch them to tea, with a cart for the personal luggage. Only the baby was left, asleep in her cradle, unconscious of all that was changing and fixing life's destiny for her; she slept while her parents and brother and sister departed, nor felt nor feared the lot of the forsaken.

Naomi stood at the garden-gate, and saw them depart; she watched them along the winding lane, and her eyes filled with tears for a home deserted. But she returned to the sleeping infant, took it in her arms without its waking, folded the cradle blankets round it, laid its scanty wardrobe in the cradle, directed the yard-boy to follow her with it, and took her way across the fields to the Mill. The fields were cleared, for it was late in September, and the still light of autumn mellowed the land. There was something in the breath of a September evening that always sent a thrill through Naomi; it seemed to her on such an evening that the air was full of the distant melodies of pealing bells. And now she carried home a treasure for which she had been scarcely able to repress the longing—a child—an object for the wealth of her affection; one who needed all that she could give; one who would repay it all;—proving a blessing by receiving now, and then by giving back when they most needed it in years to come.

At the Farm, Mistress Caxton had spread her hospitable board; a pang was in her heart, but she wore a pleasant look, as one who had too often met with trouble to feel surprise at its return. Jonathan had long felt the weight of his father's cold displeasure, and dreaded now the meeting him in this forlorn conclusion. The farmer sat by his wood fire; he did not rise to meet them; but as they stood on entering, he stooped to place more wood upon the hearth-stones, and said, "Are ye not a cold? ye had better come nigher." The evening meal was a silent one; no one was hungry, and all were glad to retire early to rest.

The sun was flushing the sky as Naomi with her burden reached the foot of the hill. Oliver from the high steps of the Mill had been watching for her return. He locked the mill-door, and came down to meet her at the gate.

"You have had a long day of it; tired out, I should think?"

"I watched to see them away, and then I brought home our treasure," Naomi said, and sat down on her low chair, uncovering the wraps, and disclosed a poor baby not three months old, in a little old bedgown that had served its elders; a little plain cap drawn with bobbins, and eyes closed in sleep.

"Isn't it such a beauty?" asked Naomi.

"You are a bit of a prophet," said Oliver, smiling. "No doubt it will be!"

The yard-boy was humbly waiting at the door with the cradle. Oliver slipped a sixpence into the hand of the poor boy, now out of place; and they drew to their tea-table beside the blazing hearth,—the baby asleep on Naomi's lap. Another name to add to their evening supplications, another head to find a pillow, another heart a home.

Amongst the farms of the parish was a large and prosperous one, rented by one Farmer Butterly. His was the hand of the diligent which maketh rich, and those were grand times for farmers, when wheat sometimes rose to a golden profit. Many a fine pasture was ploughed up in those days to grow more corn; and Farmer Butterly always had been a man for success. He had begun life in a small way; but now held a good farm. He had married rather late in life, on taking the farm, and his children were as yet very young. There were few days Susan Butterly —for so she was familiarly called—more thoroughly enjoyed than the great mouthly wash and ironing days of the farm, when she could talk freely without hindrance to work, and speak her mind to her help, Martha Hukerback, who was sure to carry abroad all that Susan Butterly said; and probably much that Susan Butterly thought or might be supposed to think.

"It puts one in spirits, I am sure, such a day of October as this," Susan Butterly said. "Take one thing with another, it's just alike good for all! There's not a horse but is at plough, and they say the moulds crumble just right. I can't tell how to work fast enough on such a day! I think long till

we get the linen hung out; the air is wholly a per-
fume, and the sun is right hot. I suppose, Martha,
you saw that poor family off from their farm, where
it just seems but yesterday they made such a grand
start? I do say, let things be as they may, one
mistake lay there in the start, for young folks who
had not learnt how it is that one and one make two.
The way to take life is to do as my good man and I did,
long before ever we thought of marrying—begin with
earning a trifle, then get on to more, and so feel your
foot firm on one step of the ladder, and hold on for
another; there is no way like that for yourself, nor for
those you bring up. Look at my three babes there! I
will answer for it they shall know the worth of every
penny, and, what's more, how to earn it! Why, those
two—they had money they never brought in, and they
only knew one thing, and that was, how to waste it.
I suppose you saw them away?"

Martha nodded assent. She had learned from
experience that such a reply was the one most pleasing to Susan Butterly.

"A fine young man like that," continued Susan
Butterly, "to be ruined, and go out of the country,
as I say, little better than a convict!"

"Never say it, mistress; never say it again!"
said Martha Hukerback, in displeasure. "He is
gone out as honest a man as ever lost a penny; and
as to the going out to those foreign parts—it is what
my Ned did, and he has risen to the top of the tree,
and is always writing home for his father and me;
and I do say Master Jonathan is as honest as day-

light. He came out to me, and thanked me so handsome for all my good service! I would never hear tongue lay a slander on him while my name is Martha Hukerback."

" You are right, Martha; you are right! I have a great respect for the young man; not but what I do say it is enough to break any man's credit to settle in as he did, and then turn out like this. The truth is—he put the wrong woman in the place, and I do say a woman has no right to the name, let her pounds, shillings, and pence be what they will, unless she can be up and doing. She may be a fine lady, but I say it that have seen it, she is no true woman for all that. Dear me! I thought it friendly to call and ask a few neighbourly questions; our two farms lie so handy I could not be off it in showing a kindness. I said, ' Do you find the dairy-work come easy to hand?' for she did not look to me as if she had ever turned up a sleeve above elbows for anything. She said, ' I have a woman for that!' ' What, for cheeses and all?' I enquired. ' Yes,' she said; ' I am glad to say I am able to pay for all work I require to have done.' I thought it would be neighbourly just to give her a bit of advice, so I said, ' You may pay out, but I warn you there will be no paying in! Mrs. Jonathan Caxton,' I said, ' let me show you a kindness, I will look in for a week, off and on, and that will set you forward with all. I would not value the time nor the trouble,' I said, 'to put you into the way.' But, if you will believe me, she would not take my offer! So I just gave her up from that day, and I said to my good man, 'The sooner that concern breaks up, the better!' I always was one for seeing the end from the beginning! Show me the way young things begin, and I will show you what it is pretty certain to end in. But the children—to turn them on charity! I do say it is shameful!"

"Ah, well!" said Martha Hukerback, determined to be heard, "the mother is just broken-spirited—down-hearted, you may say, and the grandmother always was overfond of the boy; and as to Naomi, as we used to call her—though I should say Mrs. Crisp, for all that she does smile when she hears her own name—she is as fond of the babe as if it were her own."

"For all that," said prosperous Susan Butterly, "when it comes to stowing away your children like that, I should wish I had never seen them before such a day came! Now, Dora, here's your lift; peg the linen tight, for the breeze blows up stiff. Molly, turn another screw of your cheese-press. Billy, you don't half work the dolly; you will get no wages if you slur work like that! Molly, now come! can you see your face in that copper saucepan? As I say, make your own looking-glass; and then, if you can't admire your face, leastways you can your work. Here they come in for bait! Well, I think we will all take a quiet ten minutes; we shall make that up easy when we set to again."

Colonel Gray at the Castle, said—
" Poor young Caxton is with his father, I find."

Mrs. Gray.—"It must be a great trial to them all,—he seemed a young man of such promise."

Colonel Gray.—"The drag on the wheel has been his poor wife; her ignorance of business and love of dress and company."

"What a shame!" exclaimed Conrad, "for a woman to drag a good fellow down like that!"

Colonel Gray.—"The shame may lie deeper, my son, than a woman's folly. A man has the choice; and if he chooses a wife in no way fitted for the duties she has to fulfil, the folly lies with him. Jonathan Caxton knew what would be required of the woman he made his wife: she could not tell what her responsibilities would be, and could not be blamed for accepting tne man who judged her capable. It is an oft-told tale, Conrad, this after-blame of a wife; but go back to the first link of the chain that has drawn the calamity on, and you will often find that the folly and shame censured so freely lie at another's door. I must go down and see the old man; I fear it was his love of money that led on to so unsuitable a choice; if so, it will make the blow harder for him. You and Isabelle can ride with me if you like."

Farmer Caxton was out in his fields. His house was a sorrowful place for him, with its broken-down inmates. Colonel Gray rode on to find him. Conrad went round to the rick-yard where Jonathan was stacking; and Isabelle went into the house. There, for a few moments, all her gathered-up sympathy disappeared in a flush of pleasure, at seeing Naomi seated with baby Meg in her arms. "Naomi!

I did not think of finding you here." Isabelle spoke in perfect unconsciousness of any slight in past days on Naomi, but Mistress Caxton replied, " Yes; the grandfather said, do ask of Mrs. Crisp if she would step down with the babe; they may as well see the poor rogue while they can."

" Then will the baby be yours?" asked Isabelle, eagerly.

" It is hers, indeed!" replied Mistress Caxton. " What could the poor mother do on the seas with three children? I have taken the boy, and Mrs. Crisp is so good, she will mother the babe."

" It's not the first bit of her goodness," said Jonathan's wife, in a more cheerful tone than might have been expected. The open sea and the ship, and a foreign land, and two children left behind, were all light troubles to the poor wife, now that she had dropped for ever the weary load of farm-life, which had grown heavier each day, until existence was a burden. All other ills she could face, and hope for better times; but the busy sounds of the farm, that make music for many ears, were the knell of her comfort. The impossibility had rolled from her life, and already she began to look up. Mistress Caxton also, her mother-in-law, had changed her look and tone of displeasure for one of sadness and sympathy; she thought the trial of breaking up a home for want of ability to manage it, enough to be the death of any woman, and the kindness of her nature rose to the surface in sympathy. Jonathan, her husband, no longer chafed over everything, but was kind in quiet regrets ; there was some one else to manage the children, and life already began to admit of a hope.

"Will the baby live with you?" asked Isabelle of Naomi.

"Yes, indeed, she will," replied Naomi, holding her out to Isabelle, who rejoicingly took her with many commendations ; and secret thoughts of how she really would take to plain-work, which she had always tried to escape. Even then and there she thought over her work-box, its reels, needles, tapes, and pins, and counted over the contents of her purse ; resolved that hem and sew for the baby she would ; and how glad her mother would be to see Isabelle industrious at last !

Conrad had found Jonathan, who threw down his pitchfork and came aside to the pony. Conrad shook his hand heartily, but did not quite know what to say, except, "I am out and out sorry !"

Jonathan looked away, and stroking Alaric's mane, said, "It is a bad job, but it might have been worse ; and I hope we will look up the other side of the water."

"Well, Jonathan, you know I am to be a soldier like my father, and I shall go to America. I want to see the Falls ; of course you will go and see Niagara ? and I will try all I can to get your boy, for he will be sure to like to be a soldier ; you know all boys like that, and then we two will come on and see you. Now, mind you make haste and get ready, for I shall want to stay at your house."

Jonathan smiled a slow smile, as if all visions of the future lay in one dull page for him; the bounding pulse of his youth was quite gone, and little Joe for a soldier would be no bright dream to him.

"Well, Jonathan," said Conrad, in a low, softened tone, after a little more talk on things as they were, "I have often felt glad that a boy could trust in God, and I am sure you can, and that God will bring you through your trouble," and Conrad raised his rein with his kindest good-bye. A tear was swimming in Jonathan's eye, as he bowed and turned back to his pitchfork and stack.

Farmer Caxton lived on one of the Castle farms; his father had been tenant before him, and he had looked to his son's coming after. This blow had fallen heavily, and the Colonel did not find him inclined to respond to his sympathy. The father and his children rode home reflecting on the line of thought each interview had opened. Ascending the Mill-hill they passed Mistress Crisp on her way to the Mill-house. Now Mistress Crisp had looked thoughtful for some days; she felt for the sorrows of others, and she was anxiously weighing in her mind the burden Naomi had taken. She did not grudge the poor babe a home, that was certain; but to take up another's child as your own was a thing to be looked at on all sides. There was the disposition, and the constitution, and the continuation, and the consequences, and, when you put so many serious words together, a general state of reflection was easier than any definite thought. Then the step was taken, the act was completed, and the consideration, that possibly did not weigh all before-hand, must now gather in a mist over what might be yet to come. The horse-hoofs and the Colonel's kind " Good-morning," broke up the reverie.

The Colonel stopped, saying, " We have been to see the poor Caxtons. I am sorry for them, one and all! except for the child your son and daughter have taken—that one is sure to do well."

Mistress Crisp smiled a half-smile—the lips, not the eyes, consented to smile. " I am heartily sorry for them," she replied; " ills, thee know, are sooner lamented than mended!"

" There's youth on their side," said the Colonel, "and I trust they will yet look up and do well."

" It's late in beginning," observed Mistress Crisp, who was not in cheerful spirits that morning. " 'Take the day with thee,' has been my maxim through life; don't be making thy start when the sun's at its height!"

" And yet," said the Colonel, kindly, " there is many a darkened noon-day sees a bright sunset."

" Thee art right! thee art right!" she replied, and the Colonel rode on, and Mistress Crisp said " Farewell."

CHAPTER IX.

The several classes of society are recognized in the Scriptures. Their order is of God, and every effort to overthrow that order by a general intermingling has had most baneful results. But the intermingling of spirit often found by persons of one class in society with those of another, is the result of a still higher and permanent law impressed on our common humanity. "God created man in His image; in the image of God created He him." The secret sympathy that draws, and the hidden tie that unites individuals of one class with those of another in friendship, is independent of all the temporary order of rank and station.

One cause of this may be found in the fact that refinement of mind is not confined to any class. It is a native quality of the mind, in some of the lowest as truly as in some of the highest. Refinement of mind is of three kinds. There is the first and lowest—refinement of wealth, raising the individual's social position; this refinement consists in circumstances, and observances imposed from without. There is next the higher refinement of cultivation or education, expanding the nature, and becoming more or less acute, and often fastidious and over-critical of others. The last and highest is the native refinement of mind—an instinct of the heart, not the result of circumstances, nor helplessly bound by general observances, and never fastidious nor over-critical; able to discern true heart-refinement in some by whom outward rules may be broken, and not less conscious of the lack of it in others who may observe every outward refinement.

In no stage of human life can the mind be more influenced by this native refinement than in childhood. The rules and regulations of polished society are unknown to the free heart of the child; social position may have its fetterings for the young life, and the lowlier heart and lowlier hearth may yield a pleasant and useful freshness: there is found no high aspect to awe, no self-assertion to repel, the young spirit finds nothing to impede, and the clasp of its response is often close and enduring.

It is, moreover, the custom of civilized life to class men by their trades; all thought of the man's individuality seems too often lost in his trade; a miller, a baker, a farmer, a locksmith, a cab-man—but still a MAN! This is the use of the printed page, that in quietness we may view the man or the woman in the life to which the trade is only an addition of circumstances.

We now return to the happy influence, the mutual joy and blessing, of Isabelle's intercourse with Naomi. Visits became still more frequent to the Mill-house, and Naomi was bound to a weekly visit with baby Meg to the Castle. There was no work, and sometimes little conversation in these visits, but these deficiencies were made up for by unbounded admiration of the growing baby. Isabelle was allowed by her indulgent mother to have the little cot their own baby had outgrown, in one corner of her own room, and here the Mill baby slept when Isabelle could give her up, while she talked and read with Naomi. Naomi's mind was capable of intelligent interest on any subject to which Isabelle's unfolding education could introduce her; and one interest of many a volume was, how pleasant it would be to read from it to Naomi!

Naomi's book was still the Bible, not only the Book of books, but the *one* book to her. Isabelle, with her young affections strong for every hope, learned to look onward to the glory yet to be revealed; the beauty of earth rejoicing in its King, Creator, Lord; when " the floods shall clap their hands, and all the trees of the wood rejoice before Him. When the mountains shall bring peace and the little hills righteousness; all kings shall fall down before Him, and all nations serve Him." When " He shall redeem the souls of the poor, and precious shall their blood be in His sight."

Naomi would picture to Isabelle's young eye the scenes that the earth will behold when the beasts of the field shall honour Him, and man shall learn war no more. When the slave shall be free from his oppressor, and " musical as silver bells their falling chains shall be."

They talked together of Israel's glory then, as

the typical Bride of the King of kings. When on Judah's high throne He should sit whose right it is. When those ten tribes lost, as Naomi believed, should return to their country. The thought had not risen on Naomi's soul that has flashed on many in this generation, that Israel's ten tribes may only have been hidden because we knew them not. The two disciples walking from Emmaus knew not the stranger at their side for their eyes were holden. Joseph's brethren thought him lost in some low slavery, or lower dungeon, or lower grave of Egypt, his kingly splendour blinded their eyes that they did not know him. So now, it may be, Israel is hidden only by the light of her glory, encircling the earth and possessing the gate of her enemies. But Naomi had no thoughts such as these. Only here or there, in minds unknown to her, a glimmer, a dream, a faint echo of such a grand possibility had arisen. It was enough for Naomi that He, the true Messiah, who had been despised and rejected of men, would come again to reign before His ancients gloriously. That while Christ should present the Church unto Himself, a glorious church, Israel should be a crown of glory and a royal diadem in the hand of her God. Isabelle caught the gleams of distant splendour as much from the radiance of Naomi's eyes, as from the impassioned words which fell from her lips. While their hearts glowed in the light of the sacred page, made spirit and life to them by a living faith. Their horizon was boundless ; the things of to-day were touched with the light that is eternal ; every power they possessed was expanded and ennobled, and the lowliest aim of life enshrined the energy of the infinite.

Naomi's voice of song had never been a silent one;—not only when alone, but often in the evening hour, when the open Bible lay before her husband, she sat and sang with him. Mistress Crisp thought it a dangerous gift to cultivate, but heard in silence; and secretly, when in the distance she caught the low tones of Naomi's voice, she listened, and would have missed the melody if it had ceased from earth. But now Naomi sang to the baby sleeping; she sang to the baby waking, and sang to the baby playing at her feet while busy with her needle; and baby Meg looked up with a quiet face, that told her spirit was one attuned to song.

"Naomi, thee will sing thy heart away, I fear! thee gets too vocal."

"I fear I do," Naomi answered! "I don't know how it is, only this happy life I live seems as if it must be sung."

"Thee must be careful, my daughter, how thee venture too much to please the ear or please the eye; they both let danger in. To study quietness and plainness of speech and appearance, are duties that belong to us here!"

Naomi's eye fell on the bright blue frock in which she had dressed her fair Saxon baby. She took the counsel, and sang less, and put on the little gown of drab which Mistress Crisp had bought for the child.

The baby grew a perfect sunbeam, healthy and merry to excess. Even Mistress Crisp would look on complacently as the child laid its head with its clustering curls of shining gold on Naomi's shoulder; whose raven hair, close braided, made the baby's head appear a shining gem; the little face looking upward from its hiding-place, in glee that sparkled in the blue eyes, while Naomi's looked down in their heavenly lustre; her happy tones answering the glee of the child. Oliver's observant eye often rested on the two; he sometimes longed that the child were indeed her own; but he gave as freely as Naomi, if not as fully, the kindness of his heart and the blessings of his home.

Each day was to Naomi as a Sabbath. The sunbeams slept upon the deep calm river of her life, that flowed on peacefully in its swift current to the ocean of Eternity; the sunbeams slept upon it, and it mirrored back in softened beauty every object as it flowed along—flower, and tree, and bird that skimmed its surface with light wing; and clouds that crossed the heights of blue above; all met an answering feeling in Naomi's life.

Many a friend called in at the Mill-house. A sunbeam, as we have said, rested there, and people liked to sit awhile in its light and warmth. One visitor could hardly have been an expected one: it was old Farmer Caxton. No one would have called him " old " before his son's misfortunes. His strong-built frame was then erect; the hard features unmarked by care, for all he touched seemed to turn to gold: his hair was scarcely grey, and he looked independent of all men. But a Hand had been laid

on him—an invisible Hand; it fell not as with a
blow at once, for then he might have risen again, but
he had to feel its heavy pressure for years—the
wasting away of his money, his hopes, his son's
prospects, and his own credit, as the most prudent
and successful of men. Such discipline reminds of
the expression of the Psalmist, "Thy hand presseth
me sore"; not a blow, but a long, heavy pressure,
from which there is no uprising. His stalwart
frame was bowed; he looked down, as if avert-
ing his eyes; instead of his former aspect, which
appeared ready to challenge the world. His step was
slower, and his sharp replies were less ready. Sometimes he grew angry and passionate; but you felt it
was the outburst of a troubled heart, which you longed
to soothe—not the outbreak of a proud, vindictive
spirit. None had cared for Farmer Caxton before.
All who could afford it had been ready to deal with
him; because, though his price was high, the article
was sure to be good; but no personal feeling existed.
Men sought him for barter, not for friendship; and
this keen atmosphere that everywhere existed around
him, hardened him the more. Now a pity grew up in
the minds of men for him; eyes looked on him in sympathy, and even market tones softened. This softened
feeling in others softened Farmer Caxton the more.

Not long after Jonathan had sailed, Farmer Caxton
walked to and fro at the foot of the Mill-hill, with
a strong wish to ascend it and call at the Mill-
house, but the effort was too great. He remembered
every word he had unreasonably uttered; the slight

he had put on Naomi and Oliver; and now she had taken the child, as if she owed them her gratitude; and Oliver had stood his son's friend with a kindness that ought to be acknowledged; but how to take the first step was more than Farmer Caxton knew. Pride worked against better feelings; he had never conquered self, and the Mill-hill seemed too steep to climb. Several times he drew near to the ascent, and as often turned away; until one day he met Oliver, who greeted him kindly, and said, " Won't you come up and see the child ? " and they went up together. Naomi drew the arm-chair near the door, and while Oliver conversed with Farmer Caxton on the crops and the weather, Naomi hastened upstairs, took up the baby and brought her down, with the roses of sleep on her cheeks and a sleepy surprise in her eyes. " 'Tis grandfather, baby! Shake hands! Give grandfather a kiss! " said Naomi. Baby Meg put one little arm round his neck, as was her way with Oliver; and the old man was pleased, and took the child, who looked intently in his face from the land of dreams. Her half-sleepy condition favoured the interview; and from that day the old farmer often crossed that dear threshold. He made no confession; it was not needed there. He said very little, but he felt the warm light of the home, and the little child, all his own, in its shelter, beamed on his sterile heart with a glow; and seeds of better things, long buried in its wintry soil, began to spring up and blossom ;— few, and slow in unfolding; but spring had begun, and spring leads on to summer. Every one he had

to do with felt a change in the man. On one subject it was observed he never spoke now—the subject
of money; it was a root of bitterness to him. Old
habits still held on: he still quietly took back his
sample or cattle at market if the price he asked were
not given, and would never give more for anything
than the one price he offered; but there were many
traces of kindness, and a quietness that had not been
seen in him before.

When Mistress Caxton received a letter from her
son,—for they were always addressed to his mother,
Farmer Caxton would ask at once, " Are they well?"
And when Mistress Caxton wrote, he always said,
"Tell him to write what he wants." But no want
ever came. Jonathan's good education enabled him
soon to get a clerkship; his wife could manage her
little home; and, taught by past troubles, she studied
her own pleasure less and her husband's comfort more.
After a few years they rose to a thriving condition;
but their family grew large, and their absent children
were not sent for.

And so the dark cloud broke in blessing, and
left traces of fertility. For

> Who the thunder swayeth,
> Who with lightning playeth,
> Who the storm obeyeth,
> He ruleth and schooleth
> Both thee and me.

There was another visitor at the Mill-house who
must not be passed over. It was Benoni, the Jew.
He was a pedlar, and bent with the weight of the

pack he had carried for years. In those days of sitting still, a pedlar, selling many useful and a few ornamental things, was a welcome visitor. Benoni studied always to have something new, and laid out his small returns with great caution and skill. He was not a vendor of news—an easy way for a pedlar to secure an entrance; he was a reserved and silent man. Being a Jew, he felt but little interest naturally about the people his lot was cast amongst; though it was not hard for those in distress to awaken his sympathy, and he was known to have shown kindness to many. He would undo his pack in a house, sitting down to rest, and leaving the little group, who soon gathered, to inspect its contents; but his eye was never off his goods, though he was silent in their praise. He never sold on trust, and he never lowered his price. No one asked where he lived; he was regularly expected, and he regularly came. The pedlar Jew had no home; he slept in public-houses by the highway-side, or in some hidden corner in the large town in which he replenished his store.

When Benoni first travelled his rounds, Naomi was a child; her Jewish features caught his eye as he called at her mother's door. The widow welcomed him; asked him to her frugal meal; pressed him to come whenever he returned; and as his visits became regular, the Christian Jewess spoke to him of hopes fulfilled, which to Benoni lay in the far distance. Benoni listened, but never received the earnest teaching of the widow's faith. His interest fastened on

Naomi; to her he brought the small offerings of a countryman's affection; it was her young face that lived before him all his weeks of wandering, until he returned again to mark its brightening grace.

Benoni in those days never visited the Mill-house. Mistress Crisp misdoubted him! She said that when she went to a Christian shop she knew what she bought, but she never wished to see the inside of the pack of a Jew! These remarks reached Benoni; he keenly felt the suspicion, and avoided the Mill-hill altogether.

Oliver Crisp did not share his mother's aversion. Many a commission he had given Benoni; it was Benoni who had with the greatest care procured the wedding-dress for Naomi. Shops were then chiefly confined to the towns, and travelling-men took orders from all sides; a large amount of money passed through their hands. Naomi longed for her friend at the Mill-house, and at her request, Oliver desired him to come. Mistress Crisp, who could not understand any friendship with Benoni, said, " It is nothing better, daughter, than the lust of the eye and the pride of life. Thee may as well throw thy money in the depths of the sea, as lay it out in the pack of a Jew; and better, by far; it will help no deception down there!" But Naomi would never give up a friend: such Benoni had ever been to her; and she gladly saw him resting by her winter-fireside, or amongst her flowers on her garden-bench in summer. Mistress Crisp, if there, always retired, for she never greeted the pedlar Jew.

Naomi soon ventured more than her widowed mother had done;—less in one sense, though more in another. Naomi always asked his permission to read to him; he could not deny her, and it was her habit, whenever he came, to sit by his side and read from the Holy Word. She seldom made a comment, never raised a question; she only quietly read a chapter, generally both from the Old and the New Testament; or a Psalm, with a passage from the Gospels. Benoni listened in silence; but when Naomi read of the "Crucify Him! crucify Him!" it could not be hidden that tears filled his eyes, and he would say, "Not that! not that! I never can stand it!" Still he was Benoni the Jew.

Here, in the brief calm that precedes the storm, we may quietly ask what it was in Mistress Crisp, and in her religious associations and creed, which gave religious limit, as well as religious power. The Society of Friends were devout witnesses to the Divine Person of the Holy Spirit; they were the standard-bearers of that great and glorious truth. This was the secret of their hallowing influence. But it may be asked whether their tendency was not too much to stop there—looking for inward teaching and guidance—waiting for the Divine Monitor within? The promised office of the Holy Spirit is, to take of the things of Christ, and show them unto us. The Saviour says, "He shall testify of ME." The Divine Person of Immanuel, God with us, though believed in, appears to have been less the constant object of faith and contemplation than the inward guidance vouchsafed. What the truly spiritual members of the Society sought for, they found;—Divinely-taught, Divinely-led witnesses for the indwelling Presence of God the Holy Ghost. But the yet higher advance, when the Holy Spirit reveals the Lord so fully to the heart that the apostle's words express the fact—" I live, yet not I, but Christ liveth in me "—this fulness of grace and truth has a deeper influence. It expands the life to the constant receiving from without, instead of the constant in-spection within. It is the Divine Person, perfect God and perfect man, constantly attracting—drawing out the soul to Himself, and therefore associating it more fully and freely with all that is of Him in nature, as well as in grace. There is no point in all the circle of our being, or in all the universe of God, that is not touched with Light Divine through the Humanity of Christ our Lord. The eyes that con-template Him most intently gather in most of His rays; and they learn to see all things in Him. " In Thy Light we shall see Light." " I am the Light of the world : he that followeth me shall not walk in darkness, but shall have the Light of Life."

CHAPTER X.

THE wing of softest plumage that gleams athwart the skies, still casts a shadow if it stoops its flight near to the earth beneath it. So it is with the angel of life when bending tenderly above an earthly home, to gather to his embrace the one for whom he came. Though himself light and life, the shadow of his presence falls. Even so the shadow fell on that fair village of the West, when, without warning, the husband and father of the Castle was taken from its deep affection. No embrace of earth can hold so closely that life's angel cannot loose the clasp. So gently done! no wresting from the grasp; the arms enfold as closely as before, but, lo! their treasure is not there.

The shadow fell, and the home was bereft. It fell without warning, but not without preparation. True soldier of the King of kings, his ear was ready for his Captain's call:

> At midnight came the cry,
>   "To meet thy God prepare!"
> He woke, and caught his Captain's eye:
>   Then, strong in faith and prayer,
> His spirit with a bound
>   Burst its encumbering clay:
> His tent, at sunrise, on the ground,
>   A darkened ruin lay.

Not in battle's fierce conflict, when heading his column, he desperately broke on the foe:—Not when single-handed he stood in the breach, and held it against the ranks of the enemy until succour was given:—Not in hurrying defeat, for he had never turned his back, not even to rally his fast-lessening company against the masses that gained on their lines:—Not in victory; for he lived to bear its honours, and leave them as incentives to the soldier-son of his line. Yet he fell, as suddenly, as utterly gone as if the whirring ball of the rifle had rudely broken entrance and summoned forth the noble spirit from his castle and home; the noble spirit that never wronged an enemy nor neglected a friend!

Beneath and around the Castle few knew their loss until the early morning, when the heavy bell from the church-tower tolled out a knell over hearts and homes. Then each one as they learned who was gone, gazed up to the Castle on its wooded height:—it looked unapproachable in the awe of that solemn shadow—solemn, yet soft, even then; for the eye looked up from the Castle to the heaven above,—the snowy masses of cloud standing out against the blue sky; bending like a canopy over that lofty home; and they said, each one to themselves, or one to another, "He is better off."

There was a hush over all the busy life of the farms, and the fields, and the homes. Men's voices were low, and the children were quiet in the village street. All things bore testimony that a great and a good man—a father of the people, was gone.

The poor man dies and is buried, and the wealthy around may not know. It may be, a petition is presented for decent burial, which parish economy does not always afford; or the widow and the children lack the necessaries of life, and the gold or the silver may be given, and the object of it forgotten. But it is not so when one of the upper class is taken from the village life of England. The inquiry is constantly passing from one villager to another, how the sickness is going? what turn has it taken? is there hope? And the prayer arises from many a home, that the steps of the sufferer have never entered and his hand never cheered. And when all is over on earth, where must you go for the starting tear, the words of true feeling, the sorrow and pity for the bereaved? Not always to relatives and acquaintances, to those on the same level; but surely to the surrounding homes of the poor.

Naomi had for some time seemed to lose strength, the colour had deepened on her cheek, till it became consumption's hectic flush. On this morning she was quietly preparing the breakfast, when her mother-in-law hurried in with agitated manner and shawl unpinned. Breathless from her rapid climb of the steep hill, she sat her down and said, " Hast heard the heavy news? Conrad Gray, the father, is dead! Where is Oliver ? "

Naomi stood for a moment transfixed, then her colour fled, and she sank fainting on the floor. Mistress Crisp knew not what to do; she fell upon her knees beside her, and looked in anguish to the door. It was Oliver's time, and he entered. He, too, stood pale and motionless a moment, then said, "She has fainted!" and kneeling on one knee, he raised her head, then wound his arms about her, and carried her to her bed. Mistress Crisp regained her self-possession, ministered restoratives, and Naomi revived. It was long before her strength returned sufficiently to allow her to leave her bed ; and when she did come down, it was evident that she was far weaker than before. The mournful day of interment came, and Oliver attended, as did all the country round, in sad respect. When a little time had passed, Oliver made personal inquiries at the Castle, of Mr. Howe, the butler, and mentioned how heavy the grief had laid upon his wife. Before the week was over, Isabelle wrote a note to Naomi, which came as the balm of comfort to her ; and when a little longer time was over, and Naomi was better able for the task, the pony-carriage fetched her to the Castle.

She was taken to Isabelle's room as of old, and in a moment more the young mourner, so dear to her heart, entered, clad in her heavy garb of sorrow, her face white with grief and tears. She threw herself into Naomi's arms, who clasped to her bosom the orphan weeping for a father's loss—a kind of suffering Naomi had never known.

No moment this for words ; never was uninspired proverb more true than that which says, "Speech is silver, but silence is golden." Eyes poured forth the passion of orphaned weeping, which words could not utter; Naomi's parted lips above that young head, breathed the prayer they could not speak; her arms ventured not to press too closely the form they held, with a love for the young life they encircled, even more tender than that for baby Meg;—all this was eloquence, from heart to heart. Then as the passion of those tears passed by, Naomi softly said, "Them that sleep in Jesus, God will bring with Him."

"O Naomi, he is dead! I never knew before what death was!"

Naomi, trembling with emotion, laid Isabelle upon the couch and sat beside her, and said, "Not dead! not dead! He could not die! He who is the Truth is saying even now to you, 'He that liveth and believeth in Me shall never die. Believeth thou this?' Thy father lives with his God and thy God!"

"But I shall never, never see him!"

"Never? You will see him for ever! and it may be to-day—to-night. 'We which are alive and remain shall be caught up together with them on the clouds, to meet the Lord in the air, and so shall we ever be with the Lord.' These are the words with which we are to comfort one another!"

"Yet the time, being uncertain, must seem so long!" said Isabelle.

"It will if we spend it in sorrow," answered Naomi; "grief darkens life, and we drag a heavy chain when we walk in darkness, making shortest lives seem long. But if you rise up, holding the Hand stretched out to support you; if you set not *one* step alone, but only learn to lean harder on that supporting Hand, you will find that separation is but, as it were, for 'a moment,' and that moment a golden one ; for the light of Christ's presence will shed on it a glory that will shine brighter and brighter to the perfect day of reunion. I know it, indeed, for I have tried it."

"I will try," said Isabelle, " by His help I will ! " and unfalteringly she kept the resolve of that hour.

From that day Isabelle often sent for Naomi in her little carriage, and took her through the forest drives, where the foliage sheltered from the summer heat, and the familiar deer scarcely started from their path. These summer-drives, slowly winding through woodland pathways, were blessings to them both.

There is this difference between a heavenly horizon, and an horizon of mere earthly expectation. The latter dwarfs the present, makes nearer objects of less interest, and absorbs the mind with thoughts of a desired future. But the heavenly horizon — though infinitely extended, brings out the present into clearer form, defines and brightens every claim, and sheds the softening of an ennobling purpose on every rigid line of earthly toil and care.

Sometimes when all the loveliness around brought home with a fresh anguish the thought to Isabelle, of the father who had delighted in the beauty of his home—with whom she had shared each walk, admired each varied scene—Naomi would remind her how we might expect that in millennial days the glorified may revisit the scenes endeared in earthly life ; revisit them with those who shared that love, to see them clothed in richer beauty; or if change had passed over them, clothed anew in vernal graces. Each hope that thrilled their souls, each expectation of the manifestation of the sons of God, gathered around the Man Christ Jesus:—He who must ever be the centre and the sun, the light of life in all the unfolding of the present and the future.

The harvest ripened, and bright September days saw gathered grain. Naomi had no longer strength for the little drives that had given such hallowed hours. Isabelle came down to see her now. The sun was setting on her wedding-day, and she walked to the garden-gate with Isabelle. They stood below the birch-trees that grew on either side, and looked over the valley to the western sky. They caught the distant shouts of harvest-home, the reapers' carol in the quiet air, and as they stood together, Naomi said, "It was on such an evening that they rang our wedding bells; and ever since, on such a clear September evening, I have fancied that I heard them ringing in the distance, as if they still were glad as then. I do not hear them now; only at times I seem to catch the sound of sweeter music, and I wonder, Can it be the harpers, harping with their harps, in glory?"

They never met again. Naomi had taken Isabelle by the hand, and led her on the shining way until, beyond the portals, the spiritual form receded from her view.

Naomi bore a son, and gave him to her husband's arms; and left him to his care with looks of love that lingered like evening sunbeams in his soul.

Strange anguish fills the heart that turns away, to leave alone in earth's last slumber, the form of one round whom the deepest affections and tenderest associations of life are entwined; to leave that form to rest alone within the quiet grave. O, faith divine! that then can trust its all with God. The sleeping body to His holy keeping; the riven heart, bereft of its treasure, to His healing hand; and life, made desolate of earthly joy, to His grace, which can illumine with celestial radiance the shadows that otherwise would gather round the soul in darkening gloom. Even so did Oliver turn from Naomi's grave. The sun had dipped behind the hills, and twilight reigned within his heart and home.

Slowly and calmly night came on, and when the peasant slept upon his pillow, and the lights were out in the Mill-house, and all the land around was still, a lonely man stood by the new-made grave, looking down in silence, with fingers clasped as if to grasp the struggling passions of his soul. There lay beneath that heaving sod the all of earthly love for him — Benoni; she who as the child, the maiden, and the woman, had saved him from earth's worst curse — a hardened heart. Yet he had only loved to lose; and in his lonely agony he would have welcomed the blow that could lay him low beside her there. He did not know that such a lot would then have been eternal separation.

Oliver inscribed the stone that he raised to his Naomi, with the words, "They shall be-mine, saith the Lord, in that day when I make up my JEWELS."

CHAPTER XI.

THERE are times—who does not know them?—when for us earth holds but one beloved form; the eye can scarcely wander from it, or if it looks around it is but outward seeing. The spirit trembles over the quivering flame of one beloved life; bends over it in sheltering care, that fain would breathe it back to earthly existence again; and when that quivering flame sinks and expires, a darkness falls on all around—the glory and the beauty now is dim; creation wears a solemn pall, and mourns with us— its tribute to the kingly sceptre which was man's birthright; and though the hand proved all unworthy to maintain its right, and the sceptre lies broken at our feet, yet nature, by the shadow over it, still mourns its rightful Lord.

So it was with Oliver; he fulfilled his daily task, but ever as he worked he looked upon Naomi's face. Within the Mill, amongst his sacks, or over his ledger, still he saw that face fading like summer-light away— as when you know that its last gleam will shortly fall, and then the glory gone, the quiet night comes on. His eye had never kindled in the hope that lit Naomi's—the light of resurrection-life; his sad eyes were ever turning from the Mill-hill to the tall elms round the old church tower, where she lay sleeping by her mother's side. Naomi had seldom thought upon a silent grave and sleeping dust; her eyes were on the risen saints—how soon the wilderness and the solitary place would be glad for them, and earth rejoice beneath the tread of their beloved feet. This elastic hope cheered not Oliver; no such amaranthine flower bloomed for him; he had enshrined Naomi in his heart's pure love, he still enshrined her there; but the melody her presence made through heart and home, sent back no echoes from another shore; it slept within the grave for him, and the silence that it left made Oliver a still more silent man.

The Mill-house became again the care of Oliver's mother. She left the cottage at its foot, and brought her maid to nurse the baby and do the work required. The baby had his mother's eyes, but not the light that lighted hers. He was a quiet child, seldom crying, but he also never raised the happy crow—the merry laugh of baby glee. In talking to him you might win a smile upon the little face; but no one played with him: his young nurse had been trained three years in the Quaker quiet of Mistress Crisp's small home; a strong, active girl, whose aim it was to keep the baby still. No one ever sang to him, and you could almost fancy as you looked at him that he was listening to some voice not here, whose far-away tones were falling on his ear.

Oliver would sometimes stand and look upon his infant sleeping; and when alone, a smothered groan a moment's prayer, a starting tear, told the heart's anguish and its love. Naomi was not there, from whose dear arms to take his infant; and the father seemed a stranger to his child. Mistress Crisp was always praising the baby, saying, " Never was there a stiller child upon earth ! " But praise constantly repeated loses its point, and the baby showed no signs of pleasure at the heartfelt commendations. Two friends he had who divided all his interest— Aleppo the dog, and baby Meg. Aleppo, strange to say, had made his way indoors with a most determined purpose ever since the baby boy dwelt in the Mill-house room. Aleppo slept by his cradle, or laid at his side when he learned to sit still on the floor, stooped his large head to be hugged, and gave a paw or an ear as might best suit the baby hand ; though Aleppo's paw was too large a handful for the child for many a long day.

Baby Meg had not remained at the Mill-house ; she would have been far too lively for Mistress Crisp. One event would have settled this removal if nothing else had. On the day of Naomi's sudden faintness, Mistress Crisp carried baby Meg home with her, sorely against the strong will of this two-years old child. Being anxious soon after to run up and see how Naomi then was, Mistress Crisp tied baby Meg into her little arm-chair, safe in her parlour. Not long after, a howl from Aleppo led Oliver Crisp to look out from the window of Naomi's room, from which he saw Aleppo standing by some unaccountable thing, and holding up his head with another 'long-winded howl. He went down and found it nothing else than baby Meg, who, unable to disentangle herself, had managed to get on her knees with the little arm-chair at her back, and regardless of the garden gravel-walk, made her way through the unlatched gate, and was climbing the hill on hands and knees, with a cry of "Mammie! Mammie!" Mistress Crisp said such determined self-will was all too much for her! Baby Meg was welcomed home by her grandmother at the Farm.

Mistress Caxton could hardly be silent in her laments and praises of the departed Naomi. Dame Truman, who taught the children in her private day-school—for parish-school there was not—was a heartfelt mourner for Naomi; never had she set such store by any scholar as by her! She would say, "I called her my fawn, I did!" Many a time Dame Truman stepped up to Mistress Caxton, and they sat or stood, as the case might be, while lamenting together. "I always fancied the girl," said Mistress Caxton, "and if Farmer Caxton did not, that was no fault of mine. She had those artless, simple ways, as a child, that are not manners taught, but manners natural, as you may say."

Dame Truman interrupted, "Mistress Caxton, I have taught manners from the time I taught anything. But there are some that won't learn them, let you be as strict as you will."

Mistress Caxton, scarcely conscious of interruption, continued, "You could read her heart in her young, innocent face. I have always held to true measures,—even dealing; for if you go and favour in buying or selling, you wrong them that don't, and may be that can't; but for all that, I never could help filling her milk-can up to the brim; and when I said, 'Keep your penny,' she would blush as pink as a cabbage-rose; and when I dropped an egg or two into her basket, I have often looked after her with a tear in my eye, how light-footed she ran back to her poor mother, as if you had given her a crown. There were a few words between Farmer Caxton and me, because my Jonathan was courting the girl, and as I always said, 'Not to blame, neither;' he could never have done better, only to see how that Mill-house was kept like a palace! and her husband, how he turned out like a prince! He was always before a sort of half-open man, but he came out as free and easy as you could care to see. And her dairy! you would have thought she had been born and bred to it. I'll be bound, there was not a word to be said between the Mill butter and my own; and the market knew it, too! And that butter might have been turned out on Jonathan's farm! But there is no good in wishing too late; and as I said, Farmer Caxton and me had a few words between us: he was always for money, and I was for work; poor man, he has had his lesson on that score—that money without hands to turn it round the right way is a back-door to ruin. I never bring it up against him, still it's natural that I, as the poor lad's mother, should feel it; and a better son than Jonathan I never wish to see, not so far as this life goes; and we might have all been so comfortable together! but there, it was not to be, so there is no use in my thinking it over as I do."

"I took notice," said Dame Truman, "how good she was to all! It was just as I always taught her—a good turn for a bad leaves you the upper hand!"

"Ah! 'tis too true!" answered Mistress Caxton. "She had that, any way! When I could not so much as look pleasant upon them,—Jonathan and his wife,—how she would turn things right about, if they had but had the sense to keep them so! And then to see how she mothered the babe; I could never have taken a young thing like that. I took her home here when the last illness came on, and how the poor wean did fret, to be sure! She would cry nothing but ' Mammie!' and would not put up with me. But the strangest thing of all was how Farmer Caxton turned round! Whenever he was out of the way, he was sure to have travelled up there; and the babe had got hold of his heart and, dear me, how it did please him when she cried, ' Grand-dad!' and would go straight to him, when she would have none of me. I never saw him take to a small thing before. Do you think he'll stir if she is asleep on his knee? not he! I don't think a bargain would drive him to disturb her! She has got the upper hand already, I tell him, and it may not be the better for her some day, as I say."

"'Tis teaching and training must put that right, Mistress Caxton. When Meg comes to me, there's not one above another. I rule them alike, and keep the upper hand of the lot."

"Well, I never said so much to any creature before!" Mistress Caxton observed. "There is one thing to be said, if you do have the best, you are worse off when you lose it! and that's the long and short of the comfort some have here."

It was a sad fact that Farmer Caxton never ventured to the Mill-house again. Mistress Crisp never concealed her displeasure when it was roused against any one; when out of her favour, it was enough once to have met her, to be fully aware how you stood in her opinion and feelings. Oliver would have been glad to see him; but neither Benoni nor Farmer Caxton ever called in again. Oliver himself would often fetch baby Meg, for the child seemed more to him now than before; and on any busy day Mistress Caxton took advantage of the kind offers made, and sent her up. So the child divided her time between two homes, in both of which she felt herself an object of love. She still called Oliver "Daddy," and always distinguished him from her grandfather, who was "Grand-daddy."

It was a pretty sight to see the three on the summer turf—Baby Meg, with her golden head, a dazzle of light on its clustering curls and on her laughing lips and eyes, her little head often pressed close to the baby Oliver's quiet face, with his dark eyes and close curls of raven hair; little Oliver pulling the head of a daisy or dandelion, and giving it to baby Meg, who talked in a language evidently pleasant to

him, but who for the most part threw down his daisy
or dandelion-head, which he would pick up again and
hold out once more to her hand—so early in life is
character shown, and its after-histories often spelled
out in its infant days! Aleppo would sit close
beside them, looking out in quite a different direction,
as if otherwise mentally engaged; but at any difference of sound or movement, the quick turn of his
head proved his ears were attentive. Sometimes he
lay down beside them, and baby Meg would lean the
golden lustre of her little head upon his side, close by
his noble head of black and tan; and little Oliver
would look on, and say, "Me! me!" which no one
understood.

It was a picture scene on that hill-side still,
with the far-reaching world below. Oliver on the
mill-steps, by the mill-door; Mistress Crisp sitting
in- view at the Mill-house, where Naomi's roses
clustered still; and the children at play on the turf.
It may be said that the faithful Aleppo taught little
Oliver to walk. He was not at first strong on his
feet; and Aleppo would put his nose under his
shoulder, encouraging Oliver to drag himself up, and
then moving gently with the child clinging to him.
One thing struck you—that the wistful look went
from the baby's dark eyes when Meg was at play
beside him. The look he had at other times, a half-
dreamy, wistful look, was just the same as you had
seen in Naomi's eyes in those last months, when in
her heart she knew she was departing, and looked on
into the distance, catching the nearer gleams of the

glory of the Eternal—looking also if He who shall come might come before the hour that would sever the ties of earthly association, with the life so closely blended as her husband's with her own. The reflection of this look was in her baby's eyes. The village women shook their heads. One said, " Poor child ! This world will not contain him ; he looked beyond it from his coming in." Another said, " Did ye ever see the like—how the poor thing looks after its mother, and knows she is just away over there ? You will see he'll go after her ; that far-away look is just drawing him on ! " Oliver saw it in his silence ; for the silent sometimes see more than those swift to speak ; he watched the change when baby Meg was at play at his side, and fetched her the oftener—the only way that he knew of to brighten his child.

Oliver was a man of full height, strongly built; but he stooped from the day he was left. It seemed as if the weight of sorrow bent his head, and he never recovered erectness again. He still looked upon all things around him—was as capable and quietly-decided as ever ; while across his heart lay that buried form— the softest shrine that earth can offer ; and he waited for the time that would so surely come, when he should go to her who might not return to him.

Mistress Crisp stirred but little abroad ; she felt less active than before, and she feared to lose sight of the baby. No one noticed a change, for she was as upright as ever—as clear-sighted and careful. All that utmost watchfulness could do to prevent ills to young Oliver, Mistress Crisp did ; her greatest pain was to hear him cry. "It is not natural," she would say, "for so still a child, in such health and comfortable circumstances, to cry!" She always had a ready sweetmeat to allay the irritation, and when it subsided into stillness, Mistress Crisp felt her ease of mind return.

We have seen one heart that was left desolate by Naomi's departure—the childless, homeless, friendless Benoni, the pedlar Jew. He had never known the ties of home; he could not remember any tenderness from father or mother. An early outcast from a foreign land, he had fought his way up. Life had gone hard with him. The world made use of him, but any other would be all the same if he did them like service. The cords of his inmost spirit had stiffened; no hand had cared to try if response could be there; no melody awoke until he looked on Naomi. He saw the mould of his nation in her, which left no barrier between them; in his sight, there was a glory round about this child of Israel. Her eyes looked into his very soul, and seemed to him to read the secrets of his heart,. as, with a child's simplicity, she talked with him of many things. She liked to sit upon her stool within the open chimney of her mother's cottage, and, leaning forward, with her hands upon her knees, eagerly listen to Benoni's tales of his long travels. The wood fire lighted up her form, glowed on her cheeks, and kindled in her eyes; and Benoni lost his cold reserve, and loved to tell when she, the child, was there to listen. The door of his heart, so hard to open, had unclosed to the step of the widow's child; she had entered, and the dreary cell of that poor human heart was lighted up by her bright presence. Wherever he travelled then, the child Naomi cheered his lonely way. He thought of all things as of a tale to tell to her. She loved the pedlar Jew whose best joy seemed to be to remember her, and bring her some new pleasure or new tale. All fair things bore some touch of the one flower that bloomed for him. Still stepping on his way—often with weary feet and still more weary heart—he had never, in his fifty years of life, heeded bird or blossom, earth or heaven; but now he felt the voice of Nature, and each touch of the full octave had some melody of sight or sound that brought her to his view. He heard her take her marriage-vow, hiding in a lone corner of the village church; he passed for an old man then, though he had not reckoned sixty summers, but in his heart he was a younger man by far than when he first walked with Naomi to her mother's cottage-door, twelve years before. Seven years he shared the blessings of her married lot; and then her sun went down at noonday, and his life darkened over—lighted only by the ever-living sense of what had been its blessing and its loss. It is a strange desolation when the empty heart, that one bright form has filled, finds itself left with only the vivid shadow on its walls—the living presence gone! It was this man—half-dead for other men, only a pedlar Jew to all the world, but to Naomi a friend, a father in his tenderness; he it was who stood in grief so utter by the porch of the village church, where each one passed him by, when they bore Naomi's child to baptism. He shunned the Mill-hill now; and slowly darkening over into his old heavy sense of all things, he lived once more for traffic, with the weight of his heart-sorrow.

We are sometimes struck with the way in which a self-evident fact suddenly dawns on an absent mind—a fact that lay in view, yet unperceived, until suddenly waked to a consciousness of it. Oliver Crisp, looking from the door of his Mill, saw his child holding on by Aleppo, and so supported attempting to walk, with a tumble on the turf, and a clamber up again, dragging by Aleppo's ear. The father hastily descended, and gave a hand to the baby boy who, still clinging to Aleppo, made slow and steady way. Then he took him in his arms for the first time since his baptismal day; but unused to his father's companionship, looked down at the dog crying, " Bow, wow!" Aleppo stood up, leaning his fore-paws on his master, as if to assure the child that his unusual position was a safe one, and he was close by in attendance.

This was the beginning of a new life for little Oliver, who soon took to his father's arms beyond all other means of conveyance, stretching up his baby hands at all times to be taken, and his father could seldom refuse. He went up the Mill-steps with his father, or sat on the Mill-floor by the hour together, Aleppo always entering at those times, which he never did at other times, sitting beside the child while the father was busy. The first shout little

Oliver was ever heard to give was for his father, and now having once found an object to shout for, he shouted on every fresh appearance.

He soon learnt to steady himself on his feet as far as the wicket-gate of the garden. Many an anxious look did Mistress Crisp give when busy within, to see that the latch was quite safe; there the child would stand holding by the narrow bars, his face pressed close to them, and his large dark eyes peering through; and whichever way his father came the first voice he heard was the shout of his child—that note of gladness, that assurance of heart bound to heart.

It would have been strange if Naomi's child had not been his father's delight. The cloud that bore her upward had its radiance towards heaven, its earthward side was a darkening shadow, hiding for awhile the two left behind, the one from the other. It had been so when Oliver Crisp mourned his father, and the same nature again fell into the same error. How often do faults resulting from character repeat themselves unconsciously! But they had found each other now; the child's life expanded in the father's, and the father's in the child. Blessed ties of earthly relationship—father, mother, child, bride, husband, brother, sister, friend! To many, alas! the type may be wanting; not reflecting in rainbow hues, the beauty and glory of the antitype. Yet such may learn, even by their present lack, the blessing of that which lies open to their eternal possession. While others learn more peacefully, but not necessarily more fully, the infinite in the finite—things present the earnest of things to come.

There came at length a day of high festival. Conrad, the soldier son of the Castle, celebrated his majority. He·came of age at twenty-one, and the day was to be kept by the whole village population. The bells from the church-tower awakened the day, and the villagers rose—all looking up to the Castle once more. The flag waved mast-high on the top-most tower, and the old gun of the Castle was fired. Twenty-one booms it gave, saluting the day. Then under the distant trees in the light of the morning gleamed white-plumed helmets, and horsemen rode in with dazzling regimentals and splendid horses to bear them; up the rocky street the horse-hoofs clattered, and the village gazed in awe, until, lost in the long avenues, with only a gleam here and there, they entered the old gateway, which closed again behind them. Twelve o'clock was the time for all the village guests to arrive. Before that hour large companies of men, young and old, women and children, were pressing on in groups all on foot; for horses, gigs, and carts were provided for in the village. The Castle was silent; the flag waved on high. Then the clock in the old gateway slowly struck the hour, the heavy gates were thrown open, and Conrad rode out, while behind him, drawn up in phalanx, were his military friends, such as could be there, both officers and men, and a strain of martial music broke forth on the ear. Conrad rode his young war-horse, Bavieca, noted far and near by name, a wondrous horse he was—as gentle as a lady's palfrey when Conrad was his rider, but desperate in any other hand. Not a groom liked to mount him; "his sides foam white as a sea-wave," said the one who had charge of the noble steed in his stable, "if any try to ride him, only our master;" yet to Conrad's hand he answered, scarcely needing the rein, stepping lightly along, as if hardly condescending to tread on the ground, his crimson nostrils dilated, and yet in his full eye a softness that those could little imagine who had only seen the fiery eye in his speed. Conrad rode that day in the first glory of his manhood, a noble mien he had, and a yet nobler nature. As the gates opened to let him forth, he saw the throngs of gathered people and bowed his plumed helm, greeting the village with uncovered head. The people had raised a shout, and women's eyes dimmed with tears, and children rushed on with their welcome, girls with their pinafores of gathered flowers, and boys with caps high in air; they strewed the fair emblems before him, and the horse trod so lightly he seemed not to crush them. The elders there all knew his childhood and his youth, and both were true and fair; he seemed the glory of his line, the honour of his home, his widowed mother's staff and stay, his sisters' shield and blessing. That day he took the rent-rolls of the rich lands of the Castle; the son, the brother, the master, and the friend. For him the shout was raised loud and long, while above it the pealing bells broke forth again. Then dismounting he turned, and led the people in. The old courtyard was well adorned that day with all that taste could best arrange. One sight was there which fixed all eyes; upon the broad flight of steps that led to the Castle door, stood Conrad's widowed mother; she had laid aside her heavy weeds, but wore still a widow's dress; and by her side her daughters, all in white; they formed a group that drew the eye from all the festive show. Conrad ascended the steps, stood by his mother's side, and made his maiden speech, in this his childhood's, and now his manhood's, home.

How many were entertained that day none could tell. But not one who was there ever forgot the feeling that it gave. Oliver Crisp was there, and his child held his father's hand. Mistress Crisp declined the pressing invitation; strains of martial music were unpleasing to her, and festivals had never suited the quiet tenor of her life. Farmer Caxton was there, and baby Meg was one of those who scattered flowers beneath the young Squire's horse's feet. Dame Truman had a place, and even Benoni was not forgotten. Mr. Howe, the Castle butler, had full supremacy on all hospitable occasions, and Benoni did much business in the servants' hall. Mr. Howe could trust him; and if you had referred to Mr. Howe's private book, you would have found, stretching back over many a year, on such and such a day, breakfast, or dinner, or supper to Benoni. To the upper house at the Castle, he was only known as a pedlar Jew; but Mr. Howe took care that he was not forgotten. Indeed, who could tell of a creature forgotten that could lay claim, near or distant, to remembrance that day!

CHAPTER XII.

EACH sequestered village, each homestead, and each
heart, has its own history, which, if the pen could
tell, would find a listening interest beyond the
village limits. It does not need some great event
to wake responsive feeling. The simplest tale of
human life, if true to character, can arrest the noblest
mind; heart echoes unto heart in true vibration, and
the highest power only more quickly answers to the
lightest touch. And so the summers came and went
in that woodland village of the west, with its laughing river, its steep and rocky street, with here and
there a rustic cottage more outwardly attractive than
comfortable within; and yet they wore a pleasant
aspect through the open door—the bits of polished
furniture, the old china ware, the fire on the hearth-
stones, and the neat attire of the good mother
with her rosy children. All went on in quietness,
and passers-by could mark no change. The Castle,
amidst its lofty trees, looked still the stronghold and
the guardian of the land; the high mill-sails went
round upon the sister hill, telling of peace and plenty.
The cuckoo called the summer in, then left it to its
glory. The nightingales sang to the stars in the
ash-trees that shaded then the low thatched roofs

where the cottagers lay sleeping. The children nestled in the primrose-banks, and gathered violets and daffodils. They tossed the hay with merry laugh, and gleaned the scattered ears of corn, and crimsoned their cheeks with blackberries, and eyed the rosy nuts that clustered on the hazel-trees; then filled the chimney corners by the blazing logs till spring returned again, "sowing her lilies o'er the land."

Now and then an aged head lay down in weariness to sleep beneath the church's shade; and infants at the font told that another generation was coming in to take their place. One aged head the village mourned and missed with more than common feeling —old Joseph Richards. There was scarce a villager he had not counselled, nor a child he had not tried to lure to holy things. They crowded round the old man's grave, and many a heart felt thoughtful there, that had not heeded his simple words before. His illness had been short; and Mistress Crisp, with her accustomed kindness, had ministered to his daily wants.

There was a fervour and a glow of feeling in him she could not understand; and sitting down one day beside his bed, she questioned him.

"How is it, Joseph Richards, that thou art so confident? I do not hear thee speak as a poor sinner should. Let me ask thee, dost thou think upon thy sins?"

"Ah, Mistress! Every thought old Joseph has is fixed on Him who saved me from them! My thoughts, at best, arn't many nor great, and such as they be they gather close round Him; there's not even one that can be got to lag behind and delve for sins He covered long ago with His most precious blood!"

"But art thee sure that He whom thou hast sinned against in past times may not have them in His eye?"

"Yes; certain sure! I mind the words, 'Thou hast in love to my soul delivered it from the pit of corruption: Thou hast cast all my sins behind Thy back.'"

"Friend Joseph, I should like to see thee more humble and less confident. There is a Judgment-seat! Canst thou be sure thou wilt be clean before it?"

"O, Mistress! what's the worth of me, a poor old sinner, for you or I to fix our minds on? He is clean who stood for me; and isn't that enough?"

Mistress Crisp could make no impression on old Joseph. He had no thoughts of self, good or bad; it was no use asking him of anything save of Him who was all his salvation and all his desire. He slept himself away; his departing hour was like an infant's slumber. Mistress Crisp was the last friend to look upon him when the neighbours gathered round for the last office to the mortal body. His favourite tree was thick with summer-roses; and Mistress Crisp, through the open lattice, gathered those that grew around the little chamber-window, and laid them reverently upon the sleeping body; —emblems of those drops of precious blood that had made the blood-red rose so sacred to old Joseph.

The miller's man was Richard Dolman. He had served both father and son, and was the main-stay of the Mill. He had a thrifty wife, who, being rich in sons, had long desired a daughter. A daughter came at last, and Hannah Dolman was much engaged with the question of the name. She thought on all she knew, but none appeared just right; until, in her large Bible, she one day lighted—as it seemed to her, by happy chance, or happier direction—on the verse that gives the record of Job's daughters. She took the first — Jemima — for her infant girl, remarking, " Maybe, I'll come again, and have the other two ! " Another daughter and another came, and took the names in waiting, Kezia and Keren-happuch. Richard doubted as to the second, and objected to the third; but Hannah Dolman said, " Mind ye ! there were no women found so fair as the daughters of Job; and how could I go for to part them ! " How could she break a daughter off from such a group ! When the name was given at baptism, not being pronounced quite correctly, the minister asked Hannah if she could spell so unaccountable a name? upon which Hannah replied that " it was no unaccountable of hers ! as the minister would find if he looked in the Bible." Richard was displeased that his wife should speak up to a parson ; but Hannah was lifted up in her mind by what she felt her knowledge of the name ; whence it came, and the merit it had.

Hannah Dolman felt a constant satisfaction that her three daughters were settled in one verse of the Bible. But when her youngest grew up into practical life, her name became a subject of difficulty. Poor Richard Dolman declared that he could not turn it round on his tongue to get it out right, nor, indeed, to get it out at all; he was in danger of beginning where he ought to end. Hannah, too, when in practical haste, found herself in danger of forgetting the order she wished to give by the time she had said, "Keren-happuch!" In consequence of these necessary considerations, Hannah found that it behoved her to shorten the name for the daily appliances of life. So after some thought, she said, "Take the first letter, and just call her 'K.'! 'K.' stands for kettle, and kitchen, and king; it's a letter, to the best of my knowledge, that heads words that are honest, and useful, and grand—if you go to the top of the tree!" (For how should the good Hannah Dolman suppose that "knave" had anything to do with the honest letter "K"?) It was settled to be the only resource; and the poor girl was not sorry, for the troublesome boys of the village would shout "Keren-happuch" more distinctly than she could enjoy. In time, Jemima became an under-nursemaid at the Castle; Kezia entered Mistress Caxton's pleasant farm-house; and Keren-happuch was engaged by Mistress Crisp, who said, "I suppose thy name must be Kate, short for Katherine?"

"No, ma'am, my name is Keren-happuch."

It must be confessed that Mistress Crisp was

caught in ignorance or forgetfulness, and declared the name a heathenish one. But little K. said, " Please, ma'am, mother named me after Job's youngest girl; she said she could not part the three, they all lay together so handy in the Book."

Mistress Crisp was silent a moment, but no one ever saw her confused. She now replied with a slight addition of dignity, " If thy mother hunts out the names dead and buried, no one knows how long, she should put chapter and verse at the end of them. Let me tell thee, girl, those old names don't lie in the Book to be pinned on to the pinafores of babies new born ! I will call thee K., as others do, but let me hear no more of thy name, or thou wilt not long be my servant, I can tell thee ! "

Little K. heard most humbly, and when questioned in future, she only said her name did not please her mistress, who would have her only called K. It was K. who was kind and good to the baby when her mistress returned to the Mill-house; she had grown a stout young woman now; faithful in service, and capable of relieving her mistress of many of the cares of the Mill-house and small farm-yard in point of work.

As Oliver's years of childhood increased, he sometimes showed the faults of a child. He was of a sensitive nature, with strong feelings, not often ruffled; but when they were, they were strongly moved. His father's arms and the Mill put all things right; but when alone with his grandmother, if there came an outbreak her trouble was great. On these occasions

she thought it wisest to bring up, as she expressed
it, a feeling for his departed mother; with the idea of
its having more effect, and keeping up the vanished
influence. She would say, " Olly, (that was the name
by which he called himself), thy poor mother would
never have overlooked thy bad temper, she would
have punished thee for this!" Poor little Oliver
never heard of his mother except in this way, as
a departed terror. Well meant but most sadly
mistaken. Names of the blessed departed cast no
shadow. They should not be left as Oliver Crisp left
his Naomi's name, in the dark mine of sorrow; still
less should they be used as a distant terror. Such
names should shine in open day as the gems of the
home; they should emit the diamond's rays; we
should let the light fall for others on their many cut
facets;—each emitting a radiance from having been
perfected by the purifying fire; that their memory,
like themselves, may be blessed.

Little did Oliver Crisp think that even then a
hard feeling was growing up in the heart of his boy
for the mother whose tenderness would have been
the shrine of his childhood ; and little did Mistress
Crisp imagine that by calling up an unknown
authority she was steeping the blessed memory of his
mother in bitterness to the child. How wondrous
the power of words ! Who can venture to live without the prayer—" Let the words of my mouth, and
the meditation of my heart, be acceptable in Thy
sight, O Lord, my Strength and my Redeemer !"

But there is a love more tender than a mother's,

often breaking by slight incidents the evil spells of life! It might be thought that Isabelle would have taught the child to know his angel-mother: she had made many attempts, both at the Mill-house and the Castle, to win the child to confidence, but the quiet stiffness of the grandmother, and the shyness of the child, baffled all her attempts. The only place where little Oliver was at home, away from the Mill-house, was Farmer Caxton's;—there he was always quite happy with baby Meg. One day a young son of Mrs. Butterly's was there, familiarly called Dick. Mrs. Butterly had what was called a long family, but she often said she took a mother's pride in each one; for her part she did not mind how many, it would only help her to show that the training is the making. O, mother, boast not thyself of to-morrow! There are roots of bitterness even in children's hearts that yet may spring up to trouble thee. Thou mayest water them with thy tears, but find the evil root too strong for all thy power and skill to over-come. Rather look up in humble prayer to Him who hath said, " I will take away the heart of stone, and give a heart of flesh."

Dick was older than Oliver by two years; of an even age with baby Meg, with whom he liked to come and play. On one occasion Dick was trouble-some; he was not ready at any time to submit except to his mother. Kezia reproved him in vain, and then added, "If you do it again I will just take you off to your mother." On hearing this, Oliver said with great decision, "I's glad I's not got a mother!" The sound of these words seemed to break Farmer Caxton's light sleep in his arm-chair by the fire. He turned his head quickly, caught Oliver by the arm, and holding him before him, said, "Thou dost not know what thou sayest, child! There is not such another on the face of the earth as thy mother was! Pay her weight in gold, and you would have bought her up cheap. Boy, she would have made a man of thee; a better man than without her thou art ever likely to be!" Oliver stood fixed in attentive surprise. Farmer Caxton rose up disturbed by the strong emotion and went out; baby Meg ran after him, and catching his coat-tails, followed his steps.

The "making a man of him," sunk into Oliver's mind, and dispelled the dislike he had felt to the thought of his mother. Now when Mistress Crisp said, "Thy poor mother would never have allowed thee to do this!" Oliver considered that it might be because it would hinder his being a man, and the reproof became more effectual.

Thoughts and feelings are woven together in strange combinations in the mind of a child, and none can fully tell the effect that words are producing in the misty realm of the young imagination. Where the objects are few, they fill the space in proportion, with undefined forms and long shadows; the shadows and the forms scarcely known apart. How happy the child who early learns what it is to walk with a hand held in His—the man, Christ Jesus, the way, the truth, and the life; to know the clasp of safety and tenderness; and, so led, to walk through the mists of life's morning, the glare of its noonday, and the shades of evening, with Christ,—" I will fear no evil, for Thou art with me ! "

One day in the Mill, Oliver ventured out to the door, and looked down the steps. "Come back," said his father; "you must not go there alone until you are a man !"

"My mother would have made me a man !" said Oliver, looking up in his father's face.

"My mother!" How the words thrilled through the silence of Oliver Crisp's soul! "Who told you so?" he asked.

"Grand-daddy told me," replied Oliver.

Oliver Crisp felt bewildered awhile, but the iron spell had been broken, and from that day he talked to the child of his mother. There was a willing heart in the boy, ready to open and receive; and so at length it came to pass that perhaps few living parents ever grew into more influence than that departed mother— departed, but not dead; that is not death which is but " absent from the body and present with the Lord."

<blockquote>
"He is not dead whose holy mind
Lifts thine on high,
To live in hearts we leave behind,
Is not to die."
</blockquote>

Mistress Crisp knew nothing of the quiet Mill-talks between the father and the child; and when she marked the growing reverence in the boy at any mention of his mother, she would say, "It has always been my way to keep the feeling for his mother in him!"   Alas! our mistakes are the last things that we learn to read aright.

The step was easy from the mother to the mother's book, the Bible. Oliver Crisp always kept a Bible and a copy of Wesley's hymns on a shelf in the Mill, and now, instead of little Oliver's playing at his father's feet, his father sometimes read to him, saying, "This is the book thy mother loved the best—God's Book." And the boy listened with the tender awe of childhood, linking in one the Bible, his absent mother, his father, and his father's God. This was blessed training, but he did not learn to read, and his grandmother said it was high time for him to be sent to school, if he was not to be a dunce. What a dunce was, young Oliver had no idea; but it was evidently something to be avoided. Baby Meg also was to go to school, and this alone was a reason for Oliver's going. She was much more advanced in the art of reading and spelling, but not in any way trained, nor opened in mind. Baby Meg had long become the little tyrant of the farm-house; she must never cry, never be punished, if her grandfather knew. Whenever a letter came from abroad, it was his first, and perhaps only fear, that they might want the child. Had they wanted her, it is certain Farmer Caxton would have bought her with gold; the lustre of her little head was brighter to him than his once highly-prized wealth; but Mistress Caxton said, "'Tis certain things can't hold safely that way; 'tis Meg rules the day, and Farmer's nought but a child!"

Dame Truman, who **taught** the village children, was a tall, elderly woman, of upright figure, with a white mob-cap, and rather austere manners, but a kind and ruling spirit. She kept strict discipline; two punishments constituted the penalties of disobedience or inattention—no graver fault was ever contemplated. "If they be naughty," said Dame Truman, "I set them up in the corner till they be rid of their ill-convenience; but if they be outrageous, I beat the table with this rod; it makes more noise and scares them more than if I laid it on them!" School-days began for Oliver and Meg. It was no easy task to restrain baby Meg's wild laughing glee within bounds; but she at length fell into place and order, and submitted herself as every other child had done, to Dame Truman's consistent and impartial rule. Out of school she was still the child of frolic and fun; her clean print-frock was stained or torn with each day's wear, and her white cotton hat hung off her head over her shoulders; a picture-child she was, but not a pattern-child. The two children on summer evenings often went home to the farm together, until K. fetched Oliver, lingering herself for a talk with her sister Kezia.

The incidents of life were small, yet marking character. The two children were left alone in the dairy; baby Meg swept her fingers over the cream covering a pan of milk; then, hearing her grandmother's returning step, she ran away. Mistress Caxton's eye fell on the milk-pan. "Is this your trick?" she said, with sharpened tone, to Oliver, who replied, in a decided voice, " I won't tell a lie!" Supposing this to be a confession, Mistress Caxton asked no more, but said, " Now, let me see you out of the dairy, and never see you in again!" Another day, Meg's frolic overturned the buttered toast for tea as it stood on the steel cat before the kitchen fire. Meg ran away, leaving her little substitute as before. Kezia questioned hard, but Oliver only replied, " I never did tell a lie!" and would say no more. Meg saw him not allowed any buttered toast at tea, while she was quietly eating her own. This selfishness of nature was cultivated in the child by the fondness of the old man, who let her escape all correction, until she began to feel that escape was the thing to be expected at all times. Well is it for us that life's lessons come sooner or later from a Hand that cannot be mistaken! Happiest for them who learn them readiest; for the unready learner strains the measure, and makes a jarring discord in the melody of the Divine teaching! Much that stamps its character on life arises out of what seem trifling incidents.

Oliver Crisp never left the village churchyard on the Sunday afternoon without standing by the grave of Naomi. He had often done this silently with Oliver in his arms, or holding his hand; but when the words, " My mother!" had passed the lips of the child, and his father had begun to speak to him of her, as he stood by the grave holding Oliver by the hand, he said, " This is where thy mother sleeps!"

" Is my mother asleep? Will she wake again ? "
Oliver asked, eagerly.

"Yes, she will wake!" and as Oliver Crisp
repeated the words, " She will wake!" the grave, so
dark and sad to his heart, glowed in the light of resurrection. "She will wake, she will arise!" he said
again, not heeding the earnest uplifted face of his
boy, as he felt how he had dwelt with the darkness,
while already on the silent grave lay the promise of
life—" Thy dead shall live ; my dead bodies they shall
arise. Awake and sing, ye that dwell in dust, for thy
dew is as the dew of herbs!" (or of the dawn).

"When, father, when will my mother wake?"

"When Christ shall call her!" answered Oliver.
" I cannot tell you more, but we will read together
in the Mill."

What were those readings to the two—the eager
child, the father in whose heart bereavement still lay
fresh, his boy the rainbow-span across that sorrow's
cloud? Earnestly they read, with many pauses,
many a question from the child ; and many a thought
and feeling Naomi had breathed came back in
strength and blessing now on her husband's soul, as
slowly, week after week, they made their blessed way
through such glorious passages as 1 Thessalonians
iv., 1 Cor. xv., John xi., Isaiah xxv., xxvi. And
Oliver Crisp found that the light of resurrection-life
shines forth on earth for those who believe the
blessed words of man's Redeemer—" I am the
resurrection and the life. He that believeth in me,
though he were dead, yet shall he live ; and whoso-

ever liveth and believeth in Me shall never die " ; and from that time, as he stood beside the grave, he thought how soon the sleeper's form would rise in radiance on his sight; raised from the dead to die no more, but to be as the angels of God in heaven. And the child learned to know that over those who sleep in Jesus the grave has no victory ; it is but the bed of rest, on which the dawn of the resurrection-morning is sure to break.

" Blessed Lord, our souls are longing,
    Thee, our risen Head, to see,
And the cloudless morn is dawning
    When Thy saints shall gathered be :
        Grace and glory,
All our fresh springs are in Thee.

" All the joy we now are tasting
    Is but as the dream of night :
To the day of God we're hasting,
    Looking for it with delight.
        Thou art coming,
    And wilt satisfy our sight.

" True, the silent grave is keeping
    Many a seed in weakness sown ;
But the saints, in Thee now sleeping,
    Raised in power shall share Thy throne.
        Resurrection !
    Lord of glory ! 'tis Thine own.

" As we sing, our hearts grow lighter ;
    We are children of the Day ;
Sorrow makes our Hope the brighter ;
    Faith regards not the delay :
        Sure the promise,
    We shall meet Thee on the way."

CHAPTER XIII.

One summer day in every year Dame Truman was invited with her school to the Castle. It was a grand day, one of the few yearly events in the village. The feasts and games were out of doors, and nothing was left undone to make the day a happy one. Dame Truman gave her instructions many times over, and always the same. "Now, children, you will all be in the presence of the Quality, and you must one and all behave yourselves accordingly. Now, remember, none of your round-about ways, frolicking from beginning to end; that's not the thing for the Quality! You must keep minding of me. If I smile, you may smile too. Remember, I may seem to be taken up with the Quality, but my eye will be on you all the same. And when you are called up to repeat your chapters and Psalms, remember, none of that natural way you get into with me will do for the Quality! You must say them up in a sacred, hollow voice, as the Quality would!"

The instructions were learned by heart; but, alas! when the eventful time came, the wild woods, the stately deer, the noble trees, and swings that flew high as the tree-tops; the bowls that rolled down hill, while boys despairing to catch them by a run, rolled after them; and that would not roll up the green slopes without returning again. The aviary, the gold and silver pheasants, and fish that swam after them round the large reservoir, and the golden eagle; the out-of-door feasting — pies, cakes, syllabubs and fruit; the sweetmeats that boys tumbled and climbed and jumped for, while the girls looked on, and the winning boy presented half to some delighted girl, but not to the same twice over. Girls were not then allowed to tumble in shoals with the boys; and it used to be a saying in after life, "You gave me the leaper's sweetmeat, you know!" And in truth, the fun of looking on pleased them best. All this world of merry-making kept the children as natural as nature, and very unlike what Dame Truman considered the right thing for "the Quality." Yet when the day was over, she could never find in her heart to reprove or correct them; only expressing a hope that each one would remember next time! Each and all were too happy for blame. Dame Truman made excuses for them, saying that "the kind words and pleasant smiles of the Quality, and the books and work-bags, and 'the altogether' quite carried them beyond themselves and their manners!" And there was always a present for Dame Truman. So the woods and the lawns rang with happy shouts and laughter, and the echoes of gladness came back on the summer air, which delighted the children, and made them laugh louder, and echo laughed too. And then they shouted, "How do you do?" and echo returned the inquiry; but the little ones wondered that the old man of the hills never said, "Quite well, thank you." So the bigger boys taught him, and then he said the same. But when the boys asked, "Come and play!" echo only said, "Come and play!" and the children replied they would rather not! They thought he must be a big man to answer so far, and wondered if he would be there and talk to them that way next year. But when they asked Dame Truman, she said, "My poor children, it is your ignorance to think it an old man,—it is the hill itself that says back what you say to it; it is by means of a long word, children, called circumbocution! That is five syllables, and you can none of you spell beyond three; but you will some day, if you live and do well." This voice of the hill did not lessen the mystery, and every year it was one of the wonders of the day.

On these days there was one child of all children for Isabelle—young Oliver. Baby Meg was too wild in her glee to be caught and won to any quiet converse. Isabelle would draw young Oliver away to some quiet seat or walk with her, and they talked together of some wonder of power and love in the blessed life of the Lord. Oliver still learned with his father far more than even Dame Truman could teach. Or Isabelle taught him to sing some of the hymns his mother loved best; he had her rich voice and her ear for music, and caught a tune quickly; and then in the Mill his father would sing them with him, as he had with his mother. Isabelle would talk to him of his mother, who was already to the heart of her boy all that could draw forth his reverence and love.

One day Isabelle gathered him a beautiful rosebud which he noticed, for his jacket button-hole, and he said to her, "I take care of my mother's flowers! Father says I must, and he helps me. Father says they answer to my hand as they did to my mother's!"

"Shall I come and see them?" asked Isabelle.

"Yes," answered Oliver, eagerly; "come on Saturday, for I have no school that day. We have such beauties!"

We often see the power of affection to impart tastes unknown before. Isabelle found Oliver quite a florist—trained by his father. Who could have guessed that Oliver Crisp had no love by nature for flowers, who saw him evening after evening with his child, watering, weeding, and carefully tying up the trees and climbing-plants! It was not long, by Isabelle's aid, before such a spot was not to be seen for its size, of gay blossoms and fruit, as the Mill-garden. The great variety of gay colours rather tried Mistress Crisp, who kept her herb-garden large in proportion; but she made no remark; remembering only too well the far fairer flower that had faded on earth, for whose sake every blossom was held dear.

It was a happy life they lived, more happy than they knew while the current flowed peacefully on. Every life has its unexpected events, and those who yield themselves to the training of the Heavenly Father have, it may be, most of life's discipline.

After quiet years, a crisis often comes, when events meet together as though combining to produce the difficulty or trial; and no doubt they are combined for that purpose by His wisdom and love who alone knows how to train the many sons He is bringing to glory.

It was to such an unexpected crisis that the Mill family came. Oliver was almost nine years old. The reapers were busy over the harvest in August, a month before the time of his birth. Baby Meg was eleven, though a stranger would have reversed the ages, for Oliver was tall, strongly-built, and a thoughtful child, which gave a weight to his early years, while Meg was baby Meg still. It was a day of the week at the end of which Dame Truman's school broke up for the general interval of harvest, and the gleaning for the cottage children. Oliver Crisp had left home—a most unusual event; the decease of an aged uncle, and the settlement of his affairs, detained him. All promised well as on any day before; but on the way home from school, Dick Butterly got baby Meg in close talk, or rather, close listening to him. This alone drew young Oliver's attention, and he heard baby Meg say, "You bad boy! if you talk like that I won't walk with you!" Still baby Meg did not go, and Dick whispered in her ear. "For shame, Dick!" said baby Meg; but at that word, young Oliver collared Dick from behind and drew him down on his back, saying, "You bad boy! you shall not talk to Meg!"

"I will talk as I like," replied Dick, with a blow

of his fist in Oliver's face which fetched a stream of blood from his nose. Baby Meg, seeing blood, ran home, crying and screaming; the younger children looked on, and the boys struggled together. Oliver had the best in position, though the worst in blows; yet he would not give in until Dick had given his word that he would not talk bad any more. Then Oliver gave up his hold, and Dick ran off, bespattered with mud, but nothing the worse. As he went, he took up a stone, which he threw back at Oliver, cutting open his forehead. Oliver hastened home, torn and bleeding, though conqueror—which satisfied him.

But no father was there to understand the boy-rights of the case. Mistress Crisp was appalled, and K. said she was frightened out of her life, though she hastened to wash off the blood; and Mistress Crisp, with her lily leaves, dressed the only wound on the temple, and put Oliver, sorely against his will, to bed—that being the place, Mistress Crisp considered, for a hero. Mistress Crisp said it was all over for school until the holidays were gone, but Oliver maintained that he must go. He had worked hard for his prize; and, what Oliver felt still more, it would look as if he were afraid of Dick if he stayed away at home! So a compromise was made—Oliver to keep quiet the next day, and go on the Wednesday, and have the three last days of the school; but Mistress Crisp had made up her mind to impose some restriction which should be effectual to prevent another outbreak.

"To see the child take to fighting!" said Mistress Crisp; "who could ever have thought it? I am sure neither father nor mother ever raised hand against any; and this child must turn ruffian, and fight out to the end! If this evil be not nipped in the bud he will be enlisting some day, for it is plain the fighting-nature is strong to show itself so early! We never had a fighting man to disgrace my own family, since first Friends came forward to teach the world peace; and I don't believe that the Crisps had, either. I have no notion how it comes in the child; but however it came, it is a rank weed, and must be cast out at once!"

Mistress Crisp addressed her remarks partly to K., but still more to herself. K. was mostly at the bedside, giving such comfort as came to her mind, but not such as Mistress Crisp would approve. "I would not care, Olly!" she said. "You had the best of it, and made that bad boy give his word, and if he don't keep it, that's no fault of yours; and, may-be, a stronger than you will take him in hand! I know I would not see evil get the day if I had the name of a boy! And sometimes I have thought, if the men would not fight, why, the women must; but I suppose it would not be right, for all that!"

Baby Meg ran in with her consolation—"O, Olly! they say you did it like a man, and they only wish every man would put down bad till there was none!"

This was dangerous praise for Oliver, that he had done like a man! and all the more so as coming from Meg, who had sometimes made him feel that his years were younger than hers. But he said, "I say, Meg, you must not hear bad talk; if you do that will make you bad! and you know a bad boy will talk bad. I have fought hard for you, Meg—I don't mind that; but this lying a-bed, I hate it, and it's all for you, Meg. Now promise you won't hear bad talk, nor talk to bad boys any more!"

Meg promised, and Oliver never doubted the word when a promise was given.

Farmer Caxton had never entered the Mill-house since Naomi departed. Mistress Crisp had made her feeling against him too plain to encourage him to venture; but now his anxiety for the boy could not be restrained. Mistress Crisp saw him entering the gate, and withdrew into the back-room of the house, saying to K., "I do not see Farmer Caxton; but if he chooses to see the child he can do so." K. went to the door, and received him. Oliver was sitting, with his head still bandaged, in the arm-chair; the old man sat down beside him. After a few kind enquiries, he said, "'Tis a hurt from the hand of a coward! But, take my word for it, there is little good to be got in fighting the right out; it has turned right to wrong before now, and may end up worse than is thought of. If the lad acts ugly by you, have nought to do nor to say to him. You have settled it once; they know you can stand for the right! Don't lay hands on any again, for your mother's sake, child! She ruled down the wrong by a word or a look. Evil never held up its head before her. You may buy peace, as they say ; but she made it ! Ah, child ! if you be your mother's son, you will find a better way than blows to turn evil off hand ! "

The next morning the wound was ready for a plaster, and Oliver was up for his breakfast. His little bag of books was ready for school, and he was himself ready to start when the early meal was over. Mistress Crisp had before instructed K. " I shall send thee with the child to school, K. Thee shall see him safe there, and then fetch him safe home, till the break-up on Friday."

" It is not a bit likely," said K., "that Olly will be tied to my apron-strings ! "

" K., thee hast forgotten thyself ! I tell thee to do it—let that be enough. The boy has got a notion that it is manly to fight ; if he finds that it leaves him only a mistrusted child, he will not fall to fighting again. If I had my way, I would have every soldier sit down to make his red coat before he could fight in it ; aye, and knit the stockings to march in ! It is more than men know what the needle can do ! I have worked off many a chafing of spirit. When you sit down to sew or to knit, the ferment works off in a way you scarce notice. I have made up my mind that I will not see this winter gone without the child knitting his own stockings—if for no other reason than this ! "

K. had the greatest respect for her mistress ; she felt that the needle must be better than the sword— perhaps the law of the land could order it so ; yet how to take Oliver to school was more than she could see clearly. She had a misgiving that evil was coming, and could not make a breakfast.

Oliver took his cap and his bag. "Now, Oliver," his grandmother said, looking full at the child through her large tortoiseshell spectacles, "thou hast forgotten thyself in this fight, and thou canst not be trusted alone for awhile. K. will take thee to school and fetch thee safe home, and I hope thee will learn to forbear!"

Oliver's white cheek flushed red. "Granny, I will never go to school like a baby! I fought like a man—father would know I did! I will go alone, as I have always gone!"

But Mistress Crisp had her hand on the door-latch, and she said, in her tone of strictest authority, "K., thou knowest thy duty! If the child won't go quiet, thou must carry him there!"

K. thought it the most hateful measure of safety, but she never disobeyed her mistress. She was strong-built and of full height, and she swept her strong arms round the boy and carried him off. Now, let it be said to his honour, when he got his arms free, he gave no blow for liberty to K. Too manly to strike a woman, he only wriggled like an eel to worm himself out; but the clasp was very tight, and the arms were very strong. Still K. had more than enough of her burden, and going down the steep hill-side had much ado to keep steady; and when out of sight of the Mill-house, she said, "There! you will walk quiet now?" and loosened her hold. The boy struggled to his feet, panted a moment, then started full speed, not the way to the school, but along the foot of the hill, straight to the river. K. stood still with horror as she saw him rush through. The dry harvest-time favoured his desperate attempt, and the spring of his step carried him safe from one stone to another in the river's rocky bed. He reached the further side, coming down on his knees, but was soon up again, and, without looking back, made for the wood.

The wood was a forest in those days; the trees thick and large then, where now only pleasant avenues lead the eye on to distant glimpses of scenery. The grassy paths of the forest interwound, and those who did not know it well would soon lose their way. It was, perhaps, never crossed on foot except by gipsies, and men of worse character, who in those days haunted lonely places undiscovered. K. hastened as fast as her feet would bear her to the bridge, where the water flowed deeper and turned the wheel of a mill; she crossed it and hastened towards the forest, but Oliver was quite out of sight. She called, but all was silent; she shouted, and the far-off echo did but mock her with an answering call of "Olly!" Poor K. had never known before the feeling of despair; she sat down on the grass, breathless and terrified. Some one might come by who knew the forest. It was useless for her to venture, and would be reckless—sure to lose herself, and her poor mistress distracted at home! But no one came; so, with many a backward look on the heavy mass of foliage, **and many a** lingering step, she returned, thinking, "Sure, he will never go far, child as he is —he will be afraid! He will get over his tantrums, and come home again !"

Then a fear of returning seized K. What would her mistress say ? How could she pacify her ? She did not know. She sat down on the old wooden bridge to consider, and said to herself, "I wish I had been off and away like master, and never had in hand such a business as this. The child has such a spirit, it don't hold with women to rule it, and yet he never denied us before. I have heard Dame Truman say he is a lamb of the fold if ever there was one. I wish enough she had had the carrying, or any one but me; he stood like a young lion, and just seemed to say, 'Take me up if you dare!' I didn't like it I am sure, but I was afraid to be crossed in my mistress's order; and now who knows what may happen; he may be caught by the spring-guns or gipsies, or die of hunger in the night-time. 'Tis a terrible job! I don't believe you can trample down nature; my mistress is so set against fighting, and to see the wars in the Bible; but my mistress says that was never meant to be now since the Prince of Peace came, and no doubt she knows. Then there is our young squire, what a soldier he is ! Oh, if only Miss Isabelle would come! I'll just ask my mistress to let me run up to the Castle; they would not be so hard on the poor child, for they be all fighting men. And to see how he never raised his hand against me; he'll be a brave man if ever

there was one, and women will just have fair play.
Poor child! I doubt he has not had it from us.
Well, I just wish his poor father were home, he
would have ordered the thing very different to this.
But I know I would not be in at the telling, no,—not
for a guinea paid down."

K. rose from her seat on the old wooden bridge,
and slowly made her way up the hill. She had but
little opportunity of speaking her mind to any one,
and she found it necessary sometimes to have things
out with herself, generally coming to some conclusion in this way; as now she resolved to ask
leave to hasten on to the Castle as the best thing to
be done.

"Why, girl, what a time thou hast been!" said
Mistress Crisp, who stood on the door-step with a
very anxious face.

"Yes," answered K., "and the wonder is I am
come back at all; Olly ran right out of my arms
through the river. I saw him rush in, and I thought
I should have dropped, he made off to the forest. I
hurried off after, but I never got a sight nor a sound.
And now let me run to the Castle and just tell Miss
Isabelle, they will find him in no time, for he may be
dead by to-morrow; there are foxes and serpents and
wild folks they say, who stop at nothing!"

Mistress Crisp sank down in a chair. "Hold
thy tongue, girl, let me think;" and K. looked out
at the door. The forest stretched away in the distance. Mistress Crisp sat with set lips, and eyes
fixed, yet seeing nothing the while; at length she

spoke. "Thee must not do it, girl! The disgrace it would be—the fight, and the temper, and the child running away; our families on both sides have been so respected, and never heard speak of an outbreak like this! Thee must not make it known. The boy is quiet enough—if the fight had not set him on fire; only to see what it leads to! Let them that encourage fighting answer for that! Mind thy work, and hold thy tongue, and the boy will come home and say, 'Granny, I am sorry,' and go peaceably with you. It is only the fight that has brought him to this."

When baby Meg ran up between school to see Olly, she was only told she could not see him then, and sent home in a troubled surprise. Mistress Crisp had many a sharp word with poor K. that day. It was true, as K. freely owned, she had lost many looks from the window, but her mistress scarcely looked any other way, by reason of which she thought K. wrong when she was not. Poor Mistress Crisp! she was all ajar, but her outward composure refused to give vent to her inward trouble of mind. No child returned.

Dinner passed almost untasted. Mistress Crisp watched until the sun was sinking in the west. The tea-things were set. Mr. Crisp might return; they waited, and at sunset he came. K. hurried out at the back, but her mistress soon called her in; he stood just by the door, as she left him coming in, and saying, "Where is the child?" those were always his first words on coming home. Mistress Crisp sat down in her chair. K. said she did not believe her poor mistress could stand. Her master scarce spoke a word, and she told it all clear from the first to the last, for she said, as she stood there she thought, if it should have to come up before the Justice at the Court she must tell it all, and had best do it at once. "My master," she said, "he never took his eyes off me, and when I had done he never spoke a word, but he just came forward, drank up the pitcher of milk, put a cake in his pocket, called the dog, and went off."

"Dear me!" said K. to her mistress; "the dog to be sure! If mortal could find him it would be the dog. They say women are not wise, I never thought of that; or we would have had him home by this time; 'tis like he don't know his way, and the dog will just lead him; and here the poor brute has been sitting all day on the watch, and we never thought of sending him off. Well, he's gone now for certain. There is master taking straight through the river, and Aleppo is after him!" This K. said at the door, as she shaded her eyes from the last radiance of sunset to look over the gleaming water to the dark reaches of wood; but she could see no further, and she turned in to try and cheer her poor mistress, and persuade her to take some food.

CHAPTER XIV.

K. soon returned to her station at the open door, looking on into the fading radiance; looking on into the gathering gloom. The moon rose grandly over the forest trees, the night-wind bore in the fragrance of the jessamine that grew about the porch, and the white owl of the Mill swept by on heavy wing. Still K. leaned against the door-post, her feet close set together, her arms close folded, her eyes fixed on the gloomy forest, and the moon-lit river, whose ceaseless murmur as it flowed over its rocky bed, was the only sound that broke the stillness; the reapers had sung their evening song, and the tired village lay asleep. The lights of the Castle went out one by one, and the church clock struck eleven.

"Canst thee see, girl?" asked Mistress Crisp for the twentieth time from her chair.

"I can see," answered K., without altering her fixed gaze for a moment, which took in bridge, river, and wood; "I can see, but there's nought to be seen. I say, mistress, won't you just go to bed? I'll watch till they come, if it be till the dawn."

"I don't know, girl; I feel as weak as a babe, I don't think I can get myself there."

"I' I just settle you there," said K., "and then

trust to me." K. laid her poor mistress to rest as she would have laid a child. It was the first time in all her service that her most independent mistress had needed her help. K. gave it tenderly, and when her weary head reached the pillow, Mistress Crisp said, "There, leave me now, my good girl, and don't come again; I don't seem able to bear the news, either way. Let me sleep till I wake, and then, may be, I'll feel better able to hear it."

Oliver Crisp had crossed the river reckless of where. Aleppo followed his master, and both made for the forest. Those were days of strange terror to parents, when gipsies stole children, and wandering travellers stole children, and sold them in towns and cities to chimney-sweepers; there was fear that a lost child was lost indeed in those days— terrors of more than half a century ago, that do not trouble parental hearts now. Yet "lost in a forest" had terrors enough, if none other haunted the heart.

Before entering the forest, Oliver Crisp said to his dog, "Olly! Olly! Where's Olly? Hie, boy! find the child!" Aleppo sniffed the ground, caught the scent between the river and the wood; running with nose close to the ground, he entered the forest. Oliver followed hard; the dog took this path, then that. Oliver forced back the crossing underwood, to make way for his tall figure when the path was shut in above; but all in vain, he could not keep pace with the dog. He dared not call him back, but he lifted his voice, and amidst the dark forest-trees he shouted, " Oliver !" and the echo repeated his cry. Awhile he struggled on, following as well as he could the fleet steps of the dog, but he soon lost his track ; he whistled, but the dog did not return ; he whistled again, and heard an answering bark in the distance, but far too uncertain to guide him in the darkened forest.

He had reached a small grassy glade, where no underwood grew ; the full moon cast the shadows of the trees in close tracery across it, and the giant stems of 'the forest showed pale in the moonlight, giving each shadow a defined, sharpened outline. He could go no further ; he might as well have been alone on the trackless sea without compass or chart. A strange horror seized the heart of the father—a horror that has no name save despair ; he leaned against a tree-stem, through whose top the pale moon-beams quivered, and the shadow of death passed over him !   He had felt it before in early manhood, when the father, the friend of his youth, was taken from him.   It had come again when golden sunbeams lighted the sky, and he could almost see his blest Naomi enter the gates of Rest ; but now a horror of great darkness came over him—his child, his only child lost in the gloom, the danger ; lost, it might be, in cruelty and evil ; lost, perhaps, for ever !   From the father's heart rose a groan deep and intense ! no echo caught the sound, it fell to earth in that dread silence !   Not so ! the echo of a groan from broken or crushed hearts on earth, rises to the heart of the Eternal Father :

"Full many a cry has reached Thee from the wild,
  Since the lone mother weeping there,
Cast down her fainting child ;
  Then turned away to weep and die,
  Nor knew an angel-form was nigh."

He knew not how, but over his spirit stole a calm, intense and holy. He saw, in thought before him there, the grass, the trees, the moon-beams, of Gethsemane! Was it not so alone, in such a scene, on such a night, He suffered who came to seek and to save that which was lost?—Lost doubly, soul and body! Lost utterly! Lost! The word re-echoed in Oliver's soul. He gazed on that lone glade, as if he saw that sacred form—the Holy One laid there in prostrate agony, and bathed in His own blood. He heard the cry, " Father, if it be possible, let this cup pass from me; Father, not my will, but Thine be done ! " He had made no effort to recal the sacred scene, of the Highest sinking to the lowest deep of woe unspeakable, to save the lost ; he leaned in silence there against the giant fir, his eyes and heart alike intent on what he spiritually saw. It was as Jacob when alone at Bethel ; he found this solitary glen the house of God, the gate of Heaven.

Then, in the stillness, there passed before his spiritual sight, the form of One, with mangled brow and hands and feet, bearing in His folded arms, close pressed upon His bosom, a lamb, on which the tender eyes looked down with love intense. No voice fell on the outward ear, but through the listening soul of Oliver the words breathed out in undertones from depths of joy, "Rejoice with Me, for I have found My sheep which was lost!" Oliver sank upon his knees in speechless adoration. He saw but one object, the Shepherd, wounded and torn, bearing the lamb in His bosom, with a heaven of love in His divine yet human eyes. He heard but one voice, "Rejoice with Me, for I have found!"

He knew not how long he kneeled, but he kneeled till the blissful vision changed. A glorious Man was wafted afar on clouds of dazzling white—a glorious Man, yet in His hands and feet He bore marks of the cross, prints of the nails; and resting on His breast, Oliver saw himself, Naomi, and their child! There seemed no other object in creation; cloud above cloud veiled all horizon, concealing all above, below, only that glorious Man—the very same who lay in the moonlit glade alone, amid the darkening trees, in prostrate agony, breathing the cry, "Thy will be done!" The very same who had passed by with wounded hands and feet, with head bent down in love, with gaze no mortal eyes can give, on that one rescued lamb. The very same now wafted on the clouds, His seamless robe of dazzling white, Himself as calm in His majestic tenderness as when He passed through that lone glen; and Oliver knew and felt himself, with his Naomi and his child, laid safely on His breast, without a care, without a fear —not thinking how they came, nor whither they were going, but safely there, laid on His bosom, in perfect rest! The dark waves of anguish rolled heavily around him, but above them rose the glory of a Presence, the Light of the world, in whom dwelleth all the fulness of the Godhead bodily ; and the calm of fellowship with Jesus stilled the rush of the tempest, and illumined the dark waves with radiance. All around lay the havoc of those surging billows, the wreck of uncertainty and loss; while his spirit was hid in the secret of His Presence, with whom is the fountain of life, and in whom there is no condemnation and no separation.

Think it not strange that such visions are given. To those who walk with God (albeit imperfectly, with many an erring, stumbling step), yet, in their heart's desire—walking with God—He showeth great and mighty things that they have not known. "The secret of the Lord is with them that fear Him, and He will show them His covenant." When the eyes of the spirit are Divinely enlightened, they behold what mortal vision cannot trace. " Eye hath not seen, nor ear heard, neither hath entered into the heart of man to conceive, what God hath prepared for them that love Him ; but God hath revealed it unto us by His Spirit." Why should any suffering heart be wrung with lonely anguish, in utter desolation, when such a Comforter is nigh—the Man of sorrows, the Incarnate Son, the Consolation of Israel —even He who says, " Come unto Me, all ye that labour and are heavy laden, and I will give you rest;" " As one whom his mother comforteth, so will I comfort you ; " " When thou passest through the waters I will be with thee, and through the rivers, they shall not overflow thee " ?

The night wind rose and swept the forest-trees; their branches creaked beneath its power; clouds chased their hurried course, veiling the stars and darkening the moonlight. Oliver Crisp felt the chill that creeps over the earth before the dawn of day. He rose, and by the fitful glimmer made his way as best he could, until he reached the open ground; crossed the bridge, and climbed the hill-side. Bereaved he felt, but not desolate. An aching heart, yet in its depths a deeper trust than he had ever known before. Nor did the vision fade, but lay before his inner sight in its eternal blessedness. So spake He when He said, "My peace I give unto you. Not as the world giveth, give I to you. Let not your heart be troubled, neither let it be afraid."

Poor weary K. sat by the open door, leaning her head against the door-post, sleeping in her lengthened watch. Her master woke her with a quiet voice, saying, "Go and rest now; we must wait until the day breaks. The dog is gone, and, there is little doubt, will find him."

When K. heard that the dog was gone, the sense of the child's utter desolation passed from her heart. "The dog," she said, "will not come home without him!"

She crept to the bed of her mistress, still sleeping in exhaustion of mind and body. K. feared to leave her alone, and, wrapping her shawl round her, lay down by her side, and was soon in sound slumber, forgetting the trouble that had darkened the day.

Oliver went to the stable; gave Depper, the good

horse, another feed of corn, for his past day's journey had been long; then came in, and waited for light to break over the hill. He left the door on the latch—the child was outside! and many a time he went out to look abroad. He saw the morning-star rise over the hill, and thought on the lonely nights of wakeful sorrow when it came as a messenger of peace to Naomi; but a Presence was with him in which the morning-star grew pale. His eye could find no earthly rest away from the forest, the river-bridge, and the hill-side, yet no little figure was there—no sound save the breeze that blew the rose-buds against the lattice window-panes, and the first chirp of waking bird beneath the eaves. Strange contrasts filled the soul of Oliver Crisp—the living grace and glory of the things eternal, and the desolation of all things temporal; sustained by the one, he sank not under the other.

When the sun had risen he called K. She hasted and prepared his breakfast; he packed in a basket a bottle of milk and two harvest-cakes thick with plums (K. knew for whom!); then, breaking a loaf in half, he laid some cheese in the centre, for himself, and said, "Tell Granny not to fear."

"Shall I say you will be home to-night?" asked K.

"I shall not come back again until I hear of the child; but let that alone—you cheer her with hope!" And he turned out; and K. heard Depper led out of the stable, and the master was gone, while the world still seemed sleeping. K. took her own breakfast in better cheer; the rising sun of itself was reviving, and her hopes rested even more on the dog than on her master—the dog would go where he could not! She made a comfortable cup for her mistress, and went to her room with a little tray prepared in as tempting a way as she could devise.

"'Tis time to feed, mistress," said K.

"Is the child home?" she asked.

"Not yet," answered K.; "but Aleppo's with him by this time, and master is off with Depper to bring them both home."

Mistress Crisp looked hard at K., who only said, "It is time you should feed. Master made a breakfast, and 'tis certain you must."

The little meal was taken silently, and then the weak and weary head lay down again, and she said, "If the child does not come home I just hope I'll sleep on and not wake up again!" And K. left her, sleeping for sorrow!

With the morning, the tidings of the lost child flew like wild-fire. Richard Dolman, the mill-man, had told the night before on leaving the Mill that the child was lost somewhere, but he did not know where. All were late in the fields, and the tidings were not spread until morning; then many steps were astir. All the facts of the case now became known, for Meg, in her sorrow, told all. Farmer Butterly gloomily promised Dick the horse-whip, if Oliver did not come home safe. Dick slunk off to the harvest-fields, not without thoughts of running away himself. K. stood at the gate of the Mill-house, and told all the particulars to all who came up that way; she could not leave the premises with her mistress ill in bed. Farmer Caxton could not rest within doors, nor without. The weather was dry, and the corn shelling on the ground, but he sent his son off on the fleetest horse they had. "I would turn out every man that I have," he said, "if it would not be just a sin to let the grain perish, for which so many mouths will be hungry." It was affecting to see the restlessness of the old man, in and out, inquiring of all. He came in and asked for his "bait," but before the harvest-cake was cut, or the cider on the table, he was out again, no one knew where. It was no use to speak on any other subject, he did not understand what you said. Mistress Caxton went about with a tear in her eye, but to those who lamented she said, "Don't tell me that Naomi's child can be forsaken and lost!"

Dame Truman could not teach in her school. She said "It's of no use to talk of your prize-day! There will be no breaking-up, I can tell you, till school begins again; and if the child be not found, Dame Truman can never keep school any more!" She turned the children all back, with orders to be on the watch and listen, and she stood on her door-step, and asked of all who passed by, "What! have they heard of the child?" As to Dick Butterly, Dame Truman, with her extremest native dignity, said, "Don't ask me if he will come back to school! 'Evil communications corrupt good manners.' If he were the son of the Castle, or the Lord Mayor of

London, I would not receive him while I am Dame Truman!" Susan Butterly keenly felt the discredit on her son. She said "there were faults on both sides, and a child made such a fuss about as the boy Oliver, was likely enough to give plenty to fuss over!" But in her heart she knew that Dick was a wilful and wicked boy, and the one reason why she had blinded herself to his faults was because he flattered her pride by always obeying his mother. Alas! he had found that if he submitted to her, she would excuse his evil ways against others. A boy's obedience to his mother is not always a test of a hopeful character. Baby Meg was an April-day, now crying for Oliver, now riding in empty waggons with glee. Farmer Caxton did not count his sheaves, nor reckon the gold they would bring; he would have given all they were worth to lay his hand once more with a blessing on the dark clustering curls of the young head that lay, like Baby Meg's, in his heart as its treasure.

At the Castle, its lady had walked down at the butler's request, to look at some thirty young pigs, unequalled in beauty, his particular interest. Mr. Howe, the Castle butler, was a portly man, quite beyond usual dimensions, but his benevolence was as expansive as his size. There was not the creature that Mr. Howe did not care for; ever on his feet, he was the kind patron of all living things. The fowls he watched over flapped their wings with a crow or a suitable cry at his approach. The culture of pigs was a favourite pursuit, but never preoccupied his time. There was not a guest at the Castle, from the highest to the lowest, who was not the better for his attentions and care. Man and beast were befriended by him. The poor fly-horses, generally scorned and left outside, had a special wooden building for their reception; they knew the excellence of the Castle corn, and people remarked on the quickened pace of the hired horses when the Castle rose in view, for Mr. Howe had a headship over things without doors as well as within. Yet Mr. Howe was no careless purveyor. He kept a daily diary in which everything was recorded; the work done by each man, including himself. Every promiscuous meal given, every additional horse or man, the birth or death of poultry, pigs, etc., etc., every event that occurred. A book might be written from Mr. Howe's diary!

His private room was a museum of interest, the unfailing delight of many a boy. Its curiosities could not be enumerated. We can only allude to a clock of remarkable history, and a Bible inscribed with a name of eminent worth, for which he gave two pounds, and when offered five for it he answered, "No, not for ten would I part with it!" It may well be thought that the love which the Bible reveals to us as of God, moved his universal kindness to all.

His lady had come down at his personal request to look on his young pigs, which were of eminent quality. Not having the least idea which to admire, she had singled out one which Mr. Howe found it necessary to tell her was the worst of the lot. At this moment one of the gamekeepers came by, saying he was off to the woods, for Mr. Crisp's boy was lost and supposed to be there.

Then Mr. Howe forgot the pigs, and instantly asking his lady's pardon, hastened to do all that could be done. He had a donkey of sagacity and beauty, quite capable—not of carrying him, but of drawing him out in a small convenient carriage, also his own, which he also used for giving the maids an airing when they were dull; for no one was forgotten by him. He ordered his donkey, then looked for Miss Isabelle, he found she had been the first to hear it while feeding her parrot on the lawn, the gardener had told her; she had ordered her horse, and was seeking her mother. The coachman, by his lady's wish, took another direction. Mr. Howe said, "The slowest was sometimes the surest," and set out with his carriage and donkey. Hearts were stirred on all sides, and hurrying steps trod the road, and the harvest-men looked from their wains to the forest, and the women rested on their rakes in the barley-fields, talking it over each time with the same conclusion. Isabelle rode to the Mill, and poor K. at length had her outpour to the Castle; but small hope was in Isabelle's heart, which sank within her, when she heard the whole story; yet she gave her palfrey, Lufra, the rein, and took the lanes that skirted the forest, hoping to meet some bringer of tidings to comfort or direct.

K. took her mistress a little dinner, but she refused to eat or raise her head, and the faithful servant's trouble began to pass from the child to her mistress. Early in the afternoon she made ready a tempting little tea-tray, which she carried up, saying, " Do, mistress, sit up a bit and eat ! If only you had seen how quiet master came in and went out, I know you would have hope."

" Ah, girl ! 'tis the quiet kills me; the voice of the child if it don't soon come, there will come the voice of an angel for me ! "

Poor K.'s tears flowed with a feeling of desolation ; the child gone and the mistress going. Persuasion was a thing that none had ever ventured to try with Mistress Crisp, but K. felt she must try it now. " Now don't ye take on like that, I say mistress, as if the poor child might be dead and buried. I am pretty sure he and the dog be nestled up somewhere, if we could but see. Take a bit morsel, and drink up the tea, and you will seem well when 'tis down ! "

" 'Tis no use to lift up the head if thee can't lift up the heart, girl ! "

" Well now, mistress, I do say it will be nothing less than a sin to starve the life out of us, because we be not sure if the child be on earth or in heaven. We know for certain he is in one or the other, and if we go affronting the mercy that feeds us, we may never see the mercy that brings him safe home." Mistress Crisp took the little meal, and she lay down again with a pink flush of life on her pale cheek.

There was no self-reproach in the extreme sorrow of the grandmother. She had no feeling of having made any mistake in the discipline she imposed. She considered the punishment a very mild one, only a safeguard. She did not know that the correction which makes a child an object of ridicule and laughter to other children, is far worse than the severity that would make him an object of compassion. A great mind or a comprehensive heart would never lower a child by correction. It is certain that the mind is a small one, and the heart equally narrow, which can consciously make a child the object of laughter and ridicule. It was with no such idea that Mistress Crisp had devised the remedy; she thought it a necessity of the case to lower the boy's manly feeling, lest it should break out again in a fight.

How many a mistake marks the course of human life—mistaken acts that seem to lead to evil; mistaken words that leave a wound; causes of pain that even the softening touch of time does not heal! Yet are they mistakes? In one sense they are, arising from a mistaken judgment or feeling in those from whom they come; but in another sense no mistake—for they come by His permission who numbers the hairs of our head; they are part of His appointed discipline—to show us what manner of spirit we are of, to make manifest the hidden evil of the heart, that being made manifest it may be confessed and cleansed. If received as from man they too often irritate and embitter the spirit, the object of them feels not understood, and the lonely heart grows narrower and harder. But if received through

the Heart of divine tenderness, they fulfil the highest
purposes of the will of God concerning us.—Con-
forming to the mind and will of Christ; softening
the spirit until it bears without resentment, and
enlarging the charity until it rises to cover with
the full tide of love the things that naturally tend to
check its exercise.

I LEFT it all with Jesus
    Long ago;
All my sins I brought Him
    And my woe;
When by faith I saw Him
    On the tree;
Heard His still small whisper
    'Tis for thee!
From my heart the burden
    Roll'd away,
    Happy day.

I leave it all with Jesus,
    For He knows
How to steal the bitter
    From life's woes;
How to gild the tear-drop
    With His smile,
Make the desert garden
    Bloom awhile;
When my weakness leaneth
    On His might,
    All seems light.

I leave it all with Jesus
    Day by day;
Faith can firmly trust Him,
    Come what may.
Hope has dropped her anchor,
    Found her rest
In the calm, sure haven
    Of his breast;
Love esteems it heaven,
    To abide
    At His side.

Oh! leave it all with Jesus,
    Drooping soul!
Tell not half thy story,
    But the whole.
Worlds on worlds are hanging
    On His hand,
Life and death are waiting
    His command;
Yet His tender bosom,
    Makes thee room,
    Oh! come Home!

CHAPTER XV.

OLIVER did not stop to recollect himself until he was far in the green paths of the forest. Then he stood still to think; he had never been far in the forest before, and he had never been allowed to enter it alone. Great trees were around him on every side, and he knew not which way to turn; as he looked around in the loneliness he felt frightened, and turned back to see once more the hill's green side and the corn-fields that skirted the forest—then, when safe, he could think what to do, whether to go home, or to Dame Truman, or to Farmer Caxton. "Oh! if father were but there!" thought Oliver. But his father was not there, and he was alone in the wood. He tried to return, but the paths came to no ending; he had to give up the attempt, and could only wander on helpless and hopeless. He saw everywhere the same great trees, and the same green paths. Sometimes the path was lost amidst brushwood, and the blackcock and the wild rabbits crossed his path. The squirrels played in the branches, and ran before his feet. Great birds flapped their wings in the trees and startled him by flight. Frightened and tired, he could only press on; he dared not sit down to rest, he had no guide and no helper on earth. His legs seemed too weak to carry him further, and his feet too tired.

There was only one thing that could be done in such a plight—to pray! Oliver often prayed with his father. His father had taught him the Lord's Prayer, instructing him to look out for himself all the texts of Holy Scripture he could find which seemed to him to be like each petition, and so to add from memory one or another text to each petition. To add also any special want he might feel, or confession or thanksgiving. In this way prayer became a real thing to the child, not a few sentences hurried over, but a prayer.

What now could he do in the lonely forest but kneel down and pray? He had one way quite his own of beginning the prayer; no one had taught him, nor had he, probably, ever heard it; it was the instinct of a child's heart linking the Name through which alone we can draw nigh to God, with the uttered prayer, "O Lord Jesus; O our Father!" He also of his own accord used constantly the pleading words, "I beseech Thee!" The little weary knees sank down upon the grass to pray.

"Our Father, which art in heaven,—

"I beseech Thee, comfort my father when he comes home, and take me back to him.

"Hallowed be Thy Name,—

"I beseech Thee, for Thy Name's sake, lead me and guide me!

"Thy kingdom come,—

"I thank Thee, Lord Jesus, for saying, 'Fear not, little flock, it is your Father's good pleasure to give you the Kingdom.'

"Thy will be done on earth as it is in heaven,—

"I thank Thee, my Saviour, for saying, 'It is not the Will of your Father in heaven that one of these little ones should perish.'

"Give us this day our daily bread,—

"I thank Thee for saying, 'He giveth food to the hungry'—I am hungry.

"Forgive us our trespasses,—

"Forgive me, my Saviour, for running away. Look upon my affliction and my pain, and forgive all my sin.

"As we forgive them that trespass against us,—

"Forgive Dick, and make him a better boy.

"Lead us not into temptation, but deliver us from evil.

"O Lord Jesus, I beseech Thee, deliver me out of this trouble.

"For Thine is the Kingdom, the Power, and the Glory, for ever and ever, Amen."

With his father, Oliver generally added a Psalm of praise or prayer. He often chose the 23rd, which he called the Good Shepherd's Psalm; or the 25th, or 32nd, or 65th, or 133rd, or 146th. For prayer was no hurried necessity with young Oliver, but a breathing his heart to his Father in heaven, and generally offered at his parent's side. The interest of first finding the texts that answered to the petitions, then remembering them according to his need, gave a constant freshness and force to his prayers. Oliver was never allowed by his father to use the expression, " I have said my prayers," but " I have prayed." Oliver Crisp's devout and reverent spirit was one to guard the use of words which have their influence on the mind. While some children weary with a text or two, others, like Oliver, learn to delight early in the Word; their memories being well stored; knowing from their childhood the Holy Scriptures, which are able to make them wise unto salvation.

Oliver was weary, and did not add his Psalm; but he rose with comfort of heart which helped his tired body. For the child can as truly as the prophet Daniel kneel before his God, praying and confessing his sin, and as surely as Gabriel, the angel of Jesus, was sent to the Prophet, so surely will God in His own time and way send help and deliverance to every heart confessing and praying in the name of the Lord Jesus. The bad feeling of being a runaway boy was gone from the heart of Oliver now, and he went on more steadily, keeping one pathway, instead of restlessly wandering from one to another.

The effects of our faults follow us here, even when the sin is forgiven; the effects of our faults are often painfully sad; but when sin is forgiven, we may take the suffering and sorrow in patient trust, that it will be amongst the all things God has promised shall work together for good to them that love Him. Oliver still thought of his father returning and finding him lost; and he longed to sit down and cry for sorrow at what he had done; but he was too frightened to sit down, and too faint to cry, so he still went on his way; wandering on, hour after hour.

Presently he heard a gun, then a flutter down through branches near him, and a ring-dove with bleeding wing fell at his feet. He did not know what to think of the gun—he might be shot himself, hid amongst those great trees, or wounded like the poor bird, and unable to go on. Some one else must be in the wood; he knew that bad men, as well as good ones, shot with guns; this might be a bad man, and if a bad man found him, what could he do? There was no place to run to, and if there were, he was too weak to run. He could only remember our Father in heaven, and trust to His care. He stood still and looked down at the poor struggling bird. He did not like to leave it there to die; so he took out his pocket-handkerchief, and tied the corners in the button-holes of his jacket, and laid the wounded bird gently in this small swinging bed; he had to use his hands to push away the low branches when the path was not clear.

He did not hear the gun again, though he listened in fear; but the sun's declining rays began to slant bright gleams along the tree-stems, and the poor worn-out boy began to look for the first place in which he could lie down, unable to keep his feet any longer. As he struggled on, the path widened, and he found, to his comfort, that he was near to another side of the forest. He pressed on until he saw a cart-road along the forest-side, and a field of beans on the other side of the road. There was a little glade at the edge of the wood, and there at length he sat down to rest and to wait, hoping that some cart might pass;—some one who would take him to safety if not to home. How he wished he were at home—wished he could only see K., or any one who would care for him, a poor helpless boy!

He sat down, and leaned against a tree-stem close by the road-side, but while waiting and watching he fell asleep. He was awakened by a dog pulling at the handkerchief that held the poor bird. He got up with difficulty, for he was very stiff, and clasped the bird in both hands to protect it, for the dog was of a kind accustomed to steal, and did not look at all inclined to take a friendly denial. Close by, Oliver saw a covered travelling-house, a boy loosing the horse, a woman breaking sticks for a fire, dirty children running about, and another sight he could never forget—a man lying full-length on the grass, his black eyes fixed on Oliver, and a gun by his side. They had all come up while Oliver was asleep. The man was resting on one arm, his head raised, a short pipe in his mouth, and a terrible look in his eyes, which were fixed on Oliver. It was the first time that Oliver had known what it was to feel afraid of any human being; but those eyes had a look of desperate evil that struck a terror through the boy, and seemed to fix him where he stood.

But he did move. With a fast beating heart he walked on—his terror grew greater—he could not run —he thought the man would come after him—those

evil eyes seemed to glare on him still—he was giddy,
and tottered along. The grisly dog followed him
close—perhaps he would seize him, and drag him
back to the man! He struggled on, and saw a gate,
and men in the next field cutting the corn. The gate
was not fastened; he went through, and, quite spent
with fatigue, hunger, and fright, he fell down by the,
first stand of sheaves that he got to. He felt the
grisly dog drag at his handkerchief—felt the poor bird
flutter in terror, but was too weak and faint to lift up
his little hand to protect it. It was well that he could
not, for the dog's fangs were sharp; they were soon
astened in the poor bird, which was dragged away,
and the dog disappeared with his prey.

The reapers soon saw a child lying there, and a
man came up to him, and said, " What art ailing,
lad ? " But Oliver could not answer; he heard a
voice, but could not tell what was said. The man
saw a bloody handkerchief tied to his button-hole,
and lifted it to see if the child had a wound. It was
only the empty bed of the ring-dove he had tried to
save. Then the man took him up in his arms, and
went back to his gang, and said, " Here is a child,
more dead than alive! What shall we do with him?"

The men gathered round. " Can't leave him to
die!" said one man, a father; " here, lay him down
on my coat. Mother Tibby will soon be here; I'll
be bound she will know what to do! Here comes
Matty Trundel with beer. Here, Matty! try your
hand on this bit of a chap lying here; bring him to,
if you can, and let Mistress Tibby know."

"Who is he?" said Matty, turning to him with her can.

"You must give him a tongue," said the first man. "and then, maybe, he will tell you. I reckon you might spare him a bit of your own! "

Matty Trundel paid no heed to the compliment, but turned to the child, and the men gathered round for their ale.

"Here is a bit of bread," said the fatherly man ; "'tis dry with the sun, but make a bit sop, and you may get it down."

Matty Trundel tried, and the child swallowed, and she tried again ; still the progress was slow. The men drank their ale, and returned to their sickles. At length, one shouted, "Here's Mother Tibby ; she will know what to do! "

Mistress Tibby came on through her fields. She walked with a long oaken staff that reached above her shoulder ; she had a strong, decided step, that seemed to know no difference, whether treading the stubble or green sod. She gave a look at her reapers, and saw Matty kneeling down beside something, and looking after her.

"What's got there? " said Mistress Tibby.

"A child, just a-dying! " shouted Matty.

Mistress Tibby came on, and looked down on the white face, the closed eyes, and the little hands stretched lifelessly out.

"And ye be drenching the poor babe with ale, girl! " said Mistress Tibby to the woman of fifty. "Ye will just finish him out, girl, I say! Hie home

with him, do ! and I will be after ye soon.   Lay him
down on my bed, I say, and give him a wee drop of
spirit in a wine-glass of milk, with a tea-spoon ; wait
a bit in between-whiles, and keep on till I come.
Here! give me the can, and you lug home the child."

Matty Trundel's strong arms had a heavier weight
than poor K.'s, for the child lay like one dead.   But
the burden was no way heavy to Matty, who could
toss a sheaf or a forkful as high on the waggon as
any man on the farm.   Matty prided herself more on
the skill than the strength, saying, " It was the
knack of the thing, if the men did but know !"   So
she carried the boy in her arms to the little, lone
farm-house, and laid him down on Mistress Tibby's
own bed, and did as Mistress Tibby said.

It were long to tell how Mistress Tibby and
Matty Trundel kept watch all that night beside the
bed on which Oliver lay ; how they blessed him while
he slept, and fed him when he woke !   It was that
night on which Oliver Crisp was alone in the forest ;
on which Mistress Crisp was sleeping for sorrow,
and K. sitting in the doorway at home looking on
to the river and forest.   In the morning before noon
of the next day, after some long hours of the sweet
sleep of a child, Oliver was able to get up and walk
to the open chimney-hearth, and feed himself with a
bowl of bread and milk.   You might have thought
the child was their own, so glad were those true-
hearted women over the young life they had saved.

Poor Oliver was glad to lie down again, and did
not stir from the little farm-house on that day ; his

head was weak and wandering, he grieved for his lost dove, but seemed too weak to think of his home. When Mistress Tibby questioned him, he said he lived at the Mill. Mistress Tibby said, "What Mill?" he could not tell what Mill. "But what is thy name, child?"

"Oliver Crisp," he replied.

Then Mistress Tibby knew who he was. But what could be done? There was only a post two days in the week; happily one was the next day. The distance was long round by the road, and the claims of harvest could not be set aside; the horses were tired in the night-time in carrying the corn, and the men had only five hours' sleep. All this was talked over in the fields, and the man who was a father said he did not value a night, though he was tired out, to set a father's heart at rest, if Mistress Tibby would let him off the two or three hours more that he could get there and back in. But Mistress Tibby said it was more than mortal could do to walk all the night through to and fro, and harvest a day on each side of it. The child was safe, and there was no merit in killing a man and a father in order to say so. The next day was a post, and the tidings, though slow, would be sure.

"My poor dove!" said Oliver, as he lifted up his blood-stained pocket-handkerchief.

"There, there," said Matty Trundel; "I will just rinse out the blood-stains, and let the bird be, as 'tis best that it should be out of the way, and you be saved to do good in your day to many."

How many feet were astir on this day of quiet rest to young Oliver! but none took the cart-road through the field, or if they did they saw not the reapers who had left their sheaves standing, and were gone elsewhere. The only one who heard tidings was Mr. Howe with his donkey. He heard tell that a child had been picked up dead, and carried off by some reapers, but no one knew where. Mr. Howe would not mention this to any without desiring them not to tell, and they in their turn said to those whom they told, "Do not speak on it to any," he would not tell his young lady on any consideration. But each telling another, the tidings soon spread. Oliver Crisp was away, and so did not hear it; he was seeking his lost child on all sides of the forest. One is easily lost, but is at hard cost found. Poor K. heard the tidings, and cried torrents of tears, till she could hardly lift up her head.

"What ails the girl?" said Mistress Crisp from her bed, at sight of swollen eyes.

"I take it hard," answered K., "that mistress won't feed; there's poor master away, roaming no one knows where, and he will just find you a skeleton, and lay the blame all on me."

Mistress Crisp took her food, but she looked hard at K., and said, "Girl, if thee knowest more, thee will find the blow fall the heavier from far off than near."

At evening, as Oliver sat up for his bread-and-milk supper in the open chimney-corner, Mistress Tibby said, "Child, can you write?"

"Yes," answered Oliver.

"Then we will order and send a letter by post to-morrow. My belief is it will be two days on the road, for this place lies out of the way, but all are main busy now; and Oliver Crisp will get a letter as soon as any man in the place, for there's no end of the respect felt for them all the country-side round; you came pretty nigh as the crow flies, but 'tis a long many miles, if you take the road-side round. But sleep well to-night, and you will be a man by to-morrow, and give thanks to Him who delivered you when you were brought nigh unto death."

This reminded Oliver that he had not kneeled to pray, as his habit was at morning and evening; indeed he was too weak when he rose; but when Matty Trundell began to take off his jacket, to lay him in a little bed made of chairs alongside of the settle in the farm-kitchen, Oliver said, "I must pray."

"Quite right," said Mistress Tibby, as she sat close by the wood-fire that burned on the hearth that August evening. Oliver kneeled with folded hands a few moments in silence, he could not feel so free as when with his father, or alone. He waited between each petition, as he had been taught, but added nothing more until he prayed "Give us this day our daily bread," then adding: "I thank Thee for these good grannies who feed me. Forgive us our trespasses —forgive me for running away; as we forgive them that trespass against us; forgive the man and the dog who took my young dove! Lead us not into tempta- tion, but deliver us from evil,—I thank Thee, my

Saviour, for delivering me, and bringing me here. I pray Thee to take me safe home, and bless these kind grannies; for Thine is the kingdom, and the power, and the glory, for ever and ever.   Amen."

"Shall I say the Good Shepherd's Psalm?" Oliver asked, looking up at Mistress Tibby.

"Say all that is in thine heart," she replied. And how sweetly rose its melody of thanksgiving and trust from the heart and the lips of the child who had experienced its truth!

When Oliver rose Mistress Tibby drew him close to her side. "God bless thee," she said. "It is He who teacheth the heart to know Him as our Father in Jesus—the Son of the Blessed!"

Matty Trundel was wakeful that night, and crept in once or twice to look at the child, but he did not awake, and seemed not to have moved. The farm was early astir, but Oliver was up and dressed when Mistress Tibby came in; he had prayed his morning prayer aloud, as he always did at home, greatly to Matty Trundel's comfort, who said nothing ever so troubled her heart before, for she never knew we could put things together in that way, but now she would try from that day!

Taught by his father to pray from his own knowledge of the Scriptures and the daily experience of life, his prayer was never a mere repetition, while the brief and blessed frame-work of the petitions taught by our Lord kept in his mind the great points of prayer and thanksgiving.

After breakfast Oliver had to write his letter. It

was his first attempt, and he was quite a stranger to the art; but he knew what he wanted to say, which is the principal point in a letter, so he wrote:—

"Father, do come for Olly! I am here with Grannies at Dell Croft, who saved me from the man and the dog; the dog took my young dove which I found. I am so sorry I ran away from Grannie and K."

It was done up and directed, and a wafer put on, and it was sent to the post. Oliver sat on a stool outside the door, watching the life of the farm, so familiar to him. At length an old man, bending beneath the weight of a pedlar's pack, came in at the wicket-gate of the garden. It was Benoni, the Jew! Oliver ran to meet him, for though Benoni never even crossed the Mill-hill, he was well known to every village child, and his special feeling for Oliver gave him a tenderness of manner which had won the heart of the child.

"O, Noni, I am so glad to see you!"

Old Benoni stood still and looked at the child. "What, all this way from home, with Mistress Tibby, of the Dell?"

Oliver did not answer to the surprise, but slipped his hand in Benoni's, and they walked up to the house. Benoni laid down his pack, wiped his forehead, and sat down with Oliver on the settle outside, and learned how all had happened. Mistress Tibby and Matty Trundel came in, and they all took a noon-day meal together, for Benoni was well known at the Dell—he was the walking shop of the neighbourhood. When the traffic was ended, Benoni, after considering awhile, said, "Why should not I take the child home with me? I am working my way round, and sleep only two nights on the road. The child can have a being with me, and we can rub on together!"

Oliver was glad, and Mistress Tibby relieved at the thought of certainty for the child. And Matty Trundel said it was a main chance to happen; for as to trusting to a bit of paper getting safely so far, with all the hands it was pretty certain to go through, and half of them not able to read, it was a poor look-out at the best! Not but what to keep the child would be wholly a pastime to her; but it was right to consider nature, and the father no doubt had his feelings.

So, all things considered, the old man and the child were to set off together. Oliver stood ready, hat in hand, while Benoni settled his pack; then the child looked up for a kiss to Mistress Tibby, saying, "Thank you, dear good grannie!" "Bless the lad!" said Mistress Tibby, and she laid her weather-beaten hand upon his head, and her lip quivered with a passion of deep feeling strongly restrained. Matty Trundel caught him in her arms and said, "If thou be lost again, may Matty Trundel find thee!"

"I'll never run away any more, and then I shall never be lost any more," said Oliver; and he and Benoni went out at the gate. Matty Trundel watched them as far as eye could see, but Mistress Tibby sat down on a chair—the child had laid hold of her heart, and it did not feel steady in its old life of much labour and few thoughts. We may have chosen our own way, without regard to the will of our Father in heaven, or to the feelings of others; we may have found that the way of transgressors is hard; we may have repented and confessed our error, and found the full and free forgiveness which flows through Him who purchased it for us with His own blood—and yet we may have to find that the chastening follows us still, for it is to make us partakers of God's holiness. This is the experience of childhood, youth, and old age. We cannot undo the act, recal the word, or retrace our steps. So far as we are concerned, the past is still the past, and its lengthening shadows follow us through life. But in Christ there is no darkness at all, " I am the Light of the World, he that followeth Me shall not walk in darkness, but shall have the Light of Life." The eye on self recals the shadow; the eye on Christ leaves no part dark, but the whole body full of light, even when we have still to eat the bitter fruit of our own way.

Young Oliver started in gladness with Benoni. To travel with Benoni was a great thing to do, and to be sure of getting home again a still greater. Benoni's traffic lay quite as much in lone houses as in villages : there were few that had not some dealings with him. He took the field-road by the forest, but Oliver did not remember it until they reached the bean-field; then all came back on his memory; the little glade, the man, the dog, as all connected with that road. "Noni, do not go that way !" he said.

But Benoni answered that it was quite safe, he had often gone that way, and he could not reach his places of call any other way. Poor Oliver's pleasure was all gone, he kept close to Benoni, remembering the man too painfully for any ease of mind. But they went quietly on their way, and passed the dreaded spot remembered by Oliver. Soon after, his quick ear caught the bark of a dog; he looked round, but no dog was in sight. The bark was no savage bark, but eager and repeated; he still looked anxiously round, and presently exclaimed, " Ally! Ally!" —he had always as a little child called himself Olly, and the dog Ally, which names still clung to both. On tore the dog, with a rope about his neck, and such speed that his shape could hardly be seen, and none but the child might have known him. Oliver shouted for joy, and stood to welcome the dog. But in the still further distance the man with the gun came out from the wood, and the ragged children shouting; the man levelled his gun and shot the dog as he ran; then he turned into the wood, and the ragged children and they saw him no more.

Oliver forgot his terror of the man, and ran to the dog; he lay down beside it, put his arms round its neck, saying, " Ally! Good Ally! Poor Ally!" The faithful dog licked his hand. Benoni was afraid to go back with his pack into such company, but he stood watching the child, and vainly wishing some friend would come by. The poor dog lay panting. Oliver ran with his straw hat to a little stream that flowed close by under the trees, but Aleppo could not lift his head. Oliver wetted his fingers, and laid the drops on the poor dog's tongue, which he seemed to like, but he soon shut his eyes, stretched out his limbs, and was dead. Oliver sat down beside him and cried.

"Poor dog!" said Benoni, who had in pity slowly retraced his steps. "But we must not stay here."

"I can't go! I can't go!" said Oliver.

"I am afraid of that bad man," said Benoni. Oliver looked round in terror, and got up from the ground.

"Don't leave him there!" said Oliver, entreatingly.

Benoni, touched with compassion for the grief of the child, laid down his pack. They drew poor faithful Aleppo on to the grass under the trees, and then with many a backward look from Oliver, they went slowly and sorrowfully on.

CHAPTER XVI.

OLIVER CRISP had not returned to his home since
he left it at dawn on that eventful night; he had gone
the extreme length of the forest, enquiring at every
village and scattered dwelling that met his view; he
had turned the far end of the forest, and was now
making homeward with a weary weight of sorrow.
The earth lay around him, wondrous in beauty; corn-
fields still waving in the soft wind of August, or
looking richer still in gathered sheaves; hill-sides
clothed in the massive foliage of summer, throwing
out from their dark background the glory of harvest;
or softer hill-sides, where the white flocks were feeding, and verdant pastures with cattle; blue hills in
the distance, of which no details were seen, yet
giving the beauty of form and hue.

But Oliver Crisp felt not the beauty,—his eye
sought only one object, that one little form, the child
of his heart—the child of his home, filled the great
world for him. Yet he could not fail to see the
earth filled with the goodness of the Lord, and at
length the words rose in remembrance: "The Lord
is good!—a stronghold in the day of trouble, and He
knoweth them that put their trust in Him!" He
felt his restless heart had been unthankful, and look-

ing off from his sorrow unto Jesus, the scene took instantly one of those blissful aspects the Holy Ghost the Comforter will show to the troubled heart, that is willing to cast its care on Him who careth for us. He saw in spirit the divine Son of Man standing as once He stood on the green hill-side, and heard Him saying, " They need not depart, give ye them to eat." He saw as then the gracious eyes uplifted in blessing ; and as the loaves and fishes then multiplied in the omnipotent hands, Oliver Crisp saw Him, the Lord of all power and might, still standing in the midst of earth's fallen children in blessing; saw the year crowned with His goodness, the little hills rejoicing on every side, the pastures clothed with flocks, the valleys covered over with corn, to fill the hungry with good things ; and as the scene carried back his thoughts, familiar with Scripture, to the glowing picture of the Psalmist, he remembered the opening words, " Praise waiteth for Thee, O God ! O Thou that hearest prayer, unto Thee shall all flesh come ! "

The soul that sees Jesus standing in the midst, may be troubled on every side and perplexed, yet not in despair. Trust in God regained its blessed influence over Oliver Crisp.

The sun was declining, and he and his child were now not far apart ; he was on the very field-road which the boy had trod that afternoon with Benoni ; but there is often in life a strange lengthening of trial, for a purpose sometimes hidden, sometimes shown ; and so it was, Benoni had turned out of the road into a bye-way across the fields to a distant farm where he had **custom**; glad to escape the forest-side in the day's decline, from fear of the man who had already done them such wrong. Oliver Crisp drove slowly on that very road-side, passed over the footprints of his child, and did not know it. Aleppo's keen instinct would have soon told him this; but as he passed on, hard by the road-side, under the trees, the faithful Aleppo lay dead. Oliver sprang from the cart, took the dog's head in his hand; he lay lifeless and stiff. "My dog! my poor dog!" he exclaimed, with a tenderness of feeling, as past scenes of a blessed life—scenes associated with that faithful dog—rose to mind. Oliver examined the cord; it was tied first in a noose and then in a knot, showing that the dog had been caught. The other end of the rope looked as if gnawed by the dog, no doubt to free himself. A cold shudder of fear for his son passed over him, as he lifted poor dead Aleppo into his cart—a dead dog instead of a living child—and went slowly on.

At some distance a man lay at the edge of the wood, and ragged children played under the trees. Oliver Crisp stopped, "Do you know this dog?" he enquired. "Yes," replied the man, without looking up, "he was shot by a gamekeeper along this road." "I know better," said Oliver Crisp. "The Castle gamekeepers know the dog, and would not make away with him. Have you seen a young boy about in the wood?" and a terror, as he asked, chilled his heart; feeling his child might have fallen into the hands of this ruffian.

"Yes," answered the man.

"What was he like?" asked Oliver Crisp, with intensity of feeling.

"Dark clothes, straw hat, dark curls on his head, and dark eyes," said the man.

"Where is he?" asked Oliver, with a feeling as if death and life hung on the lips of that man.

"I don't know," said the man; "but mayhap I could find him."

"Find him now!" said Oliver, with a terrible imperativeness.

"I can't," replied the man; "but if you come here to-morrow, or tell me where to take him, I will find him up, if you care to make it worth my while to be after him."

Oliver sprang from his cart, saw the man's gun, and seizing it, said, "Wretch! You have shot the dog and hid the child! And if you don't tell me, I will just bind you hand and foot, and carry you where you will have to tell!" And Oliver's powerful form looked well able to do all he had said.

"Will you?" replied the man, without looking up; "you lay down that gun where you found it, or you will find yourself worse off than you think!"

The man quietly whistled, and from the wood came out men, ill-looking and strong, able to work their own will.

"Lay down the gun where you found it," said the man; "I know you for a better man than you show yourself here, or you would not be let off as you are!"

"I don't care a straw for your let off!" said Oliver. "Tell me, where is the child? You are none of you fathers, or you would have a feeling for one!"

"For the matter of that," said the man, "I scorned the advantage when I might have got a king's ransom for the child; and to show you we can do a good turn to one who don't deserve it, you may just ask at yon farm in the Dell for the child; and when you have found him, you can act fair by us, since you have rough words to answer for."

"Take it now," said Oliver, "to prove I can trust!" and he emptied his pocket of its silver and gold, into the hand of the man, laid down the gun, and drove hurriedly on. Before he left the road through the fields, he saw reapers at work. They confirmed the tidings, and he hastened to the farm in the Dell. There he heard all! So it was that comfort dawned when his terrible night of trial was blackest; when his worst fears were awakened, peace flowed in like a river; and the strong man whose harrowed feelings had carried him away, sat down and wept like a child.

No one could tell him the way that the travellers had taken, but his heart was at rest; he stabled poor weary Depper, and accepted the kind cheer of the farm for the night. All the house was up with the daylight, for harvest makes short nights. Oliver

Crisp started for the long miles home, in the happy trust that all would be well. And now as he looked around on the rich fields in the sunbeams of morning, he still saw the form of the gracious Son of Man, as He stood in the midst multiplying blessing, and heard again the word of peace from His lips, " They need not depart, lest they faint by the way, for divers of them came from far ! " He remembered his prayer for the child at his baptism ; how truly had it been answered now to the boy,— " As one whom his mother comforteth, so will I comfort you." Mistress Tibby, Matty Trundel, and Benoni—what arms of compassion for a little wanderer to rest in !

It was much for the child to walk the five miles of Benoni's travel on that sultry day. But Benoni took his path chiefly by fields and shady lanes, where he found the scattered homesteads with which his trade lay. Oliver had many a rest, and sometimes a sup of milk and a cake, from farm-house hospitality. At length, after set of sun, they completed their journey, at the little road-side inn at which Benoni had stopped for many long years. Here they sat to their evening meal. Oliver shared Benoni's room ; but before he lay down he looked at Benoni, and said, " I must pray."

Benoni, as he sat by the bed on the one chair in the little room, took his hat from his head. The child knelt to his evening prayer,—

" Our Father, which art in Heaven,—

" I beseech Thee take care of my father, and Meg,

and Granny, and K., and Noni, and me, and take us safe home.

"Hallowed be Thy Name,—

"A Name which is above every Name, that at the name of Jesus every knee should bow, of things in heaven, and things in earth, and things under the earth, and that every tongue should confess that Jesus Christ is Lord, to the glory of God the Father.

"Thy Kingdom come,—

"When my mother will wake out of sleep.

"Thy Will be done on earth as it is in heaven,—

"For Thou hast said, 'Whosoever shall do the will of my Father in heaven, the same is my brother and sister and mother.

"Give us this day our daily bread,—

"I thank thee, my Saviour, for the kind Grannies, and Noni, who feed me.

"Forgive us our trespasses, as we forgive them that trespass against us,—

"If any man have a quarrel against any, even as Christ forgave you, so also do ye."

At this, Oliver waited and looked up in silent distress at Benoni; he seemed unable to add, "Forgive the man who shot poor Aleppo!" Accustomed to look up into his father's face when at a loss, he looked up at Benoni. Tears were rolling down the aged face of the Jew. Oliver thought Benoni was crying for poor Aleppo. He found no response to his look, but the silent sympathy of tears helped the struggle of his young spirit to pray,—

" Forgive the man who shot poor Aleppo !

" Lead us not into temptation, but deliver us from evil,—

" We thank Thee, Lord Jesus, for keeping us safe from the man who shot poor Aleppo !

" For Thine is the Kingdom, the Power, and the Glory, for ever and ever.   Amen."

The child was soon asleep on Benoni's pillow, but the old man sat weeping. He had heard such a prayer, with a silent wonder, in the Mill-house, when Naomi sometimes constrained him in his rounds to make his rest there for the night; the simplicity and power of its all-comprehensive petitions had gone home to the heart of the Jew. It was true that Naomi and her husband believed in a Messiah rejected by the Jews; and rejected, as the Jews believed, by God; yet Benoni could never resist the feeling that of such as Naomi and Oliver Crisp, Jehovah was the Father ! And now, when, after nine years, he heard those petitions again from the lips of Naomi's child—heard them mingled with the child's natural feelings and words, all uttered as to a God ready of access, inclining His ear to hear, and believed in as ready to do all that was asked in that prayer— the past impressions and feelings that seemed to have withered, revived in his heart, and, overcome by deep emotion, while the child slept he fell on his knees, and longed, like him, to say, " Our Father ! " But he could not ! His tears fell like rain, and he could only groan to the God of Israel for light in his darkness, and help in his utter sense of need.

At length, he rose from his knees, and lay down, but not to sleep. He thought of the aged Eli, and the child Samuel who ministered before him; and the voice that called not to Eli, but to the child; and that Eli perceived that the Lord had called the child, and how the child had made answer, "Speak, Lord, for Thy servant heareth!" In the morning, as he hoped and expected, such a prayer was offered again. Oliver seemed to offer it with less effort than the night before, and Benoni had wept his tears dry. They had their breakfast, and set forth on their way.

As they went by the way, the old man longed to talk to the child, but his solitary life had left him an unready speaker. He had not shed a tear, since he wept alone, with the September moon above his head, at the grave of Naomi, until those tears rained from his eyes the night before. He could recal many a dark, despairing hour, many a revengeful feeling and bitter hatred, but never, save then, a tear. He had long given up all hope of getting rich, which had been his early ambition; he had of late had only one wish— to gather money together to reach the Holy City, to weep at the wailing-place there, and be buried amidst the dust of Jerusalem. A troubled feeling crossed his mind, that the tears he would only have shed under the old stones of Jerusalem had flowed, once at the grave of one who was an apostate from the faith of a Jew; and once at the prayer of a child,—that prayer offered in the Name he had been taught to abhor— the Name of Him who was rejected and crucified in

Jerusalem. And yet he felt in his lonely heart that the only love that ever lighted his soul had been for the child Naomi; and that it would cheer his way with sunshine from Heaven if only he could keep her boy as his companion day by day. His darkened mind was bewildered. All the love he had ever met, glowed in hearts that enshrined the Name of Jesus as Messiah—the Name he had been taught as a Jew to despise and dishonour.

Benoni, amidst these thoughts, was more silent than ever. Oliver, too, was not ready to talk. His thoughts went back to poor Aleppo—he should not find him at home. He must tell his father; perhaps poor Aleppo had come looking for him? Oh, if he had never run away! He had never known grief nor fear before; and now he had lost his childhood's friend—lost, perhaps, in looking for him! So true it is that whatsoever we sow, that we must reap, if we sow trouble for others, we must reap grief for ourselves!

So passed the day; and the sun set again, and the moon rose in calm splendour over the wealth of harvest strewing the earth. They reached a little inn where this last night would be spent, and young Oliver's heart grew full of his father and his home. Benoni sat by the bed that he might gather up the prayer of the child. He had no prayer himself; he had tried the night before on stiffened knees—he had longed to pray as the child had prayed, but he could only raise a groan; he did not mean to try again. Prayer, he thought, was not for him; he said in his heart that there was nothing for him but to hold on in the darkness to the hope that he should yet stand in Jerusalem, and wait for the promise made to his fathers.   Yet still he felt that nothing on earth had been to him like the prayer of the child.   It seemed to water the seed Naomi had long since sown in his soul.   The child, too, had wept in his infant prayer; his young spirit had struggled against anger and revenge, to ask forgiveness for him who had done so cruel a wrong as to shoot the faithful dog on its way to his arms.   This was real; it was no mere lesson taught to his lips.   Benoni would listen again, and feel for a little that softness come over his heart which, even in despair, was far better to him than the hard stone he had long felt within him.

Oliver thought not of Benoni; he was a stranger to all that filled that life-long wanderer's soul.   As he kneeled to pray, he thought of his Father in Heaven, and thought how soon he would now be again with his earthly father in the Mill—those hours coming again of close union of heart and brief converse of words.   In the silence of the little inn-chamber, old Benoni sat by the bed while Oliver kneeled to pray.

"O Lord Jesus!   O our Father, which art in Heaven, we beseech Thee take us home to my father, and comfort him, and Granny, and K., and never let them be unhappy any more!"

But the thought of home so near, not only touched the child's heart with deep feeling, but brought thoughts of how he must tell them that Aleppo was dead; and his tears came again, and he got bewildered, weak and weary, too, with his long day's walk. He could not remember what came next, so he looked up to old Benoni, as he would to his father, and said, "What comes next?" The Jew remembered the words, but how could he say them? The child was praying in a Name he had lived, not to hallow, but to hate—the Name of Jesus of Nazareth. The pleading eyes of the boy were uplifted to him; the prayer, he thought, would not be his own—it would be only helping the child. All this was the thought of a few moments, and as Oliver waited Benoni said, "Hallowed be Thy Name!"

Oliver did not repeat it after him, but went on as if the prayer united them in one. "Thy kingdom come!" Then the question rose in Benoni's heart, Was not this the prayer that every religious Jew had been praying from generation to generation? He had not prayed it, but why not? Because he had never looked for that kingdom to come to him; he had only thought of dying in captive Jerusalem! He saw how low he had fallen; sunk in ignorance, sin, and despair. Lost in these thoughts, he heard no more of the prayer. Oliver having ended his petitions, rose, and embracing Benoni, as he always embraced his father, after his evening prayer, laid down to sleep.

Benoni was up with the dawn, and sat in thought by the bed. He was accustomed, on summer mornings, to start very early on his way when his places of call lay distant; but he would not awake the child who slept on, tired with his long travel the day before. This morning also was the last, poor Benoni felt, in which he should hear the voice of prayer, for, since the Mill-house had been closed to him, no voice of prayer had ever fallen upon his lonely heart. The little inn-room had now become as a sanctuary to him ; and a feeling, for the first time since his earliest years, came over him, that he wished he could open his window towards Jerusalem. Still more earnestly did he wish that he could kneel and pray, and say, with the same undoubting assurance as the child, " Our Father, which art in Heaven ! " Then came back the heavy feeling,—this morning was the last ! He should find the little room all desolate next time. A happy life would that day re-open before Oliver in his home ; a darker night would close for ever over him, when the only star in Love's heaven was hidden from his eyes.

Then Benoni thought again, " Why have I no home ? Why does the Jew wander homeless on the face of the earth ? Why have these Gentiles who follow Jesus of Nazareth, a man forsaken of God !— why have they such homes as might have been in Paradise ; while we, the favoured People of Jehovah, wander helpless and homeless—our very name a curse and a by-word ? As he thought on these things, the solemn words that Naomi had read rose to his remembrance—" His Blood be on us and on our children ! " Is it possible that that Blood can be a curse on our heads, which these Gentiles claim as their dearest blessing ? His Blood ! Ah ! no offered sacrifices pour atoning blood now, since that wild cry of "Crucify! crucify!" (Benoni did not say, "Him" —it seemed to trouble him still as when Naomi had read it.) Again he thought, "The Lamb of God!" How could it be? Then on his heart rose the remembered prayer,—"FATHER, FORGIVE THEM, FOR THEY KNOW NOT WHAT THEY DO!" The words brought back the feeling of the child's prayer—his struggle to ask forgiveness for the cruel wrong done him. "Lamb of the Fold!" said Benoni, aloud, as he looked at the sleeping boy. Then Naomi's pleading eyes came back on his view as she raised them from the Book, when she read, "I am the Good Shepherd; I lay down My life for the sheep!"

Again he thought on the prayer, "FATHER, FORGIVE THEM, FOR THEY KNOW NOT WHAT THEY DO!" The love was more than mortal, the majesty divine! That prayer, as he thought of it, seemed to enfold his spirit; it gathered closer and closer round his heart; it seemed all he wanted, it was at least a holy prayer; why might he not keep it ever lying on his soul? It seemed to bring a breathing of home—what does "Father" mean but home? What would that sleeping child feel before set of sun, when his father's arms were round him, but home! "FATHER, FORGIVE THEM!" Then, if forgiven, might he not look up and say, "Our Father, which art in heaven?"

But how could prayer put away sin? Is it not written, "It is the blood that maketh an atonement for the soul?" But when that prayer arose His blood was flowing! Whose blood? Could He be "the Lamb of God"? Abraham's reply to his son rose in

his remembrance, " My son, God shall provide Himself a Lamb!" Could this be He? Eighteen cen-
turies had passed away, and there had never been
another! He trembled, and dared not, yet longed,
that he could believe. Once more in the struggles of
his spirit, the slow tears fell from his eyes. Oliver
awoke and looked up. " Noni," he said, " why do
you cry? We are almost got home; we shall get
there to-day!"

But the old man's tears only fell faster.

" Noni, are you so sorry for poor Aleppo? Don't
cry! Father will be so glad; he won't be unhappy
when I get back home."

Benoni replied, in bitterness of spirit, " Yes,
home for you; but there is no home for me! I
shall die like a dog some day, and no one will care
where the old Jew lies buried, for they have happy
homes!"

Poor Oliver could not fathom the feeling, though
he felt the despair; and, not knowing what else to
do, he said, " Noni, shall we say, 'Our Father'?"

" I cannot!" replied Benoni. " I have no
Father."

" I mean 'Our Father which art in heaven,'"
said Oliver.

" He is not my Father!" replied Benoni, in the
same tone of despair.

" Why not?" asked Oliver, with surprise and
alarm.

" I can't rightly tell," replied Benoni, " I am a
hardened old sinner!"

"But, Noni, I have learned the text, 'Jesus Christ came into the world to save sinners'!"

"Oh that He could save me!" groaned Benoni.

"I know He can," said Oliver, rising on his arm in bed, and looking up into Benoni's troubled face. "I know He can do all things! Won't you ask Him?"

Benoni sank on his knees, crying, "Save me! Save me!"

Oliver rose from the bed and kneeled by Benoni, and the cry of the old man being silent now, the child was left to take up the prayer :—

"Our Father, which art in heaven,—

"Jesus said, 'Let not your heart be troubled; ye believe in God, believe also in Me. In my Father's House are many mansions.'"

"Hallowed be Thy Name,—

"For Thy name's sake pardon my iniquity, for it is great. Thou shalt call His name Jesus, for He shall save His people from their sins. Let those that love Thy name be joyful in Thee.

"Thy kingdom come,—

"Jesus said, 'Fear not, little flock, for it is your Father's good pleasure to give you the kingdom.

"Thy will be done on earth as it is in heaven,—

"Teach me to do Thy will, for Thou art my God: Thy Spirit is good, lead me unto the land of uprightness.

"Give us this day our daily bread,—

"Jesus said, 'I am the Bread of Life; he that

cometh to Me shall never hunger.' Lord, evermore give us this bread!

"Forgive us our trespasses—" Benoni took up the prayer, "Forgive! forgive!" lost in remembrance of the blessed words,—"Father, forgive them, for they know not what they do!" Oliver waited as Benoni still said, "Forgive!" And then, as without an effort, Benoni, in the full sense of the forgiven one, added, "as we forgive," without one feeling of bitterness left in his soul—the tide of forgiving love had flowed in,—the much forgiven! until every feeling of the melting soul was the fulness of love to God and man! Nor could he in that blissful moment distinguish the love that flowed in upon him,—the forgiven one, and the love that flowed out from his soul unto all men; the fountain was the same, it was not his own niggard nature that now forgave others, but the mighty love that flowed into his soul and flowed through it to all. He waited, wrapped in forgiveness, while the child in the silence continued the prayer, "Lead us not into temptation, but deliver us from evil, for Thine is the Kingdom, and the Power, and the Glory, for ever and ever, Amen." And a sense of blessed safety gathered around Benoni as he said, "The Lord hath laid on Him the iniquity of us all!"

Then, rising, he clasped Oliver to his heart, saying, "O child! thou wast lost that old Benoni might be found!" And they went to their morning meal with heaven opening above the soul of the old man, in the heart of our God; through Him in whom alone we can say "Our Father!" He who, having died for our sins, and risen for our justification, said, "My Father and your Father," as the inner circle of infinite tenderness, before He said, "My God and your God," as the outer circle of infinite power.

CHAPTER XVII.

It was still the prime of the morning when Benoni and the child set forth on their way; the brightness and freshness of early day. The aged man—for aged he looked, though not yet seventy—had become a little child, and entered a new world. The home of the heart is the heart of another! Benoni had found his home.—"The eternal God is thy refuge, and underneath thee the everlasting arms." Creation wore a robe of glory to his gladdened sight.

> "His are the valleys, and the mountains His,
> And the resplendent rivers ; . . . . .
> Who with a filial piety inspired,
> Can lift to heaven an unpresumptuous eye,
> And smiling say, 'My Father made them all!'"

Earthly forgiveness—the forgiveness of man to man—is the passing-over an offence. The Divine forgiveness puts the offence away as if it had never been; and, infinitely more than this, brings the forgiven one within the heart of Redeeming Love, so that it can never be an unforgiven soul again! Who can tell the change to one like Benoni; a lonely wanderer, with none to care for him, none to cherish the weary life, or cheer the tired spirit; with no fellow-feeling in any soul for him; his glimpses of affection closing in to leave his dreary life the darker!

—for such an one to know and believe the Love that forgiveth all trespasses; for such an one, who was afar off, to be brought nigh by the blood of Christ, and to be able to look up to the Highest and say, " My Father ! " to find himself inclosed within the blissful circle of a love that passeth knowledge, that hath no variableness, nor shadow of turning ; to know that nothing could henceforth separate from the love of God which is in Christ Jesus our Lord. This was a heaven of rest ! This is Life Eternal. The clasp of the Father's embrace to the returning son confessing, " I have sinned ! " the best robe, the shoes on the feet, the ring on the finger, the outcast no more—the son with the Father. Benoni was a new creature. Before, he was like the son whose eye was always on "the portion of goods that fell to him ;" now he saw all things as his Father's—this was their glory in his sight. But words cannot picture this new-born life. It is high as heaven, and must be experienced to be understood ; without the experience of it, words are but as idle tales which are not believed.

Benoni in his long life had never had a companion by the way before; all through a life-time he had walked silently; and while walking the road he was silent still, even though the living water was springing up in his once dry and barren heart,—springing up to everlasting life. At noon, when the sun was hot, they turned aside where a stream wound through cool meadows under aspen-trees, and there they rested and took their mid-day meal. The boy's heart was a shifting scene of changeful feeling; now he fancied himself in his father's arms, then by Grannie's arm-chair, who looked grave as remembering his faults; then K. speaking reproachfully to him for running away from her. Then Baby Meg came on the scene, and the sorrow for Aleppo. Farmer Caxton—what would he say? and chief of all, Dame Truman! Oliver felt a flutter of fear, and wished it were not all quite so near; but then again he thought of his father, and everything else was lost in his sense of the clasp of his strong safe arms. "Father will be there!" he said to himself at every troubled anticipation, "Father will be there!"

Sitting by the cool stream, eating their noon-day meal, Benoni said, "Child, I would give this pack for one sight of your mother! Would that she knew that Benoni can say, 'Our Father!'"

"My mother will wake when His kingdom comes," said Oliver.

"Ah!" said Benoni; "how often she said He came once to put away sin by the sacrifice of Himself; He is coming again as King, to reign in Righteousness! You can't tell what that means, child, as old Benoni can. Ah, that 'Crucify! Crucify!' how it rings through my soul! My heart was one with theirs in that hellish cry; how it rose like a blast from the powers of darkness, and swept Him away! But listen, listen, child! as He goes, hear Him pray, 'FATHER, FORGIVE THEM, FOR THEY KNOW NOT WHAT THEY DO!' That prayer rose for hearts as hard as Benoni's. That prayer opened heaven, and quenched the flames of hell-fire. That prayer bore the crucified thief into Paradise; and that prayer stoops its blessed wings under the lost, and bears them up to the arms of our Father! O child! that's where Benoni is, in the arms of our Father!"

Blessed type and antitype! the lost child returning could only think of one refuge, the arms of his father on earth; the lost soul returned had only one consciousness—the everlasting arms of our Father in heaven!

Still they took their noon-day rest, for the sun was hot. "Yes," Benoni said, "He is coming again! He who was despised and rejected is coming to reign. I used to think only of Israel's glory when Messiah should come; but now all that seems as nothing—I can only think of Him! How sweet those Hosannahs will rise where once they cried, 'Crucify! Crucify!' And, child, we shall see the King in His beauty! Ah! to think how I have slaved to gather money that I might die in Jerusalem! Now they may lay me where they will, for the Lord of Hosts shall reign in Mount Zion and Jerusalem; and let old Benoni sleep where he may, when He comes He will wake him, to see His glory and be with Him for ever!"

"Did my mother know all that?" asked Oliver, surprised and unable to understand the change in Benoni.

"She read to me more than ever I can tell you," replied Benoni. "It all seemed gone from me when she went; but now it is as if a light had broken over the page; it comes to my remembrance again!"

"I have a Bible, and I read it to father, and find texts by myself," said Oliver.

"That's what I have not got," said Benoni; "but I will never rest till I have one."

"But, Noni, do you know where to find the places?"

"No, that I don't!" he answered; "but I will just begin and go through, and not leave a word out. How it will come back to me—don't I know how it will! O child! you were lost that old Benoni might be found!"

"Noni, shall you always say, 'Our Father'? I always say it. Do you think my mother did?"

"Ay, child, I'll be bound she did! She was just a living prayer. Times and often, I am right certain, she has laid my name at the feet of the Merciful, and now I am there myself—a lost sinner found!"

At the Mill-house Oliver Crisp had that morning received the letter, confirming the tidings he had gathered at the Dell. The sun was now sinking to the hills, and Oliver Crisp stood at the door of the Mill; there he had watched and waited long. How lovely the scene in the glow of the evening, but Oliver Crisp saw it not. His eye was searching the distant roads, not knowing by which the travellers might come. For one little figure he looked; the great world was centered for him in that one small form. He listened for one little foot-fall amidst its countless steps, for the sound of one young voice— earth's melody for him.

K. had spread out her table with all her skill could

devise. Mistress Crisp had found life in the hope, and had risen to occupy her arm-chair; the evening was warm, but she drew to the fire. All the village knew the lost child was found, and many were watching with glad hearts for his return. At length, Oliver Crisp, from the high mill-steps, saw old Benoni slowly ascending the hill; but where was the child? The child had seen his father, had made one rush up the hill, now reaching the mill-steps—then clasped in his father's arms, as if for ever!

It was joy unuttered, untroubled! Then, without a word from his father, his little hand in his father's hand, they descended the steps. Benoni stood at the foot. Oliver Crisp could not speak; he pressed the hand of the old man, and they went in together at the garden-gate. K. stood at the door, and gave an embrace; but the child was at his grandmother's chair, his arm round her neck—"O, Granny! dear Granny! Olly is so sorry, Granny!"

The aged grandmother shook with emotion, but she spoke calmly as ever—"Hast thee walked far, Olly? Art thee hungry? K. will give thee thy supper. Where is thy good friend Benoni?" Oliver turned away to bring in Benoni, and Mistress Crisp looked into the fire, saying, with clasped hands, "He was lost, and is found!"

When Benoni came in, she attempted to rise and receive him, but sat down again, feeling her weakness, and held out her hand. Benoni came up to her, and took it. She laid her other hand on his, saying fervently, "Thee art welcome here! Thee hast shepherded the lamb that was lost; may the good Lord shepherd thee, and bring thee safe to His fold!" Benoni bowed his head, and said, solemnly, "Amen."

All was arranged for Benoni to rest there that night—and not that night only. He was brought to a promise that whenever his beat lay that way, he would sleep at the Mill-house; his little chamber would always be ready;—for the long, white Mill-house had its guest-chambers, though but seldom used.

After tea, the father took Oliver's hand, and led him out. They went alone to the Mill, where Oliver had so often longed to be. The father said not a word, but kneeled down to give thanks; and the child knew by the depth of the thanksgiving, the danger he had run and the feeling he had cost. As they walked back the father said, "There is no good Aleppo, Olly, to be glad to see thee home!"

"No, father. They shot him as he was running to me; I saw him fall dead!"

"Who shot him?" asked Oliver.

"A man with hard eyes, by the wood, with a gun. We thought he would shoot us, so we could not stay. We dragged him under a tree."

"Poor dog!" said the father; "he was looking for thee! The man must have caught him while following the scent. I found him under a tree, and have buried him here"—and they stood at a little mound close by the Mill.

"Were you there?" asked Oliver.

"Yes; thy poor father was looking for thee!" Oliver held his father's hand tighter, but was silent. Then his father said, "If my boy had not run away, good Aleppo would not lie here!"

But the passionate outbreak of the child's tears stopped all further converse. Oliver ran in by a back way, and found his grandmother already gone to her rest, and his father joined Benoni.

Oliver laid himself down by his grandmother's side, saying, "Granny, do forgive Olly! Olly is terrible sorry!"

"Thee hast never been unforgiven," she replied. "But if thou hast not found it already, thou wilt find, that the way of transgressors is hard. Thou canst not wash out a wrong foot-print with tears; thou hast need to pray, 'Order my steps in Thy Word, and let not any iniquity have dominion over me.' But don't fret! Take a sleep on Granny's pillow till K. be ready to settle thee." And the weary child fell asleep with tears on his cheek, and was hardly conscious when K. carried him off and put him to bed.

Many a thought had passed through the mind of Oliver Crisp, as to what token of gratitude he could offer to Benoni for his care of the child. He could not offer him money; it must be some better gift. He would like to give him a Bible; but would Benoni, a Jew, accept such a gift. There was one Bible he might be more likely to receive than any other: it was Naomi's, from which she had often read to Benoni; sacred to her husband, but never

used by him. Unable to utter her name, he had felt
unable to make her Bible his own. The tie to
her was strong as ever, but the earthly presence
was departed; he could not read from her Bible
without her. He had laid it up to give one day as a
sacred treasure to her child; but he knew not when,
for he could not bear to see that Bible used even by
him;—it would always seem to say—Naomi is not
here!

That Bible he thought might have a claim on
Benoni's heart that no other could possess. How
often he had seen it in her hand as she read to
him; her face lighted up in the radiance of its divine
truth and love! How often she had looked up with
an expression of tenderest pleading on the downcast
face of the silent Jew! The more he thought, the
more he felt that he had found the right gift to present.
He had taken it out when quite alone, had unfolded
the paper, opened it with trembling hands, looked
into it, could not read, for a mist dimmed his eyes;
he looked up to heaven with a silent prayer, pressed
its open page to his lips, and tied it up in its paper
again. Her dear name was in it;—it had been his
gift to her while she was yet a child. Bibles were
more scarce in those days than now;—this had been
her treasure. This Word she had taken as her heri-
tage for ever, it had been the joy and rejoicing of her
heart.

Yet the question arose, how to present it? Benoni had been a very silent man; he no doubt had
the pride and prejudice of his nation; he had

conferred a lasting benefit on them, and it might seem no time to venture a condemnation of his creed !

Such questionings are common as we walk in our blindness. But though we may walk in darkness, He who leads us is in light. His promise is sure to those who seek His guidance. "I will instruct thee and teach thee in the way that thou shalt go, I will guide thee with mine eye." The decision may be taken with much feeling of uncertainty; it may be that there is but the weight of a grain more for than against it; but that is enough for the single eye of faith, and will prove right in the end.

The hour for evening worship was early in the Mill-house. Oliver Crisp was used in past years to have Benoni present. Benoni had always sat by through the service. This night Oliver Crisp read Isaiah lv., "Ho! every one that thirsteth, come ye to the waters!" Who can read that chapter and not feel what it must be to a soul so awakened as Benoni's! To him it flowed like living waters and streams from Lebanon. And when the prayer was offered, Benoni sunk upon his knees, and a strange feeling came over Oliver Crisp that a heart was pleading with him in the supplications, and rising in the thanksgivings. When they were left alone, Oliver Crisp drew the precious Book from his pocket and said, "This is her Bible, who once read to thee! There is none else upon earth I would so wish should have it."

Oliver Crisp had meant to ask Benoni to take it

for her sake, but he stopped short, unable to say more.

"For me?" said Benoni. "Blessed token that our Father in Heaven receives the wretched sinner who believes in His Son! Her child has taught me to pray; and now my feeble steps will be supported and guided by the staff and the rod that led her in the faith and the hope of our fathers!"

Oliver Crisp listened in wonder and joy; but quite unable to question Benoni, they parted for the night. With what unutterable thankfulness did Oliver Crisp stand and gaze on his sleeping child! The little wanderer had been a reaper, and had returned, bringing his sheaf with him; unconsciously completing the blessed work of his departed mother. The soul of the aged Jew had lain in the dark mine of ignorance, sin, and death; but the rays of Divine Truth and Love had reached the hidden recesses where it lay; the fire of the Spirit of God had penetrated it, and now in the pierced hand of Immanuel, the once dull clay lay a gem of crystal radiance, reflecting those ever-varying rays of Divine Truth and Love. When the little family gathered to their breakfast, they found that Benoni had started long before on his way.

There had been no school-keeping at Dame Truman's since the sorrowful Monday of Oliver's loss. And now in the early morning Baby Meg ran up from the farm to see Oliver, and the children were locked in a close embrace. They had never been parted before. Baby Meg had been a most restless creature; not the less so from a secret sense that the trouble would never have happened if she had run away from Dick when his talk was not good. She grew more careful now, and more devoted to Oliver, who had gone through so much for her sake.

After breakfast, Oliver Crisp took young Oliver and Baby Meg down the rocky street of the village to Dame Truman. Oliver had longed when lost to see the kind old face he had looked up to so often; but now he felt afraid of the rebuke. While the child's safety was in doubt, Dame Truman had strained every feeling in her anxiety on his behalf. Dick was not to cross her threshold again, and Baby Meg dared not appear. But when Dame Truman heard of his safety at the Dell, and his expected return, she began to consider in what way it would be most befitting her position, as the instructress and trainer of the young, to receive the culprit. She stood erect, as if he were already before her, and said in her tone of sternest reproof, " Oliver! is this to be the conclusion of three years' reading, writing, arith- metic, and manners under Dame Truman; that you run away! a lost truant like this ? " This was doubtful, Dame Truman felt, so she sat down in a milder attitude and said, " I had been persuaded of better things from you, Oliver! these prognostics foretell dubious results!" That sounded better, but although Dame Truman had repeated it several times in an audible voice, as if the children were before her, it quite escaped her memory the next day. For two days the village mistress composed, revised, altered, and reviewed the address to her recovered scholar, so as might on the whole be most suitable; combining brevity with emphasis, tempering decision by mildness, and while pronouncing censure, leaving an outlet for hope and amendment. The right arrangement and the emendations of this sentence laid such hold on this village mentor that she lay awake composing and re-modelling her address by night, and could in no other way occupy herself by day. Many times she changed her position, studied her own aspect, her intonation, changed a short word for a long one, as more effective, and finally judged it better to say, either standing or sitting, as the case might be, "Oliver, is this tantrum the conclusion of all my intuitions? if so, it had been better that Dame Truman had never endued the children of this generation with education and manners!" But this was affecting, and cost Dame Truman a tear. Most earnestly she wished that the interview were over; such an occasion had never occurred before! as she many times observed; and it was by no means easy, even for her energies, to be always up to the mark for emergencies. The intensity of the composition went on without relief or release, until Oliver appeared in sight with his father. Baby Meg held back, she had already had a sharp reprimand for assorting with evil communications; she wished to keep near, but not to venture in sight. Oliver's cheek was very white as he crossed the cottage-threshold with his father, into the dreaded presence of Dame Truman. It happened at that moment that Dame Truman did not know, and could never tell, nor recal, whether she were sitting or standing; and the first sight of the child, she always said afterwards, made at the moment a clean sweep of her head; so that before she knew one thing from another she caught him right up in her arms, and wept as any child might have done! and if the poor lost thing did not cry too, and sob out, " I am so sorry ! " and hang round her as tight as ivy to oak ! And when she came to her recollection she could not for anything remember the words she had put together.

CHAPTER XVIII.

Oliver Crisp returned to the Mill-house, and the children went on to the Farm, with many a greeting as they passed along. Mistress Caxton gave a mother's embrace. Farmer Caxton looked down with a sorrowful benignancy. "Thou art but a small candle, child, yet it darkened our hearts when thy light was lost!" Farmer Caxton was standing in the farm-kitchen, with his hat on and his staff in his hand, and having said this, he went out. The two children followed him. Farmer Caxton looked at his men and his harvest-fields here and there, and then sat down on a large wooden farm-roller, with his long line of reapers in sight. Oliver sat by him, glad to be at his side again, and Meg seated herself on the stubble, playing with scattered ears of corn. The old farmer was leaning both hands on the round knob of his oaken staff, looking over the field in its harvest-glory. At length he said, "Child, I would not have thee take in hand to fight any more!"

"I couldn't help it, Grand-daddy. I didn't want to fight, I am sure."

"Thou wilt not be able to help it next time, child."

"What next time?" asked Oliver.

"Ah! the temptation will rise up unthought of, and just overmatch thee! That's what folks say, 'How could I help it?' as if they thought help against wrong lay in them. Ah! I said it to myself as free as any, all my life of wrong-doing. I knew nine things out of ten were wrong, and I just said to myself, 'I could not help it!' I used to say to myself of my gains, 'The chance was given me; I couldn't help taking it!' and when I raved like a fool, I used to say to myself afterwards, when I felt the warring within that even bad men will feel, I used to answer, 'Why did they provoke me? I couldn't help it!' Child, you are young. I warn you, I, who have lived the world through, 'tis the Devil's lie that he lays on lips that never suspect he is near. Ah! there was but one eye clear enough in this world to see him lurking behind it; and the most part walk on in darkness because the Devil, who is the god of this world, hath blinded their eyes; as I did all my born days till grey hairs were upon me. And so they just quiet the conscience left in them by saying, 'I couldn't help it!' but, child, the lie that deceives us is worse than the act it covers."

"How could I help it, Grand-daddy? I couldn't stop Dick any other way?"

"You couldn't; but there was One who could, and you might have asked Him. Mind, child, I don't say that to put down wrong by main strength may not be right; but I do say you can't go through the world putting wrong things right by the strength of your right arm. You have got a high spirit, boy, and there's one who will just hound you on, as he has done thousands before, till you get the high hand on all sides, and then have to flee at the last!"

"Who from, Grand-daddy?"

"Well, what am I, for you to sit learning from me? Here, Meg! you fetch me the Bible, and my spectacles on it. Now, child, we are as well off here as within doors, and you read up; and, Meg, I'll have you listen—you will stand in need of it yet. Turn up the fourth chapter of Matthew, and read those eleven verses."

Oliver read the Temptation in the Wilderness.

"Now understand what you read. He who was tempted of the Devil was the Holy One of God. Never did Light and Darkness stand alone together, not before nor after, as I can make out. He was hungered; He had not fed for forty days. He had all power and might; yet He waited God's time! See Him set on the high point of the Temple—such a place as foot of man never stood on before. He stood only by faith, on a point up that height 'twas misery not to fall, yet He waited God's help! See Him upon that mountain, all the world at His feet; He had power and might to rule the whole, and put wrong things right, yet He waited God's gift! That makes life, boy—God's time, God's help, and God's gift! Live so, and you will find His strength is made perfect in your weakness. That chapter lets you into the light of it. There is a Tempter, and he is just where you would least think to find him. I can't lay out words like a parson, but I can see it all clear. I always knew there was a Devil, but I just let that alone. He did not let me alone. No, no! He had taken my measure, and cut out my gear. I was all for gain : 'I knew what it was to be right hungered for gold, and the more I got the more I still wanted. No man in our markets sold the year round as I did. I held back the corn till they gave what I asked; and when I got it, how I gripped it! It was more than my children to me; it was just my god, and nothing short of it; and the wonder is, it had not sunk me down where there is no rising up! I can't tell the tale, but I will bring it round at the finish. It is a game, all the same, as I have played at the Public, scores of times. There is one who shuffles the cards who is wholly their master. He chucks gold to one, and a book to another; and for one there's the pleasures of sin, and another he sets up till he must not be crossed by a word, but must ride rough-shod where he will. They don't see him who is skulking away in the dark; but they drive on, just as I did, till their eyes be opened, and then they see where they are, and maybe no place to flee to!"

"Why not, Grand-daddy?"

"Ah, child! it is written, 'How shall we escape if we neglect so great salvation?' There is a shelter open now. It is Him who conquered the foe. You have read it—how the Tempter laid his track fair, but the Holy One would not set foot in the snare, neither in one, nor another. But He was given up at the last for the Devil to do his worst, and He was just drawn through darkness, torment, and death; but He came out as He went in—a Lamb, aye, whiter than snow!   And it is just He, and He only, who can keep the Devil away.   I can tell you he is not scared at your fighting, nor your learning, nor your gold; but if ye be hiding that slain Lamb in your heart, he will not venture nigh ye, whoever ye be, not now nor for ever!"

"Don't good men fight, Grand-daddy?"

"Aye! if it be their work to guard their king and their country, let them see they do it well when they are about it; but 'tis not the way for you, child, to be ruling the right by a blow; and I do say the bravest, if he stands alone in his might, will just have to flee from that foe at the last.   There, you read up again, 'Not many wise men after the flesh, not many mighty, not many noble are called; but God hath chosen the foolish things of the world to confound the wise, and God hath chosen the weak things of the world to confound the things which are mighty.'   I sit hours together and study the Book, and try things by it in the world I have lived through, and I see it stands out clear with them all.

"It is not often I sit talking like this, but when once I have begun I like to make a finish.   How clear I saw that my gold was all the same as a bag of stones that you hang round a dog's neck to make sure work of drowning.   'There, mistress,' I said to your grandmother, 'take the key; no more looking, and counting, and hoarding for me!   Take it, and use it, and let it do good to them that have need,

and save me from the curse it had like to have been.'
Ah! I had just got to know the Lamb, and was ready
to let all the world go. I had seen it was not my silver
nor gold, but the blood He shed for me. Deary me,
what a change! Why, the one, it just hardened to
stone; and the other, it melted me down as tender as
the love of a mother.

"I don't know how you children can take it, for
I have not the words to make it clear; but it was
your mother, boy, that helped me to see. My heart
was just broken over the money dripping away from
Meg's poor father; and I began to hate the money,
because after all my labour and heaping together it
paid me out with a hole at the bottom, and dribbled
away. Ah, child; and I saw that your mother had
a treasure, always enough and to spare! She could
return good for evil; and all seemed to grow to her,
and nothing wasted away, and her name seemed a
blessing; and I thought, 'there's a power! it ain't
money,' I said, 'nor learning, nor might.' One day
she and I were alone, for I often called in, by her
goodness, and I asked her, 'Naomi,' said I, for
she went by her christened name, 'what's the
meaning that you are always so gay (glad) and so
free?' She looked full serious at me, and she said,
'The blessing of the Lord it maketh rich, and He
addeth no sorrow unto it.' I thought I knew where
her words grew, so I just asked no more, but I set
to looking myself. I thought I never should find it
—I was ashamed to ask her. I read the Bible by
the hour, and found things I never thought on. I

could have given my word it was not there, but I found it at last. What a treasure I thought it, and the gift came with the words. I don't know how, but they do hang together in a wonderful way. Since then, I may say the Bible has taken more attention from me than the crops and the weather; and I would have you both lay it to heart,— it will save you many a snare, and many a wasted year, and many a sin; for the Evil One will be lurking and hiding where you are least aware. I do say that the grandest ending is that word in Rev. xii. 11: 'They overcame him by the blood of the Lamb, and by the word of their testimony.' So, child, I would not rule down evil by blows, but carry the Lamb of God in your heart, and He will give you a power."

The words oozed slowly from the old farmer's brain. Baby Meg heeded them not; though in after years they came back on her memory, indistinct and half-forgotten; yet with the feeling many know, of a warning unheeded. Oliver could not fully follow them, but he received an impression. He was a child whose listening face led on the dullest speaker; and made the slowest mind feel it had a power to interest and arrest.

In these days books are everywhere; they are written in a style all can follow. The tide of thought flows in and around the homes and lives of all men; not with a lazy current, but with a strong and often rapid sweep. Slow speakers and not clear would hardly gain attention now; but in those past days it was not so; many would listen when one v uld speak, and a human voice was, for the most part, clearer than the printed page. Parish preaching, too often, had no teaching, and Sabbath-schools were rare. Oliver cared to listen ; and they who care to listen are sure to learn.

In the evening-hour in the Mill, when the sails were fast for the night, Richard Dolman gone home, and before the Mill-door was locked, Oliver, alone with his father, told him all he could of Farmer Caxton's discourse. Oliver Crisp listened in silence, as was his wont. Then, giving Oliver the Bible from the little shelf of books, he said, " What text do you say when you pray, ' Lead us not into temptation '? Turn Grand-daddy's teaching into prayer; that is the only way to use it aright; and give thanks to the Good Shepherd, who faced the tempter for you. Look in Hebrews, and you will find a text to say in your prayer: read up to me.' The child read the magnificent opening of the Hebrews, the first chapter,—then the warning that follows ; and the infinite stoop of the Highest to take part with the lowest,—Jesus tasting death for earth's fallen children, that rising in Him they might for ever be delivered from him that hath the power of death—that is, the Devil ; and be brought unto glory as the brethren of Jesus and sons of the Ever-lasting Father. At length, the child's inquiring eye fell on the text—" For in that He Himself hath suffered, being tempted, He is able to succour them that are tempted." And he linked it to his prayer that evening, alone in the Mill with his father.

" Lead us not into temptation,—

" Lord Jesus, I thank Thee for facing the tempter for me. ' For in that He hath suffered being tempted, He is able to succour them that are tempted.'

" But deliver us from evil,—

" I beseech Thee, deliver me from the Evil One!"

These chapters in the Hebrews were a commentary to Oliver on the words of old Farmer Caxton; each impressing the other more deeply on his soul. Then with the brightened spirit that heavenly communion always gives, he hastened to tend the garden, which greatly needed his care. While working there, Isabelle rode up from the Castle, and this crowned the gladness of the evening-hour.

The Sunday that followed, was the first since the solemn and sacred night passed by Oliver Crisp in the forest. After the service he waited until the villagers were gone, and then stood by the grave, with his child, where Naomi slept. As he stood there a surprise of secret rapture filled his soul, as he recalled the blessed visions of that night of anguish, and remembered that while such glimpses are given to the spirit that tabernacles below, they are the ceaseless experience of the disembodied in glory. Then in the light of resurrection he saw Naomi's risen form in heavenly radiance; the glory in her eyes, the light upon her brow, the lips ready again to breathe forth blessing. So on his silent soul the gladness broke of that approaching morning, when, clothed in immortality, he and his Naomi and his child, all would arise, caught up on clouds to meet their Saviour in the air. "Neither shall they die any more, but they are the children of God, being the children of the resurrection."

It was said of old, "She goeth unto the grave to weep there!" But resurrection changed the scene. Yet that was a resurrection amidst the darkening shadows of sin and death ; the eye of faith beholds a resurrection from weakness unto power, from corruption to incorruption, from dishonour to glory. Faith's eye on resurrection has power to change the aspect of the grave. As on some solemn mountain-side that overhangs with gloomy and oppressive weight, when a sunbeam falls, its receding form is kindled into life and beauty—crimson heather, pine-forests, and dewy herbage:—so on the silent grave there hangs death's shadow ; but touched with the living light of resurrection, the shadow softens and illumes into a celestial glory, and life and immortality rise on the longing eyes. And as the sunbeam cometh from above, so comes the beam of resurrection-light ;— consoling and raising the spirit, by glimpses of the glory yet to be revealed.

Still Oliver Crisp was silent; he could not give in words the things unseen by mortal eyes. The father and the child walked home together; and when the happy meal of the Sabbath evening was over, he took his child as he was wont to do, to the Mill-steps, before the hour at which they gathered in the home for the hymns of praise and voice of prayer. With open Bibles on their knees, the father and the child sat together in the calm that breathes in Sabbath hours,—a deeper stillness and a brighter smile on earth's fair face, telling that the primal blessing lingers still, which sin and sorrow, care and toil, cannot efface; waiting in faint earnest until He comes who will restore the Sabbath of our God, creation's rest.

To those who know in any measure the power of Christ's resurrection, the week's first-day rest thrills even now with everlasting life. A risen Saviour, seen by faith, in grace and truth, amidst His children on the earth He watered with His life-blood, and on which He will yet reign in righteousness. The light of His countenance lifted up upon them, illumes all the past, and over the brief earthly future opens the splendours of Eternal Day. Oliver Crisp saw the grave as the step on which resurrection's angel waits the unfolding gates of Heaven; while even now to watching and expectant eyes the glory gleams that soon will pour its living effulgence wherever reposes the dust of those who sleep in Jesus.

Yet Oliver Crisp could not steep his child's young spirit in the glow that had suffused his own. Seldom from eye to eye can that radiance glance; each must receive it straight from Heaven. It may be long-looked for, or it may suddenly surprise the thoughtful soul, as it did Oliver Crisp's. Blissful hours are those when things eternal light up things temporal with the living hues of Heaven. Clouded again and hidden from the spiritual view they may be, but they have left their witness in the soul; they have shed a celestial radiance on life's bereaved or saddened pathway. We know that they will break again upon our sight, and gild the night of sorrow with heralds of the coming day.

The father and the child read then together John xi. and 1 Cor. xv. The infinite tenderness of personal detail in the first, veiled in the splendours of the second, met all the fulness of awakened feeling now kindling in the father's soul, and gently trained in heavenly truth the opening spirit of his child.

" Did my mother know all this ? " asked Oliver.

His father replied, " She knew the Scriptures from a child. She lived looking unto Jesus, until it seemed to me she saw beyond our earthly vision. She used to say to me, ' There is no distance to the eye of faith; it sees through time and space, and can bring all things near which it pleaseth God to reveal. It is a true word, Olly, ' He giveth more grace ! ' "

CHAPTER XIX.

OLIVER had not expressed his sorrow for having run away, in words to his father. The father was satisfied; for he had seen the grief of that young heart in many starting tears,—his sobs over Aleppo's grave, and with his grandmother and Dame Truman. Still it was well, that father felt, that some word should pass between them, expressive of the feeling on both sides. The older and the younger heart were so entirely one, that this might not be really necessary; but as father to child and child to father it was right. Right, but not easy; for there was seldom much talk between them, though they lived in true communion of spirit. And the past had sorely tried the parent. Scarcely could he have borne it but for those manifestations of the unseen presence of the Lord, fulfilling the promise, " When thou passeth through the waters I will be with thee, and through the rivers they shall not overflow thee! " And to re-open the fount of grief and tears in that young heart was a greater sorrow to him than it could be to the child. And so weeks passed away, and the current of the boy's happy life flowed tranquilly on; leaving behind it the rocks and rapids of those troubled days.

Oliver Crisp was one who waited for time and opportunity. This has its own danger, as he had more than once proved in the experience of his past life. Waiting may become delay or lingering, and then it loses its virtue and becomes a hurtful thing. Even so energy may lead to hurry, and firmness may become hard, and quickness, haste of temper. The child's confidence in his father was beautiful; the certainty that he would understand how the impulse arose that led to such results. Well did that father deserve such confidence. He did not surprise him by a reproof, but waited tenderly to train him in the knowledge of truth. It may be remarked again that Oliver Crisp never marred the lessons he taught by a hard impatience in the uttering them; sure of the heart of his child, he did not seek to arrest, but to train him. "God is strong and patient;" patient because he is strong; we are impatient because we are weak. And by the weakness of impatience many a sin is made out of a folly, and many a heart is thrown off that might have been trained into higher and truer feeling; the danger is alike on either side, and the path of balanced feeling that lies between is narrow and but rarely trodden.

The strain of the past anxiety had laid the heavy hand of age on Mistress Crisp. There was a stoop in her erect figure, the keen glance of her eye was more downcast and absent, and she was glad to leave household cares as far as possible to the faithful K. Young Oliver saw and felt the change, and knew himself to be the cause. His thoughtfulness for his grandmother extended to everything. He would sit by her chair, read or talk to her, wind her worsted; and sometimes, to her great satisfaction, knit a few rounds of the stocking. If out at work in the garden, he often ran in to see what Granny wanted, and seemed more necessary to her every day; his gentleness was all she needed. Whenever he was out, she looked often to the door, and would say to his father, " Is the child sure to be right? "

Slowly and doubtfully as the year advanced, Oliver Crisp came to the resolution to send Oliver to school at the neighbouring town. Baby Meg already went to the same town to a boarding-school; and it was full time for Oliver to follow. Mistress Crisp made no remonstrance; her quiet tears were her only reply. Christmas passed and Baby Meg came, bright as ever, to make the life of the winter hearth; but a weight of dread oppressed the Mill-house as the time drew near for Oliver to leave it.

Oliver and his father read now beside the winter fire, and Mistress Crisp would often say she found her best comfort in that evening hour. On the last home evening Oliver Crisp gave his child the thirty-seventh chapter of Genesis to read. Oliver read, but as the history went on, a consciousness broke over him, and he could scarcely command himself. When he reached the thirtieth verse, " The child is not, and I, whither shall I go? " his father said, " That was what father felt once, Olly ! " The child could not answer nor look up; he read on, but when he came to the words, " He refused to be comforted, and he said, I will go down into the grave unto my son, mourning!" the father said, "That is what father will feel if Olly runs away any more!"

Then the child threw his arms round his father's neck in a passion of tears, saying, "Father, I will never, never, never run away any more!"

It was not easy to still the outburst of grief; but after awhile Oliver stood calmly within his father's arm. Then Mistress Crisp, feeling that the father had not followed up the lesson to the root of the matter, said, "Oliver, will thee promise never to fight any more?"

But the father replied, "Nay, Granny, we will not ask a second promise. We will trust that Oliver will not raise his hand lightly against another, when doing it once has cost us all so much!"

But Mistress Crisp could not be satisfied, and said, "Thee wilt not fight again, Oliver;—promise thy granny?"

"We will not bind him," said her son, calmly, but decidedly; "there are worse things than blows; but when he remembers the meekness and gentleness of Christ, he will not lift a hand hastily. I say to thee, my son, and thy grannie says it, Suffer wrong thyself rather than resent it; but when others are in danger, I must leave thy conscience, and thy cause, to better light than mine."

They sat on in the fire-light, K. knitting on the farther side of the table. At length Mistress Crisp said, "Thou shalt rebuke thy neighbour; thy Lord did this!"

Oliver Crisp turned to the words in Leviticus xix. 17, "Thou shalt in any wise rebuke thy neighbour, and not suffer sin upon him." Oliver Crisp read the words, then after silence, said, "He did rebuke! He was holy, harmless, undefiled, and separate from sinners. There is a woe uttered against those who call evil good, or good evil. Mayst thou never make light of any sin, Olly, nor trifle with iniquity. But if thou see'st any overtaken in a fault, endeavour to convince and restore such an one in the spirit of meekness; considering thyself, lest thou also be tempted. Can you tell me what else our Lord Jesus did for those who reviled and crucified Him?"

Oliver remembered at once Benoni's deep feeling, and said, "He prayed for them!"

"Yes, Oliver, that is a safe, high, and holy way for you—to pray for one who does evil. You may not change him by pulling him down by your strength; but you may change him by lifting up a prayer for him. Your prayer will follow Christ's prayer; it will rise in His name, and the heart of our Father will receive it and answer it."

Then Oliver Crisp turned to the nineteenth of St. Luke, and gave Oliver the 41st and 42nd verses to read. "And when He was come near, He beheld the city and wept over it; saying, If thou hadst known, at least in this thy day, the things that belong unto thy peace; but now they are hid from thine eyes." Oliver, the people of that city had taken up stones to cast at Him; they were hateful and hating one another, yet our Lord Jesus did not strike them down in His power—He wept over them in His love. He wept for them who would not weep for themselves. He gave tears, as well as prayers! And what then, Oliver?"

"He gave His life," the child replied.

"Yes, he was the grandest man that ever stood upon this earth, or will ever stand in Heaven, for He was the God-Man. He said, All power is given to me in Heaven and in earth; yet the greatest things He ever did were to pray, and weep, and bleed, and die, for those who hated Him and His Father. Remember always that our Lord Jesus has given you three words to fill up your life for others; you will find them in a chapter you know well, Matthew v. 44: Love, Bless, Pray.—That ye may be the children of your Father in Heaven!"

The boy went to school, and the father and granny and K. knew what it was to live without him; but it cannot be written and printed, for it was the want and the weight of every day.

Oliver Crisp found his business oppressive. It continued to increase, and his rounds were often long. He offered to take young Jonathan Caxton as an apprentice. Jonathan's school-days were finished when Oliver's began; and his grandfather was questioning what to do with the boy, so the proposal was gladly accepted. The farm-house lay near enough for the lad to go home for his meals, and everything promised well. But unfortunately Jona-

than's ambition was to follow the young squire as a
soldier to the wars : he had grown up too dutiful a
lad to oppose the wish of his friends ; but he took
privately to the Mill a drum he had long possessed,
of which his grandfather could not endure either the
sight or the sound ; always afraid that it led on to
enlistment.　But to young Jonathan there was
nothing that gave such relaxation and relief from
labour as playing a drum-accompaniment, while
he hummed some military air. 'The drum was hid
in a safe place in the Mill, and at odd hours
and odd moments you heard the beat, now faster,
now slower, as the air ran in Jonathan's memory.
It had a singular effect, and far from agreeable, and
quite foreign to the familiar sounds of the Mill ; but
poor Jonathan had enlisted the good miller's sym-
pathies on his side, and Oliver Crisp having no
nerves, and no prejudices, and no scruples, he scarcely
knew when the drum beat and when it did not.　But
with Mistress Crisp the case was far different.　Of
all instruments of music the drum was most abhorrent
to her ; she never heard a single beat but there rose
up before her mind's eye a recruiting sergeant and a
company of lads in their corduroys, fresh from the
plough and the team, with flying ribbons on their
hats, and mothers' broken hearts in their homes.
The irritation to her of this uncertain drum,—the fear,
when it was silent, that it wou'd be beginning again ;
the arbitrary way in which the performance went on
without any arrangement—you might have three
beats, or thirty, none could tell ; no calculation

could ever avail to estimate how long or how short
the performance would be; nor when it might begin;
nor when it would end.

It had been one of the strictest principles of
Mistress Crisp, in her practical life, never to interfere
beyond her own line of things; therefore, whatever went on in the Mill, she left alone, and the
force of this life-long principle was all-constrain-
ing still.

"That horrible drum!" said Mistress Crisp as
its beat came full on her ear in the breeze of a fine
autumn morning, when the mill-door faced the door
of the house.

"It is very mon-no-to-ne-ous!" said K., in sympathy, as she supposed, with her mistress's feeling.

"Mon-no-to-ne-ous, girl!" said Mistress Crisp.
"Thee talkest without understanding. I say it is
the hatefullest sound that ever was invented, and
what on earth can possess the lad nobody knows!
One would think he was turning the heads of the
fowls round the Mill-house to enlist for the war. I
heartily wish he would be off there with his drum;
there is no such thing as peace in the air since he
came. It aggravates me to that degree that I can
no ways rise above it, nor knit it off on my pins.
It's neither one thing nor another, and there's never
an end! When he comes to a finish, he may go all
over again, or wait an hour, or a day, while one sits
on the stretch, always waiting in dread for its beginning again."

The trial was a sore one, for when the nerves

once resent a thing, let it be what it may, they quiver and shudder in dread of repetition, or at the least symptom of return. Mistress Crisp was at length constrained to speak her mind to her son; but to her distress and surprise, having gone from her principle of non-interference and made an appeal, he only said, "It meant nothing, and was a harmless amusement that pleased the poor lad, who had given up his wish for the life of a soldier." It was impossible to make Oliver Crisp understand how every nerve of his mother was stretched in suffering irritation, until she felt that under the liability of that most irregular drum the peace of her home life was gone. But there is an Eye of infinite tenderness, that can read the secret vibrations of irritated nerves; a Heart that cares for them, and can wholly understand all that jars on the delicate chords, from the least discord to the greatest; and a Hand that can aid and send means of relief!

Benoni had become a frequent guest at the Mill-house, equally welcome to all. On one occasion, when earlier than usual in arriving, he heard at intervals the beat of a drum, now low and now loud, now fast and now slow; and his observant eye saw Mistress Crisp discomposed.

"Are they soldiering near?" asked Benoni.

"Thee may well ask!" replied Mistress Crisp; "'tis a foolish lad in the Mill; he keeps on at that drum more or less every day, till it is wholly miserable to be near him! If there be a sound that I hate, 'tis the beat of a drum; and the worst of this is, you can never say it has done. I have heard it at the cock-crowing, and could never sleep a wink more, from lying expecting him to drum out again. I have lain weary hours, and was perhaps just dropping off, when for no reason on earth another beat came! I have almost lost my senses over that detestable drum; and the strangest thing is, my son cannot see that it's next door to death to be always in hearing. I am sure I have wished I were deaf, and all because of that drum; but then I have been thankful that I was not taken at my word, for I should never hear again the voice of the child! Ah! he was made for oil on the waters; there's no outlandish ways, nor no jarrings in him! I shall never see him in peace under that terrible drum. Sometimes I have thought if we could but contrive for the wind to perform, as they say it does on a harp—not that I ever heard it, for such things are no practices of mine, and never were;—but if only we could tell when that drum, drum, would come, and when it would cease; or if it would go on for ever, one might get accustomed; but now the stop is as bad as the start; for you never know where you are, nor what will be next!"

"It is very mon-no-to-ne-ous!" said K., taking her mistress's part.

"Hold your tongue, girl; you know nothing about it; a drum is a drum to you and nothing more; but to me, aye, and to many, it means bloodshed and death!"

Benoni stood in reflective silence. At length, he

said, "Sure, a drum is a small thing to settle! I think I can engage it shall end."

"Friend, thee must not destroy it; my son gives consent, and the act might lose us thy company, for he is full as indulgent to Jonathan Caxton as ever he was to our Oliver."

"No, no! I'll not use any violence, nor risk my one earthly home," said Benoni, with a smile; and he walked away to the Mill.

K. watched, and he entered it; they soon heard the drum, now fast and now slow, now stopping, then beginning again.

At length Benoni reappeared, and with him the drum, the terrible drum, the mar-peace, the discord of life!

"Friend, what hast thou done?" asked Mistress Crisp, in alarm.

"I have not stolen nor begged, only borrowed," said Benoni. "I find the lad can carry many an air in his head; he has plainly a gift in music. I possess a flute, 'tis a black ivory flute with silver keys. I never would sell it,—it was given me once by a young fellow whom I tended when dying. He had known better days, and had parted with all except this flute, which he loved like a friend. I did not leave the inn while he needed help, but ah! I knew not then Him that hath abolished death, and brought life and immortality to life. I have talked to the lad, he is to lend me his drum to be held in safe keeping; as I tell him he has mastered it now, and I am to lend him my flute to keep till Benoni asks it of him

again; all as pleased as is possible, and the drum
will be far away soon. Yet I will write you a slip
that he may know where it is if some day Benoni
does not return; but rest safe that he will never go
back to drumming again, when he has once learned
his part on the flute."

True to his time came Benoni with the beautiful
flute; it lay in its box, and he lent it with strict
charges to Jonathan, and a golden piece in the lad's
hand to pay for a few lessons when he went to the
town.

The first effect of this peace-making at the Mill-
nouse was, that Jonathan felt himself kindly welcomed within doors. The discord was gone, Mistress Crisp had a pleasant word that made all easy;
and the quiet lad grew sociable there; it became
a second home, and a happier one than his own, for
Farmer Caxton had never taken Jonathan to his
affections—Baby Meg had filled his heart; and Mistress Caxton, though kind in everything, was a grave
woman, greatly taken up with the business of a large
farm. Oliver Crisp was a most fatherly man, and
treated Jonathan as a son, and when the drum was
safe away, Mistress Crisp became the more cordial
from the contrast of relief.

The home of our birth has the chief part in
moulding, it may be, unconsciously to ourselves, our
nature; but the home to which youthful life may
ally us has a power of influence hardly second to the
first. Jonathan had lived a boy's life with his one
silent dream of a soldier's career; this had closed in

the Mill; yet he had still thought of the life as the only one to be desired; his drum, his sole sympathetic companion. But the flute opened a new taste before him; he learned to play well, and you might constantly see him somewhere about the Mill-house when not in the Mill; he was always welcome at its hospitable board. And on winter evenings the group might have attracted a painter's skill; when Oliver, with Baby Meg at his side, sat singing together the carols of Christmas, like young betrothed bridegroom and bride, while Jonathan performed on his flute; Oliver Crisp joining in, and sometimes Benoni's deep voice giving a note here or there when he was a guest.

The sweet melodies lulled Mistress Crisp into slumber; the flickering fire-light played on her face, and the children sang softer, until as they paused at the end of hymn or carol she looked up dreamily, and said, the music was good, and pleased her well! she had heard it in dreams, peaceful dreams, disturbed by no sound and no thought of earth's tumult.

Or in long summer evenings Oliver sang amidst his flowers, and Baby Meg on the door-step where Naomi once sat, and Jonathan leaned on the paling with his flute. And only one fear awoke in the mind of Mistress Crisp; which was, that the lad played so well, and the children so sweetly sang, that some day they would be tempted away to make music for money; and a musical life was only second to a military one to Mistress Crisp. So after this fear had once arisen in her mind, she spoke in a more decided tone, and said, the performance was very well considering all things, but was not likely to take with those better acquainted with such things than they were; and she hoped they would content themselves where they could be approved, and not go farther to fare worse.

And the happy life flowed on of holiday and school, and Oliver and Meg were as one, sharing every interest and joy, and Jonathan grew into the home and forgot his soldierly ambition. How slight a thing may change the current of a life,—open or close the heart, expand or narrow the whole being! Some discord keeps asunder those who might have strengthened life by blending; some door is closed or only half opened that might have changed the aspect of existence; hard thoughts are woven in the fabric of our being when softer might have deepened every hue. There is no refuge from such facts save in the thought of "Our Father."

CHAPTER XX.

Benoni was now a frequent visitor; to none more welcome than to Mistress Crisp. In the absence of the child nothing cheered her like converse with Benoni. He had not, like herself and her son, grown up slowly and imperceptibly into the life divine; he had, as it were, taken one bound into the glorious liberty; this gave a freshness and a fulness to his experience, which made it a powerful influence. The contrast is sometimes met with in life; those who have grown up in the knowledge of and obedience to the divine precepts, appear to lack the full assurance and the intense consciousness that may be seen in some who were once hardened in their reckless unbelief. We know it cannot be, that God is less willing to give to the one what the other so richly possesses. " God is not unrighteous to forget your work of faith and labour of love, which ye have shown for His name's sake." May it not be that the one, like the returning prodigal, can look at nothing in self? " Father, I have sinned!" sums up all the personal consciousness; to him the Father and the Father's love must be all in all. In the other case there may be a feeling of a life divinely regulated, a self-consciousness—" Lo, these many years do I serve Thee, neither transgressed I Thy com-mandments." The Father may be even then saying, " All that I have is thine;" but the self-introspection excludes the joy. Joy in the Father can only be in measure as self is left outside, accounted dead, and the life hid with Christ in God.

Mistress Crisp was conscious of a life of effort and desire to do and be right in all things; a sinful nature she knew she had, but right principles and right motives she felt had been hers. She did not doubt the freeness of salvation, the all-sufficient Saviour; but hers was not Benoni's experience, as recorded in Psalm cvii.: " He satisfieth the longing soul, and filleth the hungry soul with goodness." General truth, more than individual appropriation, had been her aim. She rested not in a Divine Person, so much as in a divine fact; not so much in a Saviour, as on a finished salvation; therefore her soul lacked the expansion, and her spirit the glow, that Benoni had, in self lost, and Christ found. He would sit in converse with Mistress Crisp, and in the fulness of his heart scarcely notice how far she might enter into his apprehensions as he spake of Emmanuel, God with us. She could not fully understand, but she felt the reality, the glow of a Presence that was filling the aged Jew with a life and a power not his own; and the longing and the hunger of her soul began to awake, that she too might drink of the river of God's pleasures; that she too might know the fulness of rest in the Lord.

When the Easter of the following year drew

near, Benoni, sitting in the Mill-house with Oliver Crisp and his mother, said, " I have to ask baptism, and where can I seek it but here ? "

There was silence awhile, then Oliver Crisp replied, " It can be had, but couldst thou not find it elsewhere with more comfort ! "

" I know not where," replied Benoni; " and here, at least, I have you, and the child, and Mistress Crisp, my best friends on earth ! "

" It is the sin of the system, son," said Mistress Crisp, " tied up to a man ; if he fail you, where are you then ?   You should meet and let them speak, to whom the grace and the power are given, instead of following the ungodly to lead where they will ! "

" Ah ! " said Oliver, sorrowfully, " 'tis often hard to know what course to take."

" 'Tis not the man that I want, good Mistress," said Benoni.   " It is the Christ's name named upon me, in the ordinance appointed of Him—in whom I believe.   That three-fold blessing I reckon will be sealed to me then:—' The Lord bless thee and keep thee ; The Lord make His face shine upon thee and be gracious unto thee ; The Lord lift up His countenance upon thee, and give thee peace ; ' ' And they shall put My Name upon the children of Israel ; and I will bless them.'   It is the putting on of that Name to the sealing of that blessing.   I can't answer for the man ; 'tis the divine ordinance I crave."

At Easter the children came home, and in its resurrection-light of life, old Benoni, with young

Oliver's hand in his, and many a friend beside, with Mistress Crisp and her son Oliver as witnesses, accomplished his desire, and took the Christian name. He would keep the name of Benoni still, for he said, "I had been a son of sorrow for ever, but for Him, the true Son of the Right Hand!"

At that time, whenever Benoni came, they had evening worship at the Mill-house; reading of the Scripture by Oliver Crisp; sometimes Benoni would speak, and prayer was offered there; and Dame Truman would come, and Mistress Caxton sometimes, and Richard Dolman and others, and the children sang a hymn when at home. It was a church in the house, blessed to many, and an ever-increasing comfort to Mistress Crisp. For the one Teacher and Guide is bound to no man, but freely imparts heavenly grace. And probably you will never find a parish, however desolate and forsaken of all teaching by man, where some soul is not shining, a solitary light and witness for God.

On that baptismal day, who did not recal the baptism of the child, when Benoni stood alone at the porch, and dare not enter unasked; and there was no voice of invitation nor welcome,—not one to say, "Come with us, and we will do thee good"? The solitary Jew had wept his bitter tears alone in the night-wind, by the grave of his one only friend; yet not alone, a pitying Presence stood beside him unseen, One whose voice said of old, "I know their sorrows;" "I have seen thy tears;" and that child had become the guide of his long-wandering feet into the paths of peace. A frequent surprise of earth is to find that one to whom our steps have been led, has been waiting for all that our presence may bring; or the reverse,—to find our own need supplied in those who may cross our pathway. Yet why should it surprise us, if we believe that our Father in heaven directeth our steps, and delighteth in our way? "Are not five sparrows sold for two farthings, and not one of them is forgotten before God? But even the very hairs of your head are all numbered. Fear not, therefore, ye are of more value than many sparrows."

That evening, even the children sat silent within; impressed by the solemn ordinance and deep feeling they had witnessed that day. And as Benoni, who had a habit of short ejaculations, said fervently, "He loved me, and gave Himself for me!" The "He" and the "me" so wondrously linked, came home to the soul of Mistress Crisp with closer power. One habit Benoni had acquired, as he dwelt alone, was of repeating from time to time the confessions of faith in Jesus, Messiah, that lie in living light in the gospels. Such as "Behold the Lamb of God which taketh away the sin of the world!" "We have found the Messias, which is being interpreted the Christ!" "Rabbi, Thou art the Son of God; Thou art the King of Israel!" "Thou art the Christ, the Son of the Living God!" on to the confession of Thomas, "My Lord and my God!" Almost unconscious whether alone or with others, there was ever an exultation in his tone, a fervency of adoration, that raised in the devout listener's heart a measure of the sacred emotion that filled his own. In no other words could he so truly express his feeling, as in those of Holy Scripture. The Holy Spirit is the sublimest master of language;—all the highest and deepest emotions of the soul towards God find their fullest and truest utterance in words inspired by Him.

When summer verdure clothed the earth, when summer's sun glowed on the green corn-fields, and the crimson poppy answered to its rays, and gardens wore a blaze of colour, and the care of their young families stopped the full song of birds; when the blue-bells no longer purpled the woods, and the stately fox-glove grew up in their place, when the night air was laden with perfumes, and the fruit was beginning to ripen, there came another grand day at the Castle. The Squire returned home to his mother; and not a maternal heart in the village but throbbed for her with a feeling, and many with a thanksgiving. He came home to give away as a bride a younger sister of his house. Gay carriages and white favours, and flags flying, and wedding-bells, and wondering people, made the village astir; but it was not their own Miss Isabelle, as they always called her,—so their hearts were at rest. Their attention was chiefly given to their grand young soldier Squire. How fine a soldier he made, his sword by his side, his helmet and plume! There could be no fear for the country while their young Squire looked after it; the very sight would daze any man that could be after striking at him! And Bavieca, his noble steed, seemed a part of himself, and able, no doubt, to take his place in the wars!

Mistress Crisp would not look on the show; she shook her head sorrowfully. Conrad did not forget to make a call upon her, but his pleasant way made her painful feeling the deeper. He was seen on the top of the Mill-steps with Oliver Crisp—the friendship between them was not forgotten by Conrad. Jonathan felt a slight stir of the old longing come over him; but Conrad was charmed with Jonathan's flute, made him play to him, promised him music, which came without delay; and finally asked Jonathan, if he did not really think that it was far better to stay at home and live to feed people, than it would be to go out of the country to kill them? Jonathan had never seen it in that light, and thought there could be no question; and only felt a slight wonder that the Squire did not see this for himself; and he secretly hoped that Benoni would never get tired of the old drum, and want the flute back instead.

Farmer Caxton said, when Conrad had paid his visit to the Farm, " He is like his father, all over, and carries a brave heart for his God and his country. He'll be safe for the next world; but I am no certain for this. I know the ways of him that's the god of this world—'tis just by a red coat he clears off many a fair blossom that would ripen to fruit if he had not been a mark to be shot at!"

" 'Tis a thousand pities," said Mistress Caxton,

"to think he should risk it. You may take up the
Scripture, and say, 'The only son of his mother,
and she was a widow!' So free, too, and pleasant as
he is, to be hacked down by good-for-nothing fellows
not fit to hold his stirrup—'tis a thousand pities, I
say! The good be not so plentiful as to cast them
off in their prime, when the good Lord who sent
them marked them for blessing."

And the pageant all passed, the young bride was
gone, and before the year closed in, Conrad was
away, and the village was quiet again, and the Castle
lay still in its woods. Isabelle was grown into a
woman now; though all the simple manners of her
childhood clung about her still. It was of her, Mother
Dumbleton said, "I call her a pink of a lady; you
may say a clove! for there be that about her that
sweetens your senses if she do but smile on you."
True it was that Isabelle kept every pathway she
trod more verdant and bright for her presence.

And so the quiet months and years passed away,
working slow changes. Isabelle had now a Sunday
school at the Castle, in which the village children delighted ; and sometimes those no longer children in
years were sitting with them to learn. Dick Butterly had gone to sea ; his mother said he wanted
freedom and space, and she considered he was likely
to find both on the ocean. The pride of Sally Butterly's heart, her youngest—she, too, was named
Margaret—was still under Dame Truman's tuition.
Meg was a sunbeam, and Oliver's quieter nature
responded to the lighter glee of her spirit. Once a

year Oliver Crisp took his boy to see Mistress Tibby
and Matty Trundel :—those were happy visits to
Oliver, and dear to the hearts of the old women,
who felt a tenderness for the child they had saved,
beyond what they had ever felt before.

There was much to feel in this quiet flow of life,
though but little to tell, until the summer of Oliver's
thirteenth year. The children came home as before
to enliven the village, and make the sunshine of the
hearts loving them best, when suddenly tidings like a
thunder-clap fell. The young Squire lay low, with
wounds, none knew how many; fighting in the breach
he had fallen; the dead lay beneath and around him,
almost single-handed he stood. He kept the breach
open until friendly bayonets were behind him, then
yielded the post of danger and death, and sank into
arms stretched out to receive him. They unclasped
his sword, to which his fingers were clinging, un-
braced his helmet, with its white plume dyed in blood.
They bore him down the steep bank, laid him by the
stream, gave him water, and pillowed his head on a
veteran chieftain's breast. He looked up, gazed a
moment on anxious faces bending over him, then
upward to the skies, their blue depths calmly tra-
versed by the white clouds of summer, floating in
their stillness and beauty, as over the wooded
heights of his castle home, where his widowed
mother might be gazing upward with thoughts of
her son; his sweet smile grew sweeter as he softly
murmured, " Home! home! home!" and "his spirit
passed in that happy dream, like a bird in the track

of the bright sunbeam." His eyes closed like a child in quiet slumber, and his head drooped on the old soldier's arm : they wrapped a cloak round him and returned to the fight.

When sunset crimsoned the west, and the red blood crimsoned the stream, and England's flag waved on the heights in victory, they returned to the sleeper. Too deep was his slumber for the roll-call to reach him ; he slept his last sleep, for his king and his country! Not even the voice of his mother could have wakened him now. The next voice he will hear will be His voice who said, " I go to awake him out of sleep." A comrade kneeled and cut a lock from his brow, reverently kissed the cold forehead, and while men all around were burying the dead, they bore him further down the windings of the stream, and turned the sod where the trees were thick overhead, and where the rippling waters over the clear stones would keep a low music by that pillowed head, and where the sound of the trumpet, and the clash of war, would reach him no more.

Words cannot picture the grief that swept through the Castle and over the village. He was gone—the hope of all hearts, the stay, the prop, the head, the blessing of his home—his young life cast away, with none to succour, none to save. The cry of anguish that followed him was almost tearless in woe. It came, it passed, he was gone ; no prayer could detain or recal him ; no love win him back ; it was over for ever ; the blessing, the beauty, the hope of his home was departed.

It was long before the widowed sonless mother was seen by any, and when Isabelle at length drove and rode out again, a paleness was on her cheek, the smile that gladdened those on whom it fell, though it lingered on her lips, seemed gone from her eyes. Oliver Crisp, who had never spoken abroad of his own past troubles before, spoke now, saying, "There be many deaths in this one; I seem to know the feeling. I knew it once when I could only say in my heart, 'The child is not, and I, whither shall I go?' and I am sure they know it now!"

As golden autumn rolled away with its rich treasure from the land, word was brought that his war-horse Bavieca was coming home to the Castle. Oliver and Meg were fetched home, partly that they might not lose the impression of what to that secluded village was a national scene; and partly because Oliver Crisp feared the further effect on his mother, whose grief had been silent and deep.

When the sorrowful procession drew near, the bells rang a muffled peal, and the Castle gun slowly fired; glittering armour was seen in the distance, and as the company advanced, Bavieca was led on by a dismounted soldier on foot, in advance of both officers and men. The noble steed stepped on lightly as ever, but his fiery eye was downcast. Well he knew that his rider was gone! Bavieca bore the battered helmet and arms. Not a labourer had gone to work on that day; all had turned out to meet the grief-sealing procession. Men in tears threw their arms round the neck of the steed, children sobbed at his side, and women, unable to stand, sat by the roadside hiding their faces in their aprons as they wept, unable to bear to look on such trophies of sorrow. Tears may water the memory, but cannot win back the treasure.

> " Violets plucked, the sweetest showers
>   Will ne'er make grow again ! "

Meg cried abundantly, but Oliver's large eyes were fixed in tearless grief upon those touching records of a loss which, like every good and perfect gift from above, nothing can replace, save Him, Himself who is the giver.

The utter silence of Mistress Crisp in her sorrow made her son uneasy about her. She spoke not a word against war ; said nothing of her past expectations fulfilled ; she only wept her silent sorrow. Oliver Crisp could not hide from himself that she was failing more rapidly than before, and he promised that Oliver should leave school at Christmas to cheer the house for her. She took no notice of the promise, and Oliver went with his grandmother's tear on his cheek when he left her to return to his school.

OLIVER had returned to school, but he could not stay; his grandmother seemed to fail day by day. Her appetite failed. "Thee need not persuade me to take more food," she said; "I cannot eat for sorrow! The beauty of Israel is slain upon the high places. Would that my old life could have gone for his!"

"I think thou art better to-day, mother," said her son, seeing her knitting in her arm-chair.

"It pleases thee to think so, my son, but life here is too heavy a load. I have borne it long, and am weary. I am going to Him who has promised me rest."

When Oliver came home she revived for a time, and even sat at the table at her meals. The boy's pleasant ways made her take an interest in many things that without him she would have passed un-heeding. The days were short, and she seldom sat on through the long evening, but went early to rest; and Oliver always went in to see her before he laid down to sleep.

One night, as he sat on her bed, she said, "Child, thou dost pray with thy father; canst thou not pray with thy granny?" Oliver kneeled. His prayer was still his old prayer, ever fresh in its infinite feelings, and dear to his young heart, as his life year by year had linked itself with it.

"Our Father, which art in Heaven,—

"'Like as a father pitieth his children, so the Lord pitieth them that fear Him; for He knoweth our frame, He remembereth that we are but dust.'

"Hallowed be Thy Name,—

"'He sent redemption unto His people, He hath commanded His covenant for ever, holy and reverend is His Name.'

"Thy kingdom come,—

"'Lord, remember me, when Thou comest in Thy kingdom!' 'They that love His Name shall dwell therein.'

"Thy Will be done on earth, as it is in Heaven,—

"Jesus said, 'Whatsoever ye shall ask the Father in my Name, He will give it you; ask, and ye shall receive, that your joy may be full.' If it be Thy will, make granny well, I beseech Thee!

"Give us this day our daily bread,—

"'Your Heavenly Father knoweth that ye have need of all these things.'

"Forgive us our trespasses, as we forgive them that trespass against us,—

"Jesus said, 'Thy sins are forgiven thee; go in peace.' 'Be ye kind one to another, tender-hearted, forgiving one another, even as God for Christ's sake hath forgiven you.' 'Having forgiven you all trespasses!'

"Lead us not into temptation,—

" Jesus said, ' Because thou hast kept the word
of my patience, I also will keep thee from the hour of
temptation, which shall come upon all the world, to
try them that dwell upon the earth.'

" But deliver us from evil,—

" ' The Lord shall preserve thee from all evil ; He
shall preserve thy soul. The God of peace shall
bruise Satan under your feet shortly.'

" For Thine is the Kingdom, and the Power, and
the Glory, for ever and ever.   Amen."

" Can thee tell where those texts are, child ; to
find them in the Bible ? "

" Yes, granny, I know them all."

" I will have thee turn them up for me to-morrow.
Now kiss thy granny ; and mayst thou sleep well ! "

Oliver found all the places, and put slips of paper
in, and wrote the chapter and verse on the paper in
his grandmother's Bible, and she was often seen
studying them over.

One day, when Oliver was sitting alone with his
grandmother by the winter fire, she said, " Child,
thou art so like thy mother ! Granny could talk to
her, and she can talk to thee. I have thought a deal
over those texts thou dost thread on the prayer that
they call the Lord's Prayer. There is one of those
texts that has wrought a change in my mind that
nothing ever could bring me to come to before."

" What text, granny ? "

" It is that text marked down here. You read it
up, and the verse that lies before it."

Oliver read Eph. iv. 31, 32—"Let all bitterness, and wrath, and anger, and clamour, and evil-speaking, be put away from you, with all malice. And be ye kind one to another, tender-hearted, forgiving one another, even as God for Christ's sake hath forgiven you."

"Now read up the other."

Oliver read Col. ii. 13—"Having forgiven you all trespasses."

"I have a word, child, to say to you. Don't it say that the Word of God is quick and powerful, sharper than a two-edged sword; and like a hammer that breaketh the rock in pieces? That's what it did for me that night you prayed by your granny! It was that little word 'as' that fixed in my mind like an arrow—'Forgive one another, even AS God for Christ's sake hath forgiven you;' and then came upon it—'Having forgiven you all trespasses.' I seemed never to have known it before! When you were asleep on your pillow I kept saying over, 'Forgiving one another, AS God for Christ's sake hath forgiven you.' Ah, I thought, that's what I have not done! I wanted to say, But I will! yet I couldn't say it. I thought, I never have hurried over anything; I will wait and consider; it may not mean all I seem to think it does now. Sometimes the day alters the feelings we had in the night; I'll not be in a hurry. But, oh, child! I have just been miserable, for that 'as' lies as clear in the day as ever it sounded by night. I can't get away from it, and, what's more, I don't want. Why should I find it so hard to say out the truth, and confess that I have carried a stone in my heart?"

"Have you carried a stone in your heart, granny?"

"Aye, child, years afore you were born! You are no child now, but your old granny's best friend; and I will just tell you. You may have taken notice that Meg's grandfather and your granny were not over-friendly to one another. In truth, it is twenty years since I have shaken hands, or said, 'How art thou, friend?' or so much as looked on him! I took ill some few words he let drop. I believe he said them when hasty and hot, for he once was a man that a feather would ruffle. He is wonderfully changed since that time. I know that, though I have shunned him. There is no call to bring the words up now, but I held off from that day; from that day, as you may say, he has had nothing from me but my shadow. I said I would not be friends where I did not feel friendly. I did not see that the wrong was in letting words settle, and fret, and fester, until I got a sore and then a hardness against an old friend. I thought I was right in having nothing to say to one who could speak hard, and hasty, and untrue, as he did. Ah! I never considered that he was hard and untrue in his hasty temper, but I was hard and untrue to the Saviour I followed in my cool mind— which is worse, I do say it, twenty times over!

"Child, your mother did plead with me. 'O, mother,' she said, 'let us forgive and forget!' I said she might do as she liked; I, for my part, liked to show I knew wrong from right, and I would have nought more to do with him that spoke them unless such words were first taken back. But now I say, Where were I if I had to take back all my hard words before my Lord would have aught to do with me? Just lost, lost for ever!

" You see, child, granny's weak, and she can't make a short tale out of a long one. How your mother would plead with me! doesn't it come back to me now! 'Only think,' said she, 'if He who so loved us were to keep before Him all our hardness; the things we say or do before almost we know what they are! I am sure we don't go confessing to Him not one half of the ills that He sees in us; and yet He says He has forgiven us all, and He'll not remember our sins!'

" Once she said to me (she was sitting down on that door-step with her work, and the red roses that clustered the casement hung their blossoms just over her dark hair, and she looked up like a white rose herself, and said,) 'Those hard words of Farmer Caxton, they be just like a stone in your way, mother, and you won't heave your foot over, and go on in the pathway of love; you roll the stone on before you, and it keeps your pathway so hard! Oh, think of the hard stones in His way! our blessed Lord whom we follow; what false things they said, and He only poured out His life-blood to cover them! And just think of Peter—that was the hardest of all—to deny Him in death, with a curse; but it was His look of love brought confession and.

sorrow.'　But I would not! that was just my pride; I would not turn from the way I had taken. It seems to me strange how I thought I was right; it was blindness to think so. I see it now—'forgiving one another, as God for Christ's sake hath forgiven you!'

"Now, child, I could not say all this to any but thee. Thou art thy granny's friend. Don't take notice of this to any. Let by-gones be by-gones. But you go to Farmer Caxton, and tell him granny is not long for this life, and if he can step up and see her it will just be her comfort; he might come this afternoon when we have a chance to be alone. I would not let to-day pass; for we know not what shall be on the morrow."

Farmer Caxton did not wait for afternoon, but returned with Oliver to the Mill. He took a seat by the fire near Mistress Crisp's arm-chair, and Oliver went off to Jonathan in the Mill. How changed were the two since they last met together, twenty years before! Mistress Crisp's hair, now snow white, lay smoothly under her cap; the old farmer's hung down to his shoulders; both faces had once been hard, both were softened now; the eyes of both had been keen, both looked kindly now.

"I am glad to see thee, Jonathan Caxton, and I thank thee for coming."

"I hope, Mistress Crisp, you are getting the better of this weakness?"

"I don't take much notice of that," she replied, "I have found worse ills than those of the body. I have carried a hard heart within me, and set up my pride, and thought it a virtue, and held it right not to look over things said or done wrong. I don't want to look back, nor dost thou, I am sure, but only to say to thee, I am heartily sorry for all my hardness and pride. O, Jonathan Caxton, I have lost many a blessing your humbled heart has won! They do say the highway to kindness from you is to do you an injury now! So I hope I may find it not too late to repent."

"Mistress Crisp! Mistress Crisp!" said the old farmer, without trying to hide a falling tear, "I have that respect for you that I could not sit under your words if I were not right sure that 'tis God's holy will that we should confess our faults one to another. A thousand times over I have wished that I had never said what passed from my lips—aye, I have never ceased to grieve that ever I said it, and I would have said so to you if I had not felt your kind respect gone, and never a chance given me to see you. But we both know it now, and I believe the good God lets us have many a slip and brings us down low, just to humble us together, as you and I are now. Aye, Mistress Crisp, you and I may just say, 'Father, I have sinned!' and find peace in His pardon; which was more than he had who could say, 'Neither transgressed I at any time Thy command-ments.' My old woman lays your sickness much to heart. She begs her respects, and she would hold it a favour if you had anything wanting she could provide."

" I am sure I am bounden to her, and will thank thee to say so ; but it is just all given me, far above my need. I am hasting away, and am lighter for going now I have had these few words with you. I shall take it kindly if you will look in again. I know your goodness to the child. I hope Meg and he may some day be one ; but that's no ordering of ours."

" I reckon that has long been a settled thing," replied Farmer Caxton ; " they have so grown together there's nothing but death now could part them. I fear our loss of our young Squire has been a great hurt to you ? "

" Well, I do believe it was the finish ; and I can say it now, I have been hard on the fighting men— harder than on anything else. But I see there are tender hearts go to war, and I am not just able to judge, for the world is the world still, and I suppose might must compel right for them that are in authority. The kingdoms are not yet become the kingdoms of our Lord and of His Christ. But they will, Jonathan Caxton, they will ! and then, it comforts me to think, ' they shall learn war no more.' I have done with that hardness. I pray God order the right ; and if their hands must deal death, may their hearts breathe His Peace ! "

The flame of the aged life flickered long ; sometimes reviving in a softened brightness, sometimes sinking away in patient meekness. The perfected work of grace often lingers in beauty, as if to be a witness to the immortality of the soul, which brightens and expands in Nature's decay. Once more she filled her chair at the Christmas hearth, and listened to the carols there. Once more she saw the New Year in, and smiled upon the frosted beauty of trees of dazzling sheen, and every blade and every straw and leaf strewn with its crystal gems.

Oliver's was a busy life, divided between his books (for his father directed his lessons and book-keeping now), his happy time with Meg, and his quiet hours with his grandmother. These last were never wearying to the boy. His thoughtful mind received all that she opened to him in frequent converse: he would linger with her,—never willing to leave unless others were there, or she were resting.

"Oliver!"

"Yes, Granny, I am here."

"I want thee, child, to take a word from my lips; they can't counsel thee long. Come here on thy stool by my side. Don't let it vex thee, what I am going to say; it will be for thy good when thy Granny's away. Once, thee knowst, thee ran away from her correction! Maybe, I did not fit the burden right to the back; but, child, let me tell thee that the good God makes no mistakes; thou art His child, and be sure He will chasten thee. Don't thee run away from the correction He gives! Let His stripes be what they may, be sure thee don't run away! There is no saying which way the Heavenly Father will try thee; it may be in body, it may be in mind, it may be in circumstances. It may come straight from His Hand, or through others. Let me tell thee the last is the hardest to meet; thou wilt be ready to chafe at thy fellows, when thou wouldest submit to thy God! But I can tell thee it is all one and the same; there is never a word, nor an act, no, nor a thought, that can trouble thee, except it were given it to do so from above. For the very hairs of thy head are all numbered; much more the joys and the sorrows of thy heart. Take all straight from whence it comes; have little or nothing to say to them that stand in between. Take thy joys and thy sorrows from thy Father in heaven, and He has passed His word for it they shall all work for thy good. But now promise me, whatever God sends thee, thou wilt not run away, but stand still and receive it humbly from Him. Wait, and thou shalt see His salvation!"

"I will promise, Granny. I wish enough I had never run away! I don't think you have been just right ever since I did."

"Don't thee lay that to heart, child! I tell thee, don't vex when I am at rest as if thou hadst helped to send me there! Our times are in His Hand who will loose the silver cord at His will, if we don't let violence and war break the golden bowl in its beauty. Ah, me! I can't think on it! May they have comfort that need it so sore! I will just gather back my thoughts; they go wandering so, and I can't mind now what I was going to say. But I think I am tired; we will talk another day."

It was a New Year of bright frosts, sunshine without, and warm crackling logs on the low hearth;

and sometimes on clear days the sun's descending rays lit up the distant sea with a glory that seemed like the verge of a Land whose radiance was far excelling this. It was only seen from the Mill-steps, therefore Mistress Crisp did not see it ; but she had dwelt by the shore in her childhood, and the feeling came back on her heart. She often spoke of the sea. One day she said to Oliver, "The sea is full-tide, and lies calmly outspread, just a silver ripple, and no more. I can't see it break on the shore; it is up level to the grey rocks ; and I am floating away to where yonder glory lies dazzling. The rough waves are no more; only ripples that just bear me on. You will lose me when I enter yon glory, but you will follow me there. Never heed whether the distance be dark or bright. It's all one, for He stands at the door Who opened it with His Life, and Death can shut it no more. Keep looking unto Him, and your entrance is sure."

The earth wore a mantle purer and whiter than any that fuller can whiten;—sparkling snow on the hills, and the fields, and the thatched cottage-roofs, and the low graves in the churchyard. Through the village a company moved, still gathering in number. Slowly, silently, and tenderly, they gathered around the sleeping form of one whose life had been purified whiter than snow, washed white in the Blood of the Lamb. Some mourned in true love; all mourned in respect. How strange to young Oliver's heart the vacant chair, the silence of home, the thought of the grave where his Granny slept near his mother ; and then, when they would wake! Many a thought filled his heart, and many a tear filled his eye. But for him his Granny still lived, as his mother had done since he learned to know her; and the world of the blessed was too near his young heart for those who had entered it to be thought far away. He grew at his father's side, a blessing from Heaven; dear to Jonathan as a brother; cared for by faithful K. at every turn, and the child of old Benoni's heart. Meg's sunny life rippled over his, while as yet she seemed to lean on his love in all things.

> "Oh! for the robes of whiteness;
> Oh! for the tearless eyes;
> Oh! for the glorious brightness
> Of the unclouded skies."

> "Oh! for the 'no more weeping'
> Within the Land of Love—
> The endless joy of keeping
> The bridal feast above."

CHAPTER XXII.

Oliver and his father now dwelt alone. Yet those who knew the Mill-house felt that no love had departed from it; scarcely could you feel that they were gone whose presence once had blessed it. On those remaining, lingered the reflection of the departed. If you had known that house in all its changes, you could not now fail to see the father, mother, and Naomi in the younger and the elder Oliver. We sometimes find a home of which the depth is more felt than the surface; a consciousness of power and tenderness comes over us beyond all that we see; a strange, mysterious sweetness silently testifying that all that has been, still breathes in all that is : past elements of life blending in present influence, around those still left in the broken circle whose brightest gems may be set in Heaven.

The older and the younger heart were linked in perfect confidence and most devoted love. The boy grew in mind beyond his years, sharing all the silent wealth of his father's thoughtful mind. And the father forgot his often cold reserve,—drawn out into expressive life by the bright and buoyant spirit of his child. When perfect sympathy exists between an older and a younger mind, the union is close and the mental blessing great; each receives its need from the other—the wealth of the older love, and the play of the younger affection; the depth of the one, and the sparkling surface of the other; the sympathy of the older heart and the trust of the younger; the restfulness of the one, and the activity of the other, form an exquisite blending of age and youth.

The evenings at the Mill were full of gathered life, when Jonathan lingered, and Meg came up and presided at tea, which K. prepared. Meg was a most trusty helper at the farm; taking the large dairy entirely, and would never leave until her work was done; but then it was her chief gladness to be off to the Mill and spend her evenings there. This self-indulgence was never checked, it being her grand-parents' comfort to see the young lives strengthening in one; and Jonathan was there as well as Oliver to see her home. Meg read from Oliver's Bible, and Jonathan had one of his own. They never parted without the evening worship, and often lingered longer over their hymns and simple songs. Jonathan liked to share Oliver's work in the garden; every niche of which seemed to make some return of flower or fruit or vegetable, and Meg upon the door-step sat and sang to them; Oliver Crisp within, intent on his ledger or his books. And when Benoni joined the circle, the gladness brightened round him; age with him was rich with a glory his youth had never known. Each outward form obeys God's law of nature sooner or later; but many a heart grows younger in its age than in meridian life; all who meet its freshness feeling that it has the dew of its youth.

So at the Mill the days flowed on in peace and plenty; neither want, nor care, nor sorrow, now marked their onward way. The village had its history, but we can only follow the selected few. One event disturbed its ordinary life. A single woman, who called herself a school-mistress, came from a distance and took a house, and canvassed the farms and tradesmen for scholars; professing to teach "Grammar, History, and Geography,"—in short, "the rudiments of all things human and divine!" This raised much questioning and not a little feeling on all sides. The more aspiring parents sent their children to the higher educational training. Others inquired what grammar might be? for village schools knew little of such accomplishments in those days; and when informed that it was to teach the manner of right speaking, they were highly affronted, and said, if they could not teach their children the use of their tongues, they did not know who could! One would think that the new schoolmistress took them for dummies or fools! Dame Truman had never thought such a thing was so much as to be named. As to geography, they were quite sure that the less that children knew of foreign parts the better; for it only tempted them to be wandering away, when they were a thousand times better at home. And as for history, they could most of them go back as far as their great-grandfather; and what they could have to do with those dead and buried before them, it was not easy to see. They surely had enough for simple folks in the Bible; if they knew more of that it would be all well; but for the rest, it must be for want of something to do, that any took up their time and their thoughts with what was over and gone long before they saw light !

An opposition began, and the children of one party were often not on the best terms with the children of the other. It was expected that Dame Truman would rise in offended dignity, and say something crushing and equal to the occasion ; but with advancing age the good old woman had learned meekness, and she only observed that " her best was quite ready to give way to what might be better; that she would still do all that was in her power; but as to 'the rudiments of all things human and divine,' which the new schoolmistress held herself able to teach, she believed, for her part, that it was nothing else than a taking up of the elements, which she had always taught meant wind and weather, and were best left alone to a Wisdom better than our own ! She had seen many honest men and women grow up in the world, whose learning had all come from her ;—they had done well in their day, and were thought well of when gone; but she was quite sure they had never so much as heard say what 'rudiments' were ! She must leave all to be proven when another generation should grow up, and it should be seen if they were more worthy of respect than those trained up by her !

" If any liked to stay and learn her old stock over

again, she would do her endeavour so to train them
they should never be ashamed to meet the eye of the
Quality ; and what was far better, she would learn
them the good and the right way; to fear God,
honour the king, and meddle not with them who
were given to change ! But if the pretty dears liked
to be after the new learning, she would think no ill of
them until she saw how it turned out. If they did
well she would praise them all the same as if they
had had it from her; but if they did not, she would
not praise them, so there was an end of it ! ”

At length, a shadow of uncertainty and care
crossed the happy life of the Mill-house. Meg's
friendship had been gradually changing. She came
up less often,—never took a long wandering walk
with Oliver, nor seemed to care for his presence as
before. This growing coldness on Meg's side went
on, notwithstanding all Oliver's efforts to win
and retain the former confidence and warmth
of affection. Their difference in age was not
shown by a visible difference in person :—Oliver
looked the older of the two, and certainly was
so in character and mind. In the winter Meg
paid a visit to her grandmother in the town ;—an
old woman with daughters who took the lead.
Mistress Caxton had never favoured Meg's visits
there ; she could not altogether hinder them, but they
had always been short. This winter the visit was
lengthened by various excuses to several weeks. It
was a heavy time for Oliver, who greatly missed, and
a little feared for, his companion. On her return,

Mistress Caxton reproved her, and Meg did not take it well ; things went wrong for a time ; but as spring advanced they seemed to brighten, and past troubles were forgotten in present hope.

At length delay was no longer possible to Oliver. He drew Meg out for a walk where the broad forest skirted the corn-glades ; and when seated alone under the shadow of the trees, where no eye and no ear save that of nature were near, he said, " I say, Meggie, my own Meggie,—father says I may ask you to promise to be mine, if we only wait awhile before we marry. You always have been dearer than life to me! I want you to promise, for I cannot tell how to live on unless I am quite sure! "

Earnestly he looked into her face ; but Meg turned away her head as if in surprise, and said with a decision that she seldom showed,—

" My brother ! Oliver, but never my lover ! "

Oliver rose and threw himself at her feet with all the half-uttered entreaty of a nature whose depths of passionate feeling could not find utterance in words ; but Meg only repeated her " Never ! " and turned suddenly away and left him alone.

What were they, those two hearts thus abruptly parted ?—One the chastened and disciplined child of the heavenly Father ; his native nobility of nature regulated by earthly training and heavenly grace ; the other the undisciplined child of indulgence : could the closer union have proved a blessing ? Yet Oliver never doubted it would. We need not closely follow the events of that day. Meg was silent and distant to all. But for Oliver creation had changed; he scarcely knew where he was nor what he did; the one earthly hope, the one earthly love he had cherished, lay faded and dead at his feet. The crown of his manhood had fallen from his head, he must toil as a mere trafficker for ever on earth; every duty a labour, and every claim a painful pressure. A cloud had suddenly descended and wrapped in its chilly mantle his home, the mill, and the very earth at his feet.

It was a paralysing blow; such as made the strong man quiver, and left him with the feeling of one suddenly forsaken, to whom the light and hope of youthful love must be for ever a stranger. Alone in the darkness of a withered life-time,—blighted ere its noonday had come, with a heart that could for ever enshrine but one object as the chosen of life; and a home that a woman's presence could never brighten again! The troubled river of his life lay shrouded in darkness; no sunlight glowed on its waters; no moonbeam shone there; not even the pale star of a hope reflected in its depths; all dark and gloomy it must break away through life's rocks, it must force its way onward—one wild rush to the ocean.

But, " He knoweth the way that I take; when He hath tried me I shall come forth as gold," was as true as ever: though the troubled heart could not hear the whisper, " shall come forth as gold," life's river, now dark and troubled, would again shine in golden light, reflecting the radiance from heaven. He who laid Isaac on the altar of sacrifice, Jacob with a stone for his pillow, and Joseph in the low dungeon, each in youth's brightest morning, has the same discipline now, for "those whom He loveth He chasteneth, and scourgeth every son whom He receiveth." And well can all tell the difference between the chastened and unchastened soul!

Meg had turned from the clasp of a love that she still believed would be hers, as it had ever been; it had satisfied her as it was, it had been to her as a brother's; she knew not her need of its shelter, she felt not her want of its fulness. She would like to retain it, but at the same time be free for a new affection and interest; something her fancy and the romantic talk of others had pictured as unlike anything she had known before. She knew neither her own heart, nor the world. It might seem coldness in her, but it is an experience of constant return towards a love that is far higher. "My son, give me thy heart," is the appeal of the heavenly Bridegroom; but the soul. that knows not its danger, feels not its need, would keep the divine love as its own, and yet hold itself free to yield to the attractions of a world at enmity with Him. Many see it in its true light in the type, while unconsciously acting the same towards the great antitype. Where were our hope, if the heavenly blessing were as readily lost as the earthly often is?

With a colourless cheek and quivering lip did Oliver tell his father that night that Meg had said, "My brother, but never my lover." Oliver Crisp was hardly less surprised than his son; for awhile he was silent; then he said, "Take comfort. It is a woman's way."

"A woman's way," replied Oliver, "not to know her own mind?"

"It is not her mind, son;—that she did not know, but thy mind. Thou hadst made up thy mind, and taken thy time, but on her it came suddenly; taken like that, there's many a woman says No. They hold it too great a thing to take up with at once. She had thought to keep thee as a brother, free as the sunlight; and win a husband besides. You must give time for these changes, and all may yet come right."

It was hard to refuse comfort; yet harder to take it. The subject dropped into silence, and the weary days dragged out their heavy length. There was but one other friend to whom Oliver could speak, —old Benoni. He had given up his pack, as now beyond his strength; but he still travelled the road, taking small orders and bringing the things required, without keeping a stock for choice, and all were glad to trust him with commissions of all kinds. Many a lover's gift he had chosen for Oliver, to bestow upon Meggie; and like others he had never doubted that the two were one in heart.

Oliver knew his day for calling; and he had walked to meet him. Benoni saw him in the distance of the wooded lane; it was not the first time Oliver had come to bring to him his welcome; but the old man saw at a glance that to-day there was sorrow.

As Oliver drew to Benoni's side to walk with him, Benoni said, "My son, is there trouble?"

"Yes, a living death! O, Noni, my life is gone into darkness and almost into death!"

"By what cause?" said Benoni, stopping short and looking earnestly into Oliver's face. "Is all well with thy father?"

"Yes, he is well," replied Oliver.

"And Meggie?" asked Benoni.

"Yes, well, but never to be mine! Meggie will be another's!"

"Whose?" asked Benoni, and his eye lighted up in a fire of indignation. "Who dares to rob thee of the jewel thou hast worn on thy heart from thy birth?"

"No other yet," replied Oliver, "but Meggie denies me; she says, 'My brother, Oliver,—but never my lover!' And I never heard her speak half so firmly. I am sure that she holds a settled mind."

Benoni trembled, he took Oliver's cold hand and said, "I am weary, and was just holding on until I saw the dear old Mill. Let us sit on this fallen tree, for I cannot go further."

Oliver felt ashamed of his haste to pour into the old man's tender heart the anguish of his own. They sat down by the road-side and he said, "Father says it only wants time, and I may wait on in hope."

"Thy father never yet spoke an ill-considered word," said Benoni; "what comfort he gives thee he feels, rest assured. But, my son, there is only one course for thee."

"What course, Benoni?"

"The thing is from the Lord! Now take an old

man's counsel. I know how often thou hast earnestly said when praying to our Father in heaven, 'Thy will be done.' I know it is as death to thee to say it now without any holding back, but for all that, those words are the arrow that must go through thine heart. Let Meggie's words alone for what they are worth. A settled mind may be unsettled,— thou canst not tell. This is what thou hast to do— let those words, even those, 'Thy will be done,' go right through thine heart. They will pierce as they go, but they will bring thee a peace none can give nor take away. Thou canst not do it now at the word of an old man, but thou canst do it at the feet of Him who said it in 'an agony.' Let that be thy first care,—thy one only endeavour. Those words are an arrow; let them go right through,—don't block their way; not even with a prayer that things may be other than they are, until thou hast said them full and free to thy Father in heaven. O, son, if thou dost not do this, Meggie's words will always be pricking and fretting and making thee sore, and thou wilt be a withered man in thy prime! Let her words alone, and take these fresh from the lips of thy Lord and warm with His life-blood. I say, take them straight from His heart, which they pierced through as He said them, and let them go through thine own. I can tell thee, though thou lose all the colour from every blossom below, thou wilt live to bless Him who sent thee both the sorrow and the grace. And when thou seest His face thou wilt forget thy life's anguish."

It was the word in season to Oliver; days of terrible darkness had passed, in which wild thoughts had crossed his heart, of flying from his father, and his home, and the Mill, because he could not live to see Meggie another's. Each desperate thought had been stayed by his grandmother's words rising up in remembrance, " Promise me, Oliver, that thee wilt never run away from the chastening of thy Father in heaven. He makes no mistakes!" Still so terrible was the struggle that he felt his sacred " I will promise," would be overwhelmed by this continued agony; until Benoni showed him the arrow. Not the poisoned arrow of unresponsive human affection, that had entered to wound, almost to slay; but the arrow that had passed through the strongest, tenderest heart that manhood ever knew, the heart of Immanuel! That arrow enters only to heal—softened by the Saviour's life-blood; could Oliver refuse? He could not; and that night, prostrate like Him whose prayer he now prayed, he said to the Searcher of hearts, without one reserve, unfettered and unfenced by any other petition, " Thy will be done on earth, as it is in heaven ! "

A joy mingled with awe followed that prayer, and flowed in the depths of his grief-stricken soul Amidst his heavy sadness, with the mist still hanging around and clouding all the gladness of earth, he yet felt the peace of God which passeth all understanding, keeping his heart and mind. He wondered at himself. He knew the arrow of the Almighty will had pierced through his spirit, but he knew not

fully then that a pierced Hand had been laid on his
spirit's trembling weakness, to stay its anguish
the while, and make it possible to say, "Thy Will
be done." That pierced hand, that is always so laid
on every human heart that is made willing to be
purified by the Divine Will. Truly Oliver knew himself to be another man, the fevered restlessness and
the fearful chill were gone; he went into the day
strong and calm, and, though heavy and sad, he was
able to live, a blessing to others, a man of purpose
again.

> " Calm me, my God, and keep me calm,
>   While these hot breezes blow ;
>   Be like the night-dew's cooling balm
>   Upon earth's fevered brow.
>
> " Calm me, my God, and keep me calm,
>   Soft resting on Thy breast ;
>   Soothe me with holy hymn and psalm,
>   And bid my spirit rest.
>
> " Calm me, my God, and keep me calm ;
>   Let Thine outstretched wing
>   Be like the shade of Elim's palm,
>   Beside her desert-spring."

CHAPTER XXIII.

MEGGIE CAXTON'S was not a character which
written words can readily describe. Nothing save
life's surface had ever been cultivated in her. The
deeper powers of her nature lay untouched. She had
been the object of indulgent love from her infancy—
more used to receive than to give. Yet there was a
charm about her young life, a brightness that lighted
up others; it seemed by constraint that every one
smiled upon her. Her mirth was never noisy, but it
was ever-flowing, rippling over life's pathway with a
melody; her absence always left a blank;—all missed
the voice of song, the gleeful eyes, the ready word
that made things pleasant, the willing step and hand
of Meggie Caxton.

But all was changed now. Meg had spoken her
denial; and at her words a chasm had opened. It
yawned wider, until a gulf lay between her past and
present life. For awhile she knew not what she had
done, nor hardly where she stood. But slowly it broke
upon her that her old life was gone, when Oliver
came not, and a secret fear held her back from the
Mill. When, after peace had calmed the wild
tempest of Oliver's feeling, he came to the farm
and spoke kindly to Meg, as if he would let her

feel no change, she only felt it the more because it was kind; each day made her more fully know what her past life had been—what her present had become. Sometimes she longed to rush back to his side, and say, "Forgive me the past, and let us both live again; for this is not life to me now!" And if she could have seen the deep anguish that still wound its slow current through his lonely heart, she would, she might have done so. But who will reveal the depths to one who has made them life's Marah? She saw him calm and kind, as though he took her at her word, satisfied to hold himself her brother. This was unendurable; and she resolved to shun him.

If Oliver went to the farm, she did not see him; she avoided every place where she was likely to meet him. The hours of service in the church had seldom but one thought, one feeling for Meggie—that Oliver was there, and how could she avoid the disquiet of meeting him! Oliver had accepted her "Never!"— he believed its repetition real on her part. He had accepted it from the Heavenly Father; he did not, therefore, seek her, seeing her unwilling to be found. The near or distant sight of her sent a faintness through his heart; the very thought of her unnerved him. All things were blended with her; she mingled in all that made life to him. All earthly joy was darkened; the mirth of the land was gone!

But from that night in which he was enabled to say, "Thy Will be done!"—even though it rent his heart as the tearing thence a rooted tree whose closely-woven fibres could not be withdrawn without rending in every part the heart in which they had rooted and grown—since that night his life had changed; its circle moved in another orbit. Meggie had been his central point on earth; his very life had flowed around her: but in that night in which he surrendered himself without reserve—in which, at the feet of his Father, he simply prayed without a single limitation in thought or feeling, "Thy Will be done on earth, as it is in Heaven!"—the current of his life, of his being was changed, and flowed to the Heart of God revealed in Jesus Christ. Slowly, with heavy tides of suffering, but surely, it circled round the Man Christ Jesus; He who had been the Man of sorrows, touched with the feeling of our infirmities; in His infinite sympathy, knowing the depth of suffering and underlying it, there was the balm of healing. The Christ of God had power and will to draw the bitter poison from life's woe, and to strengthen Oliver's suddenly-divided life by union with Himself. It was this rest of spirit, calming the countenance, and giving a depth of quiet to the whole character, which made Meg shrink away in deeper misery, at the tone and aspect strangely unlike her restless feeling.

Mistress Caxton had soon guessed the truth. It broke more slowly on the old farmer, whom his wife had feared to tell. He would ask Meggie where Oliver was? or what ailed him that he did not come? Meggie put off his questions. But one day he raised his eyes, and fixing them on her, said, "Hast thou blown out the candle that would have lighted thee through this world to the next?" Meggie was silent. "O foolish, wicked wean! I tell thee thy night will be dark, and thou wilt fret for its light when it cannot be kindled again!"

He said no more to Meggie, but to his wife he said, "Mind my word! I will have no fools of men come courting our Meggie's gay face! They that will have none of the best are like to come to the worst. If Meggie takes to folly, I will have her sent right away over the seas to her father. I will have no frivolations and dolorations here, you can see with half an eye; and I lay it on you to do what I say."

Mistress Caxton heard with a silent tear. The disappointment to her was a real one. But she thought to herself how a rank seed sown long ago will spring up and bear fruit in an evil hour! How dead-set he was against our poor boy taking Naomi—just a priceless woman was she! and now Meggie won't have her son—just such a man as she was a woman! "Poor Farmer!" she inwardly said, with a sigh; "he, at least, has reason to know that word is a true one, 'Whatsoever a man soweth, that shall he reap.'"

Meggie felt her grandfather's fond indulgence gone; her grandmother, always kind, looked as if a weight of care had suddenly fallen on her; but Meggie still said, "Why am I to marry Oliver because I have loved him as a brother?" She did not ask herself, "Can I ever be happy without the outward expression of his love?"

Oliver had been drawn more closely than ever to the aged Benoni, who had become his spiritual counsellor in this hour of need; and as winter set in he proposed to his father that they should ask Benoni to share their home. Oliver Crisp gladly consented, for Benoni was to him as a brother. The old man shed tears of thankful joy at a home—and such a home!—on earth for him; but nothing would induce him to take it as a gift. Why should he, he asked, do so, when he made much and spent little, and had no kindred save the one Family in Heaven and Earth? "Why should I keep this perishing gold together? I have no son but Oliver! Jerusalem, which is but a heap of stones—I have no wish now to be gathered to my fathers there. 'Our Father, which art in Heaven,' and the Jerusalem which is above—it is there my heart and treasure are; it is there I am already sitting in Heavenly places in Christ." So the home received Benoni, to be blessed and made a blessing there; but Meggie, who might have been its life and light, its joy and comfort, held her place outside.

The Lord leaves no man His debtor; whatever is done for His Name's sake receives a hundredfold even in this life. The child Oliver had ministered to the aged Benoni; and now Benoni's heart is his earthly shelter, counsellor, and rest. His father felt for him, but his calmer nature and comparative silence could not give all that Oliver had needed. The Jew had a depth of passionate feeling, a strong nature which the hard world had crushed under its feet, but through the scent of the living water it had revived, and poured forth its fervent affection to heaven and earth. The old man's heart, with its deep and tender feeling, and yet its strong, unwavering allegiance to our Father in Heaven, was the one earthly pillow of rest for Oliver's aching spirit.

The winter evenings came, but they did not sing their hymns. Oliver could not sing; he said his voice was gone. It was true it had lost its higher notes, but its deeper tones—were they not fuller and richer than ever? One early winter's day, a well-secured parcel arrived for Benoni. In the evening he directed Oliver to open it; it was a trumpet of finest quality. "You have a musical gift," said Benoni, "and must not leave it silent. There are jarring sounds enough on this earth—too many for any who have the gift to neglect it. This is the chosen instrument of the Lord God Almighty. By the voice of the trumpet he proclaimed the giving of the Law; the voice of the trumpet waxed louder and louder, as do the commands of the Law to the awakened conscience, until all the people trembled. It was the melody of the silver trumpets that called Israel to the door of the tabernacle, where stood the blood-sprinkled ark of the Mercy Seat; and the voice of the silver trumpets, in the day of their gladness and their solemn days, rose above their burnt-offerings and peace-offerings to Heaven. The same silver trumpets directed their march, for the Angel of the Covenant was in the pillar of the cloud. It is a sacred instrument, the only one that the Lord God will breathe through Himself, for it is written in Zechariah, 'He will blow with the trumpet.' It was the voice as of a trumpet that revealed the Lord to John in Patmos, and the same trumpet-voice that called him up into Heaven. It is the trumpet sound with which the Lord shall descend; and the trumpet is the voice of resurrection. It should be as dear to the Christian as to the Jew! It is long years since I have heard one," said Benoni. He had spoken with his hand laid reverently on it as it lay on the table. Now he raised it to his lips, and blew a blast loud and long; then changed to low tones that thrilled Oliver's soul. "I think I can be your master yet," said Benoni, as he laid it down with a smile. "We will have no more silence, my son, for the Lord God Omnipotent reigneth, and hath done whatsoever pleaseth Him."

They had no lack of melody now; to Oliver the rich tones of the trumpet were like Meggie's voice, which he ceaselessly longed for. His trumpet became a friend. Guests would often drop in of an evening—Dame Truman, when the evenings were lengthened; and Farmer Caxton sometimes; for he loved better than anything the evening hour of the Scriptures and Prayer at the Mill. He would sometimes say, "Meg, art coming?" but she ever said, "No," though her heart was there before him.

Farmer Caxton and Benoni were both men greatly changed, but the contrast was singular. Farmer Caxton had been a tall, stout, tough man, who fixed his iron look upon everyone. How often he had looked through the anxious buyer of corn, and seen that he could not refuse to buy at a higher price than he offered; wanting the corn too much to let it go. Then Farmer Caxton's grip was upon him, and the corn went at a price almost loss to the buyer, but Farmer Caxton had his gold. Now there was a stoop in the strong figure of the man, since his son's ruin at home, and a downcast look had come over him, but his face was a softened one, and no one could ask help of him in vain; even the worthless he could only deny by making them over to his wife's better knowledge. Benoni, in past years, had walked with a figure bending under the weight of his pack, with a shuffling step and a face that never seemed to look up. He now trod the ransomed earth a consciously-redeemed man; with a face lighted, and lifted on all. There was even a majesty, as well as meekness, about the aged Jew; he walked as one new-born to a kingdom, a yet uncrowned king on the earth. "He lifteth the beggar from the dunghill to set him among princes, to inherit the throne of glory."

The strength of manhood had come to Oliver early; the strong-built frame of his father, with his mother's height of person and her courteous manners, he was already felt to be the man of the place. His father sent him out on all business journeys; glad to create the variety he now felt necessary for Oliver, and to escape them himself. The custom grew more rapidly—the wind had as much to do as it could possibly accomplish, and Jonathan worked as a son under Oliver Crisp in the Mill.

Two yearly balls were given in the neighbouring town; one at Christmas, and one at the Whitsuntide holidays; for the world has its gaieties when the Church has its festivals. Mistress Caxton had always refused to let Meggie go; but Meggie was of age now; she persisted and went. It was her first public dance—a night, too often, of sad memories to many a town and village girl! It passed with its pleasant excitement, but it left Meggie with a more restless spirit than before. She did not see Oliver before she went, nor did she see him after her return; for it was her study to avoid him; but Oliver knew she was there—wherever she was she was followed by a sheltering prayer.

The leaves were thickening in the forest, the blossoms thick on orchard-trees, the hedges gay and the fields green, while birds poured forth their gladness in a ceaseless tide of song. Farmers had then no sparrow-club—at least it was not spoken of as now, nor did men poison singing-birds by hundreds on the garden-side. They shared the freedom of the forest glades. A restlessness had come over Oliver; you did not hear the thrilling trumpet at the sunset, or beneath the star-lit sky from the far Mill-steps, or from under the roof-tree. If he had heard ill tidings he did not say, he never told, but it was plain that his mind was burdened. His father thought he knew, and did not question why. Benoni was sure none knew, yet would not question, for well he knew, when ready for sympathy or counsel, Oliver's trustful nature would confide its trouble. The lover's eye had caught a glimpse of what none other might have seen.

One evening he followed, as he had often done before, the river's rocky bed; he crossed the bridge and skirted the forest; it had been his favourite walk in happier years. He entered the forest shade and passed the outer glades. He heard low voices in the distance, and bound as by a spell, he leaned against a tree. Two figures passed in the wood's winding pathway. He saw them, he heard them, and he saw and heard no more; his head swam as when a child he had tottered in faintness in the forest-shade. But his was manhood now, and he roused himself to greater strength. One look of anguish through the tracery of summer branches up to the calm evening sky, and he entered the pathway and followed slowly out of sight and out of hearing.

As the shadows deepened he saw, as he expected, one figure returning alone. A man, raised above him in station. Walking with hurrying step he came suddenly upon Oliver, in the narrow path between the tangled brush-wood.

" Stop, sinner ! " said Oliver, in a voice of terrible power.

" Who are you ? " demanded the other, " who dare address me so ? "

" I am Oliver Crisp, of the Mill, and I say, stand and hear me."

" Man, what mean you ? What right have you to block my way ? "

"The right of **a man to resist** the devil!" replied Oliver, in the white calm of his anguish.

"I will have you taken up for assault, libel, **and** villany.   Hold off, **I say!**"

"I will lay **no hand on you,**" replied Oliver. "Your life could yield no recompense for the evil you **have done.**   But in the Name of the sinner's Saviour, **I say, stand and hear me!**"

He stood, and Oliver, calm in **his** agony, said, "You are poisoning the soul of Meg Caxton, as the Serpent beguiled Eve under the trees of the garden. Rob not **earth** of its beauty, **and** Heaven of its **glory!   How dare** you pollute her soul, and darken **a jewel of the crown of the Eternal?** She is shielded **by prayer,** and will be **rescued for** ever! but you, where **will your lost soul repent?   O** man, by Him who is **Jesus the Saviour,** who died and rose between the **sinner and his sin, I charge** you **repent and forsake** your iniquity, **and thou, yes thou, shalt find mercy!**"

Oliver stepped aside and the other passed on.

Motionless for awhile, Oliver stood in **the** forest, to recover strength to return.   All **was** darkness in his soul, until a thought of **peace arose, dawning on** the terrible gloom.   Had he not **been used as a** shield, led across the pathway of **danger** to one dearer to him than life?   This **was a** hope, breaking the iron chain of despair; he returned home in the strength of **it.   Benoni** was walking in the garden beneath the spangled skies; as Oliver entered, Benoni stood, then taking Oliver's arm he led him on; they paced the garden-path silently awhile, then Benoni said, "The Lord is good unto them that wait for Him, to the soul that seeketh Him. It is good that a man should both hope and quietly wait for the salvation of the Lord. For the Lord will not cast off for ever, but though He cause grief yet will He have compassion, according to the multitude of His mercies." Then entering the house Oliver pressed Benoni's hand, and they parted, each to his chamber, neither to sleep.

Benoni to plead for Oliver, the son of his love. Oliver to wrestle in prayer that his Dove might be saved from the fowler's snare, that the snare might be broken and she be delivered. O human love, the type of Love Divine, which still endures through all, which many waters cannot quench, neither can the floods drown it! for love is strong as death. This was a sorrow none could share, his heart's desire that none might know except the One who knows us altogether, "yet loves us better than He knows." It was a woe that cast him alone on Him who understandeth our thoughts afar off, with whom is love to atone, power to help, grace to cleanse, and mercy to forgive. "Light is sown for the righteous, and joyful gladness for the true-hearted."

He who has once been cast upon God alone in sorrow that none can share, that none may know, has a depth of knowledge and experience of the God of his life that none can have with a more divided heart. Alone with God, able to pour out the soul before Him, able to receive from Him, in whom all fulness dwells, the supply of all his need; to find this enough in the soul's deepest anguish, is the grandest and noblest standing that the creature can have. It is breathed in the words, "My flesh and my heart faileth, but God is the strength of my heart, and my portion for ever."

> "Bear with the night, in hope of the morrow;
> Bear with the seed time, in hope of the corn;
> Bear with the winter, and bear with sorrow,
> In the hope of spring and a happy morrow.
> Bear, though the right be overborne,
> Though the thoughts thou lovest be theme for scorn,
> Though thy cause be weak and old and grey,
> Bear till it win to a brighter day.
> For falsehood and wrong shall not last for aye,
> They shall pass like snow from the mountain head,
> And truth and right shall be green in their stead."

CHAPTER XXIV.

A FEELING of sheltering care led Oliver again to the Farm. A terror had passed over Meggie's soul, and she was thankful to be again in his presence; a sense of safety came over her in it, and day after day it was her one hope he would come. He did go, yet she was silent—a further distance between her poor heart and his noble soul. She knew it, she felt it, she could never be his! yet there was nothing like his presence; her one longing that she could be always in it. She never shunned him now, but a shadow lay over her; her brightness was gone. She was a beautiful woman, and capable in every household need, and her time was never wasted, and her spirit less wilful, but her glee was all gone; and she looked graver than Oliver; while all things around her seemed grave and cold. How often she longed that her grandfather would but once say, "Meggie, child!" again, if only to soften her heart, which felt so hard; or that Oliver could be once again as he was before all that had passed between them.

One day, at Oliver's request, she went up to the Mill, but it did not fulfil her hopes. She could not rise to her place, nor rally her spirits. She said she could not sing—that she never sang now. The evening dragged heavily to all. Oliver walked with her home. The walk was as heavy as the evening had been. When they reached the bridge they stood there, for Oliver was arrested by the moonlight on the river; he leaned over the parapet, and looked down on the golden light of the hurrying tide.

"It is a long time since you and I stood here together, Meggie!" he said.

"You are so dull now!" Meggie replied; "there is no getting any cheer."

Oliver stood upright, and looked at her. "So I am, Meggie!" he answered; "I am always telling myself so. But look down on that shining river—how it leaps over the stones, and gains force by the blocks in its way, and keeps up a ceaseless music for all who will listen!"

"What has that to do with it?" said Meggie, glad to lead on the subject, which she felt was from Oliver's heart.

"O, Meggie! if you parted that river in two, and made separate streams, it would lose its life and force, and creep more sluggishly down?"

Meggie well understood the questioning tone, and she longed, even then, to say, "Let the stream of our lives flow as one!" She had felt the world's hollowness; the tempting words of flattery still rung on her ear. She was woman enough to know herself in danger, and Oliver's side was the tenderest shield; but she could not say it then. She was not ready to meet him with joy; a shadow lay over her heart—the shadow of willing contact with evil. She had lost her brightness of spirit; she had better go on as she was—at least, she thought, she would wait awhile.

And so she was silent, and the two, walking side by side, knew nothing of what was passing in either heart. Two hearts in full confidence may dwell in a silent communion of spirit, with continents and seas lying between them—may know what fellowship of spirit is when one is dwelling above, and the other on earth; but when once a separating feeling has arisen, they may be in the closest outward connection, and yet such a chasm between, that nothing can be known of what passes in each heart by the other; —so it was with Oliver and Meg.

As they crossed the green approach to the Farm, Oliver said, "Do you remember, Meggie, the wounded dove I tried to save when I was lost in the wood? I shielded it once, but my hand lost its power, and the cruel dog had it at last! Do you remember, Meggie?"

He did not see the deepening blush as she answered, "Yes;" and with a brother's kind "Good night," he left her at the door.

And so the months of autumn rolled on into winter's frost and snow, and the fires blazed on the hearths, and gathered families spoke of the world outside, which, though but a small world, was large to them. Only at the Mill-house no such converse passed, for there were none there to take up the village talk. A question arose at Mistress Caxton's fireside as to Margaret Butterly. Mistress Caxton said "she had a great respect, no one more, for Anthony Butterly and his wife. Theirs was the hand of the diligent that maketh rich; they had worked up from nothing, and brought up their children to work. Dick had turned out a bad fellow, but there was generally one crook in the lot; still, for all the respect that she felt, she must say she did not approve Margaret's dress. She could not understand how a sensible woman, such as Susan Butterly had proved herself to be, should encourage such dress in her daughter. She knew she was the youngest, and a bit of a favourite, but that was no reason why she should come out in such tawdry follies. Things that were well and fitting for the gentry—that might, as you say, have grown to them—when you hung them about a farm-house, did but make its daughters a gazing-stock, like stalking-horses or figures of fashion. One thing was certain—that the dress of your station was the only dress you could become or really look well in,—least-ways going up the ladder. She would not say anything as to coming down it; for she believed the gentry might look as much gentry as ever in the dress of a farm, or a farmer in the dress of the cottage. But for Margaret to go and copy the forms and the fashions of the gentry, was like feathering a barn-door fowl with the plumes of a peacock! For all she knew, the barn-door fowl might be the best of the two, but certainly not when bedizened with folly and finery."

Kezia replied, "Mother Dumbleton said she had heard say it was the gentry that helped Margaret to finery!" This much displeased Mistress Caxton, who said, "It is a poor way of working, from outside to in! Let the gentry instruct her to know her place and her station, that she may know what becomes it, instead of rigging herself out in their flashy favours. No one ever rose higher by taking tinsel for gold; but many a poor soul has lost all with the glitter!" At length, Mistress Caxton wound up by saying, "I do not intend to have new-fangled ways brought inside my doors; therefore, Margaret Butterly may just keep her distance until she learns to know true friends and true behaviour!"

The winter dragged on more heavily with Meggie than even the summer had done. She found that her mirthful fancy had no strength to stand under trouble; it was withered like a flower trampled under foot, and what had she left? a desolate heart! She had lived on the surface, and that now lay barren. Her Grandfather called her Meg now, not "Meggie, child," as he used to do. Oliver had dropped all the free warm converse of heart, all the delight in her that he had once made her feel; he spoke in kind tones it was true, but in quieter words, and she missed the tender glance of his eye. Yet she thought to herself that she could bring it all back any day, when the shadow that had fallen would be a more distant thing; when she would feel less afraid of Oliver knowing,—less oppressed by the presence of an undefined danger.

Whatever our aspects of thought and feeling may be, the seasons delay not their change. The warm

breath of spring wandered again over the hills
and valleys. The silvery buds of the birch-trees
glistened in the blue sky, and on all sides the larks
were singing unseen above in the blue. The may-
blossoms scented the lanes, the primroses clustered
in the green banks, and young life was rejoicing on
all sides. It was a season to wake every heart to its
gladness. The feeling of its beauty stole over
Oliver's soul; for nature, beneath the blessing of its
Maker, helps the sad-heart that will yield to its
influence. Even Meggie looked brighter in the busy
life of the spring; hers was a hand never idle, she
tended well all the creatures under her care. Old
people crept out in the sunshine, and the children
made garlands for the queen of the May.

Then a shock passed over the village,—a thrill of
horror. Margaret Butterly, the fair child of the Farm,
only sixteen years of age, was lost from her home, gone,
no one knew where, but all soon knew with whom,
when the wail arose from the forsaken and desolate.

The father sat transfixed in mute anguish on his
chair; her brothers rode wildly in different directions;
her mother wrung her hands in an agony; her burning eyes refused a tear. But friend and counsellor
there was none.

The lonely village stood appalled; there were
none to whom appeal could be made. Helpless
parents, helpless people. It was the third time of a
lost child from its home and its love. Oliver of the
Mill had been lost, sought, and found. Conrad of
the Castle had been reft away, and tears had dimmed

every eye for that noble heart. But now for the
child of the Farm it was woe dark as sin ; it was loss
that might be deep as hell. A sorrow on which hope
cast no gleam and Heaven gave no smile.

When Meggie heard the tidings she almost
fainted ; she staggered to her chamber, where after
awhile a torrent of tears gave relief. She could only
wonder how she herself had been drawn from the
snare, and grieve for another caught in an evil hour.
She had never known the strength of prayer, and
now brought in terror to her knees, she could only
weep her thankfulness for deliverance, and her
entreaty that Margaret Butterly might return to her
home. When Oliver heard it he could hardly
breathe. Had Meggie indeed been scarcely saved !
But this was not all. Had he rescued one that
another might fall ? How earnestly did he review
his words ! Could he have used that solemn
moment for other warning or entreaty than he had
uttered ? He did not know, yet feared he might
have erred. Such questionings may be seldom
unknown to deep natures ; their estimate of what
might be, what ought to be, being always deeper than
what is. One thing he knew,—that he had prayed ;
and when we plead with God for any, we may trust
to His grace and mercy our pleadings with man.

Over all the neighbourhood was questioning sorrow and dismay ; but there were none to act ; all
inquiry seemed vain, and the woe of a living death
darkened the life of the busy Farm.

Meggie still felt as if the ground were hardly safe

under her feet; as if she too might yet be swept away beyond recal. While night and day her thoughts followed the unhappy child, drawn from the shelter of her home none knew where, for her return she wept and prayed; nor thought nor felt how much she herself needed prayer, nor knew how her heart's prayer for another was softening her own proud, impetuous nature. And even as she thought on these things she found one earthly end to every feeling, and that end was Oliver. Yet too distant he seemed to her for any renewal of the past; each event had in her self-reproachful feeling left her further from him. Vainly she longed that she could blot out the present and restore the past; that she felt was impossible, and therefore she often longed that she could be far away; cross the seas to her unremembered parents, or find another home. She did not know the grace and love that can restore the years the canker-worm hath eaten; she did not know that the Heavenly Father can take up his lost and wandering child at any point. We may have left our earthly blessings withered in the path we have trod, but He who gave them ever liveth to make intercession for us, and can make our very loss yield in us the richest fruit.

What we look for we are likely to see,—what we seek for, to find. How often is this seen in earthly things!—" He gave them their desire, but He sent leanness withal into their souls." The world is ready for us, but for the Lord we often have to wait. God keeps us waiting to prove that no substitute can be found; that nothing apart from Him can satisfy; the world gives quickly, lest we should weigh its gifts too closely, and reject them for objects of infinite worth.

It was the summer of the year when a horseman came by a bridle-path upon a small secluded glade, a spot of wild but perfect loveliness; it lay off from the road a little way, but on the farm of Meggie's grandfather. She had gone to fetch her cows, and was returning through this summer glade, shaded by oak and ash; a sparkling stream flowed through it, and the depths of green were lighted up by the fourteen red cows, each one of the same rich colour, driven by Meggie with a giant fox-glove. It was a picture to charm any eye, for all was loveliness; and the quiet beauty of Meg Caxton's face was more impressive than its girlish mirth would now have been.

The rider asked his way, then enquired about the Farm, and finally requested short rest there for his horse; all he asked was granted, and he made himself welcome,—an easy thing to do in England's hospitable farms. He came again, which raised a thought, and yet again, which raised a question; a question as to who he was. He was an architect in the neighbouring town, residing with his mother and sisters. A few visits revealed his object; he asked the hand of Meggie Caxton, which she did not refuse him. He was a man whom, in earlier years, Farmer Caxton would have welcomed, but he looked coldly on him now; he felt that the best was lost, and what had he to do to welcome any other ? Mistress Caxton had a different feeling. She had shuddered over the thought of Margaret Butterly so often, that a man of known character was welcome to her,— welcome as a necessity of circumstances.

Meggie now had found the object on which her fancy rested. A lover, one who was to be her husband ; one fresh and unknown before. But what was its reality ? Far other than her undefined imaginations ? Too soon she found she had lost the reality and waited for the shadow only. It was true he often came, he talked, he wrote, he brought her gifts ; but evermore her heart was weighing the emptiness of all with the worth of all that had been. What was a paltry present, some tinsel finery or useless gift to Meggie, who had known Oliver's self-forgetfulness with every thought for her ? What were the words of flattery and promise, to one who had lived in the outpour of the love of Oliver's soul ? She must forget the one before she could love and honour the other.

Oliver would sometimes meet her lover at the Farm, and always spoke with kindness, and talked of passing things. Meggie wished he were not able to be kind and free ; thought all his love for her must now be dead, and tried the more to crush her own. Was she likely to know the inward strife midst which he sought to lend a brother's shelter to her still !

Amidst the wedding-gifts sent in came one on which, when she opened, she found on an inner paper inscribed, "**Meggie**, from her brother Oliver."

She scarce could read amidst her blinding tears. It was a wedding-dress, so suitable for her, and yet so costly, of finest woollen fabric and softest hue, with miniature white doves on finest tracery of branches, and, wrapped within, a Bible of clear type and perfect binding, with a clasp of silver, and on the clasp "Margaret Caxton" was engraved. Within was written, "Margaret, from her brother Oliver," and underneath, the words, "In all thy ways acknowledge HIM, and He shall direct thy paths."

This Meggie knew she had not done in any one of the past eventful acts. She felt as if she could not do it now. She refolded the parcel; none should see it. The dress she could not wear; it would just break her heart. The Bible, his gift, she could not read, that would just break it too. She did not know that *that* was the one thing she needed—a broken heart, which God will not despise. She only wrote in answer—

"Meggie thanks her brother Oliver, whom she will ever love," and hid away her gifts and waited for her expected lover. That evening he did not come; he had never missed an appointment before. No tidings followed for some days,—days of strange suspense; then he wrote to say that an opening with better business-prospects had called him suddenly to London, and he would write again. Again they waited. Meggie wrote, but no reply; they sent through his clerk, but no answer came. Meggie waited in burning indignation; her heart that had never been warm in love was hot in anger.

Oliver came to offer his aid ; she would not see him, and refused to have any further inquiry made. But after a delay of weeks a letter came, saying, that his present position was one requiring full attention ; he must for the present give up all thoughts of settling in life ; he was sorry for what had passed ; present circumstances were then quite unforeseen, and he feared that the position he was likely to fill might not prove suitable to one brought up in the retirement of country life ; he should ever think of her with affection, and " begged to subscribe himself ever her friend."

Meggie tore the letter to shreds and threw it in the fire ; then, spent with all the mingling feelings of weeks, laid her head upon her grandmother's shoulder, and her consciousness fled. She knew no more for days. The struggle and the conflict of years of feeling, with the grief cherished for Margaret, and hopes of happiness she all the while felt were vain for herself, had proved too much for her, and rest on her pillow was the blessing given. Yet when consciousness and memory woke, and she saw her kind and patient grandmother sitting by her side, and Kezia moving about, the feeling of rest and home was lost in the sense that she was now a forsaken woman ; cast off and rejected. She felt it too terrible to bear ; how could she face the village ? how could she meet Oliver ? The only refuge would be her distant parents and Canada. It was hard to leave her aged grand-parents when most they needed her ; harder far never to see Oliver again ; truly as she thought him now the noblest of men ; the greater in her eyes because the joyousness of youth had mellowed into manhood's calmer grace. His home appeared a heaven on earth after all she had passed through, but *that* she felt was lost for ever. He would see her now a rejected woman, cast off as not worthy to share the lot of one whom none could compare in excellence to him. The further from lost happiness, the less, she thought, should she be reminded of it. Every tie that had endeared life, every association that bound her, even the presence and love of Oliver as a brother, must be cast aside, because he could not now be her lover.

CHAPTER XXV.

"Who is that under the casement, Kezia?" asked Meggie, the first day that she sat up in her chamber. Through the open lattice many sounds of the farm came in, and amongst them one voice that Kezia heard not.

"It is only master out there; he is just home from market, and some of the men have waited to see him."

"Kezia, just go to the window and look; I am sure some one else is there!"

Kezia gave a glance. "Oh, yes; 'tis Master Bucklebury come about buying the roan filly."

But a voice came in upon Meggie's ear that was not of this world's business, but of that world's love to her. It was gone again, and there was silence in her heart; for the men that talked of yesterday's work and to-morrow's, their voices were nothing to her—they broke not the dreary stillness that had reigned around her so long; they were less than the lowing of her cows, or the bark of the household dog. But that one voice brought back to her dreary heart the dreams and the gladness of childhood; and in her weakness as she sat propped up with pillows, she fancied herself back in its happy life; stepping over the slippery stones of the river flowing low in its summer-bed, and Oliver holding her hand and taking the worst himself, that she might walk safely over; and she could not weep—too weak for tears, but she wished in her heart that that river were life, and her hand in Oliver's to lead her through!

" Has any one been here to-day, Granny?" she asked, when Mistress Caxton sat by her bed.

" Any one, child! the world goes on the same, and the back-door latch is on the go all the day."

" I thought I heard Oliver's voice," said Meggie, and her pale face flushed she knew not why.

" 'Tis like you did, he is not long away. Morning, noon, and night he has crossed the river, to hear of you.   I have told him he may just rest contented away, for the turn has come for the better, and you'll be looking up now."

" Don't close the lattice, Kezia; the night is warm, and I see the stars as I lie. I am tired of sleep, and shall wake and watch."

" I dare not for the life of me let the damp in."

" It is only the evening dew, Kezia, and the breeze blows fresh: the day has been hot, and the freshness will give me strength."

" Then I will leave it awhile, and come back again when the night has cooled the air."

The stars were shining large in the blue heavens, and the nightingales sang in the old ash-trees that grew round about the homestead, and the breath of flowers came in on the night wind; but it was not the song of the birds, nor the breath of the flowers, nor shining stars, that stilled Meggie's soul—it was the thrilling tones of a far-off strain, the trumpet's notes she heard.

In two days she crept down-stairs, almost too weak, yet longing to be there. When left alone with her grandfather, he said, in his old tone of tenderness, "Meggie, child, I would not be so sore of heart. It is mercy's hand that held thee back. It may show thee the curse of money! It is the gold he is clutching now. Meggie, my poor wean, thee would have found it a hard pillow to lay thy young head on—a heart choked with the base clog, and hungering for more. Meggie, child, 'tis mercy stops thee!"

And Meggie felt that she could not leave her grandfather, all that had ever made life dear in the Farm came back with that "Meggie, child!" Meggie sat in the chimney-corner all the next day, but Oliver did not come. Now he knows my life is safe, thought Meggie, he does not care! Again she thought, If he should ask me now as his bride, it might only be from pity, seeing me forsaken and cast away. I hate to be pitied! I would never marry a man who pitied me, and I am quite sure that Oliver must.

So in her folly she steeled her heart once more against the love that was true, with this fresh invention of "fancy's mis-shaping tool." "He that trusteth in his own heart is a fool," and countless thousands have proved it, blocking out and warding off the blessed reality of love in daily life by some false mist

·of self that bent the ray of affection's light, making it appear a broken beam.

Early the next morning, while still in her chamber, a letter came to Meggie. Her trembling hand could scarcely open it. She read,—

"MY SISTER MEGGIE,

"I hope this will find you better, as it leaves me, your devoted brother. I know you have been troubled in mind. I wish I could speak to you like a comforter! There is One who can do this; I believe He will bring your heart to Himself. Meggie, this has not been the hand of man, it is the hand of your Saviour. He has been a Saviour to you against your will. I have seen that you can never truly give yourself to another until you have given yourself up to Him. We are not our own to give; we are bought with a price. All our giving will come in the end to losing. But when the Lord gives it is for ever and ever!

"Meggie, have you no will to be His who loved you, and gave Himself for you? You will never be truly your own until you are His. You will never find yourself until you find Him. I have seen it is all a losing game that we do not take from Him. We may think we are getting and holding; but for all that, it is just slipping away, and some day we shall open our hand and find it empty.

"Meggie, I can hear a voice calling you, 'Come unto Me, and I will give you rest.' He stops you short in your own way, that you may give

Him your hand and let Him lead you in His way.
I can see that the Lord Jesus won't let you alone.
That's the end of all hope, when we be let alone to
wander and perish!   Other things may turn up, and
you may get a step further, and find it too late to
turn back, and have a long learning of a short lesson.
O, Meggie! we have been parted for many a day,
for I am not walking now where you are if you are
still in the way of your own heart.   I have seen Him
who, when once you have looked on, you will never
leave Him more, for He is fairer than the children
of men.   When once you are His, you will let Him
do what He will with His own; and He will do you
only good, and that continually.   I hope I shall see
you soon.   I have just waited, for I thought you
might like these few words on paper, from your
devoted brother,   OLIVER."

This letter was not what Meggie expected.   She
read and re-read, and sat and considered.   The
words were plain against her, and yet there breathed
from them a comfort and peace.   There was a hope
for her—not Oliver—but a hope higher than earth.
There was a heart waiting to win her—not Oliver's
—but One all power and love.   There was One
to whom the shadow of evil was no block, for she
knew that He could wash the reality away.   She
thought of Oliver's gift, never opened since the day
she received it.   She took out the parcel, she did not
heed the dress now, but the Bible.   She opened it,
the ribbon was in at Matthew xi., and the words

were underlined in red ink, " Come unto Me, all ye that labour and are heavy-laden, and I will give you rest." "Take my yoke upon you and learn of Me, and you shall find rest unto your souls ; for My yoke is easy and My burden light." Meggie said to herself, "Oliver thought, then, that I should be just weary-hearted and restless, but how did he know? Ah! but there is One who knows that I am weary-hearted, and it is He who says 'Come unto Me, and I will give you rest.'"

Meggie kneeled, but felt as if she knew not how to pray. All that at length she could say was, " I am weary, O Saviour; I come to Thee!"

There was rest in the prayer, for it breathed the heart to Him who is its only rest. She put the letter in her pocket, the Bible in her drawer, and went down. She stirred about a little until all was clear, and then went again to her chamber, and sat by her casement, reading Matt. xi. Every word went home to her heart. She came to the verse, "At that time Jesus answered and said, I thank Thee, O Father, Lord of Heaven and earth, because Thou hast hid these things from the wise and prudent, and hast revealed them unto babes !" Oh, to be a child again in heart! how often she had longed for that ;—to lose the sense of all this weary questioning of earthly love, and live again in unquestioning affection! " Revealed to babes !" Meggie knew the text of Holy Scripture, and re-membered the words, " Except ye be converted and become as little children, ye shall not enter into the

Kingdom of Heaven." But how can these things be? The answer was there. "All things are delivered unto Me of My Father, and no man knoweth the Son but the Father; neither knoweth any man the Father save the Son, and he to whom the Son will reveal Him." Then it is the Father whom the Son will reveal to babes! O blessed hope, to see, to know, to have the Father! I, who never knew a father's love! My father left me, but the Father whom the Lord Jesus reveals to babes has said, I know He has said, "I will never leave thee nor forsake thee!" The prayer was ready on Meggie's lips, "Lord, show me the Father!" but she heard the voice of Jesus saying, "Have I been so long time with you, and yet hast thou not known Me? He who hath seen Me hath seen the Father!" Wondrous thoughts of heavenly light and love, breaking in on Meggie's long-darkened, half-dead heart! The great thoughts rolled in like waves of the mighty ocean, and seemed almost too much,—not gloomy, troubled waves, but glowing in light divine. Who knoweth what it is for a poor empty heart, robbed of its sense of early purity, of love, of home and hope, to find such blessings flowing in with the fulness of the ocean-tide!

She sat by her low casement awhile with the open Bible, in deepest feeling rather than in thought. Then calm and rested she read again, "Come unto Me, all ye that labour and are heavy laden, and I will give you rest." What rest? Why, it must mean what she had so long wanted—rest of heart! It must mean what He was giving her now, filling her empty soul with Himself. But was she sure it was for her? Yes; it said, "All ye!" But had she really come? On this she pondered and read again. "All things are delivered to Me of my Father." "All things." Then she herself was one of those "All things" which God had given to his Son, our Lord Jesus Christ! Could it be that she had not to wait to be given, but had been given long ago, and was His already, in His hand, in His heart, to save her, to keep her for ever?

The blissful fact was there. "He says it, 'All things are delivered to Me of my Father;' then I am His, and I have just been pulling and dragging to get away if I could, and did not know He was holding me back and would not let me go! I see it! I see it! I am His, and His I will be!" And she threw herself at His feet with overflowing tears of repentant sorrow; and the love was deeper than the sorrow; for the sorrow was temporal, but the love of God shed abroad in the heart by the Divine Comforter is eternal.

Meggie could not leave her chamber again that day; still weak, the infinite love, the eternal joy, had overpowered her. She laid her head on her pillow, too exhausted for food. But the same kind care was ever ready at the Farm; she was tended again as in the days of past illness, and as a tired child weeps itself to sleep on its mother's arm, so Meggie wept herself to sleep in His tender keeping, whose love is greater than a mother's. She was down the next morning; pale and wan was the face that had once been so bright in its bloom; but a light on her brow, her eyes a quiet sunbeam, and the smile of love and peace on her lips, which had so long worn a heavy discontent.

"Blessings on thee, Meggie, child! Where hast thou borrowed a face?"

"O, grand-daddy," said Meggie, "I was just weary-hearted, and I have heard Him who speaks to the weary, and He has given me rest!"

"Well, that's just the blessing. Ye sore needed it, child, and 'tis just His way to give to them that have need. And you are a deal better off, if you have given up to Him, than if you had all a prince could bestow. You will never see the wrong side of that blessing; it will lie warmest at heart when the wintry day blows the coldest. There is a beginning of it, as you have found, but there is never an end. Himself hath said it—'None shall pluck them out of My hand.'"

In quiet hours Meggie returned to her treasured Bible. As she read and thought on these things, the light that shone on her soul grew steadier, and every time she read she saw something she had not seen before. She had reached the Divine words, "Who is My mother, and who are My brethren? And He stretched forth His hands towards His disciples and said, Behold My mother and My brethren! For whosoever shall do the will of My Father which is in Heaven, the same is My brother, and sister, and mother." The word Brother had a heart-arresting force for her now. Could it be that such was the tie that the Lord of Glory would own? "My sister!" Could it be from the Divine lips of the Son of God? There it lay, in the page of Divine inspiration, "My sister!" breathed by Him to whom all power was given in Heaven and earth, and whose love passeth knowledge.

She could not read on. A word will sometimes fill the heart to overflowing. But as she sat in the summer evening, watching the steady soothing flight of the birds above the trees to their nests, the grace and glory of the divine words, "My sister!" echoing everywhere around her—she saw Oliver crossing the green with her grandfather. She laid her Bible back in the drawer and went down. No wish was felt now to avoid him; glad at heart, glad in face, and in word, to see him again. He looked at her as if with surprise, then said, "O, Meggie, it is comfort to see you again!" Again he looked, and she met his earnest eyes with a smile, for she knew he saw in her face that all was changed now to her, from earthly unrest to the peace that passeth understanding. "It was a good letter you sent me, Oliver," she said, "but 'the Bible you gave me has spoken home to my heart."

"O, Meggie, can it be? Are we one in His love?" And she answered, "He has given me rest, forgiving me all trespasses, and filling my soul with His peace." And the old look of deepest tenderness came back to Oliver's eyes as he said, "It is like life from the dead to hear this from thee!" And he

did not say, " My sister Meggie " any more, and
Meggie was glad. But Jesus had said to her heart,
" My sister ! " and He had given her rest, and would
teach and enable her to do in all things the will of
His Father in Heaven.

  " One there is above all others—
    Oh, how He loves !
  His is love beyond a brother's—
    Oh, how He loves !
  Earthly friends may fail or leave us;
  One day soothe, the next day grieve us,
  But this friend will ne'er deceive us—
    Oh, how He loves !

  " Through His name we are forgiven—
    Oh, how He loves !
  Backward shall our foes be driven—
    Oh, how He loves !
  Best of blessings He'll provide us,
  Nought but good shall e'er betide us,
  Safe to glory He will guide us—
    Oh, how He loves ! "

CHAPTER XXVI.

THERE came at length a change; a brighter day dawned on that lonely village than it had seen for at least a century. The darkness had rolled in heavy clouds away, and light divine broke over all the land. Who can tell the blessing, when the pastor is a minister of "the true sanctuary which the Lord pitched, and not man." The minister came at first to the Castle, and was seen the next day walking down the wooded slopes of the park to the valley in which the village lay; he wore a broad-brimmed hat, beneath which his silver locks flowed freely; his face was such an one as angels might love to gaze on; but dearer still to the eyes of the suffering and sorrowful. Within his open coat lay the broad and snowy frills of cambric, fastened together by one sparkling gem. He wore silver knee-buckles and silver buckles to his shoes, and walked with a silver-headed ebony cane. The feeling of the villagers who looked on him was, Who is this? It was a question soon answered.

The old clergyman's steps were closely followed by the large collie-dog of the Castle. Nero was a dog of unsociable manners, and supposed to be of no interest to any one except as a guard; but the old clergyman had said to him, "Nero, wilt come shepherding with me?" and the dog bounded forward and they went together. From that first day Nero watched for this his first friend, and always accompanied the pastor's steps. He never quarrelled at the farms, nor showed any unseemly curiosity at the cottages, but lay down outside the door, waiting quietly.

This aged pastor was truly one whom having looked on once, you would wish to look on again. Day after day you might see him in the early afternoon coming down amongst the homes of the people. He was tall in person, but with the slight stoop so often seen in those whose heads are bent above the beds of suffering. His step was the gentle tread that had learned its measure by the couch of pain. All were struck by his appearance, and won by his manner. When he took off his hat as he entered a cottage, and they looked on his head, white and shining almost as snow in the sunbeam, and heard him say in kind tones, "My people!" or "My friends!" or "Dear sheep of the flock! whom I trust the Good Shepherd has gathered, or will gather!" all thought, and some said, "'Tis a father indeed!"

In his call at the Mill he sat long with Oliver Crisp and Benoni. When the distance was too far for walking, he was driven in the Castle pony-carriage—in some way he reached all. Farmer Caxton said, "He never had set eyes on one whom he should take to come so near to the Good Shepherd

Himself!" To Meggie the pastor said, "Is thy heart opened to attend to the things that are spoken in the Scriptures to thee?" and Meggie answered, "Yes;" and the venerable face lighted up with a smile and said, "The Lord bless thee, and keep thee!" Dame Truman wept under his good words when he called upon her, and she said, "Seventy years and more I have lived in this place, but never did I see nor hear tell of such a blessing as this! Who could have thought it!" Mother Dumbleton had many tales to tell, which she had heard on one side of the parish, and told on the other. She had heard say that he lived when the martyrs were burnt (only changing where for when), and the people did say he would have been burnt himself, only he was always hidden, so that when they went to take him in one place he was safe in another! which she said was not hard to believe, for she had not met the person already with whom he had not had a word, let them bide where they might. Also Mother Dumbleton said, it was plain the Castle dog knew it; "for if there was not some miracle of mystery, a hasty beast as he was would never lie quietly at his feet by the half-hour together, without so much as turning an eye on your cat!"

But a greater surprise was to follow. The folk scarcely believed their own eyes when they saw the venerable man riding down the village street on Bavieca! It could not be! yet it was! Bavieca had run loose in the park—no one thought to see him ridden again; but the old clergyman had soon made acquaintance with the noble steed, now grown old; and had asked to be allowed to ride him on his more distant visits. The grooms said, "There never was but one hand he would answer to." "Ah!" he replied, "I am a soldier, not less than a shepherd, and noways afraid but he will answer to me!" And they came down the rocky street together, with slack rein; the rider seated at ease with unconcerned eye, and Bavieca attentively choosing out the way, with arched neck and gentle step, seeming glad of such a service of love. His rider just laid his hand on his neck when he stopped to speak to any one; but he was soon through the village, and on the high road at pleasant speed. The grooms had run to view amid the trees, and returned in surprise. The people said, "Did you ever hear tell such a thing?" and Mother Dumbleton remarked, "Did not I say it was a miracle of mystery?"

From that day Bavieca served his new master, and served him well. There are those still to be seen whom creation owns, as if some trace of the sceptre given in Eden remained with them yet; a few links of the broken chain yet to be re-united when "the wolf shall dwell with the lamb, and the leopard shall lie down with the kid, and the calf and the young lion and the fatling together, and a little child shall lead them."

There was much discourse in the village, and many wished to hear him speak in the pulpit; but as yet he was only a worshipper. One of his first calls was an evening visit to Susan Butterly and her husband. They were seated in their farm-kitchen, and received him coldly. "Lost!" was the one word that was always wringing anguish from the heart of the mother, and finding low echoes of trouble in the soul of her husband. The Pastor took their hardly-offered hands kindly in his, and then sat down beside them. "I know your trouble," he said, "too well! too well! It is a trouble which may shut the lips and close the heart."

The parents looked silently into the fire and shook the head, but made no reply. There they all sat silent awhile, for their grief was very great. At length the Pastor gently said, "There is One with whom is power, comfort, and hope. I never yet found the sorrow He could not reach the bottom of, nor a wound too cruel for His hand to heal. God says of Him, 'I have laid help upon One that is mighty.'"

Still all was silence. Several of the family were there, and the servant-girl sewing on the other side of the farm-kitchen. Then the Pastor rose and said, in the calm, tender tones of authority, "Let us seek comfort and help from Him who alone is able to give it. Have you in your house any other beside those in attendance here?" "Call in the woman," said Susan Butterly, and Mother Dumbleton drew down her sleeves and came in. The minister reached down the Bible from the high shelf where it lay, lightly blowing off the dust, and laying it on the table opened and read, "What man of you having an hundred sheep, if he lose one of them,

doth not leave the ninety-and-nine in the wilderness
and go after that which is lost until he find it. And
when he hath found it he layeth it on his shoulders,
rejoicing. And when he cometh home he calleth
together his friends and neighbours, saying, Rejoice
with me, for I have found my sheep which was
lost."

He paused, and then repeated again in tones of
deep feeling, "'Rejoice with me, for I have found my
sheep which was lost.' He, the Good Shepherd,
goeth after it until He finds it! Have you considered
that His tender eyes rest at this moment on your
lost child? He sees her more clearly than you and
I see each other. He feels for the lost one far more
than even you can. He is able to save to the utter-
most all that come unto God by Him. And when
he saves He rejoices over the lost; which, perhaps,
even you could hardly do if at this moment brought
before you. Raise your eyes and your heart to this
tender, this merciful One, mighty to save. Your
poor eyes have been straining on into the darkness
where you could not see her, nor trace a step she
had taken. Look on Him who is shown to us here,
Jesus the Saviour! When you look on Him, you
look on One who looks on her—see how near this
brings you! You look upon Jesus, and He looks
upon her. It is weary, heart-breaking work to look
on into the distance, vainly longing that you could
see and could know. Your poor wandering hearts
find no rest. Look unto Jesus, and the Holy Spirit
will give you light to behold Him. His eye follows

her. His arm can save and restore. His heart is waiting to receive."

> "Come home! come home!
> You are weary at heart,
> For the way has been dark,
> And so lonely and wild :
>   O prodigal child!
> Come home, oh, come home!

> " Come home! come home !
> For we watch and we wait,
> And we stand at the gate,
> While the shadows are piled :
>   O prodigal child !
> Come home, oh, come home !"

Then inviting them to pray, he kneeled in their midst.

"O Saviour, Son of Man, Son of God! Who came to seek and to save that which is lost! Thou seest the lost one for whom we come to Thee. Within the home before Thee here are father, mother, brothers, sisters, and servants, but where is the lost one? Thou knowest where, Lord; Thou knowest her downsitting and uprising. Thou understandeth her thoughts afar off. Thou knowest her desires ; it may be tears, repentings, and prayers. We look on Thee, and Thou lookest on her. Thou art able to save and deliver. Thou art able to cleanse from all sin. Thou canst yet make her holy in heart and life. We commit her to Thee. Thou wilt rejoice over the lost one found, more than over the ninety-and-nine that went not astray. Save her !

Lay her on Thy shoulder, that, gathered to Thy fold, she may be Thine for ever. And, seeing we may be lost to Thee when we are not lost to one another, look down on this home, on the dear father and mother, on each son, daughter, and servant. If they be lost to Thee, draw them home into the arms of Thy love and mercy, that we may each one, absent and present, be found eternally with Thee, O Father, through Thee, O Lord Jesus, our Saviour. Amen."

He left them with words of comfort.

. Mistress Tibby was now in her ninetieth year. Oliver always went over to see her when harvest was crowning the year. On these occasions all the old scenes were renewed in his memory :—the forest, the little glade where he laid down and slept, the man with the evil eyes and the gun, the ragged children, and the dog who stole his dove; with poor Aleppo's death, all these scenes rose in vivid remembrance. The corn had grown in the same field and been reaped every year, and the very sheaves had stood in the same place where he sank that day in exhaustion. The farm in the Dell looked the same, but Mistress Tibby never visited her harvest-fields now, she sat in her arm-chair by the fire both winter and summer. This year Oliver found her by the fire-side, the wood batlings glowed red and fell in white ash on the hot stones, which kept warmth in her limbs. Oliver stabled his horse, gave him his corn, as if it were home, and then went in.

"I thought, may be, it was you," said Mistress

Tibby, "when you glanced by the door. I can't make out any distance now. Are ye just about as ye should be ?"

"All well, thank you." And the tall, stalwart man sat down on the low form by Mistress Tibby as when a child saved by her care. He took her hand tenderly in his, and said, "How be you keeping, Granny ?"

"Well, well, I am just holding on; the Lord knows for why; but it can't be for long, and sometimes I be just a-wearying to be gone, for it is a deal better there than it can ever be here; but I must just wait with patience His time."

Mistress Tibby had a beautiful hand, it might have graced the chords of a harp in its day. Her features were refined, and her mind had a tone of elevation that might have been trained to adorn any sphere. But she had been born, lived, and was now waiting to depart in an obscure little farm, with no social influences to draw forth her powers. How many such souls will expand in brightness and glorious beauty, when this mortal shall put on immortality !

Oliver raised the dear hand, now stiffened and a little swollen, to his lips, and reverently kissed it, with a silent blessing, remembering how that hand had fed him and soothed him to rest.

"This hand has done its day's work now, Granny," he said.

"No! no! Not yet!" she replied, her old spirit waking up; "it's no laid to rest yet ! He knows why I wait, and I shall know hereafter. We brought nothing but sin with us into this world, and we must leave that behind us afore we be ready to go."

"But, Granny, you left that behind you long ago. You know it is written, 'The Lord hath laid on Him the iniquity of us all.' You believe that, I know. When you think of your sins you must look upon Jesus; the Lord laid them on Him, and they can never be found any more, for His precious blood has washed them away."

"That is good—I believe it! I believe it! It lies clear as you say it; only sitting on here I sometimes have a fear."

"Do you remember what the Bible says upon that, Granny?"

"No, I cannot say I do; my memory seems short, and my eyes are but dim, I cannot read for myself; and my poor Matty is just messing and muddling about the best way she can; and then when she sits down a bit, and I want her to read, she just drops off to sleep at any word as it happens; and it scares me to know why she stops on a sudden. So thinks I to myself, I'll just not ask her again; but I do when the time comes—I am sore longing to hear."

Oliver got the old Bible and turned to the 56th Psalm, and read, "What time I am afraid I will trust in Thee!" He read it two or three times, and Mistress Tibby repeated, "What time I am afraid I will trust"—"in Thee," said Oliver.

"Aye, 'in Thee!' Where else could we trust? Then it does not seem a sin to be sometimes afeared?"

"Not a sin if it does not break our trust, Granny. Sure there is nothing the blessed Lord who died for us cares for, like the trust of our poor hearts! I seem to have been learning that, Granny. He can get our best service done some other way; but no one else can give Him the trust of my heart and yours. It is written over and over again that we should trust in the Lord. Our best doings are just sinful and poor; but we can trust Him with all our heart, and that I know pleases Him best."

"Does it?" said Mistress Tibby; "then I will. Yes, I will! Why, I have just been afraid wholly to trust; it seemed taking it too easy for a poor sinner like me."

"But, Granny, does not He say, 'Come, buy without money and without price'? The price has been paid—it cost the life-blood of the Lord Jesus— it is all paid, and we have only to take it in trust, that all is paid by His death!"

"Now all that you say was just what I wanted to hear. I just wanted somebody to come and say, 'Mistress Tibby, trust Him!' And to think the poor weakling I saved should have been preserved to say that! I, strong and able, was feeding you, as weak as a babe; and now I am come to my farthest, you in your strength sit here feeding and nourishing me to life everlasting. I sometimes get a glimmer of a light that shineth brighter than any light here ; but I have a deep, swelling river to pass through, I know."

" No, Granny—no river. What makes you think so ? "

" Aye, yes—a river," she still said, " and may be, I shan't feel the bottom."

"That's not written in the Bible, Granny."

" Yes, I think so," she said. " Does it not say, ' When thou passest through the rivers ' ? "

" Yes, you have passed through them many a time when trouble came in like a flood ; that's over and gone, and the good God brought you through, and they did not overflow you. Now you have only to be carried home in the arms of Jesus."

" But not through a river ? " asked the aged saint again, earnestly.

" No, no river. The blessed Saviour says, ' Even to old age I am He, and even to hoar hairs will I carry you ; I have made and I will bear ; even I will carry and will deliver you ! ' He bore the sheep right home on His shoulder, and never laid it down again. O, Granny, He says, ' My sheep hear My voice, and I know them, and they follow Me, and I give unto them everlasting life ; and they shall never perish, neither shall any pluck them out of My hand.' Won't you trust Him, Granny ? "

" I do, I do ! There is no cold, dark river, nothing but the arms of Jesus."

" Yes, Granny, Himself hath said it, ' Underneath thee are the everlasting arms ! ' You can only be where He carries you, and you won't fear any evil in the arms of Jesus?"

"Good words! good words!" she replied; "will they stay by me? I crave that they may."

"Yes, Granny, they are the words of the Lord Jesus, and He has promised that the Holy Spirit shall bring His words to your remembrance. He knows your hunger and thirst for them, and He says, ' you shall be filled.' "

"Does He? 'Tis just like Him! He knew it when He sent you to-day. I am thinking I shall not hear your tongue again."

"Oh, but I am vexed I have been so long away. I will just come once a month and see you; and if you want me sooner you send John on the old grey. Never mind harvest, that will be gathered in right enough, and the old grey will do the distance every bit as well as my young one."

"I am thinking I shall be the first sheaf gathered in, but I don't rightly know," said Mistress Tibby.

"Why, Master Oliver," said Matty Trundel, hurrying in as if she felt that all responsibilities of business now lay with her, "I saw you come off the road ever so long ago, and you have not had a bit of anything to take! This comes of being o'er busy; there is no doing of one thing but you are slighting another."

"No," said Oliver, in his pleasant tone, "when we do one thing as to the Lord, He takes care of the other things. We have been better off here than any feeding could be."

"Aye, that's a sure thing," said Mistress Tibby. "The Bread of Life!"

Three weeks had not passed away when the old grey came to the Mill door. Mistress Tibby thought herself departing, and craved to see Master Oliver. Oliver hastened; his good horse soon distanced the grey, and he reached the farm-house in the Dell before he was expected.

His heart beat as he saw the open door—should he see her again? A labourer ran and took his horse, and he entered in; he waited a few moments alone. How much passed through his mind in those moments! Her hand and her tending had been more maternal than anything he had known. The ready roughness of K. in her earlier years (she was a softened woman now), and the half-distant stiffness of his own grandmother, were not in Mistress Tibby. As a child he had felt the depth and power of her nature, even as he felt the depth and strength of Benoni's. In the better world to come how many a nature amongst the lowliest in place here will expand in a greatness and dignity for which it has had to wait, until the surroundings that shut it in here should enlarge for it there. And we have reason to fear that many to whom resources were open, but who shut themselves within self's narrowing limits, will find that the expansive powers entrusted to them but not improved, are now lost talents, that cannot be recovered again.

The wood-embers burned low on the stones; little cups were keeping hot as if the food were no longer required. He heard a step, and the chamber-door opened; it was a neighbour. Oliver made no inquiry, but went in. Matty Trundel stood by the bed with a cup and spoon in her hands, and her tears dropping on the white sheet that covered her mistress. Oliver was used to sickness, he had been his own Granny's best nurse. "She does not need that," he said, gently, to Matty Trundel, as he took her place by the bed. He kneeled down on one knee, and laid his hand on the hand that had done its work now. "Let the child sleep," said Mistress Tibby, "only give a wee drop when he wakes." Her thoughts had gone back to the event of her life that had most stirred her heart. Oliver took the cold hand and pressed it to his lips. She knew him then, for none had ever done that with the half-stern and reserved Mistress Tibby but Oliver. "No river! no river!" she said, "but the arms of my Saviour! I trust Him, I do!" And she opened her eyes and looked on the face of the strong man as he knelt by her side; he was nearer and dearer to her heart than anything here. He moistened her lips, made Matty Trundel lay her cold limbs in hot flannel, and there he watched until this dim light of earth was lost in the light everlasting.

The reapers gathered in the sheaves. Then they bore to the grave a nobler seed than any earthly harvest can gather—a shock of corn fully ripe, whose fruit should yet be green on the earth, and stand in the glory of Lebanon.

CHAPTER XXVII.

THE stone-masons were busy preparing to build a small house on the rising ground overlooking the church. "I cannot dwell," the good man had said, "except in a pilgrim-tent of my own,—a dwelling hallowed to His presence, who is my sun and my shield!" He thus hoped to escape all the evil associations which hung round the old rectory,—that so the new ministerial life might begin, from the very first, quite apart from the shadow which had darkened so much of the past. At length the church was left to his care; the people won by his tenderness and grace filled the building in their wish to hear him there. The deep tones of his voice, mellowed by age, breathed forth the hallowed Liturgy. He needed no printed page, for a life-time had engraven it on his heart; it was offered as fervently to Heaven as if then first breathed forth from his soul. When the Holy Scriptures were read, his utterance cleared up the meaning to many an uninstructed mind; shedding fresh light, and showing up depths in the heavenly truth to those to whom they were familiar.

The singing in the service had been led by some men of no Christian character, and some thoughtless.

young women.   They thought they were singing before the congregation, and did not know in their darkened hearts, nor consider, that they were singing before God, and that in His awful presence, who is the searcher of hearts, their vain show was profane. On taking their seats on this Sunday, they were greatly surprised at being told that they would not be required to take any part in the service. "Will there be no singing?" they asked, as if they supposed that the heavenly melody of praise was dependent on their aid! The question was answered when the pastor, having read out the hymn, raised his voice in a simple melody all could follow, and a feeling of awe stole over their untaught minds as they looked on the rapture on that saintly face.

It had long been the custom of this holy man to keep some one subject of Scripture before his mind. On this he pondered over his open Bible, in his daily reading; on this he thought when walking. In this way, one portion of the Holy Word after another filled his soul. When preaching the Word, he took the subject to which at the time he felt most led, and poured forth the meditation of his heart and the words of his lips in a way that none could who had not made the truth they were speaking the nourishment of their own spiritual life.

On that Sunday, when first speaking to the assembled people, he took for his subject the 23rd Psalm. Having read it, he went over the office of a shepherd, familiar to the people in that pastoral land. They liked it all the better for that; they listened as if all he told them were new; they took notice that he understood the things of which he was speaking. He described the grassy slopes of their hills, the streams flowing in the valleys below, the shepherd gathering his flocks to change their pasture, walking on before them, and the sheep following him. He made them remark how the dog walked obediently by the shepherd's side, and never meddled with the sheep, except by the shepherd's order; if they wandered, or were taking the wrong way, or if the shepherd wanted to bring a particular sheep to his hand; then it might seem to be fetched up in a rough manner, but it was because the shepherd wanted it near.

He showed how the shepherd might lead the sheep by some rocky precipice, where to fall would be death; but they were safe, because they followed him closely, keeping the narrow path of his footsteps. Or the shepherd might lead them through some rocky defile; but following him, they went in and came out in safety. He told of one sheep that wandered alone, and got into a fissure with a rock on both sides; there was plenty of room for the sheep to get out—the way out was quite as wide as the way in—but because the sheep felt itself alone, and had no guide, it beat its head from side to side of the rocky fissure, and the shepherd found it dead. He told how in the wilderness of distant lands, the shepherd knew where the best grass could be found, sometimes through rough pathways, where the rocks were dark above them, or under thorns and briars: if the best pastures for them were there, there they had to seek it. In this way he showed how the goodness and care of the shepherd was ever over his sheep.

It did not strike the people that this was not like a sermon, and yet it was a clear sermon to them; for as the description went on all the way through, they caught a hidden meaning, a light here and there, or a dark shadow that made them feel they knew what it meant—they saw it for themselves, which made it more their own.

When they came to the last words, "I will dwell in the house of the Lord for ever," the minister paused and looked round on the people; every eye seemed to meet the tender enquiry of his eye. He repeated the words again, "'I will dwell in the house of the Lord for ever.' This is not the earthly shepherd and the earthly sheep," he said; "the picture fails us here. It is not that the sheep may live, that all the watchful care is given here; it is that the sheep may die, and the shepherd live; that is the end with them. But there is a shepherd, and there is a flock with whom the Shepherd dies, that the sheep may live! It is because the Lord is my shepherd, the Good Shepherd who giveth His life for the sheep, that I can say, 'I will dwell in the house of the Lord for ever.'

"The Shepherd dies that the sheep may live. 'All we like sheep have gone astray; we have turned every one to his own way, and the Lord hath laid on Him the iniquity of us all.' 'God commendeth His love toward us in that while we were yet sinners

Christ died for the ungodly.' The sheep had wandered; the Shepherd treads the path of death and brings it home upon His shoulder. The sheep was dyed with sin; the Shepherd's life-blood makes it clean—whiter than snow! whiter than snow! The sheep was torn and bleeding; with the Shepherd's stripes it is healed! The Shepherd dies that the sheep may be fed; 'hungry and thirsty, their soul fainted in them.' The Shepherd says, 'The bread of God is He which cometh down from Heaven, and giveth life unto the world. My flesh is meat indeed, and my blood is drink indeed.'

"You have been saying, 'We are His people and the sheep of His pasture.' Did you mean what you said? Can you say, 'The Lord is my Shepherd, I shall not want'? The Good Shepherd says, 'My sheep hear My voice, and I know them, and they follow Me.' Is it so with you?

"Perhaps you know that you have turned to your own way, like one who said, 'I have gone astray like a lost sheep; seek thy servant!' The Good Shepherd answers, 'The Son of Man is come to seek and to save that which is lost.' Then He is seeking you to save you. Receive Him as your Saviour! 'As many as received Him, to them gave He power to become the sons of God, even to them that believe on His name.' Have you been frightened, hurried, and driven by the dog? trial and trouble are under His command; it is only to bring you to His feet. It may be you have to be dragged there; but any way, it is love that will not lose you. Let Him not say of you, 'Ye will not come to Me, that ye might have life!' Walking on the mountains, I met a shepherd leading home his flock, with a lamb on his shoulder. 'Is it hurt?' I enquired. 'No,' said he, 'not that; it is just weary and done; so I took it to rest.' Is not that like some of you, weary and done? Hear Him say, 'Come unto Me, and I will give you rest.'

"The next Lord's-day, the bread and wine, memorials of His death until He come again, will be spread for all whose desire it is to come to Him. Do you remember that before He suffered He took bread, and blessed and brake, and gave to His disciples, saying, 'Take, eat; this is my Body.' And He took the cup and gave thanks, and gave it to them, saying, 'Drink ye all of it; for this is my Blood of the New Testament, which is shed for many for the remission of sins.' Will you come, who hear His voice of tender invitation? Come in faith to feed in your heart upon His Body, and to drink His Blood? With thankfulness, and by His grace, to live for Him who died for you?

"'I will dwell in the house of the Lord for ever.' That is home, a settled dwelling-place. There no more tired feet, aching hearts, and weary heads. It is home that the Good Shepherd bears every sheep, every lamb, of His flock. Do you say, 'Not for me; I am not worthy.' None are worthy. You will not be there because you are worthy, but because He is worthy who, when He had overcome the sharpness of death, opened the kingdom of Heaven to all believers. Do you say 'I am serving another master, and cannot get away'? Let me tell you He has redeemed you from every other master, from all the slavery of the world, of self, and of the devil. He has paid the full price, you are His, and His precious blood seen by faith, can melt every chain of sin with which you are tied and bound, and set you free for ever. Come all who can on Saturday evening, and meet me here, that we may seek the out-pouring of the Holy Spirit, to enable us to draw near in full assurance of faith, that the things of Jesus may be made manifest to us."

And so they met together there upon the eve of the first day of the week for prayer and praise. And then they gathered round the table where that feast was spread, — looking to Him that loved us and washed us from our sins in His own blood. There was the aged Benoni, exultant in faith. Oliver Crisp in his deep reverence. Dame Truman in her advancing meekness. Farmer and Mistress Caxton; and there Oliver and Meg Caxton; there the broken-hearted Susan Butterly. How blessed a group is gathered around many a village communion-table, where pastor and people are one in the faith, hope, and love of the gospel of the grace of God! Who can estimate the change when the true pastor comes where the "hireling" has been? It is a blessing that the God of all grace alone can give, and that faith in God alone can duly use. It is to a rural parish like the passing from death to life. Each heart turns in a measure to the holy heart of the pastor for instruction, counsel, sympathy, and spiritual aid, and turns not in vain. Even the ungodly know that there is a prophet among them. "The evil bow before the good, and the wicked at the gates of the righteous." The holy example and influence of such an one is in measure as "the precious ointment upon the head, that ran down upon the beard—even Aaron's beard—that went down to the skirts of his garment." Now the village lived in peace, and the God of love and peace was with them.

Dame Truman had taken her place in the Valley of Humiliation; which pilgrims find to be the best and most fruitful piece of ground in all their pilgrimage. Here, also, those who walk this way are too low for the fiery darts of the enemy to reach them. The air of this valley is wholesome and healing, amidst all words of anger, wrath, and bitterness. Over Dame Truman's spirit the mantle of a perfect meekness had fallen. It did not signify now what "rudiments" were taught in the village; she only said, "You must come and teach your old teacher, my children; but if they be only the scrapings of this world's learning, don't bring them to me, I have had enough of that sort of thing in my time; and I am trying now to spell out a heavenly lesson, 'the form of sound words in faith and love which is in Jesus Christ.' I sit and muse how I thought of nothing but teaching of others, when all the time I had need that one should teach me, that 'except I became as a little child, I could not enter the kingdom of God.'"

One of Dame Truman's most frequent visitors was Meggie Caxton. Meggie had been too wilful in her spoilt childhood and early youth for any affection to lay strong hold of her heart, but it was far otherwise now; she had learned to know her own weakness and sin, she had learned to know her great Deliverer's love and power. He had given her rest, and one of her chief enjoyments was to slip over awhile to Dame Truman, and sitting at her side, they learned those blessed lessons from the sacred page, that the Holy Spirit waits to teach each willing soul. The wonder of those lessons is that they are never outgrown. We rest on the lowest step of the ladder while climbing to the highest.

Meg, whose light-hearted glee had kept her younger than her years, was older now than age would have shown her to be. It was not only her own past experience—though that alone was enough to add the weight of years to a young life ; it was the thought of poor Margaret Butterly. As the seasons passed, and no tidings came, the thought grieved her soul continually, and the cry rose that she might be delivered.

The past of Meg Caxton's young life often drew her backward glance. Her childhood and early youth lay in the growing distance, in a confusion of sunny light. Nothing was strongly marked to her except the loss of Oliver. Nothing else had told with any power upon her heart, and even that had passed into the softening mist of distance. Then came darker shadows crossing her path. Oliver desired the first place in human relationship, and she had had slowly to learn that he could never even for her fill any other; and then followed the deeper darkness, the living death of her young heart. All the time one form, her "brother Oliver's," grew upon her aching vision until it seemed to fill the world for her, yet could not be her own. Then Margaret, lost in darkness, lost with one who had drawn her own listening ear—how awfully those shadows deepened, until the past grew terrible in retrospect. Then all was gone—feeling, memory, consciousness. Her first knowledge of returning life was Oliver's voice of inquiry. Oliver's letter, and the Bible, had led her to the "Come unto Me, all ye that are weary and heavy-laden, and I will give you rest." Then the breaking of the dense, dark cloud, a Form Divine, a voice of life, a heart of tenderness, a hand held out to save! From this Divine Presence flowed the light of life, like the clear shining after rain; and every friend and every object in her daily life was touched with beauty, tinged with the glory of His love. The surface light of childhood, the fearful shadows of her youth, these were behind her still; but she lived in another atmosphere now, even the Light that doth make manifest; it was her joy, her hope, her life, to do the will of her Father in heaven. While still, as she looked upon the darkness of the past from the depth of the present light, she drew in humble, earnest prayer the poor lost Margaret; bearing her in the arms of faith and love before the mercy-seat.

CHAPTER XXVIII.

It is beautiful to see the aged, when the joy of the
Lord is their strength;—how the spirit is upborne
as on eagles' wings, sustaining the mortal body.
Benoni's age appeared to show more strikingly the
light of life within; and not in wasting sickness, but
almost suddenly at last, it flickered and went out—
went out in this dim atmosphere to glow in dazzling
splendour where no hindering medium intervenes.
He only complained of weariness and said, "Why
should I not rest these tired limbs? There is
nothing to hinder rest."

Oliver had carried him his evening meal, but
Benoni said, "I think I have done with earthly need;
set it down and come, my son, and let me think
again how I kneeled as you are kneeling now, while
you were laid in that chamber in the road-side inn.
It was then I learned to pray. It was then I knew
our Father." On Oliver's dear head he laid his
hands in blessing; then said, "Oh, Oliver, my son,
my son! Take the testimony of a lone stranger,
motherless from birth, fatherless from childhood,
friendless in youth, wife-less, child-less. Jesus, the
Christ, Emmanuel, God with us, meeteth the need
of all that is natural in us, no less than the need of

all that is spiritual. He knoweth the heart of the stranger. He knows and He cares ! That word is true from everlasting—' My God shall supply all your need, through His riches in glory by Christ Jesus.' "

Then slowly, yet without a failing voice, Benoni said—

" OUR FATHER; O Lord Jesus Christ, who hast deigned to say, ' My Father and your Father, My God and your God!' Doubtless Thou art our Father, though Abraham be ignorant of us, and Israel acknowledge us not. Thou, O Lord, art our Father, our Redeemer. Thy Name is from everlasting.

" WHICH ART IN HEAVEN. Glory to God in the highest, on earth peace, good-will to men.

" HALLOWED BE THY NAME. Thy Name is as ointment poured forth. Thou hast called Thy servant by a new name, having put Thy Name, O Christ, upon us ! May we walk worthy of God as dear children.

" THY KINGDOM COME. Thy kingdom, O God, which is righteousness, peace, and joy in the Holy Ghost.

" THY WILL BE DONE, AS IN HEAVEN SO ON EARTH. ' This is the will of the Father which sent Me, that of all which He hath given Me I should lose nothing, but should raise it up again at the last day.'

" GIVE US THIS DAY OUR DAILY BREAD. ' Save Thy people, and bless Thine inheritance. Feed them also, and lift them up for ever.'

"FORGIVE US. Forgive—forgive Benoni, Lord Jesus,—"

While Oliver looked with swimming eyes upon the saintly upraised face, Benoni passed away.

" Praise to the Lord, for they are past,
    They are gone safe before ;
They have borne the wildest tempest-blast,
    Have heard the last storm roar.
Praise to the Captain of our great salvation ;
He brings His own Redeemed
      From every nation !

Mourners they were—they weep not now,
    Sick—now they know not pain ;
But glory shines on every brow
    Of that once feeble train.

There are Judea's martyr-band,
    There Cappadocia's sons ;
And bright and beautiful there stand
    Our own belovèd ones !

Yes ! blest, and beautiful and bright,
    How fair their white robes gleam—
Oh, to behold the glorious sight
    With not a veil between !

Yet once, like ours, each aching brow
    Throbbed in the sultry noon ;
Their spirits sank, as ours do now,
    'Neath midnight's chilling moon.

And once, like us, with trembling fear,
    Their unknown path they viewed ;
Now God hath wiped away each tear
    From all that multitude !

Rejoice ! they've gained their rest at last,
  The Home where they would be;
Mid adverse gales and tempest blast
  Their followers still are we—
Hasten, thou Captain of the saint's salvation,
Bring home Thine own redeemed
    From every nation !

And now, again, the procession passed down the green hill-side, and a waiting people gathered and followed, with many a feeling and many a tear for the pedlar Jew they had known from their childhood. They had seen him changed from a " man of the earth " to a saint of God; and, forgetting this world's traffic, they thought of the light that broke on him here, which now he had entered for ever. He had stood by the porch, and none had asked him to enter, when the motherless babe of the Mill was carried in for baptism; now that babe in his manhood, supporting his father, followed Benoni with the grief of a son. As they entered the church-yard there stood in the porch the white-robed form, emblem of resurrection;— the Pastor, true son of consolation, waiting to receive the honoured dust, and the company of the mourners, with the joyful greeting of immortality. " I am the Resurrection and the Life, saith the Lord, He that believeth in Me, though he were dead, yet shall he live, and whosoever liveth and believeth in Me shall never die." Who can tell the blessed comfort that is felt when the Pastor stands as a father re- ceiving his children ; the sleeping form of one, and the living forms of the others, dear to his soul !

They laid him, Benoni, to rest, where slept Naomi and her mother, and the mother and grandmother of the Olivers. The younger Oliver lingered until the last sod was re-laid, and the children around him wept for their old friend, whose kindnesses had been so many, and whom they remembered from infancy. Then in the distance, where the witch-elm lent its foliage to the stems of the tall ash-trees, Oliver saw a form that he knew; Meggie Caxton was lingering there; he joined her, and as they walked slowly on she leaned on his arm. She knew that the one to whom he had been life's blessing was left sleeping in the quiet church-yard; and the silent token that another found the need of his support, even if only as a brother, she felt might be a comfort then. Oliver felt the token with a trembling joy. No other earthly form could lean with such welcome weight on him.

The summer had past and the golden harvest had waved, as it had waved each year through all the changes of human hearts and homes. Oliver's birth-day returned; all that was linked with it lay fresh as ever in his father's soul; the son all unconscious of what that month had been, and what it was to his father. The Mill-house had been grave and sad; the trumpet and the flute were silent there. Oliver had not made the air melodious since Benoni ceased to hear. For two years he had not cared to heed his birth-day; on this he came of age, and to the faithful K.'s contentment he said, " Make ready, I will have a party." "He thinks much of his coming to age," said K. "I remember I felt twice the woman that ever I felt before; and I am right glad of it, for 'twas a thousand pities he should go on like a man as had not a birth-day, when he was master's only son, and Master Benoni's too! I do believe he will be taking a turn, and forgetting the hard heart he looked after in vain. I will show up my best and surprise the folks, whoever they be. I will see if I can't outdo myself! The feast shall lie equal, as my mistress used to say, and nothing too domineering be set on the table."

Oliver pleaded with Mistress Caxton and Farmer that coming of age was but once in a life-time; that he ought to be a gainer, not a loser, because he was born in the busy harvest-time; that he had quite made up his mind not to notice the day unless Mistress Caxton, and Farmer, and Meggie all came. So consent was given, and Meggie was glad, though but last of the three. But as Oliver went out he gave Meggie his old look, the first time she had met it, and said, "Won't it be like a bit of the old time, hey, Meggie?" but she could not answer, for bits of the old time could not fill Meggie's heart; she wanted it whole and entire. Can the past come back again? No, never! Yet from its wintry grave a brighter bloom, a sweeter fruit, may spring and ripen than if that past had flowed on unchecked.

Dame Truman had a special invitation from Oliver, who would take no denial. Richard Dolman would drive her the short distance home, or see her safely there; so she made herself ready several times over, so far as arrangements went in intention; for she seldom went out, except to the church, which was filled with every one now who could enter. Jonathan of course would be of the party, and a few other friends of whom we have not found time to speak in former pages. How often Oliver looked on Benoni's forsaken chair, and missed the halo that seemed to hover round that venerated head! Oliver's father rejoiced in preparations to celebrate the day, and felt that at length the long-lost brightness of life was returning to his son.

When they met on that morning, Oliver Crisp gave his blessing to his son with deep emotion. "God give thee one of His jewels, my son, that thou mayest in His time be well married; for he that is not married doth but halve both himself and his home!" Never until then had Oliver Crisp breathed the word "jewel," his word of deepest love for his bride, his wife, the mother of his child! It was graven on the head-stone where she slept, and there he read it each Sunday. "'They shall be mine,' saith the Lord, 'in that day when I make up my jewels.'"

Oliver was down at the Farm long before Mistress Caxton had thought of preparing for the evening visit; Meggie was busy with provisions for the reapers; and Farmer Caxton was out in the fields; but his Sunday coat lay ready, and his high-topped boots; for these portions of his dress were generally put on in the kitchen.

"Meggie, I declare you are nothing but business, and here I am come of age all the day! Let Kezia see to the outside for once, and you and I have a walk to keep holiday!"

"I am not ready," said Meg, her rosy arms uncovered, and her broad white apron tied round her gown of blue print.

"I have seen you pull down your sleeves and hold yourself ready without any more fuss, times enough!"

"Oh, but you know it is a party! though you have not told me who? And, Oliver," she said, with an effort, but as one determined to say it, "I have made up a gown on purpose for to-day, and if I don't wear it for you, I never shall for another, so let me put it on."

And her "brother Oliver" knew well what gown, but he made no reply; and a few minutes brought her back to his side, and the tiny white doves on the light tracery met his eyes again. They did not turn towards the river and the forest; Meg was glad, she could not have taken that way; but they wandered on to a little lone copse-wood on the side of a hill, where they had often played together in the mirth of their childhood, and with which no bitter memory was linked. He spread his handkerchief over a fallen tree for her seat, and kneeled on the grass at her side in silence for a few moments. Then he gave her a blue corn-flower he had plucked in the wheat-field, and said,

"Meggie, blue is hope, isn't it?"

"I don't know," said Meggie; "but it is the colour of the heaven above, which looks as if it might stand for hope."

"Can you give it me back as hope's colour, Meggie?"

And she answered, "What hope?"

And he said, "That it may not be always, 'Oliver, my brother;' but that 'Never' blotted out, to leave it 'Oliver, my lover!'"

"That 'Never,'" she answered, "has been blotted out a thousand times with tears and prayers." She turned to him as she spoke, and her golden head lay on his shoulder in the clasp of his close embrace, and heart met heart in depths of loving, trustful rest.

It was but few moments. Oh, sin and evil, what are ye, that ye should have power to break in on such moments as these! But Meggie's soul had learned lessons of unflinching truth, while learning lessons of humble trust, and lifting her head, she hid her face in her hands, and said,

"O, Oliver, instead of being here in this blessedness, I might have been lost where poor Margaret Butterly is lost!"

"No," answered Oliver, calmly, and not as one surprised. "Not so utterly lost to us, Meggie, though there was danger, I know!"

"How did you know?" she enquired.

"O, Meggie! my wounded dove is not stolen away!" he said, as his look of tenderest love rested on her; "there was One who could guard it, and

did, when I was unable. That is long past, and
deeply repented, and what God forgives and forgets
we have no right to recal. Come, and let us go to
my father."

" But, Oliver, tell me; can you ever feel the same
as you would have done if those terrible days had not
come? "

" Look there," answered Oliver. "That bright
gleam breaking from the dark cloud over the hills—
is it not brighter for the darkness ?"

" By contrast !" she said.

· Oliver smiled a smile of such gladness; her's
answered it again. "O, Meggie, hard to persuade !
Tell me, are we not loved with a deeper love and
more tender, for ever, because we were sinners; and
saved by Him who has waited for the full surrender
of our hearts, which His precious blood alone could
deliver ? and is not our love like His in its measure ? "

" They are words of life to me, Oliver," she said;
" but can I ever be quite happy while poor Margaret
is lost ? I think of her day and night; next to you
she has filled my heart."

" It is our sorrow, not our sin, that she is
gone," replied Oliver; " or if in any way our sin,
it is forgiven, and our souls will be stronger in
prayer now they are bound together. Sorrow must
be comforted by prayer, or our prayer cannot
be in faith. I learned that lesson, Meggie, long
ago—that no prayer, however deep its anguish,
can go up from our hearts into the heart of our

Father but it comes back with some balm of blessing."

For all the delay, they were first at the Mill.
Oliver Crisp, in his arm-chair, rose up as they entered
—their gladness of countenance told more than
words. " My daughter! my child!" said Oliver
Crisp; for a moment he could say no more, then
added, " 'Tis our Father in Heaven unites His
children on earth ! "

Mistress Caxton and Farmer came in. She
never said a word at the tidings, but just sat down
and wept.

K. said, " I was then coming in with a whole
tray of my best; but it made both my eyes water to
see Mistress Caxton sit there and cry, and I had just
to turn back and set my tray down again and have a
good cry myself; which I should not have thought
of on the day Master Oliver came to age, if it had
not been for Mistress Caxton ! "

Farmer said, " 'Tis the best day I have seen !
and now I am no hearty at wishing many more."

Dame Truman, when she arrived, and saw the two
blessed in each other, had to wait a short time to
consider what was the right thing for the school-mistress who had brought them both up from nothing, to
say on such an occasion ; but her memory was short,
and though she felt herself in public in her old dignity, she could only say, " My children ! I never did
think of ye apart; and now, why, Heaven has brought
ye together!"   In the course of the evening she remembered one or two things that were suitable on

such occasions; but she thought as the introduction was over they might be left unsaid, though good at the right time.

To the small assembly's surprise, as the evening advanced with converse and minstrelsy, a knock was heard at the door, and the Pastor entered amongst them. There was pleasure in the general look of surprise, but the Pastor seemed to consider it a matter of course; he congratulated Oliver and Meg Caxton and the older generation, and sat down among them with that pleasant ease that made all things the brighter. He took the evening worship, and sang their hymns with them like one of them altogether. Oliver always maintained that only the trumpet could give the rich tones of that voice! Then giving his benediction, he left them, insisting on returning alone through the late autumn evening to his small parsonage, and the collie dog followed his steps.

This well-timed visit was talked of in the village, and Mother Dumbleton said it was all of a piece—it was a miracle of mystery from the first to the last. But Oliver told Meg that his hope had been so strong, he had written his request for the visit, and had it in his pocket all day, and sent it over on their return home.

And the village which had had much darkness and many sorrows had now a crowning call for rejoicing; and the Castle was glad, and Mr. Howe even began to think what arrangements he could make when the marriage-day should come. The strength of two hearts welded in one is Heaven's gift and earth's glory ; " for a man is the image and glory of God ; but the woman is the glory of the man."

> " My bark is wafted to the strand
>   By breath divine ;
> And on the helm there rests a Hand
>   Other than mine."

THE END.

LONDON :
Simmons & Botten, Printers, Shoe Lane, E.C.

www.ingramcontent.com/pod-product-compliance
Lightning Source LLC
Chambersburg PA
CBHW032148110726

47902CB00003B/737